Christmas with the
Wartime Midwives

Daisy Styles grew up in Lancashire surrounded by a family and community of strong women. She loved to listen to their stories of life in the cotton mill, in the home, at the pub, on the dancefloor, in the local church, or just what happened to them on the bus going into town. It was from these women, particularly her vibrant mother and Irish grandmother, that Daisy learnt the art of storytelling.

By the same author

The Bomb Girls

The Code Girls

The Bomb Girls' Secrets

Christmas with the Bomb Girls

The Bomb Girl Brides

The Wartime Midwives

Home Fires and Spitfires

Keep Smiling Through

A Mother's Love

Christmas with the Wartime Midwives

DAISY STYLES

PENGUIN BOOKS

PENGUIN BOOKS

UK | USA | Canada | Ireland | Australia
India | New Zealand | South Africa

Penguin Books is part of the Penguin Random House group of companies
whose addresses can be found at global.penguinrandomhouse.com

Penguin
Random House
UK

First published 2022
004

Copyright © Daisy Styles, 2022

The moral right of the author has been asserted

Set in 12.5/14.75pt Garamond MT Std
Typeset by Jouve (UK), Milton Keynes
Printed and bound in Great Britain by Clays Ltd, Elcograf S.p.A.

The authorized representative in the EEA is Penguin Random House Ireland,
Morrison Chambers, 32 Nassau Street, Dublin DO2 YH68

A CIP catalogue record for this book is available from the British Library

ISBN: 978–1–405–95041–1

For my brave and loving daughter, Isabella

'What will survive of us is love'
From 'An Arundel Tomb' by Philip Larkin

1. Nurse Libby Godburgh

Knowing that she had a full day ahead of her, Libby was out of the family farmhouse just after dawn. With her long, Titian golden-red hair flying around her sweet, oval-shaped face – dominated by big violet-blue eyes that could drift from dreamy to thoughtful in a matter of seconds – Libby stopped in her tracks when she saw the tall muscular bulk of her father at the back door. Clearly, he had been up even earlier than her.

'Dad,' she exclaimed with pleasure.

'I wanted to say goodbye, pet,' he said with a tender smile. 'I'll be thinking of thee, little lass.' A catch in his husky voice, he held his arms out wide to her. 'Come and give thee owd dad a big hug.'

Running into his embrace, Libby nestled against his broad body which always smelt of sheep, pipe tobacco and engine oil.

'I'll write, Dad,' she murmured.

'Aye, you'd better,' he chuckled, 'or your mam will raise hell.'

Exchanging a conspiratorial smile, Libby nodded. Nobody knew better than the pair of them how uppity Mrs Godburgh could get if she felt neglected.

'I'd best be off to market; sheep are loaded up and restless with it. We're proper proud of you, our lass,' Mr Godburgh said as he gave his daughter a final hug and a flying kiss. 'Take care of theeself, my pet.'

After watching her father drive the farm truck away, loaded with yearlings to sell at Kendal market, Libby ran across the farmyard to the stable block located next to the paddock, neatly hedged in by ancient drystone walls. When her fifteen-hand, silver-grey fell pony heard her steps ringing out on the worn flag floor, he popped his head over the stable door and neighed shrilly at his mistress.

'Morning, sweetie,' Libby murmured fondly as she stroked her beloved pony's long silky mane. 'Big day today,' she said as she slipped an old leather halter over Snowball's neck, then walked him across the farmyard to the paddock, tying him to a post and giving him a net of fresh hay, which he immediately tugged and nibbled at.

Once Snowball was contentedly settled, Libby began grooming him for the journey south. After using a curry comb to loosen the dirt in his coat, Libby vigorously brushed him down with a dandy brush, before applying regular sweeping strokes with a soft body brush. The regular rhythm of the brush across the pony's silvery bright rump, neck, chest and withers gradually calmed Libby's nerves. Feeling his mistress relaxing against him, Snowball nuzzled his velvety nose against her flat muscular tummy.

'We're going to a new home today,' she whispered. 'We're going to Mary Vale.'

Just saying the words made Libby's pulse race. 'Mary Vale,' she repeated the name softly.

Libby would never forget her first sight of the home for unmarried mothers and their babies, set on a high rocky trajectory overlooking the vast majestic vista of

Morecambe Bay. It was a beautiful old red-brick house, at that time of the year covered in riotous Virginia creeper, its vivid autumn-red colours blazing gold and scarlet in the intense afternoon light. The house faced due west, with breathtaking views of the turbulent Irish Sea that rolled in alternating shades of silver and grey towards the distant horizon before disappearing in a shimmering haze of iridescent blue. Closer by, a vast sage-green marsh hugged the coastline which was washed by the incoming tide twice a day. On the afternoon of her memorable interview for a midwife vacancy, Libby had stood trans-fixed watching the many squawking, squabbling sea-birds wading in the shallows of the marsh: redshanks, oyster-catchers, sandpipers, dunlins and piping curlews waiting expectantly for food; and crustaceans, worms and mol-luscs washed in by the tide.

Quite unlike her usual confident, buoyant self, Libby that afternoon had been a bag of nerves. This was her first real job interview, her first real challenge. Though she had done well throughout her nurse's training course at Lancaster Infirmary, and excelled on the midwives' course that followed, she had never faced an interview panel who might, for all her fine qualifications, reject her in favour of somebody with far more experience. Realistically, it had to be said that she didn't have much of that, apart from the work on the wards and community nursing, twice a week, that had formed part of her course.

'Somebody older and more experienced will definitely stand a better chance than me,' she recalled thinking to herself, but then her father's staunch words of support on the morning of her interview came back to her.

'You'll be alreet, lass, just be yourself.'

Approaching Mary Vale's imposing front door, Libby had taken deep breaths, then thrown back her slender shoulders and knocked firmly.

A plump, smiley-faced nun had immediately flung the door open.

'You must be here for the interview?' the young nun had said with such a warm smile that Libby had immediately smiled back. 'Come on in, I'm Sister Agnes,' she'd continued in the same warm vein. 'I'd offer you a cuppa and a few oatcakes, fresh from the oven, but Sister Ada and her husband, Dr Reid, are waiting for you in Matron's office.'

Libby was intrigued. 'It's unusual having a husband and wife team working together on the same premises, especially during wartime.'

Looking earnest, Sister Agnes explained. 'Yes, for sure. Perhaps I should explain that Dr Reid used to be our resident doctor before he was called up. Sadly, he was wounded in Tobruk, he lost his left hand, but he made a marvellous recovery. Now he's back to full health, Dr Reid and his wife both work here; they share the job between them on account of their little girl who one of them looks after while the other works. It's a splendid setup that suits everybody – we're blessed to have such a wonderful couple with us at Mary Vale.'

Following the kindly, chatty nun down a corridor with floors so highly polished the wooden tiles reflected the dust motes floating in the air, Libby had been led into an office where the interview panel was assembled. Libby would never forget how warm and welcoming the staff had been when she walked into the room, flushed with

4

nerves. Comfortable though the atmosphere was, the questions the panel threw at Libby were demanding. Had she nursed patients on the post-natal ward suffering from puerperal fever? Yes, she had. Had Libby ever attended the birth of twins with complications? Yes, in the first year of her midwifery training; one of the twins had got stuck and she had to perform an emergency forceps delivery. But she managed to answer all the questions as best she could and, when given the chance, told them all about her community work in Lancaster, an experience which had shaped her desire to do more community work, especially with the underprivileged in society.

By the end of the interview – which was brought to a halt by an urgent call requesting Dr Jamie's presence in the delivery room – Libby's eyes were alight with passion, and a small excited smile played around her full mouth.

'Would it be useful for you to know something about the history of Mary Vale, Miss Godburgh?' Matron asked as the interview came to a close.

'Yes, I'd love that,' Libby enthused. 'It's such a beautiful place in a lovely setting.'

'Well, it isn't just in its present guise that Mary Vale offers sanctuary to those in need; it has in fact done so for centuries.' As Matron spoke, her face lit up with pride. 'The building stands on the foundations of an ancient Cistercian priory. For over a thousand years, it was a stopping place for pilgrims en route to Furness Abbey. Pilgrims crossing the Irish Sea landed at Heysham, then they were led safely across the bay on donkeys by guides who knew the whereabouts of the treacherous tidal quicksand which claimed many innocent travellers' lives. After being safely delivered to the abbey, they were given food and a bed for the night before they went on their way to Furness, early the next morning.'

Pleased to see Libby so enthralled, Staff Nurse Ada, who had the loveliest dark-blue eyes, leant forward. 'We like to think we carry on that great tradition of giving sanctuary to all those in need, especially to the desperate women who arrive here in great distress.'

'Thank God for such a refuge,' Libby said earnestly. 'It would be a privilege to work in a place that helped a woman in her time of need.'

'Just like the Cistercian monks, we never close our doors to anybody.' Matron smiled. 'We're funded by the convent of the Sisters of the Holy Mother, which is right next to us; they, in turn, are funded by the rent they obtain from farmland and property. Believe me, we are by no means a rich foundation. Our burden is eased when we are able to admit self-funding residents; their fees pay for the non-funded residents who are very often homeless and destitute.'

'It would be hard to turn away such women,' Libby said compassionately.

'That's the point, we never do,' Ada assured her. 'But it does make life hard when we can barely make ends meet.'

Picking up on Ada's comment, Matron chipped in. 'We depend a lot on the charity and kindness of our local community, who are generous in their gifts of food, and we have our own farm nearby, run by Farmer Arkwright, who keeps us well stocked in milk, some eggs and local cheese, sometimes meat, and an endless supply of fresh vegetables which he himself grows for our own consumption.'

'We don't go hungry!' Ada joked. 'Not with the loving community that we're so grateful for.'

Libby shuffled nervously in her chair. 'Er, would you mind if I asked a question?' she blurted out.

'No, not at all,' Matron said kindly.

'You talk about the "community", which I have a great interest in.'

The two women behind the desk turned curious eyes on Libby who by now was on the edge of her chair.

'As I mentioned earlier, I have some experience of community nursing, and I have a real passion for it. I saw so many poor pregnant women give birth in awful conditions in Lancaster, in homes barely more than hovels, surrounded by little toddlers in rags crying out for food which their poor mothers couldn't begin to find for them. It was heartbreaking.' Libby paused. 'The fact is, those women needed more care and professional help than any of the women I was nursing on the wards – they and their families were virtually on the street. Quite a few died, and so did their babies, but some fared better thanks to our community work. I love working with those women, visiting them in their own homes, and making a difference to their lives,' she explained. 'I was just wondering . . . I hope you don't mind my asking, but is community midwifery ever something that Mary Vale might consider taking on?' She stopped herself, wondering if she'd gone too far, but she could see only warmth and interest in the eyes of the two nurses.

Though Libby's question had struck home, Matron's response was cautious.

'To be honest, community midwifery is not something we have the resources to support – as I mentioned, we struggle for funding – but it is certainly not something I would object to. Of course, any changes in our policy are always ultimately determined by our Reverend Mother.'

Not wanting to dash the hopes of such an enthusiastic young midwife, bright-eyed Ada interjected. 'We're a forward-looking team at Mary Vale. I would like to think your experience of community midwifery would interest the staff here, Miss Godburgh.'

Feeling self-conscious, and still anxious that she might have over-stepped the mark – 'put her big foot in it', as her mother would have chided – Libby nevertheless couldn't stop herself from continuing to speak her mind.

'Thank you so much for bearing with me, I know I can get carried away when it comes to nursing in the community. Not everybody can afford to go into hospital, can they? I suppose I just think that God is telling us something – if they can't come to us then we must go out to them.'

Both stunned and touched by Libby's sheer force of will, Matron and Ada stared at each other. Without a word, each knew exactly what the other was thinking – here's a young woman who is more than a nurse: here is a bright, brave Mary Vale crusader! Though inspired by the young woman's compassion, Matron again erred on the side of caution.

'It's a more than worthy idea for serious consideration,' she diplomatically concluded. 'I'll certainly mention it to Reverend Mother.'

Recalling how she had waited tensely for over a week to hear back from Mary Vale, Libby vividly remembered the day when the letter from the Home finally dropped on to the farmhouse doormat. Trembling as if it were a bomb about to go off, she had backed away.

'Mam, what if it's a rejection?'

Mrs Godburgh was, as ever, the pragmatist. 'Well, lass, there's only one way to find out.' Picking up the letter, she handed it to her daughter who resolutely shook her head.

'No, Mam, you read it.'

Hardly daring to breathe, Libby had watched her mother tear open the envelope. When she glanced up there was a glow of pride in Mrs Godburgh's eyes.

'You've got the job,' she announced. 'You start next week, lovie.'

Filled with jubilation and relief, Libby had grabbed her poor mother around the waist and jigged her up and down their flagged kitchen floor until they were both breathless.

'I'm going to Mary Vale,' starry-eyed Libby had announced.

Time had flown by in a whirlwind of frantic preparations, and now here she was, a week later, tacking up and simply raring to go. She was suddenly aware she had been so deep in thought that she had actually stopped grooming Snowball, who was now indignantly blowing into her hair.

Libby giggled, tickling his little pointy ears, and laughingly apologized. 'Sorry, sweetheart,' she murmured.

Reaching into her tack box for the hoof pick, Libby methodically cleaned out each of Snowball's hooves in turn, a procedure he liked a lot less than grooming. Just as she was finishing her task, she spotted her mother approaching out of the corner of her eye. Knowing full well that her mother tended to chide rather than confide when she was anxious, Libby braced herself.

Typically, Mrs Godburgh came straight to the point. 'I don't see why you have to do it this way, lass.'

Concentrating hard on brushing out Snowball's long thick tail that almost swept the ground, Libby respectfully held her tongue.

'You could always go over to Grange in't truck when your dad gets back from't market in Kendal.'

Libby exclaimed so loudly that Snowball snorted in surprise. 'Mam, by the time Dad gets back from Kendal the truck will be swilling in sheep muck. We'd have to spend an hour hosing it down before I'd even think of putting Snowball in it.'

Having lost the battle to persuade her daughter to travel in relative style, Mrs Godburgh pursed her lips before turning her frustration to another bone of contention. 'Why in heaven's name you have to take that pony with you at all when you're starting a new job beats me. What will folks think when you fetch up looking like a tinker on a pack mule?'

Seeing her dear mother's troubled expression, Libby laid aside the hoof pick and gently drew her into her arms. 'Stop worrying, Mam,' she said softly as she swiped a strand of grey hair off her mother's worn cheek. 'I asked Matron's permission to stable Snowball at Mary Vale; they've been kind enough to sort out grazing and stabling for him with the local farmer. It's not a problem, I promise,' she soothed. 'And anyway, Mam, having Snowball close by will be good for me. I'll be able to ride out on my days off, and blow off steam, something you're always telling me to do when I get worked up,' she reminded her mother.

Sighing heavily, Mrs Godburgh stared into her Libby's wonderful violet-blue eyes. They had melted her heart the moment she had given birth to her wild, wilful, passionate daughter. Ever since she was little, Libby had never wavered in her determination to do whatever it was she had set her mind on. Whether it was learning to ride at three years old, or competing with her two older brothers, Tom and Les, who had recently been called up for active service, Tom in the Army and Les in the Navy. Whatever it was – competing in fell-running competitions or training a sheepdog to herd the sheep – Libby never took on a secondary role; in fact, she often excelled over her brothers, particularly in the school room. Libby had a passion for learning. Though immensely proud of her beloved daughter, Mrs Godburgh regularly despaired of Libby's unconventional attitude which was at loggerheads with her own.

'I don't see why you can't travel to your new place of work on the Lancaster train. You could wear that smart navy barathea suit we bought you last Easter, and take a suitcase instead of a blinking saddle bag.'

Knowing her mother was not going to stop, devious Libby used decoy tactics. 'Could you pack a few butties for the journey, Mam?'

Alert to the soothing and practical task of nurturing, Mrs Godburgh jumped at the opportunity to busy herself. 'Cheese and pickle, or spam?'

'Cheese, please,' Libby replied, with a grin.

Mrs Godburgh bustled off, leaving Libby alone to finish grooming Snowball.

'Are you ready for an adventure, handsome lad?' she said as she wiped his face with a clean damp cloth.

Sensing his mistress's palpable excitement, Snowball gave Libby an affectionate nudge in the chest.

Smiling, Libby bent to plant a kiss on his soft muzzle. 'You didn't think I'd leave you behind, did you, sweetheart?'

Libby couldn't have picked a better day to make the fifteen-mile journey to Kent Banks. She knew that her mother had only recently bidden her sons a sad farewell after they had been granted home leave, quite fortuitously, at the same time. They had undoubtedly had great fun, the whole family together again, gathered around the kitchen table, eating meals, sharing stories, and laughing over past memories.

'I'll never forget when our kid,' Les said, nodding at Libby, 'fell in Black Moor pot that boiling-hot summer day when we were bringing sheep down from the fells. She yelled and hollered, I thought she were drowning.'

'Aye, I remember that too,' Tom chuckled. 'We both jumped in to save her, and it were so shallow we nearly broke our blinkin' ankles.'

With tears of laughter rolling down her face, embarrassed Libby had held up her arms. 'Stop! Please stop,' she begged.

'You should've tested the depth of the water before you panicked and dragged us two into the water with you,' Les jokingly rebuked his little sister.

'Always a softie,' Tom teased.

'I am not a softie!' Libby, as ever, fought back when her brothers teased her. 'You seem to have forgotten that I beat you twice at fell-running.'

'Yeah, but that were the lasses' race,' Tom relentlessly carried on teasing her. 'Different game altogether when it's fellas.'

Before Libby could open her mouth and continue the argument, Mrs Godburgh had put rice pudding and tinned peaches on the table. Gazing indulgently at all of her children, she said what she had always said when they squabbled. 'The first of you to start another argument will be the last to get served.'

Recalling sweet memories and remembering how heartbroken her mother had been when Les and Tom's leave came to an end, Libby was extra tender with her when it came to saying goodbye to Mrs Godburgh. After kissing her on both cheeks, she held her in her arms for a long time. 'I love you, Mam,' she whispered softly as they pulled apart.

Mrs Godburgh put on a brave smile. 'Write and tell me how you're getting on, lovie.'

'I will, of course, Mam, and you keep me informed about Tom and Les. They're bound to write to you, but they might not have time to write separately to me.'

'Pray for your brothers, lovie, pray they'll come home safe and sound, and this war will soon be over.'

Turning to Snowball, who impatiently tossed his silver mane, keen to be under way, Libby swung herself lithely into the saddle. Mrs Godburgh stood on the farm track waving her only daughter off, with tears in her eyes.

Knowing exactly what her mother would be thinking – that she was the last one to fly the nest – Libby called over her shoulder. 'Don't worry, Mam, I'll be back soon.'

Leaving the twinkling blue waters of Windermere behind, Libby gave her mother a cheery wave as she trotted along the track, a low-lying autumn sun turning overhead oak and beech leaves to burnished gold. On their way to Cartmel, they passed the little village of High Newton and the shadowy outline of Hampsfell before stopping beside a clear gurgling beck for Snowball to quench his thirst. Sitting on the riverbank beside her pony, Libby enjoyed the sandwiches her mother had so carefully prepared. She felt a great surge of love for both of her parents: they had always encouraged her to follow her own path even if it came at a high price, like leaving home in order to do her training and start her first job. Libby knew that they had secretly hoped she would return to Newby Bridge to work, marry a local lad, and bring up a family they could enjoy in their old age.

Libby gave a guilty sigh; poor things, yet another disappointment, she thought. Not that she disliked the idea of men and courting, but growing up with two older brothers had left her with no romantic notions about the opposite sex. She enjoyed their company and relished the physical challenges they took on together. From fell-running to mountaineering, she could compete with any lad in the valley, but romance had barely touched her. The closest thing to it had been a kiss on the lips from a boy at school whose advances had left her stone cold. If the truth be told, when most of her girlfriends were experimenting with make-up, or sewing dance dresses, Libby had made it quite clear she wanted no distractions from her studies, which were paramount to her. She gazed adoringly at Snowball who was snapping his tail to ward off flies.

'You're the only fella I want, lovie.'

Wiping crumbs from her jumper, she gave her pony the apple her mother had packed for her, then mounted up. Pressing her thighs firmly into Snowball's stout belly, she moved forward, ambling along the bridle path lined with horse chestnut trees heavy with conkers glowing in the autumnal light.

Some hours later, Libby arrived fresh-faced and breathless at Mary Vale, with her tumbling golden hair flying in complete disarray about her tanned face. She quickly dismounted and rang the bell, holding on to Snowball's reins. Though she'd been warned that Libby would turn up on horseback, Ada immediately burst out laughing when she opened the door to her new colleague and saw Snowball standing before her, shaking his long mane.

'Welcome to Mary Vale!' she exclaimed in delight.

Giving a loud snort, cheeky Snowball inched forward to brush his soft muzzle against Ada's arm.

'You're a friendly boy,' she murmured, as she caressed his warm silky neck. 'My little girl is going to love you.' Turning towards Libby, Ada added, 'You must be starving. Tea-time's at five, but I can fetch you a cup of tea and a sandwich from the kitchen, if you like?'

Though Libby was indeed starving, she shook her head. 'Thanks, but I'd like to untack Snowball and settle him down for the night, if you don't mind?'

Recalling the arrangements that had been made with

Farmer Arkwright, Ada quickly nodded her head. 'Of course, the farm's just down the cobbled lane at the back of the house, you can't miss it. I know Alf's already sorted out a stable for Snowball, and the grazing land is close by. In fact, the fields back on to my cottage, so I hope we'll be seeing a lot of your pretty pony.'

Gathering up the reins, Libby sprang back into the saddle. 'I can't wait to see it, I won't be long,' she promised with her widest smile.

'If I'm on the wards when you get back, Sister Agnes will see you to your room.'

'I'm so excited,' Libby blurted out happily.

Catching her mood, Snowball gave a shrill neigh.

'It sounds like you both are,' Ada joked as she waved them off.

Watching them trot off towards the back of the house, Ada felt a deep sense of contentment; a dynamic, youthful, compassionate nurse with an irresistible wide grin was exactly what Mary Vale needed.

When Alf Arkwright heard the clip-clop of hooves on the cobbles, he laid aside the pitchfork he had been using to muck out the cow byre, and went to greet his visitor. The sight of eager Snowball tossing his mane as he quickened his pace in anticipation of a full hay net made the old farmer chuckle.

'Welcome, miss,' he rumbled as he helped Libby dismount.

'Pleased to meet you, Farmer Arkwright,' she politely started.

'Alf'll do, lass,' he told her. 'I've got a stable ready for yon one,' he said as he nodded at the pony. 'Now't special, but it's dry and warm – and more to the point, not far from't big house where you'll be living.'

'I couldn't be more grateful, Mr . . . er, Alf,' Libby gratefully exclaimed. She could see the small snug stable just off the main yard, with a little tack room adjacent to it.

'Untack the beast and we'll get him into the paddock, he'll be wanting a roll after that long journey.'

Wide-eyed, Libby gazed at him in amusement. 'A roll is exactly what he wants,' she agreed. 'How did you even know that?'

Alf let out a loud deep laugh. 'I know about hosses, I've kept 'em for years.'

Glancing around, Libby asked, 'Have you any here now?'

'Aye, th'owd shire, Captain. He's in't paddock yonder, he'll be pleased to have a bit of company.' Alf cautiously eyed Snowball who was considerably younger than Captain. 'Just so long as he minds his manners.'

When they turned Snowball out in the paddock, Alf's old horse ambled over and nudged Snowball's rump.

'Aye-aye.' Alf grinned as he watched the two animals cautiously circumnavigating each other. 'Looks like they might be pals,' he said, with some relief.

Libby's gaze drifted across the farm fields, neatly hedged with drystone walls, and towards the imposing sight of Mary Vale, presently basking in the last of the day's rosy-gold light.

'Hopefully,' she smiled to herself, 'it won't just be Snowball who makes friends at Mary Vale.'

Once Snowball was comfortable, Libby made her way

back to the Home where sweet Sister Agnes was waiting for her with a welcome cup of tea.

'Tea's at five: corned beef fritters and roasted parsnips, and a nice rice pudding,' she said with undisguised relish. 'Just what you need after your long journey.'

'It wasn't long really,' Libby said, 'though we did stop a lot to admire the scenery, especially around Cartmel Priory.'

'That's a gorgeous place of worship,' Agnes enthused.

'And the view when we dropped down into Grange from the top of the hill was wonderful. The tide was way out, so we had a brilliant glimpse of Morecambe Bay, it went on for miles and miles. All silvery-blue and grey,' she ended wistfully.

'Oh, it's a beautiful part of the world, there's no doubt about that, God's own country,' Agnes declared. 'Now when you're done, I'll show you to your room before I fetch in the tea.'

Springing to her feet, Libby followed Sister Agnes up two flights of highly polished stairs to the second floor which was reserved for staff accommodation.

Once inside the large corner room at the end of the corridor, Libby spun around in order to examine every aspect of her new lodgings. With its two large bay windows facing south and west, the room was suffused with the last rays of the low setting sun. Out of one of the windows, Libby could see the vast sweep of the Irish Sea, presently at full ebb, while the other window looked out over the rose garden which sloped down to the marsh and the sea-birds settling down for the night.

As she stared out, a barn owl swooped out of a small wood and circled the silvery marsh where darkness was swiftly falling.

'This is lovely,' Libby joyfully declared. 'Absolutely perfect!'

2. Margaret Church

Looking around her classroom, with the late September sunshine falling on the nature table, which was littered with golden maple leaves, conkers and acorns collected by her pupils, alongside vases of downy pink dahlias from her own garden, Margaret's gentle honey-brown eyes filled with a rush of tears.

'Stop it,' she firmly told herself as she gripped the handkerchief balled in her hand. 'You cannot be emotional in the classroom.'

But in truth Margaret was often emotional in the classroom these days, as well as on the bus going back and forth to work, and on desultory walks in Bolton's Queen's Park, where she fed the ducks at the weekend. As the haunting music of Grieg's *Peer Gynt*, playing out on the school's crackly old gramophone, soared with more aching passion in every bar, Margaret's eyes swept fondly over her pupils, all forty-two of them, squashed into a room that barely accommodated so many desks and chairs, but which was (thanks to her imaginative hard work) nevertheless bright and cheerful. Along the length of one wall there were seasonal autumn paintings by the children – images of squirrels, owls, bears and foxes. On the opposite wall Margaret had arranged vibrant pictures of musical instruments; brightly and boldly drawn by her, they were interspersed with musical notes – quavers, semiquavers and crotchets – with quotes from Ancient Greek philosophers (which Margaret hoped would inspire her pupils) looped underneath.

Music has a power of forming the character and should therefore be introduced into the education of the young.

Music gives soul to the universe, wings to the mind and life to everything.

Without music life would be an error.

Music was a subject that Margaret had loved from being a child: playing the piano at home with her mother, performing simple violin duets with her father, and having singing lessons weekly with a retired opera singer, had been the backbone of her life. A precocious only child, Margaret had been the apple of her parents' eyes; their highest hopes had been that she would go to Manchester Music School to further her studies and hopefully train to become an opera singer. And she had been on track for just that. The combination of her stunning, vibrant soprano voice and her big, honey-brown melancholy eyes, long, lustrous dark hair and perfect pale skin were all more than promising, plus she was a consistently good, hardworking student who regularly practised her pieces and never failed to attend auditions. All boded well for young Margaret Church . . . until disaster struck.

Tragically, just before war broke out, she had lost both her parents within a very short space of time. Her father's sudden death from the flu sent her mother, who was weak, bereft and in shock, into a decline. No matter how much her only child tried to revive her spirits – tempting her appetite with tasty little dishes, taking her for walks in the sunshine, playing her favourite pieces on the piano – her mother simply hadn't the will to live without her spouse of forty years. Passing away only months after her husband, she left Margaret not only heartbroken but virtually penniless too. Abandoning her dreams of becoming an opera singer, Margaret had retrained to teach primary school children, which provided her with a modest but reliable source of income. Though it didn't extend to covering the rent on the large family home where she had been so happy. Her financial distress necessitated a move into a poky garden flat in a poorer part of town, where she was never truly happy.

Margaret had been teaching primary age children for several years now, which was pleasant enough, but her passion for music never faltered. It was the one subject she excelled at – and the one that Friday afternoons were entirely given over to. Every week, without fail, Margaret played pieces from Handel, Beethoven, Chopin, Tchaikovsky and Mozart on the old school gramophone: hauntingly beautiful arias from *The Marriage of Figaro*, *Così Fan Tutte* and *The Magic Flute*. She delighted in the children's naive but thrilled responses to her favourite pieces.

'Oi, miss. I don't know what language they're speaking, but I love the drums and trumpets.'

'This music makes me want to run up a mountain and make a grab for the stars.'

Or even more poignant, 'When the lady sings this song, miss, she's so sad it makes me cry too.'

Perched on a stool at the out-of-tune piano in the

corner of the room (with her pupils sitting cross-legged on the floor at her feet), Margaret also taught traditional English folk songs. 'Under the Greenwood Tree', 'Scarborough Fair' and 'Greensleeves' were the most popular with her class. Sometimes she even played jive music on the crackly gramophone, which very often sent her charges into overdrive. When the grumpy headmaster had heard Glenn Miller's 'Little Brown Jug' blasting out of her classroom just last week, he blundered in.

'What the devil are you playing at!'

Several of the children had sprung to their feet to cavort around the room. They nervously dropped to the ground at the sight of his red, scowling face, but Margaret answered calmly.

'We're comparing different musical genres, headmaster.'

'Load of old tosh,' he growled before slamming the door and returning to his smoke-filled office.

Those Friday-afternoon music lessons had attracted the attention of the deputy head, too, but in a very different way. Hearing folk songs playing out on the gramophone, genial Peter would very often pop his head around the classroom door to beam at the pupils. Obviously enjoying the music too, he would smile and make a comment.

'Lovely stuff!' Or winking cheekily, he would quip, 'Hah! You call that working?'

'Yes, sir,' a bold pupil would quip back. 'Miss Church says it's Beethoven, and dead posh it is too.'

Margaret, unfamiliar with men and very much a spinster, often blushed when Peter appeared, but it was impossible to resist his wide smile and twinkling, mischievous dark-blue eyes. He had a lovely way with the children too – unlike the headmaster, who treated them like second-class citizens. 'Bunch of bloody flea-infested hooligans,' he would snarl at the drop of a hat.

Peter, on the other hand, cared for his flock who mostly lived in abject poverty in back-to-back slum rentals. Surrounded by towering mills on all sides, the air was thick with smoke belching from the cotton mills and loud with the sound of clogs on cobbles as the shifts changed throughout the day and night. Margaret knew from other members of staff that Peter regularly visited the homes of some of the most distressed children, taking food, offering money, even driving some of them to the local infirmary for medical treatment which they themselves couldn't afford. She had always known Peter Martlesham was a good man, and secretly she had admired his fine looks too. Tall and slim, he had a kind face, a ready smile and a sense of humour that instantly put people – adults and children alike – at their ease.

'Just look where Peter's charming easy ways got me,' Margaret reflected.

The bell ringing out for play-time roused her from her brooding reverie.

'You really have got to stop this daydreaming,' she crossly scolded herself. Turning her wandering attention to her class, who were all set to bolt out of the door, Margaret instructed, 'Line up in twos, no pushing – one behind the other, please.'

When the long line of bustling, squabbling children was finally quiet, Margaret opened the door for them to pass through, knowing that the minute they cleared the corridor they would barge, yelling and shouting, into the playground. Sighing, she shut the door and started to tidy up the music sheets littering the floor. Normally, she would join the other members of staff in the staffroom for a welcome cup of tea, but the thought of tea turned her stomach these days. That and the fact that Peter would be there, puffing on his pipe, sitting in his favourite chair, laughing and chatting with his colleagues.

'I just can't face that right now,' she groaned as she slumped into the nearest chair, which was way too small for her – and especially so now, with her burgeoning belly.

WHY, she railed at herself, WHY had she let an affair with Peter Martlesham happen? Over her time at St Chad's she had regularly sought his professional advice (nobody in their right mind would consult with the head-master on any educational matter) and she had always welcomed his support when she was faced with an aggressive parent or naughty child. Much as she admired him on several levels, Margaret had known only too well that he was married; she had met his two little girls many times, as well as his somewhat harassed wife, at Christ-mas carol services, Easter Sunday church processions, school outings, sports days and prize-givings over a num-ber of years. Peter's loyal family always turned up wearing their best clothes, the girls' sweet, chubby little faces scrubbed clean and shiny, the mother's expression often tense, with pursed lips, which suggested she would prefer to be doing something else. They seemed the perfect family, envied by many, especially since Mr Martlesham was still able to remain at home with his family, with no fear of being called up, due to his poor eyesight.

With her hands pressed tight over her ears, Margaret

tried to blot out the wild screams and calls issuing from the playground; feeling weak and drained, she allowed herself to drift back to the wonderful late-spring day when she and Peter had taken the older St Chad's pupils on a school history trip to Cartmel Priory in Westmorland. They had set out early, taking the train to Kendal, then local buses to the ancient priory. The children, wild with excitement, dumped their gas masks and packed lunch boxes on the gravel path and ran like crazed beings around the grave-yard, whooping and hollering in the clear spring sunshine until Peter, aware of the sanctity of their surroundings, briskly called them back to order. Reverent enough inside the dark priory, lit only by the afternoon light slanting through the stained-glass windows, they went berserk again once released, chasing each other along the river-bank where pale daffodils bobbed in the wind. Even now, months on, she could feel the wind on her cheeks and smell the delicate perfume of early-spring daffodils; there had been such hope and happiness in that perfect day which had irrevocably changed her life. Pulling herself together, Margaret took a deep shuddering breath before unlocking the top drawer of her teacher's desk from where she took out the papers she had already signed earl-ier in the day.

With tears rolling unchecked down her face, she whis-pered, 'I've got to get well away from here before it's too late.' What an irony, she thought, to be returning to the place where she had first fallen in love with Peter. 'Cart-mel,' she said out loud.

Just a few miles away from the place she was planning on running away to. After checking the documents for the final time, she slipped them into an envelope and sealed the flap, then in her best copperplate writing she penned the address:

Mary Vale Mother and Baby Home
Kents Bank
Grange-over-Sands
Westmorland

3. Count Your Blessings

Hurrying along the hospital corridor that smelt of laven-
der polish, a smile bubbling at the corners of her mouth,
Libby gave a little skip of happiness. Hugging herself, she
whispered, 'I am *so* lucky!'

She had always expected Mary Vale to be an exciting
challenge, but what she had never anticipated was how
joyous it would be to actually work in such a special institution. On her way to the sluice room Libby ran down a
list of all the pleasing things that she had so far encountered in the Home. Already in her first few days she had
established sound relationships with women whom she
would be nursing throughout their pregnancies and hopefully assisting when the time came for them to give birth.
The majority of them were young, poor and appallingly
ignorant of the facts of life. From the confidential con-
versations Libby had had with most of them she had
come across the same tragic theme – innocent, romantic
girl falls for a lad who leads her up the garden path then
runs for the hills the moment he's got what he wanted.
Some of the residents' histories had been slightly more
romantic, involving promises of marriage and everlasting
love; all quashed by furious parents who had dispatched
their bewildered, pregnant daughters to Mary Vale where
they would have their babies in secret and bring no shame
on the family name.

Enjoying getting to know her patients, Libby spent as much time as her duties would allow chatting to them, especially at meal-times when staff and residents alike ate together. Gladys, a big-boned, red-headed woman from Huddersfield, who was always hungry, claimed centre stage in the dining room most days, holding forth on her favourite subjects, which ranged from how ruthless men were, what hard times women had endured throughout the centuries, her passionate devotion to the Labour Party, and her often slanted point of view on the progress of the war.

'I tell you, ladies, the Allies are doing a bloody good job, have you been following it?' she demanded of her friends.

'Don't be daft, Glad, course we have,' one of her pals answered indignantly. 'Our brave lads are fighting for their lives all over blinking Europe,' the resident added, with a catch in her throat.

Thinking of her soldier brother Tom, Libby also felt a catch in her throat. Was he among the troops who had recently liberated Belgium from German occupation? Wherever he was, she would just love to know he was safe – alive, please God, she prayed. Where her sailor brother Les was, she had no idea.

'It'll be Berlin next,' Glad gloated as she lit up a cigarette, which she smoked even though pregnant. Turning to Libby, she cheekily asked, 'So, how's our newest midwife shaping up?'

'Fine, thanks, Gladys, I'm enjoying getting to know everybody in the Home. And how are you today?'

'Well, seeing as you asked, I've got terrible wind, and my feet hurt. Apart from that, I'm smashing.' Gazing thoughtfully at the ceiling, Gladys added, 'A little bird tells me that you're thinking of spreading Mary Vale's goodwill to the locals.'

Startled that Gladys had picked up on this information, Libby did a double-take. 'Who told you that?'

'Walls have ears in this place,' Gladys answered mysteriously. 'Is it true?'

Libby prevaricated. 'It's under discussion.'

'Well, if you ask my opinion . . .' Glad launched off.

Actually, I'm not, Libby thought with a wry smile. But never mind, you're bound to tell me anyway.

'The more you can get out there to help other women the better.'

'I totally agree with your sentiments, but realistically a community midwife scheme takes funding.'

'It's always about money,' Glad scoffed.

Glad's closest pal, Maisie from Liverpool, tall and lanky, with straggly mousey-blonde hair, a bit slow on the uptake and with the deepest guttural accent, chipped in. 'It's bloody money that opens doors.'

'One law for the rich – another for the poor. It's not fair, I say,' Glad grumbled.

Seeing that the conversation was going to shift from midwives to politics, Libby quietly slipped out of the room. But as she left, she had words with herself.

'If I do get this community midwife scheme under way, I'd better make sure that Gladys and the other residents don't feel short-changed – there'd be a price to pay if they thought they were being neglected in favour of other women. Remember that, Nurse Godburgh – or face the consequences.'

Other, less demanding women than Gladys talked to Libby in private about their fears, their homesickness and their heartache. Poor Maisie, a simple-minded soul, told the new nurse how she had fallen for a sailor stationed in Liverpool.

'He promised me the moon and stars,' she confessed to Libby one tea-time as they shared a plate of mackerel-paste sandwiches. 'He looked so young and bonny in his sailor's uniform and cap, worn at a jaunty angle over his jet-black hair. I fell for him, 'ook, line and sinker,' she said in her rich Liverpudlian accent. 'Harry . . .' she said on a long sigh.

Libby hoped Maisie's story would have a happy ending, but inevitably it didn't.

'Once he'd left port and sailed away, he wrote to say he was engaged and couldn't see me any more, by which time it was too late, I was up the duff. Mi dad went mad, kicked me out, but mi ma found money to send me up here to have the baby.'

'I'm sorry to hear that,' Libby commiserated.

Maisie shrugged. 'My fault, stupid girl – I should've known better.'

'Have you thought about what you will you do, dear?'

'Have the baby, then get it adopted and go back home – pretend it never happened,' Maisie answered with tears in her eyes. 'Really, what choices have I got, Nurse Libby?'

Libby was also enjoying her developing relationships with the Mary Vale staff, who had accepted her into their bosom with undisguised pleasure. She had instantly taken to beautiful Ada at her interview – who could resist her warm smile and intelligent dark-blue eyes? – but she had never imagined that she would so quickly find a friend as well as a colleague in her senior nursing mentor. Ada's obstetric knowledge and experience were endlessly interesting to young Libby. While they made beds on the wards, or sterilized instruments in the sluice room, stories and experiences would be exchanged.

'I heard similar sad tales when I was nursing in Lancaster,' Libby said as she and Ada made their morning rounds prior to Dr Jamie's surgery. 'But listening to them here makes them all the more poignant. It's not like we can walk away, is it?' she insisted. 'Nursing in Mary Vale means you're involved with the residents from the moment they wake up in the morning until the moment they go to sleep at night. You see their pain, hear the tears, and pity the lost, bewildered look in their eyes. It just breaks my heart,' she added, close to tears herself. 'I feel so protective of them all, and fearful for their future too at times. But,' she insisted as she threw back her strong shoulders, 'I'm determined to do everything in my power to make what difference I can in their lives, and to help them enjoy their time here at Mary Vale while they wait for their babies to be born.'

Ada gave an understanding nod. 'If I had a penny for every tragic story, I'd be a rich woman by now. I've nursed so many good women here in this Home, from young women cruelly abused within the family, to girls who didn't even know how they got pregnant in the first place, from sad tragic women engaged to servicemen killed in action, to other poor wretches who tried to take their own lives in order to avoid the dreadful stigma of a shameful pregnancy. The best we can do, Libby, as I'm sure you know, is to always be there for our charges, ready with a smile, a cup of tea, a shoulder to cry on.' Ada gave a heartfelt sigh. 'God knows, it's hard enough for the girls in here now, but just think how much harder it's going to be for them once they leave – most of them without their babies in their arms,' she added pointedly. 'Returning to a world where nobody knows what has happened to them, nobody asks questions about their experience of childbirth, or the agony of handing your baby over for adoption. Most of our residents have nobody to pour out their hearts to, once they leave Mary Vale.'

'I know, I've been thinking about all of that too,' Libby agreed. 'But we can help them,' she staunchly insisted. 'They might leave here a tiny bit less vulnerable if we can prepare them for what's to come.'

Ada gave Libby an appraising look. Once again, she was impressed by the young nurse's compassion and determination.

'Quite right, Libby. Though we give shelter and nurture, I believe a vital part of our job is preparing our vulnerable residents for their re-entry into a world which they were cruelly banished from.'

Recalling the words she had heard at her interview, Libby said, 'Mary Vale shelters all.'

Ada smiled. 'We never close our doors.'

Sister Theresa, who worked afternoons on the wards as a trainee midwife, and Dora, in charge of the baby nursery, fast became Libby's friends too. During one of their regular nappy-washing sessions, rinsing out dirty nappies in the big sluice sink before steeping them overnight in sterilized cold water, Dora and Sister Theresa mentioned to Libby some of the staffing problems they'd had in the past.

'We've had some funny 'uns,' Dora chuckled. 'A ward sister who looked good on paper went and changed her identity, then ran away in the dead of night to start a new life.'

'It was so shocking, not to mention upsetting, completely took us all by surprise,' Sister Theresa confessed.

'Then there was another midwife,' Dora continued, 'who theoretically ticked all the boxes until we discovered, would you believe it, that she had a severe drinking problem!' she exclaimed.

Briefly stopping rinsing the nappy in her hand, Theresa said, 'You have to agree, Dora, the worst of all was that awful adoption scandal which ended up in the High Court.'

'Oh, aye, that were downright wicked,' Dora declared.

'An adoption scandal here at Mary Vale?' Libby gasped.

'It was shameful,' Theresa murmured. 'The chairman of the board of governors at the time was privately selling off babies from Mary Vale.'

'Heavens!' Libby cried. 'How did you survive all that?'

'I won't say it wasn't difficult,' Dora told Libby straight. 'But we got through it, didn't we, Sister Theresa?'

'With God's grace we did,' she agreed.

After all the nappies had been rinsed, Dora poured the dirty water down the drain.

'We're a tough team here at Mary Vale, very protective of our residents and their babies. When problems come our way, we stick together and fight for the Home's continued survival. We never give in.'

'And we pray,' Theresa added. 'Especially during the hard times, we never stop praying for God's guidance.'

Dora grinned. 'We have a direct line to Him up there.' She pointed to the ceiling. 'Half the staff are nuns,' she chuckled.

One morning, while they were sterilizing instruments, Libby asked Ada how she and Jamie had met.

'We fell in love right here in Mary Vale,' Ada answered with a romantic smile. 'He was our resident doctor. Not long after we were married – soon after, when I was pregnant, in fact – Jamie was called up. He was posted to a medical clearing station in Tobruk where he was wounded, then got shipped home. It was an awful time,' she recalled.

'But obviously he came home safe and sound,' Libby said with some relief.

Ada nodded. 'Once Jamie was back on his feet, we started sharing our little girl's childcare,' she explained. 'Which generally works, Catherine permitting. Occasionally, she has a tantrum when one of us leaves. She really doesn't know how lucky she is, having both parents close by while she's growing up, when so many fathers have been sent away to war.'

'It's such a sensible idea,' Libby enthused. 'How did it all come about?'

'We agreed on a working arrangement which Matron approved of. Alternating shifts, one of us staying at home with Catherine while the other went out to work.'

'So, Mary Vale kept its resident doctor,' Libby noted.

'And its senior staff nurse too,' Ada grinned. 'Our domestic arrangements are smoother these days, now that we know we can trust Catherine with Sister Agnes or

Sister Theresa if there's an emergency, which there very often is.'

'I've seen your little girl with both nuns, she adores them and they completely dote on her too.'

Still smiling, Ada said, 'Catherine insisted I make a tea towel into a nun's veil so she will look like Sister Trees and Sister Agee, as she calls them,' Ada chuckled. 'We are very, very blessed.' Patting her tummy, she added, 'I only hope the new baby settles into our arrangement as easily as Catherine.'

'Nobody would even know you were pregnant,' Libby observed.

'The baby's not due till May, months to go yet.'

'Well, you look marvellous,' Libby declared. 'The picture of health.'

Libby always enjoyed her time with jolly Nurse Dora in the baby nursery. Running a service where babies who were not breast-fed had to be bottle-fed around the clock, every four hours, was a huge task which could only be completed with the help of the residents. Every week a chore list was pinned up on the dining-room wall, which covered housework, laundry, sweeping out fireplaces, cleaning windows and feeding the new-borns in the nursery. Matron explained this to all the residents on their arrival, some of whom were initially indignant about having to get down on their hands and knees to clean out the sooty fire grates or wash soiled laundry.

'We cannot afford to pay outsiders, so we rely on you, our residents. Given your condition, we obviously try to make the work as light as possible. Please bear in mind that all chores — other than the bottle-feeding rota, which out of necessity runs around the clock – are conducted in the morning, straight after breakfast. The afternoons are free for those of you not allocated to the nursery to do whatever you please: rest, sleep, or walk out when the weather's fine.'

Libby noticed that feeding the babies in Dora's nursery was without doubt the most popular chore. The nursery with its tidy row of little white canvas cots attracted most of the residents. Though often terrified of even picking up the babies to start with, the residents quickly responded to Dora's experience; her instructions on the techniques of bathing, changing and feeding were clear and straight-forward, but if anybody ever failed to do as instructed, she descended on them like the wrath of God. If a baby was left crying in a dirty nappy for too long, or not winded properly, she would tear a strip off the offender. On one of her visits to the nursery Libby struggled to hide a smile when she was privy to a conversation between Dora and Gladys.

Staunchly defending her babies, Dora said, 'The poor little things might not be able to talk, but they can defin-itely communicate.'

Opinionated Gladys, never backwards at coming for-wards, bluntly asked, 'How the 'ell do we know what they want? They seem to be crying all the blinkin' time.'

'What else can they do?' Dora scolded. 'They've only just come into the world. You'll learn to understand their needs if you're patient enough.'

'Patience has never been one of my virtues,' Gladys joked.

'If they're scrunched up and uncomfortable-looking,

they might have wind,' Dora suggested. 'Or they might need a nappy change.'

'And if they're bawling the place down, they're starving,' Gladys chuckled. 'That one I do understand.'

Dora had told Libby in private that she often felt sad for the women she was instructing. 'Once they've given birth, the lasses will soon get to know their own babies' little ways, I've seen it often enough, it's a real time of bonding for new mothers. But then at six weeks, if they're going down the adoption path, they will have to start separating themselves from their babies, for their own sake. Some of the girls just get on with it, others never get over it.' Dora shook her grey head. 'It's not an easy thing to witness, believe you me.'

Everybody, staff and residents alike, admired and respected Dora, whose presence, whether it was in the nursery guarding her little treasures or in the dining hall enjoying a cup of tea and a laugh with friends, was always warm and welcoming. But as Libby got to know her better, she noticed that the bright, breezy nurse reacted badly to news of conscripted young lads being called up to fight at the Front. Whether it was announced on the big Bakelite radio in the cosy sitting room, or printed in a newspaper article, the effect was the same; Dora fell silent. Seeing her suddenly close up, withdrawing into herself, puzzled Libby deeply, and she confided in Ada.

'Early in the war Dora's beloved twin boys, barely turned twenty-one, both died fighting for their country. One lost his life in the evacuation of Dunkirk, the other in a minesweeper which was torpedoed by the Germans in the North Atlantic. Their deaths left a huge hole in

Dora's life, one that she very nearly didn't emerge from. If it hadn't been for Matron imploring her to return to work, Dora might very well have taken her own life. With much coaxing and reassuring she did come back to us,' Ada said gratefully. 'Once back in Mary Vale's nursery, surrounded by all the new-borns in their cots, Dora's broken heart slowly healed, as much as it ever can. Thank God she found a reason to live again,' Ada recalled, with tears in her beautiful eyes. 'Seeing the babies' little hands eagerly reaching out to her, nursing them in her arms, changing and feeding them, rocking them to sleep, restored her faith in humanity. But inevitably the grief still hits her hard sometimes, especially when she hears of other young lives being lost. To be honest, I think she'll live with that sorrow until the day she dies.'

'God, what a sacrifice,' Libby said with an emotional lump in her throat. 'She never talks about it.'

'It's far too painful for her to go down that route,' Ada answered knowingly. 'We're lucky to have her: apart from being a wonderful nurse, Dora is also a wonderful friend; once she takes you under her wing, you're hers for life.'

On the wards Libby was also regularly supported by Sister Theresa, the sweet, gentle novitiate who worked in the kitchen in the mornings then frequently joined the nursing staff in the afternoons. Libby heard from both Ada and Dora that the young nun had once been a resident herself in Mary Vale.

'When she was a young teenager, she was sexually abused by a member of her own family. Mercifully, she was sent to Mary Vale to give birth and has hardly left the place since,' Ada said with a fond smile. 'She has immense compassion and understanding for the residents. Who better to understand what they are going through than somebody who has suffered greatly herself?'

'When did she decide to become a nun?' curious Libby asked.

'Some years ago, now,' Ada recalled. 'The rules of her order dictate that she spends time studying and praying in the chapel. God only knows when she does that – probably in the middle of the night. Most of her day is taken up in one way or another at Mary Vale, where she is much loved and hugely appreciated.'

As the days passed Libby became more aware that there were no social boundaries to overcome in Mary Vale. There was no sense of the doctor being grander than the cook, or Matron being better than the nurses under her, or Father Ben being singled out for special treatment because he was a priest. Together they formed a solid team which Libby fitted into perfectly. The Home's open atmosphere led to an ease of communication among the staff who not only worked together on the wards but also shared three meals a day. Sitting side by side, seven days a week, led to an easy exchange; whether it was work or home news, information was quickly circulated at Mary Vale. The relaxed, open atmosphere in the dining room was very much down to easy-going Sister Agnes. Her big, spotlessly clean kitchen – which was adjacent – always smelt of something delicious she'd somehow found a way of baking in the old Aga, despite rationing, and was a magnet to all. As Libby's confidence grew, she got used to popping into the kitchen, where she was always welcomed.

'Have a cup of tea,' Sister Agnes would say every time, without fail.

Whenever she was in the kitchen, Libby was fascinated by the many skilful ways Sister Agnes eked out the Home's rationed food. By adding natural ingredients, herbs and spices, she enhanced the flavour of puddings and savoury dishes alike, and she somehow always found the ingredients to make her own delicious bread, which was served warm at breakfast with a scraping of Alf the farmer's freshly churned butter. Seeing Sister Agnes flaking fish into a bowl of mashed potatoes, Libby asked what she was making.

'My sister picked up a bit of cod for me from the fish man in Grange this morning. I'm mixing it with potatoes and some chives, and pepper and fried onion,' she explained as she rolled little round fishcakes in breadcrumbs. 'I'll fry them for supper and we'll have them with baked beans and some nice tinned tomatoes.'

'Can't wait,' Libby chuckled. 'I love your cooking, Sister Agnes, especially your mackerel pâtés, they're so tangy and tasty.'

'I couldn't make those without Alf's help,' Sister Agnes told Libby. 'He regularly fishes for mackerel and crab for me, they make a richer paste than the shop-bought ones – they taste like cardboard,' she said dismissively.

'Alf helps me with my pony, he's kindness itself,' Libby said gratefully.

'He's getting on in years but, thank God, he's fit,' Agnes

said earnestly. 'I don't know how this place would func-
tion without Farmer Alf Arkwright.'

Another element of Libby's happiness was how quickly
Snowball had settled in to Mary Vale farm. Even though
she had insisted to her mother that it was perfectly all
right to take her pony to Mary Vale, Libby had secretly
worried about how well things might actually work out.
What if Libby's hours were longer than expected, or if
there was an emergency and she couldn't visit her pony as
often as she would have liked during the working week?
The winter months were long, dark and cold, especially in
Westmorland; Snowball would have to be stabled before
it went dark, but what if Libby couldn't leave her work?
Who would bring her pony in at nightfall? Snowball was
used to a busy farm and the company of other horses;
would he get lonely and depressed on his own all day?
As it turned out Libby needn't have worried. Farmer Alf
was proving to be, just as Libby had told Sister Agnes, a
true blessing.

In the early days, anxious Libby regularly snatched ten
minutes during a tea or dinner break to run down the
farm track to check on Snowball. Arriving flushed, breathless and still in her nurse's uniform, she would be relieved
to find that Alf had already taken care of everything:
whether it was turning Snowball out to graze, always
accompanied by old Captain, who was touchingly patient
with the frisky little fell pony, or bringing the animals in if
the weather turned cold or the autumn rain had set in.

'I am so grateful, Alf,' Libby declared, one chilly evening. 'I got here just as soon as I could, but you seem to
have beaten me to it.'

'Don't go fretting yourself, lass,' Alf soothed. 'When it comes to beasts, I know what to do and when to do it. Captain reminds me too, he hates the cold weather, bad for his owd bones. He neighs until I fetch him in when the temperature drops. And when it snows,' he chuckled, 'Captain won't even leave his stable.'

Tickling her pony's velvety soft ears, Libby fondly repeated her thanks. 'I don't know what I'd do without you, Alf.'

'Get away with you, lass. You're needed more up there in the Home than you are down here. Leave the hosses to me – I'll leave the nursing to you.'

Safe in the knowledge that Snowball was more than happy, Libby did as Alf bade her; she threw herself into nursing, working even longer hours than was expected of her, especially in the vital early days when she was learning so much about the Home and the residents. Content that she would make up for lost time and spend her precious days off with Snowball, exploring the bridle paths that edged the coastline and the vast marsh, or venturing into the deep forests around Cartmel Priory, Libby thanked her lucky stars for thoughtful Farmer Arkwright.

Libby's final blessing was her comfortable accommodation at Mary Vale. Used to the old farmhouse where she had grown up, Libby loved the spaciousness of her new room. Full of shifting light, it was a private sanctuary to her at the end of every day. She took great pleasure in throwing open the sash windows and leaning out over the wide sill to catch views of the sun setting over the Irish Sea, or just to listen to the roosting waterbirds settling down for the night. It was also a perfect place to write letters home. Sitting on her single bed, with her back to the wall and her face to the open window, Libby scribbled off hurried notes home to her parents.

Dearest Mam and Dad,

I've settled in beautifully here. It's a lovely place and the staff just couldn't be kinder. I wondered to start with what it would be like working and living alongside nuns, but I needn't have. The two nuns I'm closest to are Sister Agnes and sweet little Sister Theresa. Agnes is the cook who rustles up one good meal after another. How she does it given the rationing restrictions that are getting worse all the time I'll never know. She's got a heart of gold, and her kitchen is a delight, it always smells of something cooking, apple pies, or fritters, or cheese and onion pasties, they're my favourite. It's not like our kitchen at home, which smells of wet lambs warming up by the Aga or work clothes drying by the fire. Just thinking of that smell reminds me of home and how I miss you two so much.

Anyway, back to the other nun, Sister Theresa, who is such a love. She's very quiet but once you get to know her you can see how determined and focused she is, she can be very funny too in a dry sort of way. She splits her day between working in the kitchen and on the wards, which would be enough for most people, but she's also training to be a nun and has to study as well as pray every single day. I don't know how she does it. Then there's Nurse Dora, who's not a nun, she runs the baby nursery. You can imagine how much I love that place, full of new-born Mary Vale babies. You know better than most how I've always loved babies, it's what drove me to become a midwife in the first place. I take every opportunity to pop into the nursery every day for a quick baby cuddle and a chat with Dora, who I know you would get on with like a house on fire.

Tell me, have you any news from Tom and Les? I've not had time to write to them, and even if I had, I'm not sure of their current addresses. Everything's so top secret these days. If you're in touch, please will you give them my love and a big kiss each. That goes for you too, a big kiss and cuddle, from your loving daughter,

Libby
xxxx

PS Forgot to mention that Snowball's got a new friend, an old carthorse called Captain, she runs rings round him!

Staring out at the inky-dark winter sky, Libby whispered to herself, 'I don't think I've ever been as happy in my entire life.'

Deep in thought, she watched a new moon, like a silver sixpence, slip from behind a bank of clouds then glide into full view, beaming down on to the churning waters of the turning tide and gently lighting up the night sky where the North Star flickered. 'There's only one thing more I want, and that is to get out into the community. I know it will have to be agreed by the powers that be, and nobody's quite sure where the funding is going to come from – and as everybody keeps telling me, I *have* to be patient,' she blurted very impatiently. 'But I really hope something comes of it, this project means *so much* to me.'

4. Community

After confessing her desire to find out if there was any news on the community project, Libby enlisted Ada's help.

'Let's have a word with Matron in the sitting room after tea today,' Ada suggested. 'We can find a little corner to chat in,' she assured Libby, whose tummy started to twirl with excitement.

Finding a quiet place to talk turned out not to be quite as easy as Ada had predicted. Gladys was holding forth with a couple of other residents who were raptly listening to their friend expounding her theory on the state of the nation.

'Now that Rommel's gone and popped his clogs we can all breathe a sigh of relief. Never fear, ladies,' she said as she gleefully wagged her finger at her pals, 'we'll have Hitler on the run before Christmas.'

Lowering her voice to a whisper, Matron suggested they move to the opposite side of the room where it was a bit quieter. Knowing Glad as well as she did, Matron said, 'Dear girl, she always gets fired up after a meal, it must be the amount she eats. She'll be dead to the world in half an hour – with Glad a burst of energy is always followed by a long deep sleep.'

After settling down with their cups of tea, which they had brought into the sitting room with them, Libby made a cautious start.

'I just wondered if we could discuss the community work I mentioned at my interview a little bit more?' she asked. 'I know I've not been here that long, but I'm really keen to see if it is feasible for Mary Vale to expand into the community.' She ended in a self-conscious rush.

Matron smiled gently; who could possibly resist the passion shining so fiercely in this young woman's eyes?

'Let me assure you, we haven't forgotten. Ada and I have been giving it considerable thought.' Coming straight to the point, though, she continued ruefully, 'Realistically, dear, the biggest problem is money. As you know, Mary Vale has only a tiny pot of surplus money.'

'As a charitable institution I'm sure you are stretched to your limit,' Libby responded, biting down her disappointment.

'If we spare you for an afternoon, we have to replace you with a supply nurse, and that would cost,' Ada explained.

Libby immediately said impetuously, 'I don't know how much a supply nurse's fees would be but I would willingly cover as much as I could from my own savings for a trial period. It would be worth every penny and I wouldn't mind at all,' she declared.

Matron held her hands up in the air. 'No, dear,' she strongly protested. 'That simply won't do.'

'I'm serious, Matron,' Libby passionately replied. 'I want this so much, I would willingly fund it myself for as long as I could.'

'I'm afraid that is simply not an option,' Matron stated flatly. 'I could never condone such a thing.'

Feeling desperate, Libby turned from Ada to Matron and back again. 'Are you saying no, then?'

Matron stretched over to gently pat her hand. 'Hear me out, eh?'

Libby dropped her penetrating gaze so Matron wouldn't see the crushing disappointment she was feeling. 'Sorry, yes, of course,' she muttered. Forcing herself to sit still and keep her mouth firmly shut, Libby hung on Matron's every word.

'Reverend Mother liked your idea very much. She mentioned a small charitable fund controlled by the convent, not the Mary Vale staff, which we can tap into. The Reverend Mother suggested we use this for a short trial period.'

'Really?' irrepressible Libby exclaimed before she could stop herself.

Matron held up a warning finger. 'It's a very small amount, it might just cover a supply nurse's fee into the New Year. But it would be a good way of finding out if the proposition is viable, and if there really is a need for a community midwife.'

Libby was jubilant. 'Well, that's better than nothing.'

'It will be an experiment, Libby,' Ada explained. 'If we establish that there is a genuine need then we might be able to apply for local funding in order to continue.'

'It would depend on how successful your trial run goes,' Matron expanded. 'A lot would be riding on you, Libby, to make it work.'

Perched on the edge of her chair, Libby felt her confidence beginning to wobble as she realized the immensity of what she was prepared to take on. How awful would it be to fail?

Seeing her usually ebullient colleague momentarily

fazed, Ada quickly tried to distract her. 'Tell us how your community nursing worked when you were in Lancaster.'

Libby took a deep breath. 'Well, first of all we had to establish who were the priority cases for a home visit. The hospital liaised with local doctors and social workers in order to ascertain this.'

'I'm sure Dr Reid has kept up good links with local medics over the years. They would know which women to prioritize and how often they would need a visit,' Matron pointed out.

Libby nodded. 'My previous community visits were two or three times a week.'

'That's way more than we could possibly manage,' Matron said firmly.

'I understand,' Libby hastily agreed. 'I'm just explaining how it worked in Lancaster, where community nursing was established. Once we were allocated patients, we spent time building up relationships with them,' she continued. 'It wasn't at all like being at Mary Vale, where the intimacy of living side by side, whether you like it or not, gives you almost immediate insight. It's generally the case that community relationships take longer to establish because the home visits are more widely spread.'

'Exactly,' Ada agreed.

'Many of the women nursed in the community in Lancaster were ashamed of their environment, and their children were initially frightened of me. I had my work cut out,' Libby smiled. 'But the mothers' needs generally overcame everything else. By the time it came to them giving birth, we were usually good friends,' she concluded.

Still treading cautiously, Matron said, 'If we were to

establish one afternoon of community visits a week, in the hope of building up to more, we would have to establish who those patients would be.'

Feeling a growing sense of excitement, the three women stared at each other.

'If you could get the ball rolling with Dr Jamie, Ada,' Matron said, 'I'll have a word with Reverend Mother at her earliest convenience.'

Ada nodded her head enthusiastically. Forcing herself not to fidget, Libby sat up straight and listened intently.

'It's important that we find the right patients who we could safely leave after Christmas, should our funding run out,' Ada continued. 'It would be wrong to abandon anybody halfway through their pregnancy, so we need to find expectant mothers whose due date is Christmas or thereabouts.'

'I agree,' Matron added. 'They must be safely delivered and nursed through the post-partum period.'

'Well, we have the makings of a modest plan at last,' Ada said.

'So, what happens next?' Libby enquired.

'I report back to Reverend Mother and consult with her on the viability of the initial plan we have just outlined together.'

Trying hard to hide her disappointment that they hadn't come up with a final yes on the community nursing plan, Libby asked, 'Does Reverend Mother normally take a long time to mull things over.'

Sensing the eager young girl's disappointment, Matron answered with a knowing smile. 'Reverend Mother can move surprisingly quickly when it is a matter that concerns her.'

Libby's heightened sense of excitement made her increasingly restless and impatient, so when her day off came around she was delighted to blow off steam by trotting around the countryside on Snowball. On a glorious golden October day, with leaves drifting down in showers of bronze and gold, Libby vigorously groomed her pony before setting off for nearby Cartmel Forest.

'I know you've been having fun with Captain in the paddock,' she chatted happily to Snowball, who gently butted Libby's tummy as she slipped the reins over his head, 'but today you and I are going further afield. I need to take my mind off things,' she confided.

After saddling up Snowball, Libby tightened his girths and then sprang into the saddle just as Farmer Arkwright came walking out of the barn.

'You off then?' he started conversationally.

'Yes, we're going to Cartmel Forest,' Libby announced. 'It feels like ages since I went for a proper ride.'

'Aye, you've been putting in some long hours up at the Home,' he acknowledged.

'Well, I'm making up for it today,' Libby chuckled as she pressed her heels into Snowball's tummy, urging him forwards.

'Don't get lost in the woods,' he warned. 'And make sure you head home well before nightfall.'

'Thanks, Alf, I will,' she called out as Snowball broke into a lively trot. 'See you later.'

Setting off down the back lane, with perfect views on either side of the surrounding fells, Libby gave her frisky pony his head; needing no second bidding, Snowball broke into a gallop, which was exactly what Libby needed. With the wind blowing through her tumbling golden-red hair, held back by only a ribbon, she laughed out loud as the surrounding countryside flashed by in a blur of autumnal red, gold, russet, sage and brown. Clutching tightly on to the reins, she kept her seat until Snowball started to slow down of his own accord.

Reaching forward to stroke her pony's hot sweaty neck, Libby murmured, 'Whoa, boy, whoa there.'

Snorting and tossing his head, Snowball reduced his speed to a walk, which Libby sank into, emptying her mind of all things relating to work. She let go of the tension that had gripped her throughout the week. Feeling her shoulders droop as her body relaxed, Libby reached the woods lying directly under the shadow of Cartmel Fell. Slowing her pace, she cautiously reined in her pony, who shook his pretty silver head.

'Slow down now, sweetheart,' she warned. 'We don't want you stumbling over any fallen logs.'

Following the forest trail, Libby carefully threaded her way along the winding pathways. Overhead, towering ancient beech and horse chestnut trees formed a canopy of criss-crossing boughs through which the slanting sun blazed on to leaves that slowly spiralled down. The fallen autumn leaves formed a soft bed underfoot which absorbed the sound of Snowball's clip-clopping hooves. The deeper they wove their way into the wood the deeper the silence became; from a glade swathed in golden bracken a gentle-eyed doe with her leggy fawn nervously looked out while scatty pheasants burst from the undergrowth, indignantly clattering their wings as they flew off in all directions. Libby cried out in delight when a great spotted woodpecker flashed its scarlet-red feathers at her before landing on a tree stump.

Listening to the steady rhythmic tapping of the bird's beak as it searched for seeds and insects, Libby counted her blessings. Here she was surrounded by beauty and the wonders of nature while millions of men and women of her generation, including her two brothers, were fighting for their beloved country. She'd had little time to write to them since starting at Mary Vale but she was sure that if there had been any news from Tom or Les, her mother would have kept her up to date. Tom, the eldest, had survived the D-Day landings in June 1944, but where was he fighting now? Feeling anxious for his safety, Libby wondered if he was part of the Normandy campaign that they heard on the BBC news was rapidly advancing?

As a stoker on a minesweeper, Les's whereabouts were kept strictly top secret; months could go by without a word from her younger brother, and when he did reappear for a brief leave Les never said where he had been or which ship he had been serving on. Libby wished with all her heart that she could share this moment of utter peace with her brothers. Smiling tenderly, she remembered how unexpectedly sensitive they could both be; in the middle of playing they would suddenly stop to point out to their little sister an eagle swooping over the fells, or a brilliant kingfisher zipping across a stretch of river. Though loud and rowdy lads, they had a soft side which Libby had occasionally been privy to. She hoped the war wouldn't have hardened that part of them, but how could anyone live through five years of fighting and somehow come out unscathed, whether it be physically or mentally?

As Glad had rightly said, the tide seemed to be turning, but dear God, what cost in human life had been paid to get to this point. When the heroic Polish Home Army uprising against the Nazis had ended with their surrender, the British press revealed that nearly two hundred thousand Polish civilians had died in Warsaw, mostly from mass executions. And that following the surrender of Polish forces, German troops had systematically levelled a third of the city, leaving thousands of innocent women and children homeless.

Imagine if that many civilians had died here, Libby thought to herself. Who could survive such an onslaught? How do you have the will to go on when everything you know and love has been eradicated?

Even though the day was warm, Libby felt a shiver ripple down her back. How fortunate she was to be safe, housed, fed and contented, while others laid down their lives for her freedom – something, in fact, she never took for granted. How could she, with her brothers in the thick of it? Patting Snowball's warm neck, Libby fervently prayed for Tom and Les, with an emotional lump in her throat.

'Bring them all safely home, Lord, keep them from peril and protect them with your love.'

Taking Farmer Arkwright's advice, Libby gave herself plenty of time to make the return journey home. Trotting back up the narrow lanes, hedged in with drystone walls, Libby spotted Ada, who was also off duty, with Dora, Sister

Theresa and Matron covering the wards. Ada was ambling along with her little daughter, Catherine, who at just over two years old was determined to walk everywhere.

Hearing the sound of Snowball's clip-clopping hooves, the little girl whirled around. 'Gee-gee!' she exclaimed in delight.

Reining Snowball in, Libby waited while Ada lifted Catherine up so she could stroke her pony.

'Good horsey,' Catherine gurgled as she tugged at the pony's long silver mane.

'Careful, sweetheart,' Ada warned.

Pointing to the saddle, Catherine begged, 'Up, up.'

'Is that okay?' Libby asked.

'I don't think we've got much choice,' Ada smiled.

Laughing, Libby popped Catherine on to the saddle beside her where the little girl sat transfixed with joy. Supporting her firmly with one hand, Libby directed Snowball up the track towards Ada's pretty little cottage garden which was still bright with marigolds and chrysanthemums. It took a while to persuade Catherine to dismount, and when she did, she ran indoors to fetch the pony a carrot and two potatoes.

'Will Snowball eat potatoes?' Ada chuckled.

'He'll eat anything,' Libby assured her.

After securing Snowball's reins to the garden fence, Libby gratefully accepted a cup of tea from Ada, and some Brown Betty slices that Ada and Catherine had made that morning.

'Don't you ever just yearn for a *real* cake,' Ada sighed as she and Libby settled on the garden bench and Catherine pushed her teddy bear around the garden in a little pram.

'You know, a real chocolate éclair, or a slice of fresh apple pie and ice cream.'

'If the war ends soon, we might have all of those delicious things again,' Libby said hopefully.

'I suspect not. If we're to feed a nation in peacetime, rationing must surely go on for years,' Ada added glumly. 'Maybe it's because I'm expecting again that I yearn for little luxuries.'

'Eating for two; at least you're fit and active.'

Ada nodded in agreement. 'I must admit, I do feel full of beans. In fact,' she added on a confidential note, 'I've been thinking of painting the little box room in readiness for the new baby. It makes me feel so sad for some of our residents, who don't have the luxury of planning a future for their babies,' she added wistfully.

Libby gave a sad smile. 'They're all so brave, just getting on with it, mostly unsupported.'

'I never fail to be amazed by the bravery of our patients,' Ada confessed. 'Their determination to see it through to the end, even if the final scenario turns out to be heartbreaking.'

'What touches me is how much they worry about the babies' well-being,' Libby continued. 'They want their babies to be strong and healthy right from the start, even though many of them might live a lifetime without them.'

'It's hard not to get emotional,' Ada replied. 'I always find the spirit of Mary Vale gives me great strength. Even when I'm overwhelmed with sadness, I take courage from the history of the Home and the wonderful staff we're supported by.'

'It must be odd working in a Home full of pregnant women when you yourself are pregnant?' Libby mused.

'Most of the residents don't even know that I'm pregnant, but when I start to show I'm quite sure there will be a lot of questions asked.'

Libby grinned. 'Pregnant ladies ask questions *all* the time.'

'And without a doubt they'll want to know if Jamie will deliver the baby,' Ada continued. 'He was away fighting in North Africa when I had Catherine, so it will be wonderful if he can.' She smiled fondly. 'Though, to be honest, I'm surrounded by wonderful midwives.'

Smiling at Ada, with the setting sun slanting on her long, rich mahogany-brown hair, Libby admired her wonderful sparkling-blue eyes and healthy tanned face. 'You could say you're spoilt for choice,' she grinned.

'Indeed, I am,' Ada laughed as she scooped her rosy-faced daughter into her arms and hugged her. Peering over her daughter's shoulder, she added thoughtfully, 'I hope you were encouraged by the talk we had the other day with Matron?'

'Oh, I was, I'm thrilled, though I must admit I'm impatient to hear it can definitely go ahead,' Libby admitted. 'Don't get me wrong, I appreciate everything you're doing for me, and we must proceed with caution. But . . .' she sighed, 'I am completely desperate to get started, Ada. I know, I know,' she said, before Ada could say it for her, 'I have to be patient – but I have a real sense that there are women out there who right now are in serious need of a good midwife, and I just can't wait to meet them.'

5. The Schoolroom

Margaret stood in her empty classroom where she finally let her tears, which she had been holding back since she woke up that morning, fall unchecked. It was safe to do so now that everybody, even the caretaker, had left the building. Her final day at St Chad's had passed in a series of mixed goodbyes. Awkward mothers or grannies picking up their charges had mumbled their stilted thanks, plus there were the ceaseless thanks from the schoolchildren – not just those whom Margaret taught but dozens of others, from different year groups, whom she had got to know during her time at St Chad's – arriving with gifts which they plonked unceremoniously on her desk, presently littered with little posies (mostly half-dead chrysanthemums and twigs), a few walnuts in a brown paper bag, a stale fish-paste sandwich, a curled-up black and white photograph of one of the naughtiest boys in her class, and a scattering of odd little trinkets.

Turning her attention from the desk, Margaret's brooding dark-brown eyes scanned the artwork on the wall. There was no harm in leaving up the children's paintings, but she was quite sure her replacement, a gruff, middle-aged drinking pal of the headmaster's, wouldn't appreciate Margaret's illustration of the Hall of the Mountain King alongside her giant-sized musical crotchets and quavers. Feeling suddenly mutinous, Margaret said to herself, 'I'll leave them anyway, at least they brighten up the classroom and might even remind my pupils of the fun we had listening to music on Friday afternoons.'

Sighing, Margaret recalled just how much her pupils had loved those lessons; the three R's were essential, of course, but music, as Shakespeare himself had written, was 'the food of love'. It lifted the soul and gave everything a higher purpose. To see expressions of joy or rapture in the eyes of young children from poor backgrounds had been an immense privilege. Their scrawled descriptions of their musical experiences, written in battered grubby exercise books, bore witness to this. At least she had done something to lift them from the poverty and grime of their everyday lives, albeit only fleetingly.

While cleaning out her desk drawers Margaret had come across a little card sent from Peter, written when their secret affair was at its height and when he had even thought of leaving his wife for Margaret.

'*My darling, I'm yours forever . . .*'

Rolling her eyes, Margaret considered what a romantic fool she had been at the time. Really! As if Peter would ever have left his family.

Not that she had ever really expected him to, or even intimated that it might be a good idea to do such a thing, but his blazing passion had been too difficult to resist. She had always sensed that it was only a question of time before the romance waned, and Peter's thoughts inevitably turned to his family. She was right too; slowly, Peter withdrew his attention. Though he still remained tender and gentle, Margaret instinctively knew the first flush of passion was over. They met less often, and when they did, he was more hurried, had appointments he 'simply couldn't get out of'. By the time Margaret discovered that she was pregnant, he was already (albeit guiltily) talking about remaining faithful to his wife, stressing his devotion to the children, and plans to enhance his career, all of which certainly didn't involve him breaking the news to his wife of his affair with the school's music teacher. Sensing his growing discomfort, Margaret in the end was the stronger of the two.

Even throughout the shock of finding herself pregnant, and at a loss initially about what she would do, or where she would go, Margaret knew that encouraging Peter to return to the domestic fold was the right thing to do. Realistically, she knew that he would never want her long term, as his lifetime partner; thinking back on how quickly their affair had blazed and wilted led Margaret to consider the possibility of Peter being a flirt, a romancer who regularly fell in and out of love but never deeply enough to make him want to leave his family. If so, she had fallen perfectly under his spell. In the end Margaret didn't exactly push him out of her life but she certainly eased the transition. Steeling her heart, she made an announcement one wet, desultory afternoon in Queen's Park.

'I've seen an advert for a job in Cheshire – Altrincham, in fact,' she lied. 'It's for a music teacher in a private school, just girls, quite well paid, and I've applied for it,' she ended in a rush.

Though Peter had reacted in genuine surprise, Margaret hadn't missed the flash of relief in his eyes, which had hurt her cruelly. The lie helped him accept that their relationship had run its course.

'Well, I am very sorry to hear that, dear,' he had solemnly responded.

And now, less than an hour ago, she had said her farewell to him; hiding her true feelings, holding back tears. Not being able to talk to the father of her child had been an agony, but now it was done. Compounding her lie about her move south, she had told Peter that she would be leaving town at the weekend. Wearing an unattractive baggy skirt and blouse, she kept her distance as she leant forward to briefly peck him on both cheeks. Avoiding any close embrace (though, in reality, it was all that she wanted), she watched her lover walk out of the classroom and her life too. With tears still flowing unchecked, Margaret wondered how Peter might have reacted if she had told him the truth: that she was leaving her job and her hometown because she was pregnant. Did he have a right to know? she pondered. Was it fair not to tell him the truth?

'What good would that do?' Margaret asked herself.

She knew he didn't want her any more, that his heart lay with his family. By announcing her pregnancy, she would make things messy; she instinctively sensed that he would frantically try to make amends, maybe offer her money, which she would need for sure. But that would have meant swallowing her pride, which right now was the only thing she had left. Margaret was old enough to accept the status quo, know the affair was over, and that she urgently needed to get away.

After school, on her way home, Margaret would regularly pop into the central library in Bolton's fine civic centre. Here she had researched homes for unmarried mothers and their babies, several of which were dotted around the North-West. There were a number of them in several big northern cities, which Margaret rejected; some were too expensive for her budget and some, she knew from reading the newspaper, were in areas frequently under attack from the Luftwaffe. Margaret yearned to be in the countryside, in a place of peace and quiet, where she could wait for her baby to arrive. When she saw the Mary Vale advert in a medical magazine, she seized on it immediately.

'*Mary Vale Home, Kents Bank, Morecambe Bay.*'

'It's by the sea,' she gasped out loud. 'Near forests, rivers, mountains – and Cartmel.'

Immediately applying for a place, she was accepted as a full fee-paying resident, which left her bank account depleted, but at least she now had a safe place to go – a beautiful place where, she hoped, she could finally find some peace.

Luckily, as his ardour had waned and guilt had set in, Peter had demanded less and less physical contact with his lover; if they had been more intimate, he could not have failed to notice her swollen breasts and thickening waist. Margaret, anxious not to draw attention to herself, always wore loose clothes: roomy cardigans and blouses, teamed with loosely fitted, pleated skirts. The only source of comfort throughout those lonely wretched days when she was concealing her secret was that, one day soon, she would no longer have to hide her condition. Within the week, she would be hidden away in Mary Vale along with other women awaiting the birth of their babies and subsequent adoptions. Not wanting to think about that now, Margaret slammed the desk drawers firmly shut.

'One step at a time, lady,' she admonished herself.

Right now, the thought of leaving Bolton, her job and her lover was more than enough to cope with; the thought of actually giving her baby away was something she simply could not contemplate. Turning to the blackboard, Margaret smiled as she read the sentences that she had written in white chalk, quotes from her pupils describing their feelings when they listened to Grieg's 'In the Hall of the Mountain King'.

Wild, spinning, twirling, whirling . . .
Hopping, magic music . . .
Stepping into the darkness . . . running away.

And that's exactly what I'm doing, Margaret thought as she left her classroom for the last time. I'm running away, stepping into the unknown.

The following morning, Margaret left her ground-floor flat for the last time and took a steam train, packed with exhausted troops who slept in untidy heaps in the carriage-ways or dozed in the netted overhead hangers. As they travelled north Margaret's eyes followed the line of hills that gently gave way to the rolling fertile fields of the Fylde Coast, still grazed by large herds of black and white cows. After passing through Lancaster, the vast expanse of the Irish Sea slowly loomed into view. On a clear day like today the sea was a flat sheet of metallic grey, reflecting a blue sky with scudding white clouds. The train, spewing black smoke in its wake, rumbled across the bay on metal tracks secured to stout wooden girders drilled into the seabed.

Marvelling at the eerie sensation of feeling, as if she was travelling between sky and sea, Margaret gazed down at the rushing incoming tide that broke on the margins of a silvery sage marshland where wading birds waited eagerly for tasty encrustations and sea worms.

Disembarking from the train at Kents Bank, Margaret – like many women before her – carried her small suitcase up a little lane that led into the grounds of Mary Vale. Dipping her head as she walked under the looping boughs of holly and beech trees turning golden in the afternoon sun, words from a popular romantic song suddenly floated into Margaret's head: 'You'll Never Know (Just How Much I Love You)'. It had been one of Peter's favourites, something he sang when they went for walks in Queen's Park or snatched a secret kiss in a darkened classroom. In truth, Peter would never know just how much Margaret had adored him, the only man in her lonely spinster's life. He would never really know just how much she cared, as the song went; she had loved him too much to make him suffer, but right now she had never felt lonelier or more abandoned in her whole life.

Taking a deep shuddering breath, she raised her hand and knocked loudly on Mary Vale's imposing front door. It was quickly opened by a smiling Sister Agnes. Feeling immediately at ease in her presence, the newcomer smiled back.

'I'm Margaret Church, I think you might be expecting me,' she said nervously.

'Come along in, you're most welcome,' Agnes said warmly as she relieved the newcomer of her case and coat. 'You'll have had a long journey; you must be freezing. Settle yourself in the sitting room by the fire and I'll fetch a nice cup of tea?'

'That would be lovely,' Margaret gratefully accepted, feeling a little less anxious already.

'The sitting room's over yonder,' Sister Agnes added as she nodded towards a room opposite. 'I'll fetch your tea right away and I'll tell Sister Ada you've arrived, I'm sure she'll join you shortly.'

Slipping into the high-ceilinged room which had bay windows facing south-west, looking out on to the sweeping gardens, colourful with heavy-headed golden chrysanthemums, banks of bright-orange marigolds and long-stemmed purple gladioli, Margaret was hoping nobody else would be in there. The room was warmed by a crackling coal fire; luckily, the only other occupant was the kitchen cat, who lay on the hearthrug fast asleep. Rubbing her chilled hands, Margaret jumped when the door clicked open and a beautiful young nurse with a wide smile and stunning deep-blue eyes walked in and shook her extended hand.

'Delighted to meet you, I'm Sister Ada. You must be Margaret.'

'Indeed I am,' Margaret said as she sank into a deep comfy chair by the fireplace. 'It's very nice to be here.'

Ada settled in the chair opposite. 'Most of our residents say that on arrival,' she smiled. 'I think it's the strain of the journey, and all the emotional goodbyes.'

Margaret nodded; how could she begin to explain the sense of letting go that was taking place inside her?

'I never expected Mary Vale to be quite so beautiful, the photograph in your advertisement doesn't do it justice.'

'It is truly beautiful.' Ada's ready smile revealed her perfectly white teeth. 'The fells and the forests, the marsh and the sea. They're what drew me here in the first place, and I have to admit I never want to leave. My family and I are determined to stay in this valley for ever.'

After she had finished her tea and nibbled at a coconut biscuit Sister Agnes had kindly brought for her, Ada escorted Margaret to her room on the first floor. Delighted by the view of the garden that sloped down to the marsh, Margaret exhaled a happy sigh of relief. This wasn't so bad, after all, she thought to herself.

'I'll leave you to unpack. Tea's at five in the dining room, you can't miss it, it's the noisiest room in the entire building,' Ada grinned. 'Take the opportunity to have a rest after your journey, Mary Vale's a great place to let go,' she said knowingly, before she slipped out of the room and gently closed the door behind her.

Lying on her narrow single bed, Margaret listened through the open window to the shushing sound of the incoming tide, and recalled Ada's words.

'Time to let go . . .' she sighed as she drifted off to sleep.

6. Mary Carter

In a dilapidated cottage set back off a muddy farm track on the Allithwaite road Mary Carter stared around the mean little dwelling where she and her family lived. An old-fashioned black grate provided heat to warm them (luckily, there was always enough wood in the Allithwaite area to keep the fire stoked, night and day) and cook what little food they had. Apart from the ancient rocking chair that Mary was presently sitting in, the room was sparsely furnished; just a rickety table, a couple of upright chairs, and a double bed in the far corner covered with a faded patchwork quilt. The back room, nothing but a crumbling wooden lean-to, was the older children's bedroom, but on cold nights Arthur and Joy abandoned their single bed with its dirty battered mattress to join their parents in the big warm bed, while baby Susan, tucked up in a blanket-lined wooden crate, slept next to the bed on Mary's side. Outside in the backyard stood a privy and a water pump, beyond which was a plot of land that would have made a perfect allotment, had her husband, Sam, not been too sick to dig it.

Since the day they had married and subsequently moved into North Cottage, life had been a struggle. Not that they hadn't married for love – admittedly, their nuptials were brought forward when Mary discovered she was pregnant with Joy, now nine years old, but she and Sam had been madly in love since the day they first laid eyes on each other in Kendal marketplace. Sam, a farm shepherd, had managed to find meagre accommodation with a low peppercorn rent. It was a reasonable arrangement that had lasted for some years, but sadly changed just after Susan was born, when the farm with its accompanying farmland, livestock and dwellings was bought up by a ruthless new landowner who raised all the tenants' rents in one fell swoop. With the massive rent increase, which everybody on the estate complained about, Mary had been forced to return to work, leaving Susan with an old lady who 'minded' mill babies while their mothers worked their shifts. It was a difficult arrangement which had meant introducing Susan to bottle milk so she could be fed by the minder during Mary's shift. It had ended abruptly when Mary, arriving to pick up her daughter at the end of the working day, found her on the floor where she had been left all day, lying in her own filth. She discovered the drunken minder in the backyard, oblivious to the pitiful howls of her hungry little charges. From then on, Mary stayed at home with Susan.

'And here we are now,' she muttered miserably as she shifted Susan on to the other breast. 'Stuck in this freezing-cold hovel, with water leaking under the flag floors and down the walls.'

No wonder her husband's health had failed. He had missed being called up at the start of the war because of a shadow on his lung, and he'd suffered for years with a wheezy chest. Eventually, coughing and breathless, he had (under much pressure from his wife) succumbed to visiting the local doctor, whom they could barely afford to pay, but who had immediately transferred Sam to Lancaster Infirmary. The outcome had not been good; Sam's pneumonia showed signs of the possible onset of early TB, which the doctor had explained was a disease that could be present in the body for years before its clinical onset. The information had struck the fear of God into Mary, who had already lost half of her family to the virulent disease. The specialist had advised Sam to take things easy, get lots of clean fresh air, keep warm and eat well. All of which had outraged Mary. If only they were rich and privileged, if only her beloved could do all of those things, but not one of the doctor's recommendations was achievable in their miserable circumstances. If Sam were to take things easy and rest when he needed to, he would be out of a job in less than a week. The tenant farmer, who was also facing a high rent increase, could do Sam no favours – he needed his shepherd out on the fells with his sheep if he were to meet the landlord's demands and keep a roof over his own head and his family's too. Out in all weathers – wind, hail, snow and flooding – Sam's shepherd's life was a cycle of non-stop outdoor chores. This was especially so after Christmas, which Mary was dreading, as the lambing season would be under way and Sam would be in the lambing shed twenty-four hours a day, even sleeping there among the ewes when it was too late to go home. When Sam wasn't physically herding his flock there were all the other jobs to be done: moving sheep from one valley to another, bringing them down from the fells, taking them to market, slaughtering, dipping, shearing – the year's cycle was relentless.

Rising to settle Susan in her wooden crate, Mary sighed

at the thought of how little rest her husband actually got. If he stopped to draw breath, he could lose work, which was what paid the bills. And as for eating well, did dry bread, potato hash, porridge and their sparse rations amount to a good diet? She didn't think so. Shaking her head in despair, Mary fumed over the injustices heaped on them. With most of their income spent on keeping a roof over their heads, there was little left over for food. Luckily, fish was cheaper and easier to come by in a seaside town than meat. Mary regularly walked into town to buy a cheap piece of mackerel from the fish man, which she would serve with a baked potato and fried onion gravy. Crab meat, if she could get it, she would pound into a paste for Sam's sandwiches – 'butties' (superior by far to the potted paste version that rationing allowed) which kept him going all day and sometimes all through the night too.

Stretching up, Mary caught sight of herself in the chipped mirror that dangled from a precarious hook on the kitchen wall. Although she had never been a beauty, Mary was once tall and shapely, with long slim legs, a narrow waist and a good bust. These days, she looked like a shapeless sack of potatoes, which wasn't helped by the darned grubby cardigan she constantly wore and the frayed winter skirt that needed patching. Her hair, once long and honey-brown, was prematurely streaked with grey and worn permanently in an untidy bun. The only part of her countenance that showed any life were Mary's silvery-grey eyes; they still sometimes sparkled with the old fire of her fighting spirit that had attracted Sam to her in the first place.

*

Later that afternoon, Mary was hanging up wet nappies, just boiled in a tub on the grate over the fire, when Sam popped back home with some provisions. These had all kindly been donated by the farmer's wife who had more than enough troubles of her own, these days, but she knew all too well just how destitute the Carter family were.

'Two slices of bacon, a small piece of cheese, milk, an egg, and half a nice fresh loaf,' Sam announced as he plonked everything on the kitchen table.

Immediately turning her attention to gratefully slicing the still-warm bread, Mary enthused, 'She's such a generous woman, as if they're not going through it too.'

'Aye,' Sam said humbly. 'Any kindness is appreciated.'

Mary bit her lip to stop herself from saying, 'If we weren't paying so much rent money, we wouldn't have to go begging for food the way we do.' She laid the thinly cut cheese on to the bread, which she topped with slices of onion. 'Get that down you, lovie, before you have to go back to work,' she said gently.

Mary's heart contracted with love as she watched her husband eat slowly.

'I can't stay long, sweetheart, I promised Stan I'd be back to help with fixing the pens.'

Gulping back the hot tea that Mary had put in front of him brought on a sudden spasm of coughing that racked Stan's frame, making him cough so violently and bringing him out in a hot sweat that left him weak and debilitated. As the spasm subsided Mary could not fail to notice a couple of vivid-red blood spots that speckled his hand-kerchief, though Sam hurriedly thrust it back into his pocket.

'Sweetheart,' she murmured as she laid a protective arm around his heaving shoulder. 'You really need to try and get a bit of rest.'

If she had suggested that he fly to the moon and back on a broomstick Sam could not have looked more flabbergasted.

'And leave Stan on his own to herd the ewes and fix the pens? Nay, lass, I've work to do,' he said as he rose. Packing his butties into his canvas snap bag, he kissed his wife on her tired cheek. 'I'll get some rest later, I promise.'

Knowing that he wouldn't get back until night fell, Mary gave a sad hopeless shrug. 'We'll walk up the lane with you,' she said as she scooped Susan out of her crate, then strapped her to her body with a big woollen shawl.

After she had kissed her husband goodbye, Mary leant against a drystone wall to wait for her older children who were due home soon from school. Turning her face to the sun and watching it slide slowly down over the hills, she relished the warmth of its fading light which briefly caught her face and warmed her cheeks before it disappeared entirely.

'Autumn will be gone before we know it,' she whispered with dread. 'And Christmas will be upon us.'

Christmas was a date she would have preferred to have wiped from the calendar. How were they ever going to find money for little toys, not to mention extra food for the children? It simply couldn't happen, but the thought of her son and daughters waking up on Christmas morning with nothing in their stockings cut Mary to the heart. Her melancholy thoughts were curtailed by a loud cry of excitement.

'MAM!'

Turning, she saw her son, Arthur, skipping along the farm track towards her, throwing up piles of crisp, golden autumn leaves.

'Catch, Mammy,' he called. Gathering huge armfuls of leaves, he threw them into the air, then watched in delight as they all drifted back down again.

Seeing her joyous boy's happy expression, his sparkling eyes and flushed cheeks, Mary waved and smiled at him, a smile that widened at the sight of Joy behind him, older and shyer than her exuberant brother, but throwing leaves too and spinning to catch them as they fell. The sound of a car roaring down the narrow lane towards them startled the children who cowered against the wall for safety while their mother, with Susan strapped to her breast, stood protectively in front of them. There was only one person in the neighbourhood who could drive a big posh car like that: Ronnie Thorp, the ruthless landowner who had inflicted such financial upheaval on the farming estate that had previously been comparatively untroubled.

As he flashed by, Joy, wise beyond her years, muttered angrily, 'Where does he get the money to drive a car like that, Mam?'

Mary didn't mince her words for a moment. 'By fleecing the likes of you and me for every penny he can squeeze out of us,' she answered bitterly.

7. Thorp Hall

Matron had been right when she told Libby that Reverend Mother moved swiftly when the spirit was with her. It was Matron who now beckoned Libby aside in the long corridor that led on to both the ante-natal and post-natal wards, to tell her the news.

'Reverend Mother has agreed that as soon as we can secure the services of a supply nurse one afternoon a week to replace you, we can begin trialling our community project.'

Libby, struggling with the overwhelming urge to grab hold of Matron and dance down the corridor with her, beamed as she skipped from foot to foot in sheer excitement.

'I'm so grateful,' she blurted, hardly able to contain herself. 'When might that be?'

'We'll advertise for a supply nurse immediately.'

'Good,' Libby exclaimed happily.

'Meanwhile, Dr Jamie is researching who might best benefit from your services.'

Seeing Libby's brilliant-blue eyes alight with curiosity, Matron kindly said, 'Why don't you pop down to Dr Jamie's office now and see if he's a moment to discuss it with you.'

With a fleeting smile Libby sped down the corridor to Jamie's consulting room where, taking deep breaths to steady her nerves, she knocked on his door.

'Come in,' he called. Seeing Libby, he smiled widely. 'Just the girl I want to see.'

As soon as Libby was settled in the chair opposite him, Jamie produced records of possible out-patients whom he and his local colleagues had shortlisted.

'Obviously, you can't nurse them all, but my colleagues have produced a number of names in quite a short space of time.'

Libby answered with confidence. 'I *knew* it,' she declared.

'Well, it's a good start. If there's a clear need, it bodes well for taking the community project further in the future, as long as we can get the funding, of course.'

'And *if* it's a success, given the tight time frame,' Libby pointed out.

'Why shouldn't it be?'

'It's just that – to quote Matron – I need to nurse expectant women who safely deliver and are then nursed through the post-partum period before I close the case. It really is a very tight time frame,' she repeated.

'Well,' Jamie said as he handed the reports on his desk to the young nurse, 'when you've studied these, tell me which three women you would recommend for a community visit.'

Libby didn't have a single minute to spare until just before tea-time, when she was allowed to grab a quick cup of tea and a cheese and piccalilli sandwich. Alone in the dining room, she ran down the list of possible patients. In such a small geographical area – Grange, Cartmel and Allithwaite – there were a surprising number of pregnant women who would benefit from a community nurse's visit, but after

75

narrowing down their dates Libby decided that two women in Grange and another living just outside Allithwaite village fitted the criteria. Catching Jamie before he left for the day, she explained why.

'I've gone through your list and narrowed it down to two women in Grange whose GPs have requested a midwife's visit in order to lighten their own load, plus a young woman in Allithwaite who's presenting problems.' Glancing down at the notes she had jotted down, Libby added, 'Mrs Thorp was flagged up as a priority by a local GP who treated her several times to start with, but she missed a couple of appointments and then suddenly stopped visiting him entirely.'

Jamie looked surprised. 'So, she's not seen a doctor for a few months?'

'Looks like it.'

'That's concerning, why would she suddenly stop?' He looked thoughtful before he asked, 'When's she due?'

Again glancing at the notes, Libby responded, 'Late December, so Mrs Thorp fits into our time frame, same as the other two women.'

'Where does she live?'

'A place called Thorp Hall. Do you know it?'

Jamie nodded. 'It's off the main road going out of town – a grand, rather imposing house that stands under the shadow of the fells by Saints Wood.'

'Sounds posh,' Libby smiled.

'Posh or not, if Mrs Thorp has been skipping her doctor's appointments,' Jamie responded, 'she will benefit from a midwife's visit, especially as her GP noted there were issues with the pregnancy.'

'I've no previous experience of working in such a posh situation, so it should be very interesting,' Libby answered with her typical honesty.

After appointing a supply nurse, Matron decided that Wednesday afternoon was the best day for Libby's community work.

'Leave straight away after dinner on Wednesday; with three patients to see, you'll have to make the best use of your time. And aim to be back by tea-time, before it gets dark,' she suggested. 'By the way, dear, how do you plan to travel?'

'I thought I'd cycle. I hope you don't mind, I spotted an old bike in the back of the garden shed which I think I could fix with Alf's help.' Libby beamed.

'My word, you are keen,' Matron beamed back. Casting an appraising glance over Libby's strong athletic body, she added with a kind smile, 'I've no doubt that you're fit enough to whizz up and down all those hills. You know we're all very excited at the prospect of Mary Vale's first community nursing attachment – the very best of luck, dear.'

By the time Wednesday came around, Libby was well prepared, with all of her patients' notes stuffed in her bicycle basket. She enjoyed her visits to cheery Mrs Cummings and Mrs Timms, both of whom were robust country women, mothers already, who welcomed her with open arms, grateful that they didn't have to travel to the GP. After finding both women in good health, Libby set off to see her third patient at Thorp Hall. Cycling over there, she reminded herself of Mrs Thorp's GP's notes in which he mentioned, among other things, that the patient showed signs of an anaemic condition. Recalling her midwifery training notes, Libby muttered consciously to herself as she cycled along.

'Check the colour of the patient's skin; if it is pale or yellowish, that could indicate anaemia. Check for an irregular heart-beat, shortness of breath, lethargy, and sluggish circulation when the flesh doesn't spring back after the skin has been pressed.'

Bowling through the rolling countryside that steadily rose higher, taxing her strong thighs on the uphill stretches, Libby arrived bang on time at Thorp Hall which was, as Jamie had described, large and imposing. Knocking on the door, Libby gave a quick glance around the rambling grounds steeped in a cold mist that drifted down from the chilly fells. The large metal-studded door was opened by a dour-faced, middle-aged housekeeper, dressed all in black, with a thin strip of a mouth and deeply suspicious dark eyes.

'You are?' she growled.

'Nurse Godburgh, from Mary Vale, to see Mrs Thorp, if you please.'

Clearly reluctant to give Libby entry, the housekeeper inched the door open barely a fraction. 'This way,' the woman instructed sourly.

Wriggling through the grudgingly allowed space, Libby entered a dark echoing hallway that led off in several directions. Following the housekeeper's clattering steps, she walked down several dim corridors until she was finally ushered into a large drawing room at the back of the house. What should have been a gracious and elegant room, with its tall west-facing windows overlooking forest and woodland that gave way to the soft swell of the rolling fells, was in fact a cold unwelcoming room with a mean little fire spluttering in a smoky hearth. Sitting almost hidden from view, in a huge wing-backed chair, was a slight young woman with a deathly-pale face framed in a cloud of long silver-blonde hair. Hearing the door open, she turned her face and the expression that Libby caught there was one of the saddest she had ever seen in her entire life. Feigning a cheeriness she certainly didn't feel, Libby hurried forward to shake the woman's limp ice-cold hand.

'Good afternoon,' Libby said. 'I'm Nurse Godburgh, your new midwife.'

Over the course of this first visit Libby found out little more about her patient than she already knew from the doctor's report. Yes, from her pallor it would seem that the anaemia was still a problem. And Mrs Thorp looked so anxious, sufficiently so that Libby gently asked if there was anything particularly worrying her today.

'Not really. I'm anxious every day. Maybe it's because it's my first time,' the woman suggested.

The stilted conversation stopped completely when both women heard a slight shuffling sound in the corridor. Purposefully standing up, Libby strode across the room and firmly closed the door. Looking out of the windows on to the lawn, where the rain was falling steadily, Libby regretted that they couldn't take a stroll outdoors where she was quite sure they would have more privacy.

'Next time,' she reminded herself, 'see if you can get

your patient out of the house and as far away from that dreadful housekeeper as you can.'

After restarting the conversation, Libby was relieved to hear her patient being a little more forthcoming in answer to her questions.

'How long have you lived here at Thorp Hall?'

'Only a year,' Mrs Thorp responded. 'Before that, I lived in the Borrowdale valley. Do you know it at all?' she asked.

'I know it very well,' Libby enthused. 'My brothers and I went fell-running up there, it's a beautiful valley.'

Gazing at her in delight, Mrs Thorp's stunning green eyes, which were beguilingly flecked with gold, welled up.

'It's the most beautiful place on God's earth. I've never been happier than I was when I was growing up there.'

'Did you walk the fells?' Libby enquired.

'Walk the fells!' Mrs Thorp laughed, suddenly as gay as a young girl. 'I was never off them! My family has a sheep farm in Rosthwaite and, like you, I had brothers. We were constantly up on Chapel Fell where most of our sheep grazed.' The sudden flash of unselfconscious happiness fell from the young woman's face. 'I miss it so much.'

Approaching footsteps made them both jump. When the door was pushed open by the gaunt-faced housekeeper, Mrs Thorp once more shrank back into the corner of the high wing-backed chair.

'Thank you, Mrs Grimsdale,' she muttered, after the housekeeper deposited a tea tray on a low table.

'I thought you might need some tea to keep your strength up, the master said you mustn't go wearing yourself out on useless tittle-tattle.'

Libby's hackles rose; how dare this woman speak in such a way, she seethed. 'I don't call acquainting myself with my patient tittle-tattle,' she said briskly.

Mrs Grimsdale gave a dismissive shrug of her scrawny shoulders before walking away, leaving the door standing ajar yet again.

Now thoroughly bridled, Libby shut it with a loud click. 'Is she always like that?' she fumed.

Looking alarmed, Mrs Thorp pressed her fingers to her lips. 'Shhh,' she warned. Then dropping her voice very low, she added, 'Yes, she is always like that, and worse. By the way, don't even bother to pour the tea, it will be cold. It's just a feeble excuse to interrupt us.'

Feeling thoroughly protective towards her vulnerable new patient, Libby reached out to gently squeeze her hand. 'I'm sorry to make things awkward, Mrs Thorp.'

Turning her beautiful but sad green eyes on Libby, the young woman said, 'Please call me Beth.'

'With pleasure, Beth, and I'm Libby,' Libby said eagerly. 'Now, dear, I really do need to examine you before I go. If you could settle yourself down on the sofa, I'll have more room there.' Once Beth was settled and relaxed, Libby said, 'Before I start, I read in your GP's notes –'

Libby got no further.

'Dr Fletcher!' Beth exclaimed. 'Did he get in touch with you?'

'In a manner of speaking,' Libby replied. 'Dr Fletcher referred you to us. I gather you didn't visit him as regularly as you should have done,' she said carefully.

Beth's pale face became suffused with a deep-pink blush. 'That's right,' she admitted.

Still treading very carefully, Libby asked another question. 'Didn't you get on with him?'

'I liked him a lot,' Beth immediately answered. 'He was very kind and reassuring, explaining things to me in a clear and straightforward manner. I missed his visits enormously.'

Perplexed, Libby asked, 'Was there any reason why your visits to Dr Fletcher's surgery stopped?'

Avoiding her gaze, Beth gave a little shrug. 'It was difficult to get there, I was dependent on my husband for transport, you see. He wasn't here very much, so I couldn't go,' she ended lamely.

Seeing that she had inadvertently embarrassed her patient, Libby gently moved on, referring to her notes. 'Dr Fletcher mentions in his notes that you suffered from some sporadic bleeding.'

Beth gave a quick, nervous nod.

'Is that still happening?' Libby asked.

'It comes and goes,' Beth replied.

'Is it ever heavy, or continuous?' Libby persisted.

'No, not really, but it's frightening when it happens – I always think I'm going to lose the baby,' Beth confessed.

Libby explained in a calm voice, 'Bleeding can happen at any stage in the pregnancy, and it doesn't always mean something is seriously wrong.'

Beth, starved of any medical information, seized eagerly on this vital piece of knowledge. 'So other women have it?' she exclaimed.

'Yes, it happens as the lower part of the uterus thins,' Libby explained. Seeing her patient's puzzled expression, she added, 'The uterus is another name for the womb, Beth.'

Intrigued, Beth nodded. 'It's good to know these things,' she said gratefully. 'I've not had the opportunity to talk to many nurses,' she added humbly.

'Well, you can talk to me any time,' Libby laughed. 'That's what I'm here for, to support you through the rest of your pregnancy, and to bring your baby safely into the world.'

Gazing into her patient's tender young face, Libby felt her heart contract; though married and pregnant, Beth had an innocent ignorance about her that troubled Libby. Why did this young woman appear to know so little about what was taking place in her own body? Seeing that Beth was keen to learn more, Libby tried desperately to make her explanation as clear as possible.

'The placenta inside your womb is what feeds the baby, it's over the cervix, that's what's causing the bleeding.'

'Is it bad for the baby?'

'If you were bleeding heavily, that would be a cause for concern,' Libby replied. 'But so far it is light and sporadic, from what you've said. If it ever gets more than that, you might need to go to hospital for checks,' she warned gently. 'Now lie still while I measure your tummy and listen to the foetal heart-beat.'

After examining her patient, Libby was reassured; though the size of the foetus was small, the heart-beat was steady.

'Is it all right?' Beth enquired as she peered down at Libby examining her tummy.

'You could do with gaining a little more weight, dear,' Libby answered frankly.

After Beth had rearranged her clothing and was sitting

up straight, Libby took her patient's blood pressure, which was a little low.

Continuing with her questions, Libby asked, 'How's your appetite? It's important that you eat properly during your pregnancy – especially food containing iron.' Seeing Beth's blank expression, Libby went into some detail. 'Liver, greens, fish, beans – they're all good for you and baby.'

Beth grimaced. 'I don't have much of an appetite,' she admitted.

Libby gently added, 'It's not just about you, dear, you have to eat for two now.'

'I'll try my best,' Beth shyly agreed.

'You're quite pale, too,' Libby commented. 'Are you often tired and lethargic?'

'All the time.'

'Do you get out into the fresh air and take exercise?'

'Not much.'

'Then you must,' Libby insisted. 'I know it's cold and damp out there, but it will do you good. In fact, we could take a stroll together next time I visit.'

Looking slightly more animated, Beth asked, 'When will that be?'

'I'm scheduled to visit you once a week, every Wednesday afternoon, if that suits?'

Beth looked relieved. 'I've enjoyed your visit so much, Libby. I've learnt something I didn't know before, about the bleeding, which was troubling me,' she explained.

'In my experience, the more knowledge a patient has about how her body is changing and how her baby is developing, the more confident she feels. A little know-ledge goes a long way,' Libby smiled.

'You're right,' Beth agreed. 'I look forward to seeing you next week . . . and getting to know each other better,' she added shyly.

'Me too,' Libby warmly responded, before winking conspiratorially and whispering, 'let's do our best to get as far away as possible from Mrs Grimsdale and her pots of cold stewed tea. In the meantime, please try to eat a little more, especially iron-rich products, where you can. If we don't get your iron levels up naturally, we may have to start you on iron tablets. Don't forget now: dark leafy greens, nuts, fish, liver and beans are excellent sources of iron. Red meat would be good for you too, but it's hard to come by, these days,' she added realistically.

Beth surprised her midwife by volunteering some start-ling information.

'My husband doesn't seem to have a problem getting red meat.'

Though amazed that anybody could lay their hands on meat, a rare and expensive luxury during times of increased and harsher rationing, Libby quickly responded, 'Well, hopefully he might be able to get some for you.'

Libby returned to Mary Vale, deep in thought. She felt no sense of jubilation, or even plain satisfaction, after her visit to Thorp Hall. In fact, she felt quite the opposite: deflated, and heavy with foreboding. There was no time to discuss the case with her colleagues on the evening of her return. But Libby was determined to discuss Beth before her next visit, and made sure she snatched a hasty ten minutes with Ada and Matron before ward rounds began the following morning.

'How did it go?' Ada immediately asked.

Not holding back, Libby launched in. 'It was like a chapter out of *Rebecca*! The place was dark, sinister – to start with, I hardly got a word out of Mrs Thorp,' she exclaimed. 'Beth, she calls herself, by the way. We were constantly hounded by a housekeeper who looked like Mrs Danvers.'

'Libby, dear, though I know the literary characters you're referring to, we really mustn't blur fact with faction,' Ada gently smiled. 'Can we just stick with the medical facts?'

Blushing self-consciously, Libby continued. 'Sorry, I read lots of library books when I was on night shifts – the characters sometimes pop up unexpectedly.' Seeing a look of indulgent amusement pass between the two older women, she swiftly moved on. 'The housekeeper, Mrs Grimsdale,' Libby raised an eyebrow at the aptness of the name, 'never left us in peace for a moment. She was either eavesdropping in the corridor, or warning my patient not to get overexcited.'

Ada looked sceptical. 'Could somebody have told her to behave in such a way?'

Libby nodded. 'It felt like that.'

'Did you see Mr Thorp?' Matron asked.

'No, but Mrs Grimsdale was everywhere. It's ridiculous!' Libby exclaimed. 'I'm the woman's midwife. It's going to be difficult nursing a patient who appears to be constantly guarded.' Libby gave a heavy sigh. 'Poor Beth's a bag of nerves. Mind you, who can blame her, living in a place like that?' Slightly rallying, Libby continued. 'We agreed we would try to get out into the garden on my visit next week, if the weather allows.'

'That might be a good move,' Ada agreed.

'She does have quite a few complications; she is still suffering from anaemia, and having sporadic bleeding. Poor girl, when I tried to explain to her what half the things she's suffering from are, she just hadn't a clue. I felt like I was talking to a child most of the time. She's so sweet, a complete innocent who really wants to know more and understand the changes taking place in her body.'

'I'm beginning to feel somewhat sorry for her,' Matron murmured.

'I feel really sorry for her,' Libby exclaimed. 'Stuck in that gloomy old heap with only the snooping housekeeper for company.'

'Jamie told me that Mrs Thorp was referred by her doctor?' Ada asked.

Libby nodded. 'That's right, to start with she saw Dr Fletcher in Grange, but her visits petered out. When I asked why, she was clearly embarrassed, said it was difficult to get there.'

'You'll need to keep a close eye on Mrs Thorp, especially if her problems escalate,' Matron advised. 'It looks like your idea of community nursing came in the nick of time for this particular patient. She can't suddenly drop off your list like she did with the doctor.'

'Yes, thank goodness,' Libby agreed. 'I'm astonished that she even considered stopping her GP visits – baffling, really, considering she's so concerned about her child's well-being.'

'Well, you seem to have managed all your visits on your

first community outing, Libby, even the officious house-keeper at Thorp Hall,' Matron smiled.

Libby beamed. 'It's a relief that my other community patients present no obvious problems so far,' she said gratefully. 'As for Mrs Thorp, have no doubts, Matron,' Libby staunchly declared. 'After all the trouble the convent has gone to, funding this project, and the research Dr Jamie has done on my behalf, plus the sad lost look in Beth Thorp's eyes, nothing, *absolutely nothing*, is going to get in the way of me attending my patient and doing my best to ensure a healthy remainder of her pregnancy.'

Libby was preoccupied all that week, worrying about Beth alone in Thorp Hall. On her ward rounds and in the sluice room, and even on her way to visit Snowball, first thing in the morning before her shift started, Libby's thoughts constantly ran to Beth and her sad circumstances.

'Why does that wretched housekeeper guard her so closely?' Libby addressed her concerns one morning to Snowball, who nuzzled her sympathetically. 'Why is Beth so nervous and edgy, who is she frightened of?'

8. Sister Agnes Steps In

Though there was no doubt in Margaret's mind that her decision to come to Mary Vale had been the right one, she nevertheless experienced a growing sense of low mood as the weeks slowly passed. She couldn't fault the Home, nor its dedicated team of caring staff. The food was somehow excellent, given increasing wartime shortages; she didn't know how they managed it. The surroundings were beautiful, and the fresh sea air was just what she needed. At the beginning, Margaret had been a little taken aback by some of the residents. The likes of Gladys, Maisie and their chums, who were generally loud-mouthed and rather coarse by Margaret's genteel standards, bemused her, but she soon came to appreciate that underneath their brash exteriors they were good women with hearts of gold. But in spite of all this, Margaret felt as if she was holding her breath, waiting for something terrible to happen. As her baby grew and moved more vigorously inside her, she knew she had to do the one thing she desperately didn't want to do, and that was to visit Father Ben in his office in the convent to discuss her plans after the birth.

The time finally came when she couldn't put this meeting off any longer.

'Ideally, I would love to keep my baby,' she opened with.

The sensitive priest gave an understanding nod; though

he had heard these words a hundred times before, it nevertheless still touched him to the core. He had seen so many young women parting with babies they yearned to keep, but he had also seen – and he thanked God for it, otherwise his job would be unbearable – many successful adoptions too.

'I understand,' he answered quietly.

'However, I don't seem to have any option but to talk to you about having my baby adopted,' Margaret confessed. 'I spent my savings paying for my stay here in the Home. I have no home and no job,' she sighed. 'It doesn't bode well for bringing a baby into the world, does it?' she said forlornly.

The thoughtful priest explained gently how he set about placing babies in his care. 'I go into great detail with any prospective couple, question them on siblings, background, education, religion, location, aspirations. It's very important to try and make a good match, and you can only do that by being thorough.'

Sitting quietly listening to him, Margaret wondered who her baby would be 'matched' with. A well-to-do professional couple living in a detached house in Carlisle, perhaps, or a childless working-class couple desperate for a baby of their own. Where would he or she live? Would they love her child as passionately as she hoped they would? She would never see her son or daughter start school or matriculate, but she prayed that the adoptive parents would applaud and praise their charge at every major step he or she took throughout life, whether it was learning to walk, ride a bike, play the piano – the very thought of which brought a rush of tears to Margaret's large dark eyes. How she would have loved to teach her daughter or son to play the piano, just like her mother had taught her.

Dragging her attention back to Father Ben, she heard him gently saying, 'Pop in any time if you have anything on your mind, Margaret, there's no rush about making a decision right away.'

After leaving the priest's office, Margaret strolled out into the garden, deep in thought, then walked along the sandy coastal path which followed the curve of the bay. Though it was bitterly cold, with the wind blowing in from the churning Irish Sea, Margaret was oblivious to the elements and walked in thoughtful solitude for a long time. Having felt alone and unloved for so long, the yearning to keep the baby whom she already loved with a passion overwhelmed her.

'How can I even dally with such a selfish thought?' Margaret scolded herself. 'Daydreaming about keeping it is too cruel. It will be difficult enough for me to get a job once I leave Mary Vale. I'll have to live in some mean grubby digs while I apply for work. How could I possibly do that with a baby in tow, and who in their right mind would take me on in those circumstances?'

Slumping down on to a bench that overlooked the marsh, with a pair of marsh harriers shrilly calling to each other as they hunted for food, Margaret put her head in her hands and wept. She had known that it would always come to this, but knowing was not the same as experiencing the anguish of the stark truth, which was that she had no choice but to hand her baby over for adoption.

The nagging worry of a formal adoption sent Margaret into a spiral of despair. Her former healthy appetite faded, she slept badly, and she woke every morning feeling weary and depressed. The change in her was so dramatic that the staff, always concerned about their patients' well-being, started to exchange comments about their newest resident.

'She's just not settling into Mary Vale life as well as I thought,' Matron observed sadly.

'It sometimes happens,' Ada reminded her colleague kindly. 'After the first flush of relief, reality strikes and residents start to miss elements of their former life – work, family, location, their own sense of personal identity. Then, of course, there's the grieving that comes with the fact that they're here because they have been rejected by their family or lover. That can't be a pleasant feeling.'

'So, what's brought on the change in her?' Matron pondered. 'Margaret seemed initially to settle in well.'

'She told me recently that she misses teaching,' Ada answered. 'She said she particularly loved teaching music.'

Checking her fob watch, Matron was forced to conclude the conversation for now.

'I must dash, dear,' she said. 'Can I leave you to have a word with Margaret?' Smiling, she added, 'You're the most experienced nurse in the Home when it comes to lending a sympathetic ear.'

It was later that day when Ada heard the haunting strains of *Peer Gynt* drifting from the sitting room. Stopping in her tracks, she quickly retraced her steps so that she could double-check if she was actually hearing things.

Leaning against the door, she could indeed hear music playing out, quite low but nevertheless clearly audible. Gently turning the door handle, Ada peeped inside the room where, to her surprise, she could see nobody at all.

'Somebody must have left the music on,' she reasoned.

Just as she was about to close the door and slip away, Ada heard a small stifled sob. Quickly stepping back into the room, she eventually spotted Margaret crouched on the floor by the old-fashioned gramophone.

'My dear,' she exclaimed as she hurried forward to comfort her distraught patient. 'What on earth is the matter?'

With her long, lustrous dark hair trailing around her pale anguished face and her slender fingers pressed against her swollen eyes, Margaret was too distraught to speak.

Saddened by her pitiful state, Ada knelt down and warmly embraced her. 'There, there,' she soothed gently. 'Shhh . . .'

Regaining some composure, Margaret pulled a perfectly clean, pressed lace handkerchief from her cardigan pocket to press self-consciously against her wet cheeks.

'I'm so sorry,' she gulped. 'You caught me unawares – well, in truth, it was Peer Gynt himself who caught me unawares.'

Turning to the gramophone, still squeakily revolving, Ada asked, 'Shall I turn the music off?'

Margaret shook her head. 'It's almost finished,' she said.

As the piece came to a climactic crescendo, the music ebbed away, and Margaret, slightly more composed, rose to her feet. 'It's a piece of music that was always a favourite with my pupils. I used to play it every Friday afternoon, and they just adored it,' she recalled fondly. 'I couldn't resist it when I saw it lying there with the other records,' she added as her eyes once more filled with tears. 'Silly thing to do, really; it reminded me so much of the happy times my pupils and I used to have together.'

'Well, at least you have happy memories,' Ada said with a positive smile, seizing the opportunity to talk to Margaret while she had the chance.

'You mentioned previously how much you enjoyed teaching; you must miss it awfully.'

'Oh, yes, I miss it dreadfully,' Margaret answered fervently. 'I miss the children too. Their comments about the music I played to them were always so touching and heartfelt.' Smiling, she fondly recalled one of their innocent comments, '"That music makes me want to hop and reach for the stars."' With a sigh she concluded, 'Nothing beats children for getting quite such an honest response.'

'I can well imagine that,' Ada agreed. 'Catherine's still only little, but music can fire her up in no time, it seems to release something quite explosive inside her.' Glancing down at the records scattered on the floor at Margaret's feet, she apologized. 'I'm sorry we haven't got a better collection. Most of the residents prefer listening to *Workers' Playtime* on the wireless, rather than classical pieces on the gramophone.'

'I love popular music too, and so did my students,' Margaret assured her. 'They especially loved the loud boisterous numbers like "Little Brown Jug" and "Boogie Woogie Baby". They would jive all around the classroom, spinning and laughing – that is, until the headmaster turned up and put a stop to their wild fun and games.

Teaching music and seeing the children's pleasure really was the best part of my working week.'

Seeing the undisguised yearning in Margaret's big brown eyes, Ada became thoughtful. A rather bold idea was forming.

'You know, if you miss it so much, you could offer a bit of voluntary work in the local school.'

Margaret's eyes lit up. 'Could I? Where is the local school?'

'It's at Grange,' Ada told her kindly. 'St Mark's is a little primary school that takes in children from the surrounding villages. People speak very well of it, especially Sister Agnes,' she smiled. 'Her sister, Betsie, works at the school as a dinner lady – we get regular news from her of the school's activities.'

'I must say, I would love to do that just for a few hours a week. Maybe I could teach a bit of music?' Margaret said wistfully. Remembering her condition, she added, 'That's if anybody will have me.'

'With the majority of male teachers called up, the war has undoubtedly affected staffing quotas, there simply can't be enough teachers to go around, these days,' Ada replied. 'I'm quite sure most schools would welcome all the voluntary help they can get.'

Glancing down once more at her tummy, Margaret said hesitantly, 'They might not be interested if I couldn't commit for a long period of time.'

Undeterred, Ada rose to her feet. 'Well, let's make a few enquiries, shall we? Sister Agnes's sister might be able to point us in the right direction.'

*

Excited by the possibility of teaching again, Margaret hung on to Ada's comment about wartime staffing quotas and the shortage of teachers. Wondering if she might soon be called upon to start her voluntary work, Margaret decided to revisit Father Ben while she had time on her hands and her mind was clear.

'I'd be grateful if you could start the formal proceedings for my baby to be adopted,' she told him.

'Are you quite sure?' he softly asked. 'There's no rush, you know.'

Margaret gave a firm nod. 'I've given it a lot of thought, Father,' she honestly told him. 'There's no point in delaying, adoption is unquestionably the best way forward. In fact, it's the *only* way forward.'

After her second visit to Father Ben, Margaret couldn't face dinner with the other residents. Slipping into the dining room, she took a couple of slices of buttered bread from the counter, then after pulling on her big woolly coat she went outside into the garden where the air was sharp with the tang of woodsmoke rising from a fire in Alf Arkwright's farmyard. Nibbling the still-warm bread, Margaret made her way to the front of the house to sit on a bench and gaze out over the bay, where the slanting sun coloured the restless sea a blazing shade of silvery pewter.

'What would Peter say,' she mused, 'if he knew our child was going to be brought up by complete strangers?'

Recalling how doting Peter had been with his two young daughters, always identically dressed in exquisite little home-made frocks, just like the two royal princesses when they were little, there was no hiding the adoration in their father's eyes. His seemingly perfect family unit remained safely intact at least, she thought bitterly, while she and an innocent child paid the price for their brief, secret love affair. Sick of the morbid thoughts that were getting her nowhere, Margaret headed back indoors to sit at the old upright piano in the sitting room and play Peter's favourite duet by Schubert, '*Licht und Liebe*', a delicate piece that filled the darkening room with its lovely melody and soothed Margaret's troubled soul.

After chatting with Sister Agnes, Ada tracked Margaret down to the laundry room a couple of days later, where along with a couple of other residents she was hanging wet sheets on to the wooden maiden that hung over the boiler.

'Sister Agnes has some news for you. Can you pop into the kitchen when you've finished in here?'

Just after twelve, when her chores were complete, Margaret wiped her damp red face and hurried to join Ada in the kitchen, where tea had already been brewed by kindly Sister Theresa. Sitting at the highly scrubbed kitchen table, they drank tea while Sister Theresa prepared a vast pan of rice pudding and Sister Agnes stirred a simmering vegetable stew on the Aga hotplate. The savoury ingredients were bulked out with pearl barley and flavoured with Lea & Perrins sauce, plus a large handful of fresh thyme (boughs of which dangled from the overhead kitchen rafters). Putting a lid on the stew, Sister Agnes joined Margaret and Ada at the table, lowering her substantial bulk into a chair, and poured herself a cup of tea.

'Well,' she started, 'I bumped into our Betsie, my sister, in Grange when I went to pick up some smoked herrings for the residents' tea yesterday. I mentioned we might have a resident here in the Home who would be interested in teaching music – the long and the short of it is, our Betsie thought any volunteer would be most welcome at St Mark's.'

Knowing what sticklers head teachers could be about protocol, Margaret nervously enquired, 'Shouldn't Betsie check with the head teacher first?'

'Oh, she has,' Agnes assured her. 'I saw her again this morning, when I was buying rissoles for tomorrow's tea – we usually catch up every day in town, by the way,' she explained. 'Anyway, when Betsie mentioned you to Mrs Temple, she said they'd welcome you with open arms.'

'I'm not surprised, schools are so short-staffed these days,' Ada said, watching Margaret's face carefully.

Quickly setting her cup down in her saucer, Margaret still looked anxious. 'Would it be a good idea to drop a letter in the post to the headmistress?'

Turning her attention to the bubbling stew on the hob, Sister Agnes stirred the mixture as she replied, 'Aye, that'd be a nice touch.'

'You could mention what days might suit you best too,' Ada suggested.

Margaret rolled her eyes and smiled. 'Any day that suits them suits me,' she answered. 'I'm not exactly rushed off my feet here at Mary Vale.'

9. Sam Carter

Inevitably, the fateful day that Mary had been dreading came. The morning had dawned as usual; the house was silent after Mary packed the children off to school on the bus. After changing baby Susan's nappy, she settled in the rocking chair to feed her when suddenly Mary heard the sound of horse's hooves clip-clopping down the lane. When they stopped by her front door, Mary sprang to her feet. With Susan clasped to her breast, she ran to the front door and flung it wide open. Seeing the farmhand struggling to lift Sam from the cart normally used for transporting sheep, she dashed back indoors to lay Susan down in her crate, then ran back outside again.

'What's happened?' she cried.

Breathlessly trying to lift Sam from the cart, the lad shook his head. 'Your man collapsed on't fells, we had to carry him down.'

Between them they carried Sam indoors and laid him on the bed.

'I'm sorry, missus,' the lad said, 'I'll have to leave you to it, I've got to get back to't sheep.'

Ushering him out of the room, Mary thanked him for delivering Sam safely home, then returned to her husband, who was lying prone on the bed, and looked half dead. She sponged and cooled his emaciated body, which was running with sweat, and she did her best to get him to sip some water, regularly rousing him over the course of the day to take a little more, trying to keep the children as quiet as possible around him to let him rest. Throughout the day and night, the cough never abated – in fact, it got worse.

He desperately needed a doctor, but they couldn't afford one, which tormented Mary. Weary and exhausted, she stoked up the fire, grateful at least that they weren't yet reduced to burning the furniture. With an abundance of wood in the garden and surrounding countryside they could, for the moment, keep warm. Knowing she should take the opportunity now, while Susan was sleeping, to slip outdoors to collect more kindling, Mary reached for her threadbare shawl. But worn out and racked with worry as she was, she just hadn't the will to do anything other than fall into the rocking chair by the fire, where she put her head in her hands and sobbed.

'What in God's name are we going to do?' she moaned.

The farmhand dropped in again in the morning, to check up on Sam. But Mary was terrified that he would see just how much Sam had deteriorated, so she kept the lad standing at the front door, assuring him that Sam was making slow progress but, with luck, he might be back at work soon. If the visitor had seen Sam, lying in a fever on his bed, he would not have believed a word Mary had spoken. Inevitably and truthfully, the farmhand would have passed on news of Sam's rapid decline – which Thorp, Mary feared, would inevitably pick up on. Knowing full well that Thorp showed no clemency towards any tenant on his land who didn't pay their rent, Mary wasn't looking for trouble. She would keep the seriousness of her husband's condition a secret for as long as she could.

It was obvious that Sam urgently needed to see a doctor – that had been the case for weeks – but no matter how often she racked her brains, trying to reach a conclusion as to how this could be managed, Mary never reached a solution, because there simply wasn't one. She had pawned the only jewellery she had (apart from her wedding ring) – a pearl brooch left to her by her godmother, which had paid for Sam's first doctor's visit – now they had nothing at all to barter with. Mary had made a few local enquiries about getting help from medical charities who helped the destitute, but so far she had made no real progress. There were the Public Assistance Institutions (run by the local councils), usually referred to by their terrifying former name, 'The Workhouse'. The very thought of the family being committed to such an awful place drove terror through Mary's heart, though she had been told there was a chance that, once there, Sam might at least receive free health care.

'God!' Mary fumed. 'Does it take the entire family being evicted and rehoused in an institution to get my poor Sam medical treatment?' Feeling a hot hand on her trembling shoulder, Mary started. 'Lovie,' she exclaimed when she saw her husband standing over her. 'What are you doing out of bed?'

'I heard you crying,' he murmured as he stooped to kiss her wet cheeks.

Getting up from the chair in order to offer it to him, Mary curled up at her husband's feet. 'Sam, I've been thinking,' she started cautiously. 'Shall I try being open with Thorp about your illness, and ask for a rent reduction? Just while you're so ill.'

Echoing her own thoughts, Sam answered wearily, 'Nay, lass, best keep that to ourselves for as long as we can.'

Desperate to do something – anything – Mary cried some more. 'If you're too ill to work, we can't pay the rent, it's as simple as that. What's the worst Thorp can do if I ask for a reduction?'

'He can say no and throw us out into the streets,' Sam answered knowingly. 'Listen, lovie, the less the bastard knows about our situation the better. I don't want him seeing me sick in bed, that would be the undoing of us.'

Mary nodded in agreement. 'I know, I've been trying my best, told a pack of lies to the farmhand this morning when he came calling.'

'He's a good lad, he'll only have called with the best intentions, I'm sure he wouldn't stitch me up.'

'How long can we hide the truth from Thorp?' desperate Mary whispered.

'The longer we can keep him off our backs the better,' Sam wheezed. 'Help me back to bed, love.'

Supporting him, Mary laid her husband back on the bed and tucked him up as tenderly as she would baby Susan.

'Sleep well, sweetheart,' she whispered, before creeping into the damp misty garden to collect wood before Susan woke up for her next feed.

By the time Joy and Arthur arrived home that day it was four thirty and going dark, but there was a good blaze in the hearth and a pan of thin vegetable soup on the boil, which the children wolfed back along with chunks of stale bread toasted on the fire. As they ate their supper, Mary was relieved to see they barely seemed to notice the strain on her face, or quite how ill their father looked. They chatted non-stop about school and the new teacher who would be coming in to teach them how to sing.

'She was in school today, she's not like the other teachers, she wears nice clothes and she smiles a lot.'

'I think she's got a baby in her tummy,' cheeky Arthur remarked. 'She looks like you did, Mam, before Susan was born.'

Knowing Arthur's capacity for impishness, Mary eye-balled her chubby-cheeked son. 'I hope you weren't cheeky to her, Arthur?'

'NO!' he exclaimed. 'I never said she'd got a big tummy.'

Mary smiled for what felt like the first time in days. 'What's her name?'

'Mrs Church,' Joy answered. 'She's coming again next week.'

Distracted by the sound of her husband coughing from the bed in the corner of the room, Mary hurried over to him. 'Can I get you anything, Sam?' she asked.

'Aye, lass, lift me up a bit, then I can breathe more easily,' he gasped.

Seeing the blood-spotted handkerchief clasped in his hand, Mary quickly responded to his bidding. 'Better?' she said as she settled him upright against the banked-up pillows.

Too weak to speak, Sam simply nodded, and within minutes he was fast asleep again.

Later that evening, when Joy and Arthur were in bed, Mary gently laid dozing Susan into her box crib. Warily approaching the double bed in the corner of the room, she bent to examine her beloved husband's weary face. Presently covered in a sheen of sweat, it was gaunt and drawn; even under the coats and patchwork quilt that covered Sam she could make out the outline of his poor emaciated body. The disease was gaining on her husband at a speed that petrified Mary.

When she recalled Sam's struggle to carry on working, Mary's heart ached. Of course, there had been absolutely no opportunity to take on board any of the doctor's advice. He had had no choice but to drag himself to work every day for as long as he could, venturing out in the October gales when the rivers were swollen with constant rain and the high fells already topped with a light dusting of snow. Sleeping rough while existing on a poor inadequate diet. Though she had done her best to nurse him when he did return home, warming his freezing-cold body in front of the fire, preparing him hot broths from vegetables and beef bones that she scrounged from the butcher in Grange, there was no improvement. How could there be? Mary wept as she recalled how her poor husband had staggered from his bed every morning, racked with a cough that left him weak and trembling. Though she had repeatedly begged him to stay at home, Sam had refused.

'I can't take time off work, lass, so stop mithering me, it makes things a whole lot worse,' he had wheezily told his wife.

'I have got to get work,' Mary decided now, as she banked up the fire for the night. 'It's the only thing left that might save this family from ruin.'

*

The following morning, Mary made sure Sam was as warm and comfortable as he could be, then she caught the bus into Grange with Joy and Arthur, and Susan wrapped in a warm scarf strapped to her chest. After dropping the older two off at the school gates, she briskly set off for town. She had been thinking for some time of looking for work, and with Sam now looking like he might be bedbound for some time, she could no longer put it off. After her futile talk with Sam about appealing to Thorp's better side – if there was such a thing, she thought bitterly – Mary knew that looking for work was really her only remaining option before they were evicted.

Hurrying past the shops, some already bright with wartime festive decorations, the sight of little knitted teddy bears and woolly animals, plastic dolls with blonde wigs and eyes that opened and shut, tinsel stars and crêpe-paper decorations wrung Mary's heart. What child wouldn't want to wake up to the weight of a Christmas stocking lying at the end of the bed? When she was young, dirt poor as they had been, there had always been a few gifts to delight her and her siblings. A tangerine, a few boiled sweets, some walnuts, an apple, sometimes a bar of chocolate. There would be nothing this year, Mary thought bitterly, in fact there was barely a pair of stockings in the house that wasn't threadbare and full of holes.

Determined to stick to the task in hand, Mary walked through the little town, stopping to gaze into newsagents and post offices to see if there were any job ads in the shop windows. A little bit of work, cooking, cleaning, mending, would bring in money for extra food for Sam and the kiddies. After checking all the shops, Mary slipped into the library to check the noticeboard in the entrance hall, in the hope she might find some jobs advertised that she could manage alongside Susan. Preoccupied with rearranging Susan inside her coat, Mary walked slap bang into one of the nuns from Our Lady's Convent who were regularly invited to St Mark's annual nativity play.

The smiling nun recognized Mary as the mother of the sweet little boy who, playing a cherub with a silver halo and fluttering silver wings, had captivated last year's audience with his sweet rendition of 'Silent Night'. Mary, aware of her scruffy old clothes and bedraggled appearance, was keen to get away from the small, slim, immaculately dressed nun who nevertheless politely asked after Arthur.

'How's your son who entertained us so beautifully last Christmas?'

'He's well, thank you, miss . . .'

At which point Susan stirred and started to cry.

'You have a new baby?' Theresa murmured as she peeped into the shawl to smile at the sleepy baby.

'She's ready for a feed,' Mary explained as Susan started to wriggle.

Realizing that Mary was shy about feeding her baby in public, Sister Theresa thoughtfully urged, 'Let's go and sit on the bench in the corner over there.'

Knowing that Susan would very soon be lustily bawling the place down, Mary hurried to the bench where she settled Susan at her breast. When the baby was sucking contentedly, Mary explained her motives for being in town that morning.

'Actually, I'm looking for work,' she confessed. 'What

with Christmas looming and my husband not well, we need a bit of extra cash right now.'

Theresa's tender heart contracted with pity for the woman before her, old before her time, worn out by poverty and always putting her family first. She remembered only too well what poverty was like, having been thrown out on to the streets by her own father when she became pregnant. Without the love and support of Mary Vale, not to mention her faith, Theresa would never have survived those times of cruelty and abuse. Life could be hideously unfair, but women like Mary — loyal, tough and strong — never gave up, even with the odds stacked against them.

'I'll make enquiries at Mary Vale,' Theresa promised. 'But we tend to cover most of the jobs ourselves – cooking, cleaning, washing, mending, sewing, even gardening, it keeps the costs down.'

Mary nodded. 'Of course, but if anything should pop up, *anything*, I'd be grateful if you could put me forward,' she eagerly suggested.

After Susan had been fed and changed, Mary, exhausted by her unsuccessful morning's research and with not a copper to pay her bus fare, set off to walk home in the freezing-cold misty rain. Worried that Susan would get cold – or worse still, wet – she pulled her ragged coat around the baby clamped to her breast. On her way out of town she passed Ronnie Thorp swaggering down the street; stopping to talk to passers-by, he behaved like he owned the town and everybody in it. Desperate to avoid being seen, Mary ducked into a shop doorway from which she peeped out. Watching Thorp clamber into his big black shiny Daimler, Mary's heart ached; if only the man would stop pestering them, life would be so much less of a torture.

When Mary arrived home, she found Sam exactly where she had left him, lying on the bed with his eyes wide open. 'Thorp came here,' he wheezed.

'Did you open the door to him?' she gasped.

'Of course not,' he replied. 'But he knocked and banged for ages, even tried the lock.'

'Thank God I locked up before I left,' she murmured as she unwrapped wriggling Susan from the scarf crossed over her shoulders. Feeling herself break out into a hot sweat of fear, Mary cried, 'He's not going to let it go, Sam, we're already a month overdue.'

'I know,' he answered as he slumped back on to the tangled sheets. 'We've got no choice but to stick it out for as long as we can.'

Or until we're evicted, Mary thought bitterly.

10. 'The Lord Is My Shepherd'

Just before she was due to start work at St Mark's, Margaret blurted out to Ada how nervous she suddenly was.

In her typically direct manner Ada asked, 'Are you having second thoughts, dear?'

Margaret quickly shook her head. 'Not at all, but for a woman in her mid-thirties I'm feeling ridiculously edgy,' she admitted.

Big-hearted Ada didn't hesitate for a moment. 'If you like, I could accompany you,' she suggested. The look of intense relief on Margaret's face said it all. 'I have a day off tomorrow. I'm going into Grange to do a bit of shopping then visiting a friend, so it's not a problem,' Ada added. 'That's if you don't mind Catherine tagging along with us. Jamie's on call so I'm looking after her.'

Margaret gave a happy smile. 'I'd like that very much,' she exclaimed. 'I've seen your daughter from a distance, I thought she looked delightful.'

Ada glowed with pride as she responded, 'She's adorable, but be warned – Catherine never stops talking.'

Ada was right. All the way on the train into Grange, Catherine – in a little red woolly coat and bonnet that Sister Theresa had knitted with recycled wool – kept up a non-stop conversation. Gazing out of the window, she pointed her chubby little fingers as she chanted the names of just about everything they passed on their journey.

'Duck . . . dog . . . cow . . . sea . . . sand . . . man . . . bird . . . sky . . .' she babbled excitedly.

'See what I mean? She never lets up,' Ada remarked.

'She is lovely,' Margaret replied, turning her gaze on Catherine who had just spotted a herd of sheep. She allowed herself a moment to wonder what it would have been like if Peter had, in fact, left his wife for her. Would they have rejoiced in bringing up a child as wonderful and precious as the little girl beside her? Feeling her baby turn in her womb, Margaret beat back tears. Catherine's excited cry brought Margaret's sad wandering thoughts back to the here and now.

'Look, horsey!' the little girl exclaimed as they passed a horse and rider on the coastal path. 'Clip-clop-clip-clop, pony!' she chanted in delight.

When they arrived, Margaret enjoyed seeing Grange again; she had instantly liked the small, pretty grey slate town that nestled on the edge of Morecambe Bay.

'It's charming,' she declared as she stood on the platform inhaling the fresh tangy sea air. 'The views out to sea are stunning.'

'It's a sweet little town,' Ada agreed. 'The people are warm and welcoming, as I'm sure you'll soon find out,' she added as they crossed the road that led to St Mark's School, where they went their separate ways, but not before arranging to travel back to Mary Vale together when both had completed their tasks.

*

The headmistress, clearly thrilled at the thought of having extra help, warmly shook Margaret's hand.

'Hello, I'm Mrs Temple, so kind of you to help us, Miss Church,' she said.

'Please call me Margaret.'

'I have to confess we are so grateful for your time. We have become very negligent in the area of music; there are just not enough staff to go around these days,' Mrs Temple explained.

'Well, I'd be happy to help however I can,' Margaret assured her.

Meeting the children, aged from five to twelve years, properly this time, was a complete delight for Margaret. The Grange children, though poor, were nothing like as abjectly poor as the Bolton children she had taught. On the whole, they looked better fed and much healthier, with ruddy cheeks and a curiosity about them that delighted Margaret. There were a few children who looked less well off; Margaret noticed, in particular, a boy and an older girl she'd spotted last week too, similar in looks, which suggested they were siblings. They were both scrawny and looked distinctly underfed; their clothes, though clean, were ragged, and their boots, despite a hint of shine, were cracked and worn down. Somebody obviously cared for them, Margaret thought, and did their best.

Some of the pupils apparently lived in Grange, while others travelled in by bus or walked from the nearby surrounding villages. A large number were children of farm workers, shepherds, blacksmiths, stable hands and hill farmers. They seemed to have a robust attitude to the outdoors too – regardless of the chill of the day, they ran wildly around the windy playground, with leaves blowing around them, calling out and laughing as they played tag and hopscotch.

At the end of her first working day, Margaret agreed to teach music twice a week.

Glancing briefly at her tummy, Mrs Temple said as delicately as she could phrase it, 'I hope such a commitment won't be too much for you in your delicate condition?'

'I'm strong and fit, I'm looking forward to it very much indeed,' Margaret assured her.

'Given how curious children often are,' Mrs Temple continued diplomatically, 'they might well ask a few, er . . . awkward questions.'

Gazing down at her tummy, Margaret said, 'I'm quite sure they'll soon guess that I'm expecting.'

Mrs Temple smiled. 'Most of our pupils are children of the land, brought up with cows, sheep and horses. Animals reproducing throughout the farming year is as natural to them as breathing.'

'If any questions are asked, I'll just say I'm having a baby and the father is away,' Margaret explained.

It couldn't be simpler than that, she thought to herself – nor, in fact, more truthful.

It was pleasant to travel back to Mary Vale with Ada and Catherine. While the little girl, finally exhausted, slept on her mother's breast, Ada and Margaret exchanged news.

'How was your day?' Ada eagerly asked.

'I enjoyed it enormously,' Margaret smiled. 'The children are charming.'

'I hope you're not too tired?' Ada enquired.

'I feel fine, full of ideas,' Margaret replied excitedly.

Looking thoughtful, Ada said, 'I know I suggested this voluntary work, Margaret, but my fear now is that you might go overdoing things, which would make me very guilty.' She gave a little self-deprecating smile. 'Promise me, dear, that you will take care of yourself. You are getting on in your pregnancy,' she added as a reminder.

'If I start to feel worn out then I promise you I shall cut back on my hours,' Margaret replied. She watched the tide slowly ebb, leaving the vast marsh area washed silvery bright in its wake. 'I'm really looking forward to this opportunity, Ada. I've missed music and children so much, I'm just grateful for a chance to enjoy both experiences again.'

'Well, that's a relief. I can see by the keen expression on your face that you have plans.'

'I do,' Margaret assured her. 'I only wish I had more music books; the school's supply is pitifully low.'

'Try the local library,' Ada suggested. 'The librarians there couldn't be more helpful.'

Turning to a more sombre subject, the two women discussed the latest war news.

'It was heartening to read about the massive German surrender at Aachen,' Ada remarked.

Margaret gave an eager nod. 'And so swift on the news of Rommel's recent suicide. The Germans must know by now they're losing. I wonder how many would like to give up and admit defeat?'

Ada sadly shook her head. 'How many might even dare to think such a thing with Hitler at the helm? He's never going to give up, he'll fight to the bitter end – whatever the cost is in human life.'

Gazing out across the Irish Sea that was presently rushing out across the marsh, Margaret murmured wistfully, 'Can you imagine a world with no war?'

'When I hear news of our military advances, I start to dream of it,' Ada confessed. 'But then I stop myself, for fear of going too far. Five years of fighting has taught me caution.'

After sharing so many confidences throughout the day, Ada took the opportunity to inform Margaret (while Catherine was sound asleep) that she also was pregnant.

'It's early days, the baby's not due until April or May next year,' she said. 'It's not common knowledge yet, but I'll make an official announcement in the New Year.'

'Congratulations,' Margaret said warmly. 'You must both be very happy.'

'We are,' Ada exclaimed. 'And very excited.'

'A little brother or sister for Catherine,' Margaret said with a tender smile. Staring at Ada and her daughter, bathed in the golden glow of autumn sunshine streaming through the carriage window, Margaret struggled to suppress a bolt of envy that shot through her.

Some people are born blessed, she thought sadly. I'm just not one of them.

Margaret planned for her music classes at St Marks to be based very much along the same lines as those of her previous school. On the first day, she had played pieces of music on an old gramophone player that was even more ancient than the one at St Chad's. Hoping that her present class would respond to the music of Mozart, Brahms and Chopin as her other pupils had, Margaret was not to be let down.

After a short piece from *The Magic Flute* had finished, she turned to her pupils, who gazed at her in what she thought was complete mystification. 'Did you like that?' she asked them.

The response was astonishing. Hands shot up in the air, while other pupils called out comments.

'Why was everybody whistling so much?'

'Can that lady really sing as high as that?'

'Who's Papageno?'

'Can you play it again, miss?'

Smiling, Margaret answered all their questions as best she could, before moving on to hearing the children sing.

The large class of older children shuffled to their feet, and after much coughing and spluttering began to sing, accompanied by Margaret who played the opening chords of 'Rule, Britannia!', which just about brought the roof down.

'Excellent,' she announced. 'You certainly can sing. Let's try a song that you might not know all the words to,' she continued as she pointed to the blackboard where she had chalked the first verse of 'Under the Greenwood Tree'. This was not quite the success that 'Rule, Britannia!' had been, but Margaret persisted, listening closely as she played the music. By the end of the music lesson Margaret had a good idea of the range of the class, and who were the stronger, more gifted singers. Including, indeed, young Arthur.

'Well done,' she smiled when the bell rang out for playtime. 'I hope you all enjoyed that?'

Davie, an older boy with a shock of red hair, threw her a wide cheeky grin. 'I thought the Magic Flute fella sang better than us, miss!'

Margaret was genuinely delighted to discover the number of lovely voices in the group; young and fresh, their sweet voices soared high into the hall's wooden rafters. Their combined song had been so charming it actually brought the headmistress, who happened to be passing down the corridor, into the hall.

'My goodness,' she exclaimed. 'That was beautiful singing, children.'

Beaming in delight, the children eagerly responded.

'The new miss taught us, miss,' said an older girl, nodding to Margaret, who was still sitting at the piano.

'You sang so well,' the headmistress enthused. 'I'm impressed – you sound as good as any choir.'

Spurred on by the children's enthusiasm, and the headmistress's too, Margaret went home full of ideas for her next visit, which she put into action the very next day. Taking Ada's advice, she paid a visit to Grange public library to borrow song sheets and music books, which she thought might stimulate her pupils' interest.

Carrying the borrowed books home in her shopping basket, Margaret considered how her lesson plans might go down with her new pupils. Recalling their eager excited faces – and the way they threw themselves into the music – she smiled happily to herself.

'I'm so looking forward to this,' she said out loud. 'It's going to be fun!'

11. A Stroll in the Grounds

The following Wednesday, after calling in to check up on Mrs Cummings and Mrs Timms, Libby arrived at Thorp Hall with a definite plan in mind. Luckily, the weather fell in with her agenda; Libby intended to walk with her patient in the garden, where she was determined they would talk more in private. However, after knocking at the door and bracing herself for the sight of Mrs Grimsdale, Libby got the shock of her life when it was thrown open by a swarthy, scowling middle-aged man.

'I suppose you're here to see my wife?' he barked.

'I'm Nurse Godburgh, your wife's midwife,' Libby said with as much dignity as she could muster. Seeing him literally blocking the doorway, she added, 'May I please come in?'

'Aye,' he grunted as he stepped aside to let her pass.

Though the circumstances were distinctly inhospitable, Libby continued as cheerfully as she could. 'Your wife and I thought we might take a stroll outdoors.'

'It's a bit damp for that, I'd say,' he grumbled. 'You should know my wife's not well.'

'The fresh air might do her good.' Libby diplomatically added, 'One can spend too long cooped up indoors, don't you think?'

Rudely stopping Libby in her tracks, Thorp said forcefully, 'You fail to understand, Nurse Godley.'

'Nurse Godburgh,' she corrected him.

'My wife is extremely highly strung; she worries about every little thing.'

You could try comforting her, Libby thought to herself.

'She needs to get a grip of her emotions,' he stated. 'I only hope you have some success, otherwise your time here will be completely wasted.'

Fuming to herself, Libby managed to hold her tongue and answer politely. 'Thank you, sir, now if you don't mind, I'd like to attend to my patient.' Turning her ramrod-straight back on Thorp, Libby strode away with her head held high.

Slyly admiring her slim strong legs and slender waist, Thorp leered under his breath, 'Saucy little minx.'

When Libby slipped into the drawing room, Beth was already in her coat.

'Let's get out of here.' She spoke urgently, quickly drawing Libby into the garden.

The two women made their way across the vast stretch of lawn to a pergola half-hidden from view by a bank of copper beech bushes.

Inching closer to Libby, as if for protection, Beth said, 'We can be private here.'

Not convinced that Mrs Grimsdale wouldn't pop up from behind the pergola, Libby didn't waste any time. 'How have you been this week, Beth?'

'I had one small bleed, but mercifully it stopped, though I have felt quite dizzy since.'

'Have you felt tired?'

Beth nodded. 'I could sleep all day,' she confessed. 'Sometimes I just want to stay in bed and never wake up.'

That's a classic sign of anaemia, Libby thought to herself.

'And I get a queasiness every now and again. Not like the morning sickness I had to start with, that was terrible and went on for months, this is more of a fluttery sickness that comes and goes. It gets worse when I'm upset or nervous.'

Aware that her patient might be nervous quite a lot of the time, Libby trod very carefully. 'Being on edge could make you feel a bit queasy. Does the sensation go away when you're on your own, relaxing?'

Beth gave a weary little smile. 'Libby, I am on my own all day long, you'd think that I would find time to relax, but I don't. I'm constantly on edge.' Her shoulders slumped, as if she was frightened that she had said too much.

'When you feel up to it, couldn't you pop into Grange and do a bit of shopping every now and again?' Libby asked. 'You could buy something for the baby, or have tea in a café with a friend?'

The look on Beth's pale face suggested that it would be easier to fly to the moon and back than walk with a friend in Grange. 'Never!' she exclaimed. 'I'm not encouraged to leave the house,' she finally admitted.

Wanting to say, 'That's just outrageous!' Libby bit her lip and waited for Beth to finish.

'My husband's old-fashioned enough to believe I'm better off at home, resting, and not exciting myself with visiting friends and exchanging gossip.'

'That really is a very old-fashioned approach to pregnancy,' Libby agreed. 'We're not living in Edwardian times any more.'

Beth's green eyes, with their beguiling golden lights, widened. 'I agree,' she declared. 'But my husband insists that he knows better – and to be honest, Libby,' she sighed heavily, 'I just haven't the strength or the energy to fight him any more. It's easier to comply than protest.'

At a loss as to how to best comfort her defeated patient, Libby cast around for the right words. She couldn't just say, 'You must defy your husband and do what is best for yourself,' that was far too simplistic, and dangerous too. She would never give advice that might jeopardize a patient, but surely, she shouldn't just acquiesce to something as outrageous as cooping a woman up throughout the whole of her pregnancy? Surely that was equally as dangerous?

Fortunately, Beth broke through Libby's turbulent thoughts.

'I wasn't always like this,' Beth continued in a mournful voice. 'I used to be a vibrant, headstrong young women, full of life and fun. I think that's what drew my husband to me in the first place. He was doing business in the Borrowdale valley when we met, by chance, at a local auction. He was a lot older than me but appeared handsome and powerful; I was attracted to him and flattered when he started courting me. My parents, especially my mother, warned me off, she repeatedly said he was an over-bearing man who was far too old for a girl like me.' Beth gave a resigned shrug. 'She was absolutely right, but being the silly impulsive young girl that I was, I resisted her advice and agreed to marry Ronnie . . . and here I am now,' she said as she expressively spread her pale delicate hands in the air. 'A married woman with not a friend in the world.'

Desperate to conclude the grim conversation on a more positive note, Libby said, 'I'm sure once the baby is born your husband will be relieved to see you leave the house, men generally hate the fuss and noise babies create.' Rising, she added, 'Shall we take a stroll around the garden before I examine you?'

Seemingly reluctant to leave the dripping pergola, Beth blushed. 'I'd feel more relaxed if you could examine me when my husband is not in the house.'

'He must appreciate it has to be done,' Libby pointed out. Taking her patient by the arm, she urged her to her feet. 'Come on, dear, let's walk.'

Supported by Libby, Beth agreed to take a stroll around the large garden. As before, the air was dank, with a cold mist that rolled off the fells.

'I'd give anything to return to Borrowdale and my family,' Beth suddenly blurted out. 'I'm so homesick, I miss them so much. Why, oh why, did I ever agree to leave them in the first place?' At that she burst into floods of tears.

Desperate that Beth shouldn't upset herself while her husband was in close proximity, possibly spying on them, Libby laid a protective arm around her trembling shoulders.

'Let's go indoors,' she suggested. 'I'll build up the fire, and I'll check you and the baby over, and get you a bit warmer.'

After Libby had taken Beth's blood pressure, which remained low, she felt her patient's abdomen before listening to the foetal heart-beat.

'How's my baby, Libby?' Beth asked nervously.

Libby threw her a tender smile. 'Definitely on the small side. Have you been eating properly? Do you remember the food I mentioned? Liver, greens, fish – they're all good for your condition.'

Beth gave a little nervous nod. 'Ronnie got me some beef,' she answered with a grimace.

Though startled by this information, Libby nevertheless stuck to the matter in hand. 'Your expression tells me it didn't go down well.'

'I just couldn't swallow it, sorry, I did try,' Beth said feebly.

'If your appetite's not improving,' Libby said decisively, 'it's time to start you on iron supplements. I'll bring some pills for you on my next visit,' she promised.

Like an overtired child, Beth laid her head on Libby's strong supportive shoulder. 'Thank you,' she said. 'Thank you for being my friend, Libby.'

Seeing tears welling up in her patient's green eyes, Libby answered softly, 'I have your best interests at heart, Beth. I'm going to make sure that you are properly taken care of, even if it means upsetting a few people along the way.'

12. 'Zip-A-Dee-Doo-Dah'

It was gratifying to notice on Margaret's second school visit the children's enthusiasm and excitement for their next singing class, running into the school building from the playground, and chiding each other.

'C'mon, we don't want to be late.'

'Get a move on.'

'Be quick! Miss is waiting for us.'

The hall resounded this time with songs from *The Wizard of Oz*, 'Follow the Yellow Brick Road' being the all-time favourite. The children also eagerly picked up popular songs like 'Teddy Bears' Picnic', 'Run, Rabbit, Run!' and 'Zip-A-Dee-Doo-Dah', which reduced the young singers to hysterical laughter every time they roared out the catchy chorus. Another big favourite was 'When You Wish Upon A Star', which they sang with real pathos and longing.

Having the time of her life, Margaret had to regularly remind herself that she was also expected to rehearse hymns for the daily school assembly; even these old established numbers were revived under Margaret's light artistic touch. Selecting students blessed with good voices, Margaret grouped them accordingly – there were some children who were tone deaf and couldn't sing at all, but she never put them off or shamed them before their peer group. Her system of embracing and encouraging all levels of ability was beginning to engender a joy of singing, something which Margaret relished as much as her students did.

'We've been overhearing the children singing their new songs all week,' the headmistress enthused in the staff-room. 'I've never heard anything quite like it in all my time here.'

The other staff, helping themselves to hasty cups of tea during the play-time break, nodded in agreement.

'Assembly was a joy,' one older teacher commented. 'When the children sang "The Lord Is My Shepherd", I was almost reduced to tears.' She grinned, before adding, 'Believe me, that takes some doing for a hard-bitten teacher of thirty-five years. To be honest,' she added, turning to the headmistress, 'I never even knew we had so much talent at St Mark's.'

Feeling slightly embarrassed by all the praise that was being heaped on her, Margaret was quick to speak up. 'Actually, there's a lot of natural musical talent in the school, it's just a question of winkling it out. Many of the children start off shy, but once they start enjoying them-selves, they throw caution to the wind and have fun.'

'I agree with you, Margaret,' the headmistress said. 'With your encouragement, a lot of new voices are com-ing to the fore, Joy Carter for one. She used to be such a shrinking violet, always shy and self-deprecating, but this week we've seen her singing like a bird.'

Margaret nodded as she pictured Joy, a tall skinny child, with mousey-brown hair always tightly plaited. The girl was a natural alto, with a high pure voice. Margaret was confident she could get her effortlessly harmonizing in due course.

'Her brother Arthur's a little star too,' the older teacher added fondly. 'A cheeky little devil, but standing there singing his heart out – with no front teeth – well, he stole the show this morning singing "All Things Bright And Beautiful".'

Looking thoughtful, Margaret agreed. 'Both Carter children are complete naturals. Do they come from a musical family?'

Joy's teacher answered her question. 'I wouldn't think so, father's a shepherd, they live in a rented tithe cottage up Allithwaite way. Good kiddies, bright too. Joy's reading age is well above average, she's quiet and very diligent.'

Arthur's teacher burst out laughing. 'I can't say that for her brother, little imp, always in trouble but sweet with it. I just wish he had something warmer to wear for school these days. Sometimes he arrives blue with cold, I make sure he sits by the radiators until he's warmed up.'

The headmistress nodded. 'The Carters are poor, but realistically St Mark's has a lot of poor pupils. Families that live off the land have little cash to spare – and it's even harder these days, with so many of their men called up for active service.'

Nurturing the natural talent within the school, Margaret noted there was an older boy in the top class, a big red-headed, tousle-haired boy, who had a good musical ear and a deep bass voice.

'Where did you learn to sing, Davie?' she enquired of the boy at the end of one of her music classes. She was astonished by his candid answer.

'In't pub wi' mi dad.'

'Your dad's a singer?'

'Only at weekends, miss, rest of time he drives buses to Carlisle.'

Baffled, Margaret asked another question. 'He's a bus driver?'

'Aye, he were fighting at start o't war but got shot in't th'eye during combat in France, so he got discharged from th'army and came home.'

Incredulous, Margaret continued. 'Can he see all right to drive buses?'

'Oh, aye, he's got one right good eye,' Davie told her proudly. 'And a crackin' voice, he makes a bob or two in't Crown in town every Saturday night.'

'And you sing with him, Davie?'

'If he can slip me in, I do, he makes more if we double up and duo together.'

Intrigued by this unexpected information, Margaret asked, 'What do you sing?'

'Anything by Vera Lynn, "The White Cliffs Of Dover" brings the house down, jolly songs too, "Roll Out The Barrel", "It's A Long Way To Tipperary", "Rule, Britannia!", patriotic stuff like that goes down a storm round about closing time.'

'You're obviously not shy when it comes to singing in public?'

'Nay, I love it, miss – and I love the sixpences mi dad gives me after we've had a whip-round at the end of the night,' Davie grinned.

Back at the Home, Ada, Matron and Libby were pleased to note the difference in their patient.

'I can tell from the skip in your step that you're having fun,' Ada teased as she, Libby and Margaret sat having beans on toast one tea-time.

'Heavens! The size I am,' Margaret chuckled, 'there's hardly a skip in my step these days.'

Libby, despite always being a little preoccupied by her concern for one of her patients outside of the Home, still of course kept meticulous tabs on the Mary Vale patients whom she nursed every day. Looking out of the window, she could see the outline of trees blowing in the garden, now growing dark as the sun rapidly set like a huge red orb over the churning grey sea.

'I hope the journey there and back twice a week isn't proving too much?' she asked.

'I've enjoyed it, actually,' Margaret confessed. 'It's a very short train journey, less than ten minutes, and the views every time across the bay are breathtaking. I don't know how this beautiful part of the world passed me by in my former life.'

Ada, who unashamedly adored the Cartmel Peninsula, bobbed her head in agreement.

'As Jamie always says, there's no finer place on God's earth. But returning to the point,' she checked herself, 'you really must not go overdoing it, Margaret.'

'It's early days. But I promised you I would cut back my hours if it all got too much,' Margaret assured her. 'And I will. But for the moment, given the circumstances, I'm having the time of my life.'

13. Mrs Grimsdale

Heading downstairs early in the morning before the residents appeared for breakfast, Libby helped herself to her first cup of tea of the day, which she drank sitting by the window in the uncharacteristically quiet dining room. Libby loved this early, still time when she could peacefully run through her plans for the day; they nearly always began with a visit to Snowball's stable – at this time of the year in the dark, before dawn broke. Leaving the Home by the back way, as songbirds woke up to a new morning, Libby would slip down the track to Alf's farm where she looked forward to enjoying a kiss and a cuddle with her pony. Snowball always snickered a welcome when he heard his mistress's approaching footsteps on the echoing stone-flagged corridor. Flicking on a dangling overhead light that illuminated the stables and tack room, Libby would make affectionate little clicking noises with her tongue as she hurried towards Snowball who, as usual, was eagerly poking his pretty silver head over the top of his stable door. Excited by the sight of his smiling mistress, he would paw the straw-strewn cobbles of his loose box before blowing into Libby's long, flaming-red hair (which she would later tuck under her nurse's frilled cap but for now left fanned around her lovely face).

'I know it's early, my sweetheart,' she would murmur as she opened the door and stepped into the box to run her flat palm over Snowball's sleek, plump rump. 'I just wanted to make sure we had a cuddle before I started work.'

Throwing a rug over Snowball, she would lead him into the wide tiled corridor where she tied him up beside a fresh net of hay, watching him hungrily attack it. After picking up Snowball's droppings, Libby always laid fresh straw on the stable floor, then replenished his water bucket before returning the pony to his stable. Pressing her body against his to get warm, she enjoyed chatting on.

'I've got a busy day ahead,' she'd tell him. 'So be a good lad for Alf, and don't pester Captain.' Closing the stable door, she then hurried outside into the cold dawn light. 'See you later, sweetheart,' she always called over her shoulder.

In answer Snowball would give a loud, shrill neigh that echoed around the farmyard, disturbing the chickens who were scratching for worms in the dirt.

This morning, Libby was topping up her cup with fresh tea when Sister Theresa appeared with warm bread and little pats of butter; they were fortunate enough to have any these days, with rationing now even harsher than ever before.

'We're lucky to have Farmer Alf's delicious butter,' Libby declared as she helped Theresa lay the food out on the vast dining-room table that could easily accommodate twenty-five diners at any one time.

After the young nun had dashed back into the kitchen, Libby sat staring dreamily out of the window, watching the low-lying sun appear from behind a bank of misty grey clouds. As well as her Mary Vale duties that morning she had her three pregnant ladies to visit that afternoon, starting with Beth at Thorp Hall. Just thinking of the place made Ada shudder. What a grim soulless place it was. Imagine waking up there every morning, she thought, with only Mrs Grimsdale and Ronnie Thorp for company. Poor Beth. No wonder she was so lost and depressed. What a pity she couldn't get away for a few days to her family's farm in the lovely Borrowdale valley on the other side of the fells. Good company and exercise would do Beth the world of good, but what with the housekeeper and her morose husband breathing down her neck there was little chance of Beth ever getting a break.

Apart from the miserable claustrophobic image of Thorp Hall that haunted Libby, she also had more tangible concerns, like her patient's anaemia and apparent depressive condition. Her sporadic bleeding was a worry too, but Libby knew from experience that for the moment at least there was no real cause for concern, unless the bleeding suddenly became heavy and was associated with tummy pains.

'Thank God, that's not happened so far,' Libby muttered. 'If it did, Beth would be in serious trouble. Anyway, I'm her midwife now,' she firmly told herself. 'It's up to me to support my patient and attend to her needs. If Beth is too ill and nervous to help herself then I must do what's best for her, even if that does mean getting on the wrong side of Thorp and his watchdog housekeeper.'

The dining-room door opened again; this time to Margaret, who looked immaculate in a loose-fitting, soft blue woollen dress worn with thick winter stockings and highly polished brown leather brogues.

'Morning,' she called cheerfully as she collected a cup of tea and joined Libby at the table by the window.

'Morning, Margaret, how are you?' Libby enquired.

Bright-eyed Margaret, with her long lustrous dark hair held back in a velvet Alice band, looked distinctly brighter than she had done for weeks.

'Very well,' she declared. 'I'm so enjoying my time at St Mark's School.'

'It certainly suits you,' Libby beamed.

'It's great fun, but it couldn't be more different to my former job, teaching children in Bolton,' she chatted. 'Don't get me wrong,' she smiled. 'They were lovely but, locked into an industrial environment, they had no knowledge of fields, forests, rivers, flowers – how could they, when most of their parents were working full-time at the local mill, or in the case of their fathers away fighting for their country? There was certainly no time for holidays or little trips out to the country,' she explained. 'The children at St Mark's School are just as poor but they have a different attitude to life – and so do their parents. I've barely been there more than a few times but, heavens, they know so much – they make me feel quite ignorant,' she laughed. 'I overhear them in the playground chatting about bringing the sheep down from the fells and getting ready for lambing. I'm already impressed by their natural knowledge and understanding of nature.'

Libby smiled fondly. 'I grew up with all of that. That was my world, and I wouldn't swop it for anything. Working on the farm since I was old enough to muck out the stables and sweep down the yard, I loved it. When I was big enough, I used to herd the sheep with my brothers, staying up all night during lambing time and, best of all, riding out on the bridle paths on my pony. It was a very precious time.'

Margaret cast her mind back to her own childhood days. She had been happy sitting at the piano in their rather overcrowded parlour, practising piano pieces for hours on end, or sitting by the fire in the evening, drinking Ovaltine while listening to the wireless with her parents. Happy days, but the polar opposite of what Libby had just described.

Completely changing the subject, Libby gave Margaret an appraising professional look. 'As much as you are enjoying St Mark's, Margaret, you must err on the side of caution, don't go overdoing it,' she warned. 'You haven't got that long to go – and baby comes first, you know.'

Margaret gave a happy little shrug. 'Ada's been saying the same thing but, truly, I feel better than I have done in weeks.' Lowering her voice, she added, 'I have to admit that I was very down just after I arrived here. Not because of Mary Vale,' she hastily added. 'I was just disorientated, but now I'm feeling fine,' she announced. 'It's good to have a reason to get up in the morning, I'm just not used to sitting around doing nothing all day.'

As other residents trickled into the dining room Libby slipped away to join Ada, who was waiting for her in order to start their morning ward round. Libby immediately congratulated Ada on the change in Margaret. 'She's so much improved, almost unrecognizable even after just two visits.'

Ada grinned with pleasure. 'It's marvellous,' she agreed. 'Though I have to watch her like a hawk,' she admitted. 'I have a feeling Margaret would be at St Mark's every day if she had her own way.'

'Yes,' Libby agreed. 'I've just had a little word with her about that. She said she would consider cutting back on her hours if she found she was doing too much.'

Ada nodded. 'It might just be a rush of energy that will peak soon. It happens often enough in pregnancy.' Checking the fob watch on her nurse's apron, she smiled. 'Time to get cracking, Nurse Godburgh.'

The morning sped by, and after an early dinner Libby (with her medical bag firmly strapped to the back of her bike) set off at speed for Thorp Hall and her patients in Grange. Since her last visit to Beth, Libby had enjoyed a busy and productive week at Mary Vale, where she had been kept busy and happily occupied. But now, once more heading for the gloomy hall, she felt her stomach nervously tighten at the prospect of Thorp opening the door to her. When, in fact, Mrs Grimsdale opened the door, Libby didn't even attempt to be pleasant; instead, she stepped into the hallway without being invited, then made her own way to the drawing room where, as usual, she found Beth curled up in the huge wing-backed armchair.

'How are you this afternoon?' she enquired cheerily. When no response was forthcoming, Libby approached Beth, who remained curled up in a ball with her face pressed against the upholstery. 'Beth, what is it?' she gently asked. When her patient turned towards her, Libby's hand flew involuntarily to her mouth. 'Sweetheart!' she exclaimed. 'What on earth has happened?'

Beth's pale face was puffed up and red with weeping. Unstoppable tears spilled from her big green eyes and rolled unchecked down her pale swollen face.

'Dear,' Libby murmured as she took a step closer. 'You look like you've been crying all night.'

'I have,' Beth sobbed.

Crouching down beside her, Libby wrapped her arms around Beth and rocked her back and forth, gently stroking her long, tangled hair until eventually her tears subsided and she was finally able to talk. Afraid that her patient's frail physical condition might have worsened in the week since she had last visited her, Libby asked, 'Have you felt poorly?'

'No more than normal,' Beth sadly replied.

'So, what is it, what's the matter?'

Blushing, Beth replied. 'I sleep badly when I have to sleep with my husband,' she whispered. 'He's big and heavy and noisy – he keeps me awake with all his tossing and turning,' she finished lamely.

That's not enough to make you cry all night, Libby thought to herself. Not pressing the point, she let Beth continue.

'When I ask his permission to leave his bed, go elsewhere to sleep in peace, he gets cross, says a woman's place is beside her husband, whether she likes it or not.'

With all the rooms in this wretched house, you'd think Thorp could spare one for his sick wife, Libby seethed inwardly.

Looking anguished, Beth burst out, 'I'm so homesick, Libby, I just want to go home and be with my family.' She wailed like a lost child.

Knowing they could be interrupted by Mrs Grimsdale at any minute, Libby was nevertheless determined to comfort and calm Beth. Sitting close, with her arms encircling her patient, she said tenderly, 'Tell me about home; you told me you grew up in the North Lakes, in Rosthwaite, way up in the Borrowdale valley.'

'Borrowdale,' Beth sighed, and gradually started to talk. 'The most beautiful place on earth.' She paused a little, her eyes glazing over, and Libby waited patiently, hoping she would get more out of her. 'After I had finished school, I wanted to work on the farm, like my brother. I would have made a good shepherd – and nobody in my family can build a neater drystone wall than me,' she added proudly. 'Secretly, I think my father quite liked the idea, but my mother was fiercely against such a thing. "What will folks think!" she used to scold, every time I brought up the subject. Frankly, I didn't give two hoots about other people's opinions, valley folk can be very closed in on themselves,' she told Libby, who simply couldn't equate this limp weak woman with the strong feisty girl she was describing. 'Anyway, I went to train at a secretarial college in Penrith but during the holidays I spent every minute on the fells, swimming in the becks on hot summer days after we had harvested, taking the cows to market, feeding orphaned lambs.'

'It sounds idyllic,' Libby enthused.

'Apart from having to work as a secretary in Keswick once I qualified – which I hated – it was idyllic, until war was declared and then, like every other family across the country, our boys were called up. It was only then that my dad allowed me to pack in my job. With my brother gone, we were a farmhand down and my dad working every hour God sent to make up for the shortfall.'

'So, you became a land girl,' Libby chuckled.

'That was dad's argument; he said, we've got a land girl right on our doorstep, why go looking for another?'

'You got your own way in the end,' Libby smiled. 'Where's your brother serving now?' she asked.

Beth paused, a shadow returning to her face. 'He died, in a fighter plane shot down over the North Sea,' she said quietly. 'Dad took it badly enough, but mother's never been the same since. I'm the only one she's got now, visits between us would be a blessing, but . . .' her voice trailed away.

Libby's skin began to creep. What in God's name was going on in this place? It was bad enough not to be allowed to sleep alone during the uncomfortable latter months of her pregnancy, but to be banned from having visitors was another matter. And on cue, the drawing-room door swung open and in walked Mrs Grimsdale herself, bearing a loaded silver tea tray. Seeing her scowling expression, Beth sank back into the sanctuary of the chair where she tried to hide herself from view.

Libby, livid at yet another interruption, boldly faced the interfering housekeeper.

'I thought you might be in need of refreshment,' Mrs Grimsdale snapped.

Libby forced herself to say thank you, but then had no hesitation in unceremoniously ushering the intruder out of the room. 'Thank you, Mrs Grimsdale. I would be grateful if you could leave us in peace.'

Tall, strong and thoroughly determined, Libby towered over the housekeeper who looked like thunder.

'I shall relay your behaviour to my master,' she declared.

'Go ahead, ma'am,' Libby calmly answered.

The minute the door closed, Beth emerged from her hiding place, looking white-faced with fear. 'She'll tell him what you said.'

With her violet-blue eyes flashing, Libby tossed her head. 'Let her,' she declared. 'Your treatment here is intolerable. Keeping you cooped up like a captive, forcing you to do things against your will, and allowing you absolutely no privacy. It's outrageous.'

Seeing Beth's timid expression, Libby wound in her raging emotions. It was all right for her to express herself; she was a free woman who could come and go as she pleased, whereas Beth was in effect a prisoner in her own home. Alarmed that she had gone too far and behaved unprofessionally, Libby immediately apologized.

'I'm so sorry, Beth, my temper got the worse of me,' she confessed. 'I shouldn't have reacted quite so strongly, but I couldn't help it,' she blurted. 'The woman just gives me the creeps.'

Beth unexpectedly burst out laughing. 'She gives me the creeps too,' she gasped. 'I can't stand her.'

'Was she here when you arrived?' Libby enquired. 'I can't imagine that you would ever have employed a woman like Mrs Grimsdale.'

'Never!' Beth exclaimed. 'I'd have willingly taken over all the housekeeping myself, shopping, cooking, cleaning, I'm used to that, and I love gardening too. But Ronnie said he wanted me to conduct myself like a lady,' she added darkly.

Sounds ridiculously Edwardian, Libby thought.

'He won't let me ride, or even keep a horse, which I miss dreadfully,' Beth continued.

'I would be devastated if I couldn't keep my pony,' Libby confessed. 'In fact, I brought Snowball to Mary Vale with me – I couldn't bear to be parted from the sweet boy.'

'I begged to bring my bay mare to Thorp Hall – the stables could house a hunt – but Ronnie refused point blank, didn't want me riding around the countryside attracting attention to myself. I ask you, who would even see me out here in the middle of nowhere?'

Now seriously concerned, Libby cautiously asked, 'Beth, what exactly are you allowed to do?'

'Not much,' she grimly answered. 'Certainly not visit friends and family.'

'Surely they can visit *you*?'

'My parents have been allowed to visit me twice. Once on the occasion of my brother's death; the second time was when I announced I was pregnant.'

'TWICE?' Libby spluttered.

'Since I fell pregnant, it's been the perfect excuse for keeping me more enclosed. Ronnie thinks going on visits and gadding about will be bad for me and the baby.' She rolled her eyes in despair.

Having just said too much to the housekeeper, Libby kept her mouth firmly shut, but that didn't stop her from thinking what an utter monster Ronnie Thorp was. Concerned that she had already spent far too long talking – though the information she had gleaned from Beth's confessions was vital to building up a realistic picture of her patient and her condition – Libby was impatient to turn to more immediate matters.

'Dear, let's continue with this very important conversation. But for now, please may I examine you before we are interrupted again?'

'Of course,' obliging Beth quickly replied.

As she had previously done, Beth lay flat out on the long sofa and pulled up her clothes so that Libby could examine her tummy. Surprised that Beth, at seven months, was still quite small, Libby gently moved her hands around her patient's abdomen in order to gauge the baby's position, before pressing the wide end of the little trumpet-like Pinard stethoscope that she had brought along in her nurse's bag against Beth's abdomen.

'I hope that's not too cold against your skin?' Libby said as she placed the other end of the stethoscope against her ear. 'Lie as still as you can while I listen to the baby's heart-beat.'

Though troubled by the apparently erratic heart-beat, Libby wondered if the Pinard stethoscope was totally accurate; they had a reputation for occasional inaccuracy, which only slightly allayed her growing anxieties.

Interrupting Libby's thoughts, Beth asked, 'Is everything all right?'

Knowing that this was not the right time to share her fears with vulnerable Beth, who would be left alone and unprotected once she departed for Mary Vale, Libby avoided the question by prevaricating. 'I need to finish examining you, dear.'

During the examination Libby discovered that Beth's blood pressure was lower than on her last visits, and her pulse also faster. Libby wondered if this might be the consequence of her patient's nervous, agitated exhaustion. It was clear that neither patient nor baby were doing well this week. Every instinct in Libby's body fought against leaving Beth alone again, but what choice did she have? If she stayed, she was quite sure that Ronnie Thorp would kick her out the moment he returned home, plus she had other patients at Mary Vale who were in need of her nursing.

If only Beth were one of my Mary Vale patients, Libby thought. We could monitor her regularly, make sure she was eating the right food and taking the best care of herself. Here she wastes away, showing no improvement – if anything, getting weaker – and now I'm going to leave her all on her own for a whole week.

Seeing the desperation in Beth's sad eyes, Libby said in as reassuring a voice as she could muster, 'Your anaemic condition is not improving, which is bad for baby.' Reaching into her bag for the iron tablets Jamie had prescribed at her request, she presented them to Beth. 'Here, iron supplements,' she said as she handed them over. 'One a day, don't forget.'

Libby was alarmed when her patient suddenly cried out, 'Oh, Libby, I'm so frightened.'

Taking her hand, Libby calmed Beth down by suggesting that she should be seen by a doctor.

'Why? Is something wrong?' Beth demanded anxiously.

'As I just said, you're anaemic and underweight, so there are issues that I'd like advice on,' Libby patiently answered.

Beth's face fell. 'My husband might not permit it, he doesn't like interfering doctors. That's what he calls them,' she added in an embarrassed voice. 'He wasn't keen on you nursing me, goodness only knows how he'll react to a doctor,' she added nervously.

'Surely he won't prevent me or a doctor from entering if you need medical attention?' Libby asked.

Knowing better, Beth said bitterly, 'He can't be doing with strangers.'

Not wanting to overload her patient with even more anxieties, Libby answered evenly. 'Mary Vale's resident doctor is very polite and highly experienced. I'm sure Dr Reid will take charge of the situation.'

Ten minutes later, cycling along the track from Thorp Hall to Grange, rather late for her scheduled visits to Mrs Cummings and Mrs Timms, a furious Libby gave vent to her emotions.

'Oh my God!' she said out loud as she pedalled downhill in the face of a bitterly cold wind. 'Dr Jamie must see Beth as soon as possible. But heavens,' she exclaimed as she recalled Beth's ominous words. 'It's hard enough me gaining entry into Thorp Hall – how on earth is Ronnie Thorp ever going to allow Dr Jamie over the doorstep without a fight?'

14. 'Greensleeves'

The morning assembly the following week was, thanks to Margaret, considerably brightened by another charming rendition of 'Greensleeves', which was a popular favourite with everybody. Though an ancient song with ancient lyrics, Henry VIII's romantic music delighted the children, who swayed to the music that Margaret played on the big piano in the cold school hall.

'Alas, my love, you do me wrong . . .'

The children's sweet young voices eased the words which usually pierced Margaret to the heart. But today, captivated in particular by the voices of Joy and Arthur Carter – which, when combined in perfect harmony, brought tears to her eyes – Margaret simply enjoyed the pleasure of the moment rather than the heartbreak. She wasn't the only one who was moved by the song; out of the corner of her eye she saw the headmistress and several other teachers surreptitiously wiping away tears as the haunting music drew to a close. After the music class had finished, the children lined up for dinner-time, making their way into the dining room, where they were served a school dinner of spam fritters, mashed potatoes and sprouts.

Heading down the corridor towards the staffroom, Margaret stopped in her tracks when she heard a child crying as she passed the cloakroom. Stopping to peer in, she couldn't see anybody, but she could certainly hear them. Following the sound, she discovered Arthur Carter huddled up underneath a pile of coats.

'Arthur!' she exclaimed. 'What on earth's the matter?'

Huddling further into the coats, Arthur wriggled uncomfortably. 'Nothing, miss.'

Not convinced, Margaret held out a hand and gently drew him out from the coats, only to discover that his skimpy trousers were ripped from top to bottom.

'I don't want t'other children to see mi bum,' he said, starting to cry again.

Feeling desperately sorry for the little lad, Margaret gently enquired, 'What happened, lovie?'

'I were playing tag with t'other lads when somebody grabbed me hard by the pants and they ripped, everybody laughed at me, so I ran in here to hide from them.'

'Oh dear,' Margaret said soothingly. 'I'm sure someone can find you another pair of trousers in the store cupboard. Let me go and ask.'

With tears fast fading from his big blue eyes, Arthur said, 'Really, miss?'

'Of course, come with me.'

'I can't go down the corridor like this,' he cried.

'Let's borrow a coat for now,' she said as she wrapped him up in a coat dangling from the nearest peg. 'I'll bring it back later when we've finished with it.'

Once in the school office, Margaret asked the assistant to unlock the store cupboard. Helping Arthur into the warmest pair of long trousers she could find, Margaret couldn't help but notice how pale and thin his young body was. She also saw that the soles of his boots were nothing but holes, and he wasn't wearing socks.

'Does that feel better?' she asked.

Now almost back to normal, Arthur threw her one of his cheeky smiles. 'Aye, much better – and much warmer too.'

Cautiously feeling her way, she enquired, 'Do you often feel the cold, Arthur?'

'Only when we're playing out or walking to school, that's when I'm freezing cold.'

After leaving the little boy to enjoy the last of his playtime, Margaret replaced the coat she had borrowed, then made her way to the staffroom for a welcome cup of tea. Within minutes, she found herself once more in a conversation which centred around the Carter children.

'I'm becoming so fond of them already,' she admitted. 'I know Arthur can be a handful, he's got "mischief" written all over him, but he's so sweet and sincere, and Joy seems a poppet.'

'I marvel that either of them has the heart to sing, their home life is grim to say the least.'

Thinking of Arthur's skinny little body, tender-hearted Margaret murmured, 'Poor lambs, they both look so terribly neglected.'

'Although they go around in threadbare rags and look dreadfully neglected, they're much loved,' the head assured Margaret. 'But what I've gathered recently, from Arthur actually – you know what a little chatterbox he can be – is that Mr Carter is sick and has taken to his bed. Joy's not said a thing, remains tight-lipped. Poor child, I've found her several times in tears in the cloakroom.'

'What an awful worry for two children to bear,' Margaret replied.

Dropping her voice to a whisper, Mrs Temple added, 'I hear that their landlord, a local man, is particularly vindictive towards the family.'

'Why would anybody pick on them?' Margaret exclaimed.

'You know how ruthless landlords can be, and this one sounds particularly harsh.'

Margaret's heart ached, poor children, she thought, victims of poverty, brought up hungry with the threat of eviction forever hanging over their heads. It was a miracle that they even wanted to sing at all.

Turning to an altogether different subject, Mrs Temple surprised Margaret.

'I've been thinking about morale recently. We're told we're winning the war and the enemy is on the run, which I pray to God is true, but, my goodness, we seem to have been fighting for such a long time now.'

'Five long years,' Margaret sighed.

'Exactly. That's why I am determined to do something jolly this Christmas, something that will bring a smile to our pupils' faces; make them forget, however briefly, the sadness of the last few years.'

'It's a nice idea,' Margaret responded. 'What did you have in mind?'

'Well, because of *your* input,' the head said, with a wide smile, 'I've been thinking of something along the lines of a concert.'

'A concert!' Margaret exclaimed.

The headmistress gave an excited nod. 'St Mark's school choir's first concert,' she announced. 'Put together and directed by you – if you think you could manage that, of course?' she quickly added.

Completely taken aback, Margaret's thoughts flashed involuntarily back to St Chad's School in Bolton and a children's concert she'd put on there. It was that particular event, and the children's joyful enthusiasm, that had inspired her to continue teaching and led her to St Mark's. And Peter had been part of that fulfilment and happiness. Taken completely unawares by the tide of longing that suddenly washed over her, as if from nowhere, Margaret smothered a gasp. Would she ever be able to forget Peter, the only love of her life and the father of the child she was carrying?

Seeing Margaret go pale, Mrs Temple quickly asked, 'Are you quite all right, dear? If it's too much, it's no problem.'

Collecting herself, Margaret answered, 'Yes, I'm fine, just a little dizzy.'

'Please sit down,' the headmistress urged. 'I really shouldn't be asking so much of you in this way, I do apologize. Please forget I ever even mentioned a concert, so thoughtless of me.'

'I'm fine, really I'm fine, and of course I'd love to help the children put on a concert.' Taking a sip of tea, Margaret gave more thought to Mrs Temple's original question. 'There's a wealth of natural musical talent here in St Mark's. With so many good voices, I'm sure we could put on a lovely concert, though the children might have to put in extra hours if they're to learn new carols as well as practise the more traditional ones in time for Christmas.'

'I'm sure we can find extra time for the children in the choir to rehearse during school hours,' Mrs Temple eagerly approved. 'Perhaps we could arrange for them to sing in the town centre at Christmas, the council always have a big tree in the main square, it would be lovely for them to hold a public concert there. And there's the bandstand on the promenade, that would be a perfect setting too. We could even travel to some of the outlying villages,' she continued enthusiastically.

Yet again, feeling a little overwhelmed Margaret held up a warning hand. 'Before you get carried away,' she pleaded, 'please bear in mind that I'm due to give birth at the end of January. I would be in trouble with the Mary Vale staff if I took too much on.'

'Of course, we are deeply beholden to you and wouldn't dream of overtaxing you,' Mrs Temple smiled. 'We don't have to do as much as that, it's just a rather exciting project – something St Mark's School has never done before.'

Looking thoughtful, Margaret continued. 'We would have to make sure the kiddies are well wrapped up if they're going to sing outdoors, we don't want them catching colds and losing their voices.'

The headmistress gave a sympathetic nod.

'And we could have a break halfway through,' Margaret suggested, 'so that the children could have a warm drink and something to eat.'

'That's a very good idea,' Mrs Temple agreed. 'We could have a little collection during the break, just small donations that could go to the poor of the parish.'

Galvanized, Margaret said, 'I'll draw up a list of carols, old and new, which we'll have to rehearse weekly before Christmas.'

The headmistress beamed. 'Thank you so much for agreeing to do this, Margaret. I'm quite certain it will raise morale in our local community. And, with luck, we might even generate a few pennies for the destitute in the community.'

On the steam train on the way back to Kents Bank, Margaret was oblivious to the breathtaking views of Morecambe Bay, preoccupied as she was by the Carter children. She didn't even see the tide swiftly rushing in over the marsh where sandpipers, curlews, gulls and little grey dunlins squabbled over rich pickings washed in by the tide. Taking a notebook and pencil from her brown-and-cream snake-skin handbag, Margaret made a list of winter clothing that the Carter children might be in need of. A warm coat, woolly hat, scarf and gloves, thick socks, stout boots, trousers, skirt, jumper, cardigan, liberty bodice, vest, underwear. None of St Mark's children were well dressed – the majority, like the Carters, came from poor farming stock – but they were all much better dressed than Joy and Arthur whom she had only ever seen in ragged clothes and worn-out boots. It had to be said, their meagre clothing was clean and well patched, but months of wear and constant washing had reduced them to a threadbare condition that barely generated any warmth at all.

'I can't ask those two little waifs to sing their hearts out when they are freezing cold,' she fretted.

Margaret considered the delicate situation. Getting a few second-hand items for two children in Grange shouldn't be beyond her. Though she had spent most of her savings, she still had the weekly pocket money that she carefully allocated herself and was barely spending, and there were enough jumble sales in Grange where she could more than likely pick up clothes for next to nothing.

The problem was getting the stuff to the Carters without causing deep offence.

I don't even know where they live, she thought to herself. And even if I did, would I really have the bare-faced cheek to go knocking on their door with an armful of clothes?

Still deep in thought, Margaret disembarked from the train which chugged noisily out of the station on its way to Barrow-in-Furness. With a cold wind blowing in from the Irish Sea, Margaret pulled her winter coat firmly around herself as she hurried through the little wood where berries were beginning to appear, glowing deep red on the holly bushes.

Entering Mary Vale, which smelt of fresh baking, Margaret hoped that Sister Agnes was preparing her delicious apple and cinnamon tarts for tea, though she knew it was likely to be something less luxurious, like coconut and carrot swirls. Just as she was hanging up her coat in the cloakroom, an idea struck Margaret and caused her to stop in her tracks.

'Sister Agnes!' she exclaimed out loud. 'She might know what to do.'

Margaret waited until tea was cleared before she nervously tapped on the kitchen door.

'May I?' she called as she popped her head around the door.

'Come, come, dear,' Sister Agnes beamed as she beckoned the visitor in. 'I'm just having five minutes before I tackle the washing-up.'

Sitting at the kitchen table beside the cheerful nun,

Margaret outlined her dilemma. 'There's a sweet little choir at St Mark's School, they're very good,' she smiled fondly. 'So good, in fact, the headmistress has asked me to put on a concert in town.'

'Well, that's a lovely idea,' Agnes enthused.

'It is,' Margaret agreed. 'But I have a problem, Sister Agnes,' she confessed. 'We won't just be performing indoors, where it's nice and warm, we're hoping to be singing outdoors too, carols under the Christmas tree in Grange and possibly Allithwaite.'

'Outside, under the tree, gorgeous,' Sister Agnes continued to enthuse.

Margaret nodded in agreement with the smiling nun. 'In theory yes, but I'm concerned that if I take some of the poorer children in the clothes they usually wear, they'll simply freeze to death singing around the parish. They need to be appropriately clad if they're to sing in the open air in the middle of winter,' she insisted.

'Quite right, you'd never forgive yourself if the poor little mites caught pneumonia,' Sister Agnes sympathized.

'Exactly,' Margaret agreed. 'It's a brother and sister I'm most concerned about, the Carter children.'

'That's a name that rings bells,' Sister Agnes remarked. 'I'm sure I've heard our Betsie mention that name.'

Taking the kind nun into her confidence, Margaret added, 'Arthur and Joy are the heart of the choir – without them it's just an ordinary school choir – to be blunt, the Carter children transform the ordinary into the sublime.'

'And they won't sing well if they're hungry and their stomachs are rumbling,' Agnes added knowingly. Ever pragmatic, she continued, 'Could you get hold of a few warm clothes for the little kiddies yourself?'

Shuffling uneasily in her chair, Margaret murmured, 'I've thought of that, Sister. The problem is, how do I pass them on to the children without causing offence to the family? I don't know where the Carters live, and even if I did, I couldn't possibly turn up on their front door-step offering charity which might offend their pride.'

'Aye, that's a point,' Agnes conceded.

'I just wondered if your Betsie might have any ideas on how I can go about it.'

'She might,' Agnes replied. 'I agree, you'll have to be a bit discreet, you wouldn't want the poor Carter kiddies shamed into thinking they're the only children in the school in need of charity.'

'From what I've heard, the Carters are desperately in need of all the help they can get. It's not just warm clothes they need, it's food too,' Margaret added.

'Let's concentrate on one thing at a time, for now at least,' the cheerful nun said as she rose from the table. 'If you can get hold of some warm clothes, I'll talk to Betsie about how we can get them to the family without causing offence. And then we can look at how we can feed them up.'

'You'd be doing me a big favour if you could help me in any way, Sister Agnes.'

Sister Agnes smiled. 'Leave it with me,' she concluded as she adjusted the knotted rope girdle around her stout waist, before heading towards the sink piled high with dishes waiting to be washed up. 'We'll sort something out, with God's help.'

15. Black-Hearted

As soon as she got a chance, Libby made sure she saw Dr Jamie.

'I'm really worried about Beth Thorp,' she immediately confessed.

Looking concerned, Jamie asked, 'What's the problem?'

'*Problems*,' Libby stressed. 'You may recall you pre-scribed iron tablets for her anaemia, but on my last visit her blood pressure and pulse were also slightly concern-ing. I think she might benefit from being seen by you, if at all possible.'

Crinkling his brow, Jamie looked up. 'She's due round about Christmas, if I recall correctly?'

'That's right,' Libby agreed. 'And then there's her domestic situation,' she blurted out. 'Thorp Hall is dreary enough – great big gloomy place – but it's Mr Thorp, her husband, who concerns me.'

Looking surprised, Jamie said, 'Go on.'

'Well, he seems to control Beth,' she started to explain. 'She's scared stiff of him.'

'But he doesn't scare you?' Jamie asked.

Libby tossed her head. 'He's intimidating, but I have a patient to nurse.' Coming to the point, she added, 'I'm concerned about her health, and the baby's too. I would really appreciate it if you could see her.'

'Of course I will,' Jamie said, without a moment's

hesitation. 'I'll do it as soon as I can get some time off work.'

On the day that Jamie was due to make his visit at Thorp Hall, Libby skipped dinner at the Home, grabbing a sandwich from the kitchen to save time. She cycled into Grange for straightforward visits again to both Mrs Timms and Mrs Cummings, who were thankfully in good form. Declining a cup of tea in both homes, she sped over to Thorp Hall, where she instinctively knew that her first task would be to calm her patient down before the doctor's visit. She also needed to find out who would be in the big house when Jamie arrived. She was quite sure that Mrs Grimsdale hardly ever left the building, but would Thorp be there too?

'Please God, I hope not,' she fervently prayed.

Propping her trusty bike up against the wall of the big gloomy house, Libby straightened her long curling hair, which the chill November wind had sent flying all over her flushed face. After taking several deep breaths to calm her nerves, Libby rapped on the front door. To her horror it was opened by Thorp himself, with a face as black as thunder.

Oh no, he's home, Libby thought, gasping in dismay.

'My wife tells me you're planning on bringing a doctor into the house,' he barked.

Knowing that if she showed any hint of nervousness, Thorp would bring her down like a hound tracking a fox, she managed to speak with an authority that she certainly didn't feel.

'Yes, Dr Reid will be here soon,' she answered as she stepped, uninvited, into the chilly hallway.

Thorp blocked her pathway with his threatening bulk. 'Since when has a doctor's presence been required here?'

Staring into his scowling face, Libby kept her nerve. 'I'm afraid your wife has a few significant medical problems, anaemia being one of them, Mr Thorp.'

Looking like he had never heard the word in his life before, Thorp attempted to bluff. 'She looks well enough to me,' he sorted dismissively. 'She's always been one to make a fuss over nothing.'

Recalling her young patient's frightened face, Libby struggled to control her emotions. Stick to the facts, she reminded herself. Tell him just how serious it is, and don't be diverted.

'On top of her anaemic condition, which was picked up by the doctor she saw initially,' Libby said pointedly, 'your wife is underweight, she has sporadic bleeding, and her blood pressure has become a worry.' Pausing to take a breath, she concluded, 'I'm concerned about the baby too. At my most recent examination I fear there was an erratic heart-beat, which is why I want a doctor to examine Mrs Thorp.'

Pausing to take breath, Libby held Thorp's gaze. Seeing his dark, beady eyes flash dangerously, she instinctively backed away from him. 'I need trusted obstetric advice. Dr Reid is the resident medic at Mary Vale,' she started to explain. 'He has a great deal of experience. I'm sure your wife will benefit from his advice as much as I will.'

At this point, Thorp completely lost his temper. 'You must be bloody joking, woman!' he exploded. 'Why would I want anything to do with a quack who specializes in looking after fallen women and their bastards?'

Thoroughly outraged, Libby could barely believe that she had heard such words come out of Thorp's mouth. Did the man have no compassion, no understanding of what these so-called 'fallen women' had gone through, and were still going through, what they would live with for the rest of their lives? Though Libby wanted to fight back and tell the bullying brute blocking her path that he wouldn't have a wife or child soon if he didn't start paying attention, somehow, yet again, she held her tongue. Picking a fight with Thorp would get her nowhere, and right now she was seriously worried that he might throw her out of the house without her even having a chance to see her patient. To Libby's immense relief, Beth suddenly appeared in the hallway, creeping up behind her husband.

'Hello, Nurse Libby.'

Swinging round, Thorp snapped at his wife, who cowered. 'I told you to stay out of this.'

Shrinking from him, Beth trembled. 'I'd like to see my midwife – I'm not feeling well.'

Thorp mockingly rolled his small dark eyes. 'HAH! Here we go,' he jeered. Jabbing a finger in his wife's direction, he laughed in her face. 'Other women have babies like they're popping peas, no fuss, no bother. But this one,' he sneered in contempt, 'mewls and snivels at every turn. See to her then, if you must,' he commanded Libby. 'Then get yourself out of my house, and take your bloody interfering doctor with you.'

After Thorp had stormed off, cursing the two women under his breath, Beth's knees gave way and she slumped against the wall.

Supporting her patient, Libby gently guided her into

the drawing room, where she managed to calm her down. 'Settle down, dear,' she soothed. 'The doctor will be here to see you soon.'

With so much riding on Jamie's visit, Libby hoped that he wouldn't be delayed. She also wondered, after her confrontation on the doorstep, if Jamie would even be allowed entry. Would it be better if he came in the back way, rather than approaching the front door, in the hope of avoiding Thorp altogether? Libby was thinking fast on her feet when Beth came up with the solution.

Nodding towards the French doors, she whispered fearfully, 'Libby, bring the doctor in that way.'

Libby actually smiled in relief. 'Good idea. Hopefully, that will draw less attention to him being here.'

Slipping out into the garden, gloomy with a seeping, cold low-lying mist, Libby ran around the back of the house to the driveway hedged by dense rhododendrons. She soon heard the sound of an approaching car.

Peering out to make sure it was Jamie, she frantically flagged him down. 'Leave the car here, by the side of the drive,' she told him breathlessly.

Seeing her tense expression, Jamie didn't waste time by asking a string of questions. Instead, switching off the engine and grabbing his medical bag, he hurried out of the car.

'This way,' Libby said as she retraced her steps back to the drawing room. 'I should warn you, Dr Jamie, the master of the house is all set to throw us out.'

Jamie stopped briefly to raise his eyebrows. 'I recall from our recent conversation that Mr Thorp is a bully.'

'Oh, he's that all right,' Libby assured him. 'But it gets worse. He's now livid because he thinks we're interfering. If you don't mind, Doctor,' she raced on, 'I suggest we get this examination done as quickly as possible so we can both leave before he picks a fight and upsets poor Beth even more.'

Looking concerned, Jamie shook his head. 'I'm not at all happy about leaving a defenceless woman on her own with a tyrant.'

'Me neither,' Libby whole-heartedly agreed. 'But I'm treading on eggshells here, Doctor. If I put a foot wrong, Thorp may well ban me from the house, and I may never sec Beth again.'

Jamie nodded grimly and followed Libby into the drawing room. After introducing himself to a white-faced Beth, he asked if he might examine her. Settling her patient on the sofa, Libby held her hand while Jamie checked her pulse, breathing, temperature, blood pressure and the baby's heart-beat, after which he examined her abdomen and pelvic area.

When he had finished, Jamie said, 'You can sit up now.'

With Libby's help, Beth struggled to sit upright in order to look at Jamie face on. 'Is my baby all right, Doctor?' she asked nervously.

Though concerned, Jamie (anxious not to alarm his already highly nervous patient) answered levelly, 'Your midwife was right to seek a doctor's opinion. Your baby is small,' he admitted. 'And the heart-beat is a little slow.'

Squeezing Libby's hand, Beth gasped, 'Could I lose my baby?'

Answering in the same even voice, Jamie continued. 'If your condition doesn't improve, there's a possibility that you might need to deliver earlier, by Caesarean section.'

'Oh, dear God,' Beth cried.

'We can monitor this,' he soothed. 'But if your baby is not strong enough to go full term then we would have to act promptly.'

'I want to save my baby,' Beth whispered miserably. 'It's all I've got.'

Jamie gave an understanding nod.

'But my husband, he doesn't like interference,' she gasped. 'I'm afraid he won't, simply won't allow me to leave the house – not even to go to hospital . . .' Beth's voice trailed away.

Holding Libby's gaze, Jamie went against the advice she had given him, which was to leave Thorp Hall without seeing the master of the house. 'I think I'd better have a word with your husband, Mrs Thorp,' Jamie said in a hard, determined voice. Seeing Libby's alarmed expression, he said firmly, 'There are issues at stake that he needs to be made aware of.'

A look of relief flashed across Beth's stricken face. 'Thank you, Doctor. But I know he'll give you a hard time,' she added nervously.

'Don't trouble yourself, Mrs Thorp, I can look after myself.'

'Be careful, Doctor,' she cautioned Jamie. 'He's a dangerous man.'

In the corridor, Jamie turned to Libby and dropped his voice to a whisper. 'I'm sorry I'm not slipping away as you recommended, Libby, but the man's brutish behaviour goes so much against my conscience,' he declared. 'Thorp must be told the facts – he needs to know the truth about his wife and child,' he seethed.

Thorp didn't take kindly to the sight of Jamie striding through his house, telling him his wife was gravely ill.

Thorp grunted in disbelief. 'So I've been told.'

Completely undeterred, Jamie continued. 'I'm sorry to say, sir, that if your wife's condition doesn't improve very soon, we might have to admit her to Mary Vale, the Home where her midwife and I work, where we can monitor her progress while providing total bed-rest.'

'Over my dead body,' Thorp growled.

'Or your wife's,' Jamie answered coldly. 'If she continues as she is, your wife will undoubtedly lose the baby.'

Thorp gave a loud mocking laugh. 'Do you seriously think I would let my wife mix with whores and their bastards? Get out, before I kick you out,' he snarled.

'I can go,' Jamie answered evenly. 'But that won't help your wife. Without proper treatment she could die – and the baby too.'

Looking like he was all set to punch Jamie, Thorp advanced with a murderous expression on his face. 'I'll have you know that I am more than capable of taking care of my own wife,' he snarled. 'I'll get a proper doctor to take care of her – one who treats genteel women, not those dragged in from the streets.'

Seeing that there was no way he could further his case on this occasion, Jamie had no choice but to turn on his heel and walk back dispiritedly to his patient.

'Take your interfering midwife with you,' Thorp called after him, following Jamie into the drawing room.

Totally outraged by Thorp's ruthless behaviour, a furious Libby turned to face him. 'I'll put my patient to bed and settle her down before I go anywhere,' she said through gritted teeth.

'Aye,' Thorp growled. 'Get on with it, and then get out too.' He stood over Jamie threateningly as the doctor picked up his medical bag, nodded courteously towards Mrs Thorp, and prepared to leave.

Hurrying after Jamie, and well out of earshot of Thorp, Libby asked, 'What are we going to do, Doctor?'

Jamie was careful to choose his words. 'There's nothing we can do here *officially*. Right now, being here is only making things worse for our patient. Let's discuss the case as soon as we can, once we're back at Mary Vale. Do you need a lift, nurse?'

'No, thank you,' Libby replied. 'I have my bike, and I want to settle my patient before I head back.'

'At all costs avoid Thorp,' Jamie advised. 'As his wife said, he's a dangerous man.'

When Libby returned to the drawing room, she was relieved to find no sign of Ronnie Thorp. In the absence of her bullying husband, Beth lay limply in the armchair.

'The doctor's just left,' Libby explained.

Seeing Libby's tense expression, Beth asked fearfully, 'What's the matter with my husband? Has he no heart? I don't care about myself any more, I'm well past that, but you'd think he would want the best for his baby,' she said as she laid a hand protectively over her tummy.

'We might be able to persuade him to call in another doctor,' Libby said.

'Ronnie banned me from seeing Dr Fletcher when he first said I had anaemia; he's never going to let me see another doctor,' she cried. 'I really liked Dr Reid,' she continued sadly. 'He seemed fine to me.'

'He is indeed a very fine doctor,' Libby agreed. 'But the truth is, Beth, your husband is not keen on Mary Vale, he has a very bad view of the place and the people in it.'

Tears sprang to Beth's green eyes. Panicked, she spoke in a strangled voice. 'Please, Libby,' she implored, 'don't let him stop you from visiting me – you're the only person in the world who I can trust right now.'

Praying that she wouldn't be proved wrong on this point, Libby assured her, 'Dear, you won't lose me.' Attempting a lightness she certainly didn't feel, she added, 'I'm not that easy to get rid of.' Seeing her patient so weak and exhausted, she frowned. 'Let me settle you down in bed before I leave.'

Beth vehemently shook her head. 'No!' she sharply exclaimed. 'I hate that room.'

'At least let me make you warm and comfortable in here,' Libby urged.

Watching Libby stoke up the fire, Beth murmured anxiously, 'If my baby dies because of Ronnie's neglect, I will never forgive him. In fact, I would rather die too and have done with this miserable existence for ever.'

'I promise you, dear, that I will do everything in my power to make sure that doesn't happen, and I know Dr Reid will do his best for you too. We're not unfamiliar with difficult domestic circumstances,' she added.

Full of despair, Beth sank back against the cushions

that Libby had just rearranged for her. 'I know that, Libby, but when I'm on my own here, which is most of the time, I am so frightened.'

Though deeply troubled, Libby tried to speak with confidence. 'I know, and that's something we want to help with. Dr Reid and I will be discussing your case just as soon as we can, we'll think of something, I promise. Meanwhile, you must concentrate on taking care of yourself and your baby until I get back.'

Beth gave a weak smile. 'When will that be?'

Not sure if she would ever be allowed back into the house, Libby answered breezily, 'Next week.'

After saying goodbye to her now sleepy patient, Libby collected her coat and bag, then went outdoors where heavy rain had set in. Squinting in the gloomy afternoon light, she went in search of her bike; she always left it propped up against the wall closest to the front door. Surprised to find that it wasn't where she had left it, Libby turned this way and that, confused.

'Where on earth could it be?' she muttered to herself. At which point her eyes fell on a heap of metal lying in a deep puddle of rain. 'Oh, no!' she cried as she ran forward.

Though mangled and broken, the heap was unmistakeably her bike. It had been run over several times – by the looks of things, by a heavy vehicle. Libby's only form of transport had clearly been vandalized in an act of pure malice, and it didn't take a genius to guess who had done this to her.

Leaving the bike where she had found it, Libby set off on foot, with rain beating down on her head and trickling down her back.

'If the brute thinks this will stop me, he's got another think coming,' she vowed to herself. 'I will keep my word and look after Beth, even if I have to walk to Thorp Hall every day. I will not leave Beth alone and unprotected, I will *never* abandon her.'

16. Jumble Sale

On a bleak, cold Saturday afternoon, with a chilling sea mist hanging in the damp air, Margaret queued up outside a church hall in Grange along with a crowd of other determined customers, all intent on getting a jumble sale bargain. When the doors were flung open, there was a stampede of eager buyers who riffled through the enormous piles of clothes laid out on long wooden trestle tables dotted around the draughty hall. Anxious that she might get knocked or pushed about, Margaret waited for the crowd to thin out before she patiently worked her way through the heaps of children's clothes. Happy with her choices – two woollen coats, a pair of long corduroy trousers, a knitted dress, warm underwear and two pairs of old but still sound leather boots, plus scarves, mittens and woolly bobble hats – Margaret paid what, in fact, was more than she had initially expected to pay.

'Never mind,' she reasoned. 'I don't need money here, and if it keeps the Carter children warm throughout the winter, especially when they're singing outdoors, it will have been worth every penny.'

Once back at Mary Vale, an excited Margaret showed her purchases to Sister Agnes, who was busy making fish-paste sandwiches to serve with a tomato and onion salad for tea.

'Well done,' Sister Agnes beamed as she examined the pile of clothes.

'My thoughts exactly,' Margaret exclaimed. 'I hadn't intended to buy so much, but they were just what I wanted, and in reasonable condition too, so I threw caution to the wind and bought the lot.' Gazing down at the clothes, she added thoughtfully, 'It's quite a pile. Do you really think Betsie will help deliver them?'

'Don't you worry,' Agnes advised. 'Our Betsie will know what to do for the best.'

Ironically, after all the discussions between Sister Agnes and Margaret in Mary Vale's kitchen, it turned out that there was no need for Betsie's help, after all. The very next time Margaret was in school, she found the Carter children outside the school gates long after all the other pupils had departed. Seeing them standing, cold and pinched in the sharp November chill, she approached them.

'Shouldn't you be home by now, children?'

Joy, distant and withdrawn as usual, gazed awkwardly at the ground, while little Arthur spoke with no hesitation.

'We missed the bus.'

Her heart melted at the sight of their cold, bedraggled faces. 'How will you get home now?' she asked gently.

'We'll walk,' Joy announced, before Arthur could start babbling. 'Come on,' she said as she turned to her brother. 'We'd best get a move on.'

'I'm cold,' the little lad complained.

Feeling desperately sorry for them both, Margaret suggested they should perhaps wait for the next bus.

'We've got no money, we went and spent it on toffees,' Arthur bluntly told her.

'That was a silly thing to do,' Margaret gently chided,

though she felt desperately sorry for the two shivering waifs. 'I've got money for your bus fare. Why don't you come indoors and warm up before the next bus arrives.'

Back indoors, Margaret ushered the now blue-faced children into their classroom, then went in search of something to warm them up. After setting mugs of hot milk in front of them (which she had boiled up in the staffroom), she searched around for something they could eat. All she could find was a bowl of cold rice pudding that somebody had forgotten to clear away, and her own cheese and pickle sandwiches that she hadn't felt like eating at lunchtime. Hurrying back to the classroom with the food on a tray, she found Joy and Arthur poring over some record albums that she had left on the desk.

Looking at the pictures on the record labels, Arthur, not quite so cold as he had been, excitedly asked, 'Are these yours, miss?'

Laying the tray on a desk, Margaret answered, 'Yes, I was going to play them in class earlier but there wasn't time. Here,' she said as she nodded towards the food, 'help yourselves.'

In no time at all the food and drink were demolished by the starving children. Once replete, they turned back to the records on the desk.

'Can we listen to this one, miss?' Joy shyly asked.

Margaret picked up the album with an elegant lady in a gold and silver crinoline on the front. '*Così Fan Tutte*,' she said. 'It's very long, Joy.'

'Can we please hear just a bit,' the timid girl begged.

The minute the music crackled out on the record player

the two children sat transfixed. As they listened to the music Margaret watched them in wonder; from *where* did these two poor children get their love of music? She had seen many pupils delight in music, articulate their pleasure in it, but she had never seen concentration at this level. Looking at their rapt expressions, she would have assumed that they came from a musical family who had nurtured their love for opera, given them singing lessons from a young age; not so with these two. Of course, she had read about penniless artists who had made their way against all the odds to gain fame and fortune, but these two had inherited from somewhere an amazing talent and the same intense passion for music.

Breaking through her thoughts, Arthur pointed to a record cover with a photograph of Frank Sinatra on the front.

'Can we play this one next, miss?'

Checking her little golden wristwatch, Margaret was alarmed at the lateness of the hour. 'Sorry, dear,' she quickly replied. 'It's getting late. I'd better escort the two of you home – your mother will be wondering where on earth you have got to.'

On the bus home the children sat quietly gazing out of the window, clearly enjoying the free ride home. When the bus pulled up at the stop nearest the Carters' house, Arthur diligently gripped Margaret's hand as they crossed the road, while Joy ran on ahead of them.

Trying hard to hide her dismay at the state of the dilapidated cottage with its wild neglected garden, tattered dangling curtains, and windows sealed up with rags to keep out the draughty elements, Margaret followed Arthur into the cottage where she found Mrs Carter hugging Joy tightly to her chest.

'You're late, lovie, I was worried about you.'

'Sorry, Mam, our Arthur went and spent all of our bus fare at the toffee shop,' Joy grumbled. 'Our music teacher fetched us home on't bus.'

Feeling uncomfortable, Margaret gave a small embarrassed smile. 'I'm so sorry to intrude,' she apologized.

'She gave us some tea too, cheese butties and rice pudding, right good it were,' Arthur chatted on.

Mary turned to her grinning son. 'Arthur, you've no right to go spending your bus money on toffees,' she scolded, though her eyes were full of love for her bright-eyed son.

'That's just what I told him, Mam, but he wouldn't listen,' Joy indignantly protested.

'You ate the toffees as much as I did,' Arthur quipped back.

Refusing to get drawn into their argument, Mary turned to the visitor. 'Thank you, miss, for bringing them home,' she said graciously.

'I'm sorry we're so late, Mrs Carter. They were so cold, I thought I should warm them up before they set off for home,' Margaret explained. 'And we had to wait for the next bus, of course,' she added.

Catching sight of the untidy bed in the far corner of the room, where a gaunt figure lay sleeping, Margaret felt herself blushing; now more embarrassed than ever, she started to make for the door, feeling she was intruding.

Releasing her daughter from her embrace, Mary called

out, 'That's very kind of you, miss. Please,' she added, as she remembered her manners, 'take a seat.'

Flustered, Margaret tried to explain herself. 'I help out at the school from time to time, so it was no problem to drop the children off on my way home.'

'I'm grateful to you,' Mary humbly replied. 'I can leave my husband long enough to pick up the kiddies most days, but today I was, er . . .' She paused as she searched for the right word. 'Detained.' At which point, though she struggled to contain her emotions, Mary dissolved into floods of tears.

Seeing the anxious children gathered around their distressed mother like nervous chicks, Margaret was desperate to ease the situation. 'Is there a shop close by?'

'Aye, there's a little corner shop at the end of the lane,' Joy told her.

Taking a half-crown from her purse, Margaret handed it to the young girl. 'Go and fetch us something for tea, please.'

'More toffees!' Arthur exclaimed.

Before the pair of them flew out of the door, Margaret quickly called out, 'No, Arthur, wait a moment.' Turning to Mary, she asked, 'What about you and your husband?' She nodded towards the bed. 'Is there anything particular you need?'

Too hungry and desperate to prevaricate, Mary blurted out, 'Bread, butter, sugar, a jar of meat paste, milk.'

Turning back to the children, Margaret was firm. 'Spend all of the money on food for supper.'

'ALL of it, miss?' goggle-eyed Arthur gasped.

Margaret nodded. 'Off you go now,' she urged.

Once they had gone, Mary thanked Margaret humbly before hurrying to her husband's bedside, tenderly stroking his hollow cheeks after feeling his damp forehead.

'Poor lamb, he's very sick, as you can see.' Returning to the kitchen range, which she heaped high with firewood, Mary settled in a rickety chair opposite Margaret. 'And as if that wasn't enough, our wicked landlord turned up today. Sam, poor man, tried his best to stand up to him, the effort nearly killed him.' In a voice tight with fear she continued, 'We can't pay this month's rent, but he won't give us an extension. He's threatening to evict us.'

'Can he do that?' Margaret gasped.

'Oh, aye – Ronnie Thorp can do whatever he wants,' Mary bitterly told her. Glancing over to the bed, she continued in a whisper. 'He's been on our backs since my husband took ill. Once he heard Sam wasn't able to work on the farm, and the rent was delayed, he was on top of us like a ton of bricks. Says there's a place for the likes of us who can't meet their obligations – he means an institution, you know,' Mary said, in a voice that trembled with fear. 'That's what he came here to tell us this afternoon – threaten us with, more like.' Wiping tears from her eyes, she added, 'My poor Sam, he could barely raise his head off the pillow. That didn't stop Thorp, though; talk about kicking a dog when it's down,' she sobbed. 'He carried on ranting and bullying, called us every name under the sun, and left promising to come back with an eviction order.' Unable to sit still a moment longer, she paced the room wringing her hands.

'I tell you, miss, Sam's in no state to take this, it could

kill my husband and separate me from my two kiddies.' Turning to Margaret with an anguished expression on her face, she cried, 'What if the authorities decide I'm a bad mother and take my children away from me – put them in a home or foster them out?'

Shocked that the family might be ripped apart, Margaret exclaimed, 'Surely it won't come to that, dear.'

Hearing baby Susan wail from her little box crib, Mary snatched her up and put her quickly to her breast. Immediately sensing her mother's tension, the baby resisted feeding, wriggling and struggling. Losing all control, desperate Mary leapt up and cried out wildly, 'Sweet Jesus, help us.'

Relieving Mary of the fractious baby, Margaret soothed, 'Calm down now, Mrs Carter. You're upsetting your baby.'

Obedient and utterly worn out, Mary slumped back into the chair. When Susan started to wail, she held out her arms to Margaret. 'It's all right, miss, I'll see to her now,' she said as she laid the baby on her breast.

Taking the opportunity to brew a pot of tea, Margaret set a cup down beside Mary.

'When's your baby due, miss?' Mary enquired.

'Please call me Margaret.'

'And I'm Mary.'

Smiling across the space at each other, the two of them felt suddenly at ease.

Answering the question, Margaret said, 'I'm due at the end of January.'

'That's not long off,' Mary smiled. 'And you're still working?'

'Just a bit of voluntary work at the school, it's nice to

fill my time doing something useful,' Margaret explained. Then realizing she had nothing to lose, she bluntly added, 'I'm staying at Kents Bank, in a home for unmarried mothers and their babies.'

Mary gave her a tender look. 'So, you're on your own, lovie?'

Touched by her kindness, it was Margaret's turn to fill up. 'Yes, I'm on my own,' she admitted, with tears in her beautiful brown eyes.

Swopping Susan on to her left breast, Mary asked, 'And does this home look after you well enough?'

'Very well,' Margaret assured her as she gazed down at her burgeoning tummy. 'The nuns who run the Home are kindness itself.'

'What are you planning on doing once your baby is born?' Mary softly asked.

Margaret shook her head. 'Adoption seems to be the only option,' she said, with a lump in her throat, at which point the children burst back into the cottage with their arms full of food.

'We spent it all!' Arthur triumphantly declared as they strewed their purchases all over the kitchen table. 'And we got loads more toffees too,' he said, his mouth bulging with chewy sweets.

Seeing Mary attempt to rise and make tea for her children, Margaret held up her hand. 'Stay where you are, I'll see to the children.'

After the children had been settled with huge meat-paste sandwiches and mugs of strong tea, Margaret, aware that her late return home to Mary Vale might be causing some alarm, asked the question that had been on her mind for some time.

'I wonder if you would mind me giving the children some warm winter clothes?'

Again, Mary didn't baulk at the idea of charity. In fact, the look of relief on her face made it quite clear that she actually welcomed it.

'Really, miss, er . . . Margaret,' she quickly corrected herself. 'We couldn't thank you enough. We would really appreciate it,' she added gratefully. 'The kiddies have been wearing threadbare clothes for months now, and their boots have hardly any decent soles on them.'

'I could drop off some clothes tomorrow, if you like?' Margaret suggested.

'We'd be proper grateful,' Mary repeated herself. 'The thought of Joy and Arthur going to school well wrapped up will be a huge relief to me, and them too,' she said with a weak smile. 'They've been really suffering lately, what with the lack of food, and such poor clothing – not to mention the onset of winter.'

Hearing her husband stirring, Mary laid Susan back in her crib and hurried over to his side. 'Can I fetch you a mug of tea, lovie?' she asked tenderly.

'Just water,' Sam wheezed.

When Mary had seen to Sam, as much as she could, she returned to her chair by the fire as he sank once more into sleep.

Margaret asked, 'How is your husband?'

Mary gave a heart-weary sigh. 'He gets worse by the week. I'm told there are charities run by doctors who would treat Sam for nothing, but they're difficult for the likes of me to track down, and there's bound to be a waiting list as long as your arm.'

'Are you actually on any waiting list?' Margaret enquired.

Mary looked shame-faced. 'I've only recently had a chance to look into it briefly. So far, I've been spending every spare minute trying to find work myself. I didn't think it would be so hard,' she finished lamely.

Margaret chastised herself; she could have helped this desperate family out if she hadn't spent all her savings on funding her stay at Mary Vale. Medical treatment might just save Mr Carter's life, but who was going to stump up the money for that? Feeling guilty about her own relative good fortune, she said, 'Don't worry, Mary, I'll look into it for you – I can check in the library tomorrow after I've dropped off your clothes.'

'Oh, that would be wonderful,' Mary exclaimed. 'I'm grateful for all your favours, Margaret, I really am.'

Her new friend smiled. 'Well, actually, Mary, I've a big favour to beg of you.'

'ME? What can I possibly do for you?'

'Quite a lot,' Margaret replied. 'St Mark's School now have a little choir which your two children are at the very heart of.'

Looking surprised, Mary said, 'Our Joy and Arthur?'

'Yes, they have the most beautiful voices – especially Arthur, he sings like an angel,' Margaret replied.

Mary blushed with pride. 'Sam always used to say Arthur had an outstanding voice for a little kiddie, says he inherited it from his dad.'

'Joy's voice is quite exceptional too,' Margaret quickly added. 'The headmistress is keen to cheer up the local community this Christmas, so we thought we'd organize a little outdoor carol service and share the joy of Christmas with everyone.'

'That's a lovely idea,' Mary enthused. 'And if the kiddies have your warm clothes, they won't feel the winter chill, thank goodness.'

Exactly, Margaret thought to herself. 'So, do I have your permission to take Arthur and Joy carol singing? I have to check with all the parents beforehand.'

'Certainly,' Mary answered. 'It'll be a lot more fun than sitting around here of an evening,' she finished glumly.

'I promise I'll take good care of them, and deliver them home safely,' Margaret said as she rose to go. 'And I will make enquiries about charities at the library tomorrow.'

'You're very kind, Margaret,' Mary smiled. 'Thank you, not just for our tea today but for bringing the children home and offering us help with clothes to keep them warm. Your visit has cheered me up, good and proper, I'm so pleased we've got to know each other.'

Margaret beamed back. 'Me too, Mary.' Then, seizing the moment while she had the chance, she asked, 'Would you mind if I occasionally dropped in to see you?'

'I'd be thrilled,' Mary promptly replied. 'Though,' she said glumly as her eyes roamed the room, 'you'll have to take us as you find us.'

'Don't worry about that, it will be lovely just to keep in touch.'

After saying goodbye to the children, Margaret, now utterly worn out both physically and emotionally, caught the bus to Grange and then the train back to Mary Vale, where the staff had anxiously been awaiting her return.

'We wondered where you'd got to,' Ada fretted when Margaret walked in.

'I just saw some children safely home. Sorry if I caused any concern.'

'We saved tea for you, it's in the dining room,' thoughtful Ada told her.

Sitting alone, eating her spam and tomato sandwiches, Margaret recalled the terrible conditions the Carter family lived in, and the declining state of Sam, prone on his bed and unable to protect his children. Her eyes filled with tears which she impatiently brushed aside.

'This is not the time for emotion,' she firmly told herself. 'The Carters need action not tears,' she said through gritted teeth. 'I'm going to do everything in my power to help that poor family, starting with finding out more about Ronnie Thorp — the black-hearted landlord who's ruining their lives.'

17. A New Case

Still reeling from the shock of Thorp's tirade, Libby made her way to Jamie's surgery at her earliest opportunity.

'I hope you don't mind,' she quickly said as she closed the door behind her. 'I had to see you just as soon as you could fit me in.'

'Not a problem, Libby, I was keen to catch up with you too.'

'I'm sorry I haven't got here sooner, Doctor. We seem to be in overdrive these days,' Libby said as she took the chair he offered. 'Maisie's got a stomach bug which we hope won't spread through the Home, and Gladys is complaining of lower back pains, even though her baby's got a few weeks to go.'

Jamie nodded. 'Gladys came to see me this morning, she's a great alarmist,' he smiled.

'High drama all the way, is Glad,' Libby said fondly. 'At least it takes her mind off men and politics.'

'Well, let's hope she doesn't cry wolf too often, we don't want to miss the signs when she really does go into labour. Now tell me, how did you leave Beth?'

'Miserable and frightened.'

'Poor soul, and Thorp?'

Libby grimaced. 'He flattened my bicycle, a clear sign that he doesn't want me back, wouldn't you say?'

'What an utter bastard he is,' Jamie seethed. 'You know,

Libby, if Thorp doesn't let us help, there's a good chance the baby won't survive.'

'One thing is for sure; as things stand, he's not going to allow his wife anywhere near Mary Vale. He thinks it's a house of sin, when all we want to do is help,' Libby added.

'My hope rests on Thorp consulting a private doctor. Better than none at all.'

'But how can we be sure that Thorp will do that?' Libby questioned. 'He might have thrown that out just to put us off the scent.'

'If he's as callous as he appears, he might well do nothing at all,' Jamie agreed.

'God forbid!' Libby exclaimed.

'There is a possibility that Beth could admit herself,' Jamie continued thoughtfully.

'How could she do that, with her wretched husband breathing down her neck?' Libby cried. 'She barely leaves the house, and now she's so weak I doubt she would even make it out of the grounds.' Throwing back her shoulders, Libby said in a more determined tone, 'I know I'm not welcome at the Hall, but I'm definitely going back. Even if I have to break in, I have to see Beth – she can't just be abandoned.'

Jamie looked concerned. 'Is it safe? Beth herself said he was a dangerous man. And you need to confront him about the bike.'

'The bike is seriously the last thing on my mind right now.' Libby shook her head. 'If I go storming back, complaining about what he did to my bike, I won't get anywhere.'

'So, you'll just forget that it ever happened, that he vandalized your bicycle?'

'Yes, if it helps my cause,' she told him. 'It'll probably choke me, not saying anything, but I'd do anything, literally anything, to help my patient.'

'You're a good nurse, Libby,' Jamie smiled. 'I hope you've talked to Matron about this matter, because I certainly have.'

'I'll talk to her as soon as I get the opportunity,' Libby promised.

'She might not approve of you nursing in a very compromised situation,' Jamie warned.

'Then I'll have to do everything in my power to change her mind.'

Looking up from making notes, Jamie threw Libby a knowing look. 'Be sure to monitor Beth very carefully, I need to be aware of her condition at all times – just in case we have an emergency on our hands,' he added ominously.

'I only wish I could see her more often,' Libby fretted.

'Don't push it,' Jamie warned. 'We're having trouble seeing her at all. Let's see if, in fact, Thorp does come up with another doctor. Meanwhile, you have two other local patients to see to, as well as all your ladies here.'

Deep in thought, Libby made her way back to the wards. What rotten luck that Mary Vale's very first community job was turning out to be such a challenge. Unless she could turn Beth's situation around and prove the value of her visits, there was a strong possibility that this experiment would not be deemed a success or worth the continued funding. At least Mrs Cummings and Mrs Timms in Grange are doing well, Libby thought with some relief. Nevertheless, it was depressing that a unique

God-given chance to establish Mary Vale's community nursing project might fail just because of the tyrannical behaviour of Ronnie Thorp.

A few hours later, just before tea-time, Jamie walked into the dining room in search of a cup of tea and a bite to eat, when he bumped into Margaret doing exactly the same thing.

'Doctor,' she said rather shyly. 'I wonder if I might have a word with you?'

'Of course, shall we take a seat?' he answered courteously.

Taking their tea to a table in the bay window that over-looked the garden, they sat opposite each other.

Looking rather self-conscious, Margaret started hesi-tantly. 'I hope you don't mind me asking, Doctor, but I am in need of your help.'

Thinking Margaret looked in good form, Jamie asked, 'Are you feeling unwell?'

'It's not for me, it's for a friend who is dreadfully ill,' Margaret quickly explained. 'I've recently been doing some voluntary teaching at St Mark's School in Grange, and as a result I've got to know a family who live Allith-waite way. Mr Carter, the father, has TB, he works as a shepherd but now he's bedbound and getting worse by the day. He's seen a doctor once, when they scraped the money together to go privately, but that was a one-off visit which they can't afford to repeat. His condition is deterior-ating so quickly, I just wondered if you might consider sparing the time to see if you could help? I would pay what I can myself towards the fee.'

'I'd like very much to help – and given the family circumstances, I wouldn't want to charge, so don't worry about that. The only problem is, I'm pretty much rushed off my feet here, and with Catherine at home,' Jamie explained. 'But I'll do my very best to try and see him as soon as I can.'

Looking deeply apologetic, Margaret blushed. 'I'm so sorry to trouble you, Doctor, I do appreciate that you have a heavy workload here, I wouldn't ask if I weren't so worried about Mr Carter. After my last visit, I seriously wonder if he'll be alive the next time I return.'

'And you say he's only seen one doctor since his illness started?' Jamie enquired.

Margaret nodded. 'Since then, Mrs Carter has been trying to locate some charities set up by doctors who are prepared to treat patients in extremis for nothing.'

'There are such organizations,' Jamie responded. 'But, as you can imagine, the waiting lists are long. If you jot Mr Carter's address down, I'll do my best to see him,' kind-hearted Jamie promised. 'But you'd better warn him in advance, or he might get a shock if I walk in unexpectedly.'

'Of course,' Margaret eagerly responded. 'I'm so very grateful, Doctor, I think when you meet the Carters, you'll agree they are in a desperately sad situation.'

Rising to leave, Jamie said with a smile, 'Let's see what we can do.'

Walking back to his surgery, Jamie collected his coat and bag, then set off for home. In the dark farm lane, illuminated by a clear moon, Jamie's breath was white on the sharp frosty air. At Mary Vale, he thought to himself, there was always so much to attend to: not just the obstetric care, which was significant in itself; there was also overall care of his patients, mentally and emotionally. Thank God they were a good strong team, right across the board, he couldn't have asked for a better one. From Matron to his darling wife, to ever-reliable devoted Dora, and their youngest member of staff, vibrant passionate young Libby. She's a dynamo, Jamie thought, unstoppable in her passionate devotion to her patients. In truth, he would struggle to find the time to visit a sick man in Allithwaite, a case which was outside of his medical remit. But after Margaret had so vividly described the man's condition, Jamie could hardly refuse. Somehow, he would fit a visit in – but from the sound of things, one doctor's visit wasn't going to fix a very serious situation.

Returning home, walking into the house – which, this evening, smelt of home baking – was always Jamie's favourite time of the day. Hearing the door open, Catherine always abandoned whatever she was doing and flew into his arms.

'Dada! Dada!' she cried today as she kissed his cold face and put her hands, covered in flour, on his thick tawny hair. 'I'm a good girl,' she announced as she pointed to a pie on the kitchen table.

'I managed to save up our sugar ration, so we've been baking,' Ada said as she too kissed her husband on the lips.

'I can smell it,' he answered as he set Catherine down on her feet and embraced his wife. After nearly five years of marriage he was still bowled over by her. 'I've missed you,' he whispered in her ear.

Staring into his sparkling hazel eyes, Ada's heart lurched. How lucky she was, having a husband she loved so much.

'How are you feeling, darling?' he asked as he gently swept a hand over her tummy.

Pushing her abundant long curls off her face, Ada smiled. 'Tired, but fine. Catherine's run me ragged today. We must have been to the farm at least five times to see a ewe with her premature lamb in the farm pens. Poor Alf, she never stopped asking him questions.'

'Baa, baa, black sheep,' happy Catherine chanted as she skipped around the kitchen.

Recalling recent radio news of French troops crossing the Rhine and taking Strasbourg, while inmates, more dead than alive, were slowly emerging from German prison camps, Jamie gazed lovingly at his little girl and counted his blessings. It was a cruel, unfair world. But right now, with a new baby on the way, his wife in his arms, and his daughter singing nursery rhymes, he considered himself to be one of the luckiest men alive.

18. A Good Spread

A few days later, Margaret was eager to get to school. She hadn't heard anything directly from Dr Reid about fitting in a visit and didn't like to ask again (especially as he was making the visit in his own time) so she assumed he hadn't yet visited Mr Carter. When there was no mention of a doctor's visit from the children either, Margaret didn't initiate it. She certainly didn't want to raise their hopes but, fretting to herself as she hung up her coat in the staffroom, she hoped Dr Reid would find time to see Sam soon. The way things were going, the poor man could die before he had any medical attention – and then what would happen to his family? All of Mary's worst nightmares would come true if they were institutionalized or, worse still, the children were fostered out to another family.

The children hurrying up and down the school corridor swiftly claimed Margaret's immediate attention.

'Morning, miss.'

'Are we have singing classes this morning, miss?'

How Margaret loved their freshness and innocence. Admittedly, there were bad, noisy days when her head throbbed and her back ached when she got back to Mary Vale, but overall St Mark's School and the children in it were an absolute godsend to her. The school choir was turning out to be a joy too, particularly when she saw the

Carter children thriving as a consequence of their involvement in it. The sight of her young choristers diligently learning the words to 'Away In A Manger' and 'Silent Night', then learning the descant to 'Hark! The Herald Angels Sing' convinced Margaret that singing actually made Arthur and Joy (these days looking smarter and tidier in the jumble sale clothes) briefly forget the miseries that beset their troubled family life.

At the end of the afternoon rehearsal, Margaret turned to the sixteen children who made up the choir. 'Well done, all of you, you're improving with every practice.'

'Now that it's almost December, miss,' one of the older, more responsible girls said, 'won't we have to have more rehearsals so that we're in fine fettle for our first concert in Grange?'

Smiling at her student's quaint choice of words, Margaret replied, 'You're quite right, Edith, we'll need to slip in a few extra rehearsals as Christmas approaches – possibly a Saturday morning, if your parents will allow it?'

Unfortunately, on the Saturday morning they had planned, misfortune struck.

On her arrival, the caretaker glumly announced that the basement furnace that heated the school pipes had broken down overnight. 'You'll be in for a chilly morning,' he informed Margaret.

The children duly gathered in the hall, which was distinctly chilly, and commenced the rehearsal. But as the morning progressed it got colder and colder, to such an extent that one of the littlest choristers started to cry.

'Can I go home, miss?' she wailed. 'Mi feet are freezing.'

Heavily pregnant, and hot most of the time, Margaret

was mortified that she had not registered her pupils' discomfort. Realizing that she couldn't keep sixteen young children in a freezing-cold building for the prearranged session, Margaret had a sudden thought. Briefly leaving the children, she hurried into the headmistress's office to make an urgent phone call.

'Mary Vale Home,' Sister Agnes's voice came down the line.

After explaining the heating problem at St Mark's, Margaret rather apologetically asked if she might continue the rehearsal in Mary Vale's sitting room. It was big enough to accommodate sixteen children, and she knew for sure there was a piano she could use.

'It's the only place I can think of,' she confessed. 'We shouldn't be long.'

Matron, whom Sister Agnes had called to the phone, was typically generous and agreed immediately to Margaret's suggestion. 'On condition that they don't go running around upstairs or on to the wards,' she stipulated.

After promising Matron that she would keep the children contained, Margaret returned to the still freezing-cold hall.

'How about we all go on the train, back to my nice big warm house, where we can rehearse our carols and get something nice to eat too?'

'Where's that, miss?' older Davie, the impressive bass singer, asked.

'Kents Bank, Davie, just down the line by train.'

'Aye, miss, I know Kents Bank,' Davie grinned. 'Me and mi dad sing in't Dog and Duck down there in't summer.'

Margaret smiled. Was there any local pub where Davie and his resourceful dad didn't entertain? she wondered.

'You want us to sing carols at your house, miss?' Arthur asked incredulously.

Margaret nodded. 'We'll have our practice there, Arthur,' she explained. 'And then I'll bring you straight back here after our rehearsal, though we might be a bit late back.'

'Mi mam's coming to pick me up, miss,' a little girl anxiously reported.

'Don't worry, dear, I'll get the caretaker to tell any parents who come to collect you that we might be a little bit delayed.'

When the steam train pulled up at Kents Bank station, the overexcited choir burst on to the platform where, laughing and chattering, they formed a line of eight couples. Holding hands, they obediently followed Margaret through the little wood that led into Mary Vale's grounds. Here they ran, whirling and giggling, across the sweeping lawns that sloped gently down to the edge of the sea. Then, breathless and wind-swept, with rosy cheeks and tousled hair, they gradually calmed down enough to approach the Home's front door.

The arrival of sixteen chattering children caused quite a stir in the Home. Intrigued and amused, the residents peeped out to smile at the line of children as they clattered into the hallway, to be greeted by a big welcoming smile from Sister Agnes, ecstatic at the sight of so many 'dear young things'.

Fussing over them like an overexcited mother hen, Sister Agnes (who had been told of the children's arrival) helped them hang up their coats, then bustled them along the corridor, passing heavily pregnant residents along the way.

Never one to miss a beat, wide-eyed Arthur turned to the nun. 'Is everybody in this house having a baby, miss?'

Trying desperately hard not to laugh, Sister Agnes kept a straight face as she diplomatically answered the child's question. 'Not absolutely everybody, dear, but quite a few.'

'My mam had a baby not long ago,' Arthur informed Sister Agnes.

'That's nice,' she smiled.

'No, it in't, she's always skriking,' Arthur concluded.

Hearing the commotion, Matron came to greet the children, now warming themselves in the sitting room, which was cosy with a crackling fire that Sister Agnes had hurriedly lit. Though Sister Agnes wore the same habit, she didn't cut quite such a figure (with her flapping apron and plump, flushed face) as Matron. In her pristine starched uniform, Matron momentarily silenced the children, who all gazed at her in awe.

'Welcome,' she said with a kind smile. 'I hope you'll be nice and warm here for your choir practice.' Lowering her voice, she said in an aside to Margaret, 'Knowing Sister Agnes, she'll do her utmost to give the kiddies something nice to eat.'

Margaret nodded knowingly.

Indeed, before bustling off, Agnes had informed Margaret of her plans. 'I've got a crab or two that Alf netted, in the pantry. I'll make a nice crab paste for the kiddies, far tastier than that nasty bottled fish paste. There's a little bread I can spare this week too.'

'You're an angel, Sister Agnes,' grateful Margaret had enthused and, unable to stop herself, she gave the plump nun a big hug. 'Thank you so much.'

After Matron swept away, the children finally settled down. Knowing they had a lot to cover before she took her charges back to Grange to be collected by their parents, Margaret got straight into the rehearsal.

Sitting at the old piano, Margaret waited patiently for the choir to take up their positions before she played the opening chords of 'Silent Night'. As Margaret's opening chords faded, Arthur stepped forward and, with the beguiling face of a cherub, he sang the opening lines of the much-loved popular carol. The intensity of his sweet innocent voice, soaring high, pierced the stillness of the space, and when the rest of the choir joined in, Margaret thrilled to the sound of their combined voices. Practising here in Mary Vale – in a strange place, as far as the children were concerned – seemed to enhance their performance. Loving the swelling melody, Margaret bit back tears of pride; this dear little group simply took her breath away. Striking the piano keys more powerfully, she and the choir moved on to 'Hark! The Herald Angels Sing' and before they were on to the second verse, Margaret noticed the sitting-room door slowly opening. A few residents quietly slipped into the room, listening in delight as the children sang on, ending with the shattering crescendo of the final chorus. There was a brief silence as the children took in their audience, and then the residents were no longer able to hold back.

'Well done!' cried Gladys.

'Bravo!' beamed Maisie.

'MORE!'

'That were just beautiful.'

'Never heard the like in my entire life.'

Circulating around the astounded children, the residents bombarded them with compliments, smiles, toffees they had dug up from nowhere, even a few hugs. Ever the team leader, Gladys congratulated Margaret, who was thrilled that her sweet choir were enjoying so much attention.

'They're good enough to go on the wireless,' Glad announced.

'Beltin' little singers,' Maisie enthused. 'Knocked mi blinkin' socks off.'

Davie, who was used to public attention, was the first to speak up. 'We were only practising,' he grinned. 'We'll be even better at Christmas, when we're due to sing in Grange. You can come if you like, there's no entry fee,' he joked.

'Well, there should be,' Maisie staunchly replied. 'I'd pay good money to hear you little angels sing again.'

Davie's eyes lit up. 'Really, missus?'

Before Davie could start bartering admission fees, Margaret quickly stepped in. 'Come in, all of you.' She beckoned shyly to her fellow residents. 'There's plenty of room, if we all squash up around the piano.'

'Come on, ladies,' ever-enthusiastic Glad called out. 'Let's have a right good sing-song!'

Several rousing renditions of 'Rudolph The Red-Nosed Reindeer' and 'Jingle Bells' brought Matron, Ada and Dora, followed by Sister Theresa. Knowing that somebody had to keep an eye on the wards, Theresa and Dora tore themselves away just as Glad led a rousing chorus of 'Roll Out The Barrel', which brought the house down. At this point, Sister Agnes swooped into the room with a well-deserved tea. As the children ravenously tucked in, Ada quietly took Glad to one side.

'Not long ago, you were complaining of severe back pains, dear,' she reminded her patient, who had just helped herself to a bit of cake. 'I suggest you have a little lie-down now, Glad, we don't want any more excitement this afternoon,' she smiled.

Throwing off her former concerns, Gladys exclaimed, 'I've never felt better. Margaret's little choir have cheered me up no end.'

Not convinced, Ada urged, 'All the same, dear, please get some rest.'

Meanwhile, on the other side of the room, Joy (for once not at all nervous) confessed, 'I love our choir, Miss Margaret.'

Helping himself to his fourth crab sandwich, Arthur grinned. 'I loved the clapping, miss, it made me feel proper grand and important.'

Coming up behind the little lad, Sister Agnes tousled his mop of dark hair. 'You *are* proper grand and important,' she roundly assured him. 'You're blessed with a wonderful voice, and so is your big sister.'

Charming the nun with his mischievous smile and twinkling eyes, Arthur grinned. 'You make belting butties, miss,' he said.

'I'll make you some more, if you promise to come and sing to us again,' Agnes promised, with a grin.

Watching her choir happily interacting with the residents, Margaret bubbled with pleasure. They were the dearest group of children, she thought to herself, so loving and giving. She had known from their first rehearsal that they had the makings of a fine choir, but it wasn't until now that she actually realized they were more than good – they were, in fact, extremely talented.

Behind Margaret's back, Maisie was arranging a little whip-round. 'For the kiddies,' she whispered. 'Send them home with a copper or two.'

A small bag was surreptitiously passed between the residents, who dropped in any loose change they could find, and by the time the children had consumed every crumb of Sister Agnes's carrot cake, the bag had a reasonable weight of contributions. Dividing it into equal amounts, Maisie was able to give each child some pennies to spend on themselves.

Flustered by the rather unexpected generosity, Margaret blushed. 'Really, that's not at all necessary. It was kind of Matron to let us use Mary Vale for our rehearsal, we certainly didn't expect payment.'

Nervously clutching their pennies, the choir wondered if they might have to give back the money they had only just received.

'Can we not keep it, miss?' Arthur asked the question on behalf of all of them.

Glad, now enjoying a cup of tea while sitting with her feet up, waved a dismissive hand in the air. 'Course you can keep it, lovie, you deserve it.'

'But really,' Margaret feebly remonstrated.

Grinning, Glad again waved her hand in the air. 'Get

away with you, Margaret,' she cheerfully declared. 'It's only a bob or two, stop fretting, lass.'

'Thanks for the entertainment,' the residents said, as the children packed up their things and collected their coats. 'Come back any time you fancy.'

'There'll always be something nice for you to eat at Mary Vale, I'll make sure of that, rationing or no rationing,' Sister Agnes promised as she escorted the noisy group to the front door.

Waving goodbye, the children thundered across the lawn and ran through the woods. With weary Margaret in their wake, they headed to the railway station and caught the train back home.

19. Charity

When Margaret returned from dropping the children off in Grange, she realized as she made her way across the lawn that she was utterly exhausted. Walking into the Home, the first person she encountered was Dr Jamie.

He immediately said, 'Could I have a word with you, Margaret?'

Sensing immediately that this was about Sam Carter, Margaret instantly pricked up her ears. 'Of course, Doctor.'

Guiding her into the sitting room, Jamie came straight to the point. 'I found time to see Sam Carter today. You're quite right, I'm afraid. He is gravely ill.'

Margaret's heart lurched; suspecting something was seriously wrong was not as terrifying as having the truth confirmed.

'The state he's in, I don't know how long he can go on for,' Jamie continued. 'And you're right about the Carters' domestic set-up, there's nothing good about it. Poor, damp surroundings, inadequate food; and a landlord who, I'm told, is hell-bent on evicting the entire family.'

'I cannot tell you how deeply grateful I am that you took the time to visit Sam, Doctor,' Margaret said gratefully.

'Mrs Carter seemed relieved to find me standing on her doorstep,' Jamie told Margaret. 'Her husband was so weak, he barely acknowledged me. But he did allow me to examine him.' Jamie gave a long sigh. 'I really don't know what to do for the best. A stay in hospital, if we could manage it, would help. Sam would be isolated and cared for around the clock, kept warm and well fed, but that's not going to cure him, and he'd still have to return home at some point.'

'If he's even got a home to return to,' Margaret glumly pointed out. 'If only the poor man could perhaps see a specialist.'

'My thoughts exactly,' Jamie responded. 'I've got an old pal I trained with, he's a consultant, a specialist in advanced TB. He works in Lancaster Infirmary . . .' He paused as he formulated a plan of action. 'He might be prepared to do me a favour for old times' sake. I plan to ask him to run some tests on Sam.'

'That would be wonderful,' she exclaimed.

'I can't promise anything, I'll have to speak to my pal first,' Jamie quickly told her. 'So please don't inform Mrs Carter of any of this until I'm clearer.'

'Of course,' Margaret assured him.

Jamie shook his head. 'I feel so sorry for the poor man and his family,' he admitted. 'Left as he is, Sam will be dead by Christmas, which is why I feel obliged to at least try to do something.'

'Something is far better than nothing,' Margaret replied solemnly. 'Nothing is what the Carters have lived with for too long; they lost hope long ago.'

Jamie held up a warning hand. 'If my friend agrees to do me a favour, he would need to somehow work around the issue of getting Sam the hospital bed he so desperately needs. We'll have to hope there are strings he can somehow pull. I'll let you know as soon as I have any news from him.'

*

When Matron saw Margaret leaving the sitting room, she took one look at her pale weary face, and said, 'Get yourself off to bed, dear. I'll bring you up a cup of tea and something to eat.'

'I'm fine,' Margaret started to protest.

But Matron stopped her mid-flow, insisting that she did as she was told.

Tucked up in bed and clutching a hot-water bottle, Margaret gratefully accepted the cup of tea and plate of bread and butter that Matron set down on her bedside table.

Perching on the side of the single bed, Matron's tone was soft. 'Now, dear, I'm pleased you're making progress with your little choir, but you really have to start focusing on your health a little more too. Your pregnancy is advancing, only two months to go now; I'm afraid of you wearing yourself out. I can see how much you love your choir, but you really have to put your baby first.'

Feeling stricken that she had, in all the excitement, not been putting her baby first (she had barely had a moment to even think about it), Margaret blushed guiltily. 'You're right,' she conceded, with a rueful smile. 'Today has been a very long day, and to be truthful, since I started working at St Mark's I have been very preoccupied.'

'And that's good, to a certain extent,' Matron agreed. 'But it is my job to look after my patients and their babies. I have put their health and well-being at the top of my list of priorities.'

Margaret nodded. 'I understand that, Matron, and I thank you for your concern. I will try to take it easy, but things are only going to get busier in the run-up to Christmas.'

'Then you must make the most of your time when you're not working at St Mark's,' Matron urged. 'Get as much rest and relaxation as you can while you're here at Mary Vale. You need to build up your reserves for the birth, and for the post-natal period too.'

Margaret struggled to hold back tears. 'To be honest, the post-natal period is something I prefer not to think about. It will end with me handing my baby over for adoption, which is something I can hardly bear to think of.'

Matron laid a hand on Margaret's arm. 'I understand, dear,' she murmured. 'Father Ben does a grand job of finding the right match for all our babies, but it's always hard for the mothers.'

'I agree, Father Ben is sensitive to our needs, but the fact remains that the adoption process is an agony. Carrying my baby inside me makes me feel happy, because I know he or she is safe. Once we're physically parted, we become two separate entities. To be honest, Matron,' Margaret blurted out, 'the choir helps me enormously; they take my mind off all the pain that is to come.'

Matron smiled. 'Yes, I can see that, they really are a delightful group, especially that dear little boy.'

'Arthur,' Margaret volunteered. 'He and his sister are unbelievably talented; they take the choir to an altogether higher level. God knows how they learnt to sing the way they do, it must be in the genes, they certainly haven't had any formal musical education. Singing seems to come to them as naturally as breathing.'

'They're an impressive pair,' Matron agreed.

'I just wish I could do more for the family, they're as poor as church mice,' she continued. 'I begged Dr Jamie to visit Mr Carter, who is virtually at death's door, and he's doing all that he can to help them.'

Seeing Margaret's stricken face, Matron enquired, 'Not good news, I presume?'

'It's the worst news possible, but Dr Jamie is doing his best to get him seen by a specialist. I dare not think too far ahead; my fear now is the landlord will be even more determined to evict them. What they're going through is utterly tragic,' she sighed.

'Then we must do something to help them too,' Matron insisted.

'I do as much as I can,' Margaret told her. 'At first, I was concerned about overstepping the mark, but really their state is so desperate they're grateful for anything they can get. I took them some second-hand winter clothes, which they appreciated, but I'd like to do so much more.'

'Surely we can do our bit?' Matron suggested. 'Rationing limits us, of course, but we can spare some of the farm produce given to us by Alf when we have enough ourselves – milk, butter, some eggs maybe.'

Margaret smiled. 'They would really appreciate that. And there's plenty of fish swimming out there in the Irish Sea,' she joked. 'Maybe I should learn to fish myself!'

'Not in your condition,' Matron cried. 'Leave the fishing to Alf, he's often dispatched by Sister Agnes to catch fish for Mary Vale,' she pointed out. 'But you do have a point, Margaret – fish is delicious, and not as hard to come by as meat.'

'Sister Agnes's fresh crab paste and her delicious mackerel and parsley fish cakes are a fine example,' Margaret enthused. 'If she only knew how hungry the Carter children are, the dear soul would be on the headland fishing for them every day,' she smiled.

'I think we have the makings of a plan, dear,' Matron said as she tucked Margaret up. 'Mary Vale will do all that it can to help the Carter family, on one condition . . . that *you* take care of yourself.'

When word went around the Home of the Carter children's plight, residents and staff alike agreed that they wanted to support them in whatever way they could. Money was hard to come by, but coppers were steadily dropped into a jam jar set in the middle of the dining-room table with 'Donations for the Carter Family' written on it. When offerings of cast-off clothes, plus the odd children's item purchased from a jumble sale, suddenly started to appear, Maisie, who wasn't as far gone in her pregnancy as either Glad or Margaret, took control.

'We can't have Margaret doing all the heavy lifting and carrying,' she declared. 'Us young 'uns can do that. Better still, we can get Alf to drop stuff off when he's out doing deliveries with his horse and cart.'

Alf (who had heard all about Margaret's little choir) willingly agreed to make deliveries to the Carters' home when he was going their way. 'I'll drop off any fresh veg I can spare too,' he told a grateful Margaret. 'Not much at this time of the year, mind – but the odd bit of cabbage and a potato or two would be good in the pot to make a warming soup for the kiddies.'

The small wooden crate that Sister Agnes put in the hall slowly filled up with second-hand clothes and bedding which the nuns from the convent donated, even a few knitted toys, and in the kitchen Sister Agnes carefully squirrelled away any food she could salvage from her large pantry.

Taking Margaret on one side, she whispered, 'I can't go cycling over to Allithwaite with offerings of food until I've been formally introduced to the Carters. But I don't want to wait until Alf is free to drive me over, as I've fresh food for them now.'

Margaret managed to hide a smile. Knowing how utterly desperate and in need of charity the Carters really were, formal introductions seemed completely unnecessary but, respecting the kind nun's offer, she readily agreed to go with her. After all, she herself had pussy-footed around to start with; it was only when you met them that you appreciated the extreme poverty in their life and the depths this drove the family to.

When Margaret did arrive at the Carters' later that day, with Sister Agnes bearing a small basket, there was no awkwardness. Sister Agnes immediately involved herself with the needy family. Leaving Margaret to chat with Mary, who was eagerly unpacking Agnes's basket containing the remains of a loaf of bread, more crab paste, home-made onion and potato pasties, and a slim slice of Lancashire cheese, the nun made her way to the wooden crate that baby Susan had almost outgrown. Hearing her mewling cries, she picked up the little girl from her makeshift crib and held her close.

'Goodness me, lovie, you need a nappy change,' she chuckled as she felt the baby's damp bottom. Politely turning to Mary, she asked if she could change the child's nappy.

Flabbergasted that a nun was considering taking on such a task, Mary was flustered. 'No, I'll do it,' she blushingly said.

'Don't you go worrying yourself,' Agnes smiled. 'I was the eldest in a household of ten children, I've changed more nappies in my time than you've had hot dinners.'

Margaret was moved by the nun's genial and comforting presence in the cold, uncomfortable cottage where, without being pushy or controlling, she helped Mary with baby Susan, and her sick husband too. While Margaret played with the children and chatted to Mary, Sister Agnes sat beside Sam, reading or praying the Rosary as he slept, clicking the wooden beads that hung around her ample waist as she prayed. Her soothing voice and sweet serenity soothed the sick man; and after he had drifted into a peaceful sleep, Agnes rolled up her sleeves and set about washing Susan's nappies, which she sluiced in the back-yard and then put in a big tub to boil on the stove before hanging them on the line to dry.

'You're an angel, sister,' Mary said, over and over again.

Agnes gave a cheerful shrug. 'I'm no angel,' she grinned. 'I'm enjoying getting to know your dear husband, not to mention this little darling,' she cooed as she picked up Susan, who gurgled happily in the nun's embrace.

'You know we're more than grateful to you, Sister,' Mary said guiltily. 'But really, we must let you both get back. You have your work cut out in the Mary Vale kitchen, and it's getting late.'

With a dismissive wave of her hand, Agnes said, 'Don't you go worrying yourself, I've arranged with Sister Theresa to do the teas today, and I'll make sure Margaret gets home safely.' Moving briskly on, she added, 'Now let's get this dry washing off the line and make up a nice clean bed for your husband. Then I'll be on my way and leave you in peace.'

In truth, the sense of comfort and care in the Carter home after Sister Agnes's departure – and the knowledge that she would be coming back soon, as she'd promised – made everybody in the family feel happier, leaving them with a sense of being loved and valued rather than despised.

When Jamie informed Margaret that his medical friend had not only agreed to help but had somehow secured a hospital bed for Sam and made arrangements for him to have a number of tests in Lancaster Infirmary, she felt her knees go weak with relief.

'Thank God,' she gasped.

'I'd like you to come over to the house with me later, if you are up to that, so that I can break the news to Sam and Mary; it might be better if you're there with me, if you can spare the time?'

Margaret quickly nodded her head. 'Happy to – today isn't a teaching day, so I'm free to accompany you, Doctor.'

When Margaret and Jamie arrived at North Cottage later that afternoon, Mary immediately recognized Dr Reid from his previous visit. Extremely relieved to see him again, with Margaret at his side, she said with tears in her eyes, 'My poor Sam had another terrible night.'

Desperate to ease her load, Margaret wasted no time in saying, 'Dr Reid has some news for you, Mary.'

Quickly ushering them into the cottage, Mary, fussing and nervous, offered to brew a pot of tea.

Glancing over to the bed where Sam was sleeping, Jamie quickly refused the offer. 'No, please don't bother,' he said. 'Please, sit down at the table – I need to talk to you while your husband's asleep.'

Looking tense and white-faced, Mary did as she was told.

Not wanting to waste any time, Jamie came straight to the point. 'After recently examining Sam, I have to tell you that he is very seriously ill, Mrs Carter.'

Gulping back tears, Mary could only nod.

'There's no doubt his condition has worsened due to lack of treatment. Quite frankly, if Sam isn't treated very soon, his chances of survival are very slim. I'm not an expert in this field but I do have a friend, a colleague in fact, who works on the pulmonary lung ward at Lancaster Hospital. He has far more experience than me in this area –'

Interrupting him, Mary blurted out, 'But we haven't a penny to pay for any treatment, Doctor.'

'I quite understand, Mrs Carter,' Jamie soothed. 'As an act of friendship, my colleague has agreed to see your husband without any fee – and has managed to sort him a bed.'

Mary gave a huge gasp of relief. 'That's wonderful! I am so very grateful to you, Doctor,' she cried.

'I'm not promising any miracles,' Jamie warned. 'Sam should have been treated months ago; he's now reduced to a very weak state. Who knows if he will be strong enough to respond to any treatment at this late stage?' He spoke solemnly, knowing he wouldn't be doing this young woman any favours by giving her false hope. Gathering up his medical bag, he continued gently, 'Hopefully, an ambulance will pick Sam up within the next few days, we'll have to see. You might wish to accompany him, Mrs Carter. I'm sure in your absence Margaret can keep an eye on the children,' he added, turning to Margaret. 'If that's all right with you, Margaret?'

'Yes, yes, of course,' she instantly agreed.

Overwhelmed, Mary clutched Jamie's hand in her own. 'Thank you, Doctor, thank you so much. We'll never be able to thank you enough . . . I pray to God that it isn't too late.'

In the car on the way back to Mary Vale, Jamie spoke grimly; he was more direct with Margaret than he had been with Mary.

'I have to be honest with you, Sam's chances of survival are pretty poor. I'm quite sure my colleague will do all he can, but it might be too late for Sam.'

The rest of the journey was spent in silence.

Margaret's thoughts were full of fear: if the worst happened, how would the Carters survive without Sam? Where would they go, what would they live off?

Also preoccupied, Jamie was considering the plight of the two individuals he was treating out of the goodness of his heart, outside of his Mary Vale practice: Beth Thorp, whom he was struggling to free from the grip of her brutish husband; and Sam Carter, whose chances of survival into the New Year were next to zero.

20. A Change of Plan

When Alf Arkwright spotted Libby tacking up Snowball one afternoon, straight after dinner had been served in the Home, he ambled over for a chat.

'Not your usual time for a ride out,' he amiably remarked.

Throwing the saddle on to her pony's back, Libby explained, 'I'm not actually going for a ride, Alf. Snowball is taking me to work these days.'

Alf cocked one of his crinkly grey eyebrows. 'You're travelling to work on your hoss?'

'I have to, Alf, somebody mangled my bike. Snowball is the only means of transport I've got now.'

Looking serious, the farmer asked, 'Why would somebody mess about with your bike, lass?'

Tightening the saddle girths, Libby crossly explained, 'To stop me from visiting my patients.'

'That's not right,' Alf commented.

Patting Snowball, Libby robustly replied, 'It's definitely not right!' She continued, scowling, 'I'm quite sure it was my patient's husband, Ronnie Thorp, trying to stop me from nursing his wife.'

Alf took a step forward. 'Ronnie Thorp?' he queried. 'Yon fella that lives in Thorp Hall?'

'That's him all right,' Libby seethed. 'Do you know him?'

Alf shook his head. 'Nay, I've heard about him though, came from t'other side of Windermere, from poor sheep farming stock. Once he got wed to a wealthy lass, he bought a big estate up Allithwaite way.' Dropping his voice, Alf added, 'He jacked up all the rents without a word of warning, even kicked out a couple of retired sitting tenants. Then bold as brass has the bare-faced cheek to swan around in his big fancy car when we're told there's no fuel to be had.' Shaking his head, he grumbled, 'Your guess is as good as mine where he gets it from.'

'Nothing would surprise me about that beast of a man,' Libby declared. 'I shouldn't be telling you this, Alf, but Thorp treats his wife very badly, which is why I'm determined to visit her even if I have to walk there to see her.'

Coming closer in order to soothe Snowball, who always grumbled and stamped his hooves when his girths were pulled tight, Alf grinned. 'I'll tell you what, lass, you get yourself over there on Snowball and I'll follow later in't cart. Old Captain could do with an outing. And I could pick up your bike and fetch it back here, to see if I can fix it for you.'

Libby smiled back at the old man. 'That would be so kind of you, Alf. Are you sure?' At his emphatic nod, she spoke hurriedly. 'I've a couple of ladies to see in Grange first. Hopefully, I won't be long there, then I'll ride over to Thorp Hall. Perhaps you could meet me at the Hall at four thirty? That would give me time to visit all three of my patients before we try to track down my bike.'

Alf gave another quick nod. 'Aye, I'll do that.'

Expecting the worst, Libby grimaced. 'That's if my bike is still there,' she said, 'and Ronnie Thorp's not thrown it into the nearest river.'

'There's only one way of finding out,' Alf answered grimly.

After visiting Mrs Timms and Mrs Cummings in Grange, and worried that she had spent too long there and might be late for her rendezvous with Alf, Libby turned Snowball in the direction of Allithwaite. Though she was very nervous about returning to Thorp Hall, the tranquil ride over on a frosty, early December afternoon considerably calmed Libby down. Leaving Snowball to amble along the bridle path, requiring almost no guidance, Libby's eyes followed the line of hills that steadily grew higher as the landscape of the beautiful Cartmel Peninsula gave way to the majestic rise of the mountain ranges that were the distinctive landmarks of the Lake District.

When she finally arrived at Thorp Hall, Libby trotted Snowball around the back way and secured him to a fence close to the drawing room, where she could keep him in sight. Patting her pony, she whispered, 'I don't want Thorp coming anywhere near you, lovie. If he can destroy my bike, I'm sure he won't have any qualms about hurting my pony.'

Avoiding the front door and any contact with Mrs Grimsdale, Libby made her way across the lawn to the back of the building, where she tapped on the drawing-room window. The sound didn't disturb Beth, who was curled up in her usual chair. Tapping harder, she realized that her patient was in a deep sleep.

I've got to get in there, I've got to see her, a desperate Libby thought. I've not come all this way for nothing.

Turning the door handle, she was hugely relieved when

it gave way to her touch. Anxious not to alarm Beth, she tiptoed across the room and gently reached out to her patient, who still didn't stir. Now frightened by her continued stillness, Libby gently shook her arm. 'Beth, dear, it's me, Libby.'

A deep shuddering breath brought Beth to her senses. But when she opened her eyes, they were pale and lifeless, her lips were white, and Libby was even more horrified to notice a bruise on her right cheekbone which was turning an ugly shade of blue.

'Please,' she whispered, so low that Libby had to bend to hear her words. 'Let me sleep, let me die.'

Now thoroughly alarmed, Libby took hold of Beth and tried to sit her upright. She felt her pulse, which was slow and sluggish. Thinking fast, Libby knew that she had to take command of the situation, at whatever cost. Already left alone for too long, her patient's condition had rapidly deteriorated.

Terrified that Thorp would walk in and find her in his drawing room, Libby asked, 'Dearest, is your husband at home today?'

'He'll be gone all day, he's over Morecambe way, thank God,' Beth said, with a sigh of heartfelt relief.

Thank God indeed, Libby thought. Without doubt, she was in a better position to rescue Beth without him here.

'But *she's* here. Mrs Grimsdale,' Beth added bitterly.

'I can handle her,' Libby said forcefully.

At which point, Mrs Grimsdale walked in. Scowling at the visitor, she growled, 'The master said you weren't allowed entry.'

Trying to sit upright, Beth said boldly, 'She's my guest – I invited her.'

'The master will be angry,' the housekeeper snapped.

The master's not here to be angry, Libby thought with relief. If she could only get the housekeeper off her back, she could start to formulate a plan.

'My patient is in some distress.' She pointed to Beth's bruised face. 'I need to examine her more closely, if you don't mind . . . ?'

Looking like she might well stay while Libby examined Beth, the housekeeper locked eyes with Libby until, unflinching, Libby finally stared her down.

Turning on her heel, Mrs Grimsdale left the room. 'I shall be speaking to the master the minute he's back.'

Wasting no time, Libby hurried to shut the door, and came straight to the point with young Beth. 'This is not the time for modesty. I need to know how you are, where it hurts, and I really need to listen to your baby's heart-beat.' Nodding at Beth's bruised face, she added, 'And your husband obviously hit you?'

Beth nodded. 'And he forced me to have sex.'

Smothering a gasp, utterly horrified, Libby gave herself a moment. Was there anything this man wouldn't sink to?

'Have you had any bleeding since?' she asked gently.

'Yes,' whispered Beth miserably.

Libby's heart sank. Why had she left Beth with such a man in the first place? she flagellated herself. Because I had no choice, she firmly reminded herself. Beth's married – to a monster – but nevertheless he's her husband who, by law, she is subjugated to.

'Quickly, dear,' she instructed. 'Lie down on the sofa, please.'

After seeing for herself the most recent blood loss, she took Beth's temperature, which was raised; her pulse was rapid, while her blood pressure remained low. Laying the metal Pinard stethoscope on Beth's tummy, Libby pressed her ear to the other end and listened intently. Expecting the worst, she smothered a gasp of relief when she heard the heart-beat, which was undoubtedly weak, but at least the baby was still alive.

Peering down at Libby, who was still listening intently, Beth whispered, 'Is my baby all right?'

Libby reassured her on that score, but went on to speak plainly. 'Beth, you really need to be properly looked after. Remaining here, you're at risk. Would you agree to going into Mary Vale, where we can constantly monitor you and your baby?'

A weak smile briefly illuminated Beth's wasted face. 'Yes, yes, I agree – please do that,' she implored. 'Just get me out of here before Ronnie gets back.'

Keeping her voice low and steady, Libby said, 'I just need to slip upstairs and pack a bag for you.'

'I beg you, Libby, *please*, be quick – I don't want to spend another night here with him.'

Spurred on by Beth's agonized words, Libby desperately hoped that Alf would turn up soon and help her move Beth to safety. She had to get her out of this house while Thorp was away. She crept up the stairs, praying that the dreaded Mrs Grimsdale wouldn't spot her. On entering the gloomy master bedroom, she found the bed in complete disarray, with clothes strewn all over the floor.

Ignoring the scene that spoke of a struggle, she grabbed a leather holdall and stuffed it with some underwear and nightclothes, plus a hairbrush and comb from the dressing table. As she glanced up, Libby got the shock of her life when she saw scowling Mrs Grimsdale reflected back at her in the ornate silver mirror. Libby smothered a scream.

'May I ask what you are doing trespassing in my master's property?'

Feeling like her heart was beating as loud as a drum, Libby faced the tyrannical housekeeper square on. 'I'm preparing a hospital bag for Mrs Thorp,' she said as she calmly dropped a jar of face cream into the holdall.

'She's in no need of any hospital bag. The mistress is due to deliver the child here in Thorp Hall,' Mrs Grimsdale pointed out.

Over my dead body, Libby thought. But nevertheless, she continued calmly. 'Her health has declined, which means that is no longer an option, Mrs Grimsdale. She's requested to be admitted to Mary Vale, where she can be properly monitored.' Libby spoke firmly, as she casually dropped a little hand towel into the bag. 'Now, if you'll excuse me, I must get back to my patient.'

'You won't get away with this, miss. I shall inform Mr Thorp of this matter, the minute he returns home this evening,' the housekeeper threatened, and made a grab for the bag in Libby's hands.

Though she was violently trembling with fear, Libby answered without a tremor in her voice. 'Do that, Mrs Grimsdale.'

Nimble and younger than the hatchet-faced housekeeper,

Libby sidestepped Mrs Grimsdale and made a dash for the stairs. She ran down them two at a time.

'If I don't get Beth out now, I'll never get her out at all – except in a coffin,' Libby grimly muttered.

She just hoped Alf would be on time; without his cart, her rescue plan could not succeed. Poor Beth was in no condition to walk away, and though she had Snowball tethered up close by, it wouldn't be safe to drag a sick woman, urgently in need of medical attention, on to his back, even if he was presently her only means of transport. She could ride back to the Home and alert Dr Reid, who could transport Beth in his car, but that would mean leaving Beth alone once more, and also losing the opportunity to take her from the hall while her husband wasn't there to stop her. If Libby had been more forceful, or more devious, she might have got Beth out sooner. As it was, she had played by the book, and now look what a mess her patient was in. Working against time, with her brain in a spin, Libby was relieved to find Beth sitting upright when she returned to the drawing room.

Seeing the packed bag, Beth asked the very same question that was going around and around Libby's head. 'How are we going to get to Mary Vale?'

Libby opened her mouth to speak, then sighed with relief as she heard a sweet familiar noise that was like music to her ears. Dashing to the window, she saw dear Alf clip-clopping down the drive with frisky Captain tossing his head, pulling a cart.

'Wait there, Beth,' she cried. 'I won't be more than a few minutes.'

Running to the French doors, she threw them open

and ran hell for leather across the lawn to the drive, waving her arms.

Astonished by the sight of Libby, with her long hair loosened by the wind and blowing all over her face, Alf pulled sharply on the reins. 'Whoa there, boy, whoa.' Seeing her flustered face, Alf enquired, 'What's up, lass?'

'I don't know whether I'm breaking the law here, Alf, but I need to get my patient to Mary Vale as quickly and as *safely* as possible,' a breathless Libby explained. 'If you can help me carry her to the cart, we need to drive her to Mary Vale immediately.'

'What about your bike?' Alf quickly asked.

Libby shrugged. 'Who cares? That's the least of my problems right now.'

Securing the reins to the nearest post, Alf, never one to beat about the bush, declared, 'Right then, let's get on with it.'

As they crossed the lawn, Libby added urgently, 'Alf, there's a housekeeper who will try to prevent us removing my patient – under no circumstances allow her to do that. If my patient isn't treated right away, she might die.'

The old man gave a terse nod. 'Then we'd best make sure no bugger gets in our way.'

Once back in the drawing room, pulling a warm shawl around her patient's scrawny shoulders, Libby spoke very clearly. 'Beth, listen carefully to me, we're going to take you to Mary Vale in Alf's cart, it's just outside. It won't be the most comfortable ride, but it's the best we can do.'

Weak as she was, Beth managed to stand up, desperate to get out of the house. 'I don't mind. Just get me out of here,' she repeated, in an unexpectedly strong voice. 'Let's not waste time.'

Seeing Beth swaying, knowing how weak she was, and desperate that she might start to haemorrhage, Libby looked over at Alf. 'I think we should carry her between us across the lawn, she's as light as a feather.'

Making a chair with their arms, and grabbing any blankets they could find, they lowered Beth into place, then very gently, but still moving as quickly as they could, they made their way across the lawn.

Weakly leaning her tired head on Libby's strong shoulder, Beth whispered, 'Please, just get me away from here.' Then, turning to Alf, she added a heartfelt, 'Thank you, sir.'

Looking at the poor young woman whose eyes were heavy with crying and whose pretty face was marred with bruising, Alf's old heart ached. 'Don't fret yourself, we'll soon get you somewhere nice and safe.'

When they reached the cart, Captain let out a shrill, indignant neigh.

'Shush now, lad,' Alf urged. 'We don't want the whole neighbourhood alerted to what we're up to.' Surprisingly nimble for his age, Alf instructed, 'I'll take the lass, Libby, while you drop the tailgate.'

Once the gate was down, they gently loaded Beth into the cart, which was strewn with hay.

Covering her patient with the blankets and rubbing Beth's icy hands, Libby muttered, 'She's stone cold.'

'Give her the horse blanket too,' Alf instructed. 'It's rolled up at the bottom of the cart.'

After settling Beth, Libby wiped her patient's brow. The woman's skin was glistening with sweat, and Libby noticed with alarm her laboured breathing.

'She's running a fever,' she told Alf. Stroking Beth's tangled hair, she added urgently, 'Beth, dear, don't worry, we'll get you to Mary Vale in no time now.'

Running with sweat herself, Libby swiftly covered her patient up while Alf wasted no time in climbing back into the driver's seat. After clicking Captain on, the old horse set off at a brisk pace.

'Thank God,' Libby gasped as she briefly watched them pull away, before turning back to the house to find Snowball.

At that moment, Mrs Grimsdale came running out of the house, waving her hands and hollering at the top of her voice. Remembering Libby's words of warning, Alf did not stop. Libby made straight for Snowball, who was still tied up in the drive, neighing indignantly at the sight of Captain departing ahead of him.

'STOP!' the housekeeper shrieked. 'You have no right to do this. Mr Thorp's strict instructions are that his wife must remain here,' she panted with exertion.

Grateful that Alf, ignoring Mrs Grimsdale's protests, was briskly moving forwards, Libby confronted the irate housekeeper. 'Madam, my patient is in need of urgent medical treatment. Neither you nor your master can deny her that,' she reasoned.

Thwarted and furious, Mrs Grimsdale snarled, 'You won't get away with it, young lady.'

'We'll see about that,' Libby said under her breath as

she mounted Snowball, kicked him on, and left the house-keeper standing on the drive with a face as black as thunder.

By the time they got to Mary Vale, Beth was very cold and deathly pale.

'Poor lamb,' Alf declared as he caught sight of her bruised face. 'She looks like she's been in the wars.'

Not wasting a moment, Libby dashed down the corridor ahead, to the ante-natal ward where she found Ada on duty.

'Sister, come quickly,' she called softly. 'We have an emergency.'

When Ada saw Libby's young patient – pale, breathless and dishevelled in the back of Alf's cart – she too wasted no time. In full professional mode, she instructed, 'We need a stretcher right away.'

After they had collected a hospital trolley, Alf gently laid Beth on to it.

Libby, knowing the full extent of Beth's injuries, whispered, 'We might need Dr Jamie.'

Overhearing her, Alf quickly volunteered. 'I'll pop down and tell the doctor he's needed.'

'Thanks, Alf,' Ada said gratefully. 'He'll be busy with Catherine. Please ask him to drop her off to Sister Agnes in the kitchen. I know she won't mind,' she said, with an encouraging smile.

While they waited for Jamie's arrival, Ada and Libby gently tended to their patient.

Though cold and unwell, Beth was weeping with relief. 'Thank you for helping me, Libby,' she sobbed repeatedly.

'Dearest girl,' Libby whispered, as she and Ada removed Beth's crumpled clothes and got her into a nice, warm clean nightdress. 'Try not to upset yourself,' she urged. 'You're safe now, we'll take care of you, but you must calm down.'

Ada hurried away to make Beth a cup of strong tea, while Libby tucked her patient up in her clean hospital bed and smoothed back her tangled hair where bits of hay from Alf's cart still remained.

'Dr Jamie's on his way,' she told Beth, who gave a weak smile.

'He's a good doctor,' Beth recalled. 'I trust him.'

When Jamie arrived, very soon after, he quickly drew the curtains around Beth's bed before he began to examine her thoroughly.

Panicking, and in unfamiliar territory, Beth cried out, 'Where's my midwife, where's Libby.'

'Right here, dear,' Libby soothed her as she caught hold of Beth's cold hands. 'Right here next to you, don't worry, you're safe now. Dr Jamie needs to examine you, try to relax.'

After listening to the baby's heart-beat and running his hands over Beth's tummy, Jamie immediately beckoned Libby away from the bed. 'If her blood loss increases, it would suggest that the placenta is detaching from the uterus, which is very dangerous and might require immediate surgery at Lancaster Infirmary.'

Libby smothered a gasp. 'After what she's just been through, could Beth manage another journey right away? And what about the baby?' she urgently whispered. 'Is there anything we can do?'

Looking deeply concerned, Jamie shook his head. 'It's not looking good, to be honest. I'm uncomfortable about sending her to hospital right now – her body's in no state to withstand surgery and, to be frank, I don't think the baby could withstand it either. The heart-beat is there but it's weak.'

On hearing this, Libby immediately blamed herself. 'I should have acted earlier – this is all my fault.'

Jamie hastily shook his head. 'It's nothing short of a miracle that you and Alf managed to get Beth here today, you've done all you can.'

'So what happens now?' Libby asked.

'She'll need constant bed-rest, for sure, and round-the-clock care. If we can calm her and stabilize the bleeding, that would be good, at least for the moment. Let's see how she goes. If necessary, we can give her a blood transfusion along with a saline drip. Please stay here with Beth and keep her quiet while I prepare a private room for her.'

Gazing trustingly at Libby, Beth gasped, 'Will my baby die?'

Standing at Beth's bedside, stroking and smoothing her long, tangled silver-blonde hair, Libby answered, 'Your baby stands a better chance of survival if we can keep an eye on both of you here in Mary Vale, for now at least. You'll have your own room where we'll regularly monitor you and baby – and you absolutely must stay in bed, Beth, that's doctor's orders.'

'Poor mite,' Beth sobbed as tears rolled down her weary face. 'If it weren't for my wretched husband, we would have had proper treatment long ago.' Grasping Libby's hands, she held them so tightly her nails cut into her midwife's flesh. 'I never want to go back there, *never*. I'd rather die than set foot again in that monstrous house.'

Terrified that her patient might become hysterical, Libby soothed her. 'Shhh, shhh, dear, let's not talk about that now, we're going to take good care of you.'

After Beth was wheeled away to a small private room, Libby slumped against the bed her patient had just vacated, which was where Dora found her, on her way through the ward.

'Sweetheart,' she exclaimed. 'I hear you've had quite a day. Why don't I go and make you a nice cup of tea. It'll help you relax, maybe?'

Libby gave a loud groan. 'Oh, Dora, I don't think I'll ever relax again. When I think of the state Beth was in when I arrived at the Hall!' Almost in tears, she cried, 'The thought of Ronnie Thorp turning up here tonight, demanding to take his wife back, just makes my blood run cold.'

Before she dashed off to make the tea, Dora did her best to calm her friend and colleague, nevertheless speaking with a lump in her throat. 'I think we can safely say that Beth Thorp has found sanctuary and peace here at Mary Vale, for the time being at least.' Giving an emotional Libby a brief but very warm hug, she added, 'God bless you, dear girl, for putting yourself at risk and bringing your patient here when you did.'

21. The Power of Women

Early the following frosty morning, Libby hurried down the back lane that led to Mary Vale's farm in order to check on Snowball. She found Alf already up and keeping an eye on Catherine while Ada popped into Mary Vale to check up on Beth.

Seeing her pony already turned out into the frosty paddock, Libby called out gratefully, 'Thanks so much, Alf, I came by just as soon as I could manage.'

'You shouldn't go fretting yourself,' he fondly scolded a flushed Libby. 'You've got your work cut out up at the Home, lass. How's our patient?' he anxiously enquired.

'Really sick, Alf,' Libby confessed, with an emotional catch in her voice. 'She's presently being treated in one of the private rooms. I can never thank you enough for your help yesterday. I simply couldn't have done it on my own.'

'From the look of things, you had no choice but to get that poor young woman into your care, she looked half dead to me. Though you do wonder what kind of man this fella Thorp is,' Alf mused. 'Not a thought for his wife or unborn child, it beggars belief that any man could treat his kin so cruelly.'

'Blasted arrogant brute,' Libby swore under her breath.

'The lass is in safe hands now,' Alf soothed.

Catherine interrupted their solemn conversation by crying out, 'Horsie, horsie! Ride horsie.'

Libby shook her head. 'Sorry, sweetheart, Snowball's having a nice rest today, we'll go for a ride another day. Look,' she added, as Captain came ambling up to nuzzle her pony's silver-grey muzzle. 'They're having a cuddle.'

'Let's give Captain a carrot,' Alf suggested to the little girl.

'I'd better get back to work,' Libby said.

'I'll be bringing the little 'un up to the big house soon, to see her mother,' Alf added.

'I'm sure Sister Agnes is already cooking up a storm for Catherine,' Libby smiled as she waved goodbye.

Back in the Home, Libby briefly popped into the baby nursery, where she found Dora in the process of changing a baby's nappy.

Looking up from the tiny wriggling baby balanced on her lap, Dora enquired, 'How's our patient this morning?'

Dropping her voice to a whisper, Libby said, 'So weak, Dora. Dr Jamie thought that the baby might not make it.'

'We must pray that's not the case,' Dora answered staunchly.

'What really worries me, like I said to you last night,' Libby fretted, 'is Thorp storming into the Home and seizing Beth. I'm astonished that he didn't come here last night, in fact.'

'Be grateful for small mercies,' Dora responded, with a contemptuous snort. 'Mebbe the fella was drunk when he got home – that's if he ever got home at all. Anyway, what can he do if his wife is half conscious and her baby's life is hanging in the balance?' she realistically asked. 'Drag her out of bed? He'd never get away with it.'

Libby scowled. 'You don't know what he's like, Dora. The man is mad and quite capable of anything, just so long as he gets his own way.'

Though small, grey-haired and distinctly middle-aged, Dora, ever a tough fighter, drew her shoulders back. 'Let him bloody try, he'll have to get past me first.'

'What if he turns up and is violent, Dora?' Libby fretted. 'Here we are – a house full of women, half of whom are pregnant, living in a Home in the middle of nowhere.'

'Don't ever underestimate the power of women,' Dora wisely advised before she added, with a knowing wink, 'especially *pregnant* women.'

Libby's worst fears did indeed come true. Just an hour later, a loud pounding on the front door sounded out through the downstairs rooms. Libby had had the foresight to warn Sister Agnes that they might have an unwelcome visitor who should not be allowed entry. Unflappable Sister Agnes opened the door to Thorp.

The man immediately jammed it with his boot. 'Where's my wife?' he snarled.

Sister Agnes politely but firmly held her ground. 'Your wife, sir?'

'Mrs Thorp! Don't be a bloody fool,' he swore, 'I know she's been brought here.'

Bridling at his choice of words, Sister Agnes responded, 'I beg your pardon.'

'Get out of my way,' Thorp snapped. He attempted to barge past the broad nun, who was trying to block his entry with her bulk. 'Get out of my way, woman!'

Passing along the corridor that linked the wards to the

Home, Libby heard Thorp shouting and swearing in the hallway, and came running.

The sight of Libby incensed Thorp, who pushed his way past Sister Agnes. 'There she is,' he bellowed. 'There's the bitch who stole my wife!'

Outraged, Sister Agnes faced a livid Thorp square on. 'Leave now, sir, before I call the police,' she said.

Incandescent with fury, Thorp raved, 'I'm going nowhere without my wife. How dare you take her!'

Fighting for dignity and composure, Libby held firm. 'I had no choice. Your wife had to be admitted immediately, otherwise she might have died.'

Throwing his arms up in the air, Thorp scoffed, 'So you keep saying – where is she now?'

Libby answered truthfully. 'In a private room, receiving treatment that might help save her life.'

'How long do you plan to keep her here?' he demanded.

'You must talk to Dr Reid about that.'

'And you'll be talking to the police, if I have my way,' Thorp continued to rant.

His loud angry voice echoing down the hallway alerted Gladys, who was with a group of friends – Margaret included – in the dining room. Laying aside the *Daily Herald* she had been reading, Gladys hurried to open the door leading into the hallway.

'Hell fire!' she cried, when she saw Thorp confronting Libby and Sister Agnes. Quickly beckoning her friends, she called out, 'There's a riot on our front doorstep!' Vast in her advanced pregnant state, Gladys waddled into the hallway, followed by a procession of several other pregnant women.

Margaret, at the tail end of the small procession, stopped dead in her tracks when she heard Sister Agnes protest loudly, 'Mr Thorp, you are trespassing.' When she realized who the visitor was, Margaret gasped under her breath, 'Thorp!'

The man she had heard nothing but bad things about, the ogre who had haunted a seriously sick man and repeatedly threatened a woman and her innocent children with eviction, knowing there was nothing left for them but the streets, was right here in Mary Vale. With her heart banging like a drum, Margaret took in his every detail – his dangerous flashing eyes, his angry red cheeks, his snarling mouth and wiry dark hair. He was a heavily built man too, with broad shoulders and big fists, the sort of man who would pick a fight and win it.

Seeing the women crowding in on him sent Thorp into an even more incandescent rage. 'I won't be stopped by a gaggle of women,' he shouted.

My God, thought Margaret. He's worse than I ever imagined.

Continuing to shout and rage, Thorp threatened, 'Give me my wife, or I'll have this house of sin taken down, brick by brick.'

Incensed by his words, the women moved forward as a body.

Outraged, Gladys snapped, 'OI! I'll have you mind your manners.'

Giving her a long contemptuous look, Thorp viciously retaliated, 'This is a house of whores and bastards.'

As a collective gasp of shock rose from the assembled women, Gladys crossed the hallway, supporting her burgeoning tummy with both hands, looking thoroughly incensed and clearly intent on confronting Thorp who, Libby knew full well, would have no qualms about assaulting a pregnant woman. Luckily, Matron's arrival, with Dora at her side, stopped both parties in their tracks.

With her pristine, starched white wimple fluttering around her stern face, Matron imperiously approached Thorp. 'Can I help you, sir?' she icily enquired.

Pointing a finger at Libby, who was at the forefront of the group, Thorp yelled, 'That so-called nurse removed my wife from my house without my consent.'

Matron, who had been fully primed by Jamie on recent events, replied fearlessly, 'Your wife, sir, is seriously unwell. We are treating her as best we can, in the circumstances, building up the little strength she has in order to protect her baby who has a weak heart-beat. All in all, sir, we are very concerned – as you should be – for your wife's well-being.'

'Who gave you permission to haul her off here?' Thorp barked.

Ignoring his threatening tone, Matron answered calmly, 'Mrs Thorp actually asked to be admitted, sir.'

'What the hell are you on about?' Thorp exploded.

'After Mrs Thorp's midwife explained the seriousness of her condition, your wife asked to be treated here at Mary Vale.'

'She can't do that without my say-so,' Thorp continued to bluff.

Looking him straight in the eye, Matron replied, 'When Nurse Godburgh arrived to treat your wife, your baby's life was hanging in the balance – which is why your wife was rushed here. Our entire household is praying that both mother and baby will survive. Would you care to join us in prayer, Mr Thorp?'

Looking like he would explode with fury, Thorp threw his hands up in the air. 'To hell with your snivelling prayers – you can have 'em!' he snapped, turning on his heel, to everyone's intense relief. But as he left, he snarled over his shoulder, 'Don't you worry, I'll be back, but next time with a police warrant for the arrest of the midwife who abducted my wife.'

Swearing and cursing, Thorp jumped into his black Daimler and roared off down the drive, narrowly avoiding Alf who was walking up the drive holding Catherine's hand. Clutching the little girl close in order to protect her, a furious Alf yelled out, 'Watch where you're going, you bloody fool!'

Ignoring the fact that he could have knocked the two pedestrians down, Thorp yelled back out of the open car window. 'Get out of my way, you stupid old sod!'

Still holding on to terrified little Catherine, a red-faced Alf joined the group on the doorstep. 'Who the 'ell does he think he is?' Alf seethed. 'He nearly ran me and the little lass down.'

'He's Beth's husband, and the devil incarnate,' Libby muttered, slumping with delayed shock against Sister Agnes's comforting bulk. 'Thank God he's gone. For now.'

'There, there,' Agnes soothed. 'You did well, Nurse Libby.'

'He looked all set to kill me,' Libby half sobbed. 'What must poor Beth have lived through, all these months?' Turning to thank Matron and the other women for their support, she was met with a grin from Dora.

'One for all, and all for one, eh, ladies?'

To which the residents responded with a rousing cheer.

'Like I've always said – never underestimate the power of women.' Dora gave a low chuckle. 'Especially *pregnant* women.'

After Thorp had made his dramatic departure, Matron, Ada, Jamie and Libby held an emergency meeting in Jamie's surgery.

'We might have successfully got rid of Thorp this time, but we do have a very serious problem,' Matron started. 'We can't keep a patient here without her husband's permission.'

'I think we can circumnavigate that by saying that Beth can't be moved at the moment,' Jamie reasoned. 'Her only chance of survival – and the child's too – is if she has total bed-rest until she delivers, and if we monitor her vitals around the clock.'

'Whatever happens,' Libby said through gritted teeth, 'Beth can *never* go back to Thorp Hall.'

Looking grim, Jamie agreed. 'Then there is no alternative but for her to remain here.'

'But how do we keep her safe without Thorp making a fuss, even bringing in the police as he just threatened?' Ada asked.

Matron, who had been silent for a while, finally spoke. 'We will have to be creative with reasons why Beth can't be disturbed.'

'What are you thinking of, Ann?' Ada asked, with a teasing smile.

Matron spread her hands expressively as she chanted

off a list of excuses they could give to the police, if they did come.

'Beth is sedated, Beth is with the consultant, Beth is having tests, et cetera, et cetera. We might have to fudge the truth to protect our vulnerable patient.'

Smiling, Jamie shook his head. '*Really*, Matron,' he teased.

Smiling back, Matron wagged her finger. 'Don't look at me like that, Doctor,' she chided. 'I agree this is all slightly underhand, but seeing as we're dealing with an unscrupulous bully, quite frankly I feel no qualms whatsoever in suggesting that we lie, if it means we can save Beth Thorp's life.'

Jamie gave a long slow smile. 'I have no problem with lies, if they provide us with delaying tactics,' he agreed. 'They might stall the brute of a man she calls her husband.'

Standing firmly at her husband's side, Ada joined in. 'From what I've heard, Libby has tried everything to help her patient but has been thwarted on every count.'

Gulping back tears of gratitude, Libby was relieved to hear her colleagues speak on her behalf. Throughout the whole of this terrifying ordeal, with her patient's life still hanging in the balance, at the back of her mind she had been worrying herself sick about her actions. After all, she was only a midwife, and new to community work, at least in Grange. Having braced herself for trouble, she was hugely relieved to find herself supported and exonerated.

'Thank you,' she gulped.

Seeing her youngest nurse's face tense with emotion, Matron added, 'I'm in complete agreement with Ada. I'm not sure where we stand on the matter, but as a midwife,

I believe you did the right thing. It was a life or death decision, a tough one, but you made it, Libby.'

Now really struggling to control herself at the end of what had been a truly harrowing twenty-four hours, Libby could only murmur an incoherent thank you to Matron.

Moving the conversation on, Jamie said, 'So we have the makings of a plan, which is ultimately to keep Beth here for as long as we can – and do whatever it takes to prevent Thorp removing his wife from Mary Vale, to most likely lock her up all over again.'

Ada, Matron and Libby nodded their heads in unison.

Exchanging conspiratorial smiles, the four of them held each other's gaze.

'Are we agreed?' Jamie asked.

'YES.'

'Right,' said Jamie. 'Let's do it!'

22. An Ear to the Ground

Alf's involvement in Beth's rescue from Thorp Hall, added to his witnessing Thorp nearly running over a completely innocent child, aroused in the old farmer a great dislike of the man. As he had told Libby, he had never met him but had certainly heard a great deal about him through the local grapevine. After witnessing first-hand what the man was capable of doing to a woman in a delicate state, Alf, with the bit firmly between his teeth, determined that he was going to find out more about the man – and, in particular, about where his money came from. A task that turned out to be surprisingly easy. It seemed that Thorp regularly angered the ordinary folk of the small town of Grange, who were all doing their bit for the war effort, making sacrifices every day as they struggled to get by on rationing, while he drove around in his distinctive black Daimler, flaunting privileges they were denied. His flagrant use of restricted petrol was his way of blatantly putting himself above others, in effect saying, 'I'm better than any of you.'

When Alf took himself to the Crown public house in Kendal marketplace, to see what he could pick up about the man, his drinking pals grumbled immediately at the mention of Thorp's name.

'Up to no bloody good, that flash fella.'

'Hasn't he heard there's a war on?'

'Swanks about while the rest of us go short.'

After buying a round for his pals propping up the bar, Alf made a few more not-so-subtle enquiries. 'How does the fella make his money?' he asked.

His best mate shrugged. 'It's hard to say, there's definitely not enough rich pickings in Grange to pay for a fancy new car and enough petrol to drive it.'

Another drinker chipped in. 'I've heard he's got businesses in Blackpool and Lancaster – posher places than Grange.'

Baffled and frustrated, Alf pressed on. 'Mebbe, but doing what? There's now't up here but sheep and cattle, and nobody makes a packet from building drystone walls,' he joked.

His pals gave a collective shrug.

'I'd say, at the rate he spends his cash,' Alf's mate said cautiously, 'it's summat dodgy, like the black market.'

'Bloody 'ell!' another drinker exclaimed.

'I've got no proof for saying that, mind. No proof – just a hunch, you could say.'

'Well, there's a thought,' Alf muttered. 'Who'd a thowt there was such a thing going on here, right under our noses, right here in Grange?' Pausing to consider the prospect, he challenged his friends. 'So, let's say for the sake of argument that Thorp's dabbling in't black market – my next question is, where's he storing his stuff?'

Putting down his empty pint glass, his pal shuffled closer to whisper, 'Look around you, man, there are sheds and boathouses all along this coastline.'

Alf gave a slow, thoughtful nod. 'Aye, but most of the shacks on the marsh are leaky old heaps.'

'Rumour has it that he rents a warehouse – supposedly for storing antiques. Baloney!' one of the men rather drunkenly scoffed as he accepted another pint from Alf. 'I'd lay a fiver on it being stuffed to the roof with booze, fags, food, clothes, fuel and the like.'

'If that's the case, the bastard's laughing all the way to the bank,' another said. 'He could be stockpiling a fortune right under our noses.'

Now consumed with curiosity, Alf continued with his questions. 'If he does have contraband stuff stashed away somewhere – how does he shift it?'

One of the group, a local fisherman, chipped in. 'Some boats have been spotted regularly crossing the bay at nightfall, from this area over to Morecambe way – none of 'em local fishing boats, and I would know,' he added sagely. 'Who knows what they're up to?'

Driving his cart home from Kendal market before darkness fell, Alf let Captain amble along at his own speed while he mulled over what he had heard in the Crown. There were indeed umpteen fishing shacks and boathouses along the coastline, where the railway line ran, tucked away in gullies washed by tidal streams, with tracks that led directly down to the bay. If contraband goods were stored in any of them, it would only take a quick walk across the marsh to load up a boat and sail it soundlessly over to the other side of the bay, where the cargo could be picked up and transported on, without anybody being any the wiser.

'Aye,' Alf lugubriously considered. 'That's only if you know the marsh and the safe tracks around the quicksand.'

Many a smart alec had met a bad end out there, thinking they could take a short cut through the sand dunes, and landed up dead in quicksand.

Only the locals knew the safe paths, and even then, they were cautious. But Thorp wasn't a local, born and bred; he wouldn't be versed in the whereabouts of treacherous quicksand. With all these questions going around and around his head, Alf reached home, deep in thought. Eager for the warmth of his stable and a welcome net of hay, Captain clip-clopped into the farmyard. Alf removed him from the cart shafts then led him into the stable block, to be welcomed by Snowball with a rapturous neigh.

Leaving the horses to enjoy their supper, Alf headed into the farmhouse and a kitchen that was snug with the warmth coming from the big black grate. Putting the old-fashioned kettle on to boil, Alf stoked up the fire with wood, then sat back in his rocking chair to light up his pipe. Puffing tobacco smoke that smelt of rich cherry wood, Alf decided he would keep his eyes peeled from now on. If Thorp was hoarding black-market goods somewhere on this side of the bay, then Kents Bank was well placed to spy out any action between Grange and Barrow. Kents Bank also had a number of slip yards and boathouses, while further up the coast towards Barrow there were deep caves and many abandoned fishing shacks. Fishing, as he regularly did in both directions, Alf had come to know both stretches well. Mary Vale's constant need for extra resources often drove Alf on to the rocky headland to the north of Mary Vale, where at high tide he would stand on a high promontory to fish for herrings. He decided to make time for a fishing trip the next day; if Thorp was storing his booty locally, a keen-eyed nosy parker like himself might well spot something useful.

Alf didn't hang around long on this particular freezing-cold December day, when the high tide came later with every passing evening. Though it was terribly cold – almost cold enough to snow – the chill wind blew wisps of clouds from the darkening sky, leaving it a clear, dark blue which was reflected in the fast-flowing waters of the Irish Sea. A bright half-moon rose slowly, tracing a deli-cate silver filigree pattern over the soft-lapping waves. Though Alf was familiar with the beauty of the bay, he nevertheless always treasured moments like these when, even frozen to the bone, he could bask in the beauty of the still, silent countryside he loved so deeply.

After fishing for another half-hour, and with hands now numb with cold, Alf decided he had caught enough herring – though, in reality, no matter how much fish he caught, it seemed to disappear in a flash with all the hun-gry mouths to feed back at Mary Vale.

'The ladies are eating for two,' Sister Agnes always said, with a cheerful smile. 'They'll be grateful for your contri-bution, Alf. Mackerel, herring and crab paste all go down a treat at tea-time. I'll be sure to save some for you,' she always promised.

'Thank you, Sister, I'm partial to a bit of fish paste mi-self. Better than that muck they serve up in them little jars these days.'

Giving up on his hope that he might catch more fish,

with the bright moon rising higher in the sky and casting light on to the headland, Alf clambered back over the rocks on to the sandy track that wound its way along the railway line from Barrow-in-Furness to Lancaster. When he came to the pedestrian crossing by the track, he stopped and waited for a steam train to rumble by. As it did so, the light from its windows illuminated a dark alleyway that Alf had previously never noticed. After the train had pulled away, Alf crossed the railway line. Ever curious, he took a peek into the dank alley; it was hard to see clearly without the light cast by the passing train.

With darkness rapidly descending, Alf had no desire to investigate the gloomy area. Now with his curiosity fully aroused, he made his way back along the coastal path, intrigued by the number of boatyards and sheds, tucked under the cliff's edge, that in former times he might not even have registered. His pals in the Crown were right; there really were innumerable hidey-holes around the edges of the bay. The question was, which one – if any – Thorp might be using.

23. Thank You for the Music

The morning following Ronnie Thorp's visit, while the Mary Vale staff were doing everything they could to protect Beth, still weak and resting in a private room off the busy ante-natal ward, the residents at the breakfast table were talking about Gladys. She had gone into labour shortly after Ronnie had stormed off.

'She went all funny when that vicious, scary man turned on her,' Maisie fumed. 'All she was doing was defending our good name – how dare he call us whores,' she crossly declared.

'Disgraceful spectacle!' her companion announced. 'Who'd want a fella like that?'

'Not me!' Maisie cried. 'Treating women like muck. I blame him entirely for Gladys's waters breaking when they did, the bastard,' she continued to seethe. 'The way he tore into her,' she said, rolling her eyes. Then she added, 'And of course, Glad's not the type to back down, is she? She'd have a go at anyone who was picking on us.'

'Tch!' her companion snorted. 'Men have been treating us poor women badly for bloody centuries.'

'Aye,' another woman grumbled as she glanced down at her big tummy. 'I wouldn't be here in the state I'm in now, but for the fella who knocked me up forgetting to let me know he was a married man in't first place.'

'"Love 'em and leave 'em", that's their motto,' a young girl bitterly added.

Swanning in with a tray of hot toast, Sister Agnes spotted the angry expressions on several of the residents' faces and cheerfully remarked, 'Now, ladies, we're not getting ourselves worked up, are we?'

'It's all right for you,' Maisie grumbled under her breath. 'You're a nun, folks treat nuns with respect.'

With ears as sharp as a bat, Agnes parried back, 'I haven't always been a nun, you know, Maisie. Before God called me, I was a woman of the world – and I've seen suffering, I'll have you know. I see it now, every day, here in Mary Vale,' she added, with genuine emotion in her voice. 'Real suffering, endured over and over again, by brave women, just like you, ladies.'

Mortified, Maisie quickly apologized. 'I'm sorry, Sister Agnes, just hearing that bully of a man screaming and shouting in the hallway yesterday bothered me – not to mention poor Glad going into labour as a result of all the upset.'

'Sister Ada told me Glad's doing fine. She had a healthy son in the middle of the night, with lungs like a lion,' smiling Sister Agnes informed the women.

'I'd love to see her,' Maisie said.

'Maybe you should drop by the post-natal ward later,' Agnes suggested.

Margaret, who was among the residents at the breakfast table that morning, remained silent throughout most of the exchange. Hearing her companions castigating all men in general, she kept her eyes down and her mouth shut as she buttered her toast. Her only experience of men had been gentle, tender Peter whom she could never damn or mockingly dismiss. Had he treated her badly? Not really. She answered the question honestly – not when she had wantonly welcomed his every move, and rejoiced in the physical pleasure of their passionate love-making, knowing all along that he was married. Just thinking of his lips on hers, his hands caressing the length of her naked body, and recalling the sweet words he had whispered during their love-making – 'Precious one', 'My sweet darling', 'Beloved' – even now set her heart pounding with desire.

Peter will probably be the only experience of physical love I'll ever have, Margaret thought sadly. Unquestionably, she had deceived him, walking away without Peter ever knowing that she was pregnant. Though she had felt, and still felt, it was all for the good, she also experienced some guilt when she recalled the lies she had repeatedly told him. Deep in thought, Margaret jumped when she felt a gentle nudge at her elbow.

'I'm looking forward to seeing the kiddies here later,' Sister Agnes whispered. 'I've made them a nice little custard each, for their pudding – that should cheer them up.'

Quickly laying aside her napkin, Margaret rose to her feet. 'Oh, they'll love that,' she answered gratefully. 'I'd better get a move on, Mary's expecting me soon.'

'It's marvellous that Dr Jamie's colleague managed to arrange Sam's hospital admission so quickly,' Agnes enthused.

Margaret gave a grim nod. 'Indeed, though he probably didn't want to waste time, given Sam's terrible circumstances. Anyway,' she continued on a more cheerful note,

'I thought it best to get Arthur and Joy out of the house before the ambulance arrives to collect their dad,' she added sensitively.

Sighing heavily, Agnes murmured, 'The kiddies won't want to see their daddy taken off in an ambulance, that's for sure. God bless the poor fella.'

'At least Mary will be with him,' Margaret added.

'And baby Susan too,' Agnes pointed out. 'I offered to have her, but Mary said the little baba would need feeding. Though I think myself that the baby would fare better on a bottle,' she confided. 'Mary's breast milk can't be very rich these days, not with the little she eats and the constant worry about her husband and that terrible landlord. Poor little Susan, she never seems satisfied.'

'To be fair to Mary,' Margaret said gently, 'I think the poor woman has so much on her mind, she's just not thinking straight these days.'

Before she left the Home, well wrapped up against the freezing-cold blustery wind, in her warmest coat and stout fur boots, Margaret was waylaid by Ada.

'I gather you're off to pick up Joy and Arthur,' she started.

'That's right,' Margaret answered as she pulled on her soft leather gloves. 'I asked Matron's permission to bring them here for the day while their mum accompanies Mr Carter to Lancaster Royal.'

'Are you sure you're strong enough to look after two children all day?' Ada continued to fret. 'And you've got to get there and back too,' she added realistically.

Margaret gave a cheerful shrug. 'It's only a short train

journey and a quick bus ride,' she said dismissively. 'Once the kiddies are back here, there's plenty for them to do: the woods, the marsh, the sea, the garden. They'll probably run around all day, until Sister Agnes calls them in for something to eat,' she said fondly.

Looking distinctly uncomfortable, Ada said, 'I know it was me who encouraged you to volunteer at St Mark's School, Margaret. But there are times when I wonder just how wise that was,' she admitted. 'You seem to be busier than ever these days.'

Margaret gave a knowing smile. 'Are you worried about me overdoing it?' she asked.

'I certainly am,' Ada answered, with characteristic frankness. 'What with your imminent Christmas plans for the choir, and now taking on the responsibility of looking after the Carter children, it's too much for a pregnant woman with only a few weeks to go.'

'I'm only taking care of the Carter children today, to help Mary out,' Margaret quickly assured her. 'And I've stopped all my teaching work at St Mark's – apart from the choir.'

'That's a relief, but it depends on how many choir rehearsals you're planning before Christmas.'

'Actually, not that many now,' Margaret answered honestly. 'The children have worked so hard, I feel quite confident that they could easily perform tomorrow, if necessary – though it is important to keep their enthusiasm high, I wouldn't want to lose that impetus.'

Determined to find out all of Margaret's plans while she had the chance, Ada asked, 'How many performances have you scheduled?'

'We're definitely doing a performance in Grange just before Christmas, and I'd love us to sing in Allithwaite and Cartmel,' Margaret told her. 'Alf's volunteered to take as many of us as he can transport in his big cart.'

Ada threw up her hands. 'Margaret!' she cried. 'The way you're going, you'll give birth in Alf's cart if you're not careful.' Patting Margaret's arm, she conceded, 'You're doing a great job cheering up the community with your lovely choir, I'm genuinely impressed by your generosity, but *you* are my priority, Margaret. I have to put you first, before any choir or Christmas performance. Do you understand?'

Throwing her a grateful smile, Margaret replied, 'Yes, I understand, and I take it on board. I really don't want to upset my baby in any way, Ada,' she admitted. 'But given the circumstances, odd as they are, I can honestly say I've rarely felt more energized in my whole life.'

Ada shook her head as she grinned at her patient. 'It's true, you've been transformed by St Mark's choir, which is exactly why I'm determined to keep an eye on you, miss!' she said as she wagged a playful finger in the air.

Joy and Arthur were eagerly awaiting Margaret's arrival while Mary, white with nervous tension, was busily preparing Sam for his journey to Lancaster Infirmary.

'I've tried to keep the children out of his way,' she whispered. 'Though they love to talk to their dad, their constant chatter exhausts him.'

Seeing Mary trying to get Sam into an overcoat that was far too big for his skeletal frame, Margaret made a suggestion. 'Shall I take over while you feed Susan, before the ambulance arrives? You don't want her crying all the way there, it might bother Sam.'

While Mary fed Susan by the fire, and the children played in the grubby backyard, Margaret settled Sam, now wrapped up in his overcoat, against the pillows.

Breathless, and sweating with the exertion of dressing, he held Margaret's gaze. 'I know what you've done for this family, miss,' he wheezed.

Desperately wanting the sick man not to upset himself, Margaret answered with a quick dismissive smile. 'It's been no trouble at all.'

Determined not to be fobbed off, Sam pushed on. Labouring in his breathing, he said, 'You've brought us food and clothes, and a few coppers too, and you've given my children happiness. That's something money can't buy.'

'Please, Mr Carter,' Margaret implored. 'Please don't go exerting yourself.'

Clutching her hand, he said, 'This could be my last chance to thank you, miss, I might not come out of the hospital alive.'

Alarmed, Margaret whispered, 'I beg you, please don't talk like that.'

'It's true, and we all know it,' he answered bluntly. 'During these few weeks lying here on this bed, I've heard my children sing like angels, it's been a blessing,' he said, with tears in his eyes. 'And I want to thank you from the bottom of my heart.'

Feeling overcome herself, Margaret enthused, 'Both of your children have amazing natural talent – have you any idea where that gift might have come from?'

'Aye, mi dad used to perform in the music halls, a fine

baritone voice he had,' Sam said proudly. 'He must've passed it on to Joy and Arthur.' Starting to cough, he gasped. 'Thank you for all your music, miss, and the singing, it's brightened my last days at home.'

Swallowing hard, Margaret squeezed his clammy hand. 'It's been nothing but a pleasure, Mr Carter.'

Trying to get the children out of the house quickly (and hoping to avoid the sight of the ambulance) wasn't altogether easy. First, Arthur and Joy wanted to kiss their father goodbye, and Susan too. And then Mary got emotional, which was not how Margaret had hoped things would pan out. Determined to catch the next bus that would drop them off at Grange railway station, where they would catch the train back to Mary Vale, she offered the children sweets she had tucked away in her coat pocket. Then she hurried them out of the house, leaving Mary and Sam in peace to prepare for their journey.

When the children tumbled off the train at Kents Bank, Margaret – knowing they had plenty of steam to blow off – let them run through the woods and then out across the lawn.

'YEAHHH!' they called out to each other. 'Can't catch me!'

After ten minutes of running around playing tag in the sharp frosty air, they finally slumped down on to one of the garden benches, where they lay red-faced and breathless. Arthur, ever restless and ever hungry, suddenly shot off indoors. This gave Joy the opportunity to ask a question, completely out of the blue, which virtually took Margaret's breath away.

'Will my daddy go to Jesus, miss?'

Frantically trying to think of something to say that might ease the child's worries, Margaret gazed into Joy's eyes, old beyond her tender years, and answered as best she could. 'Your daddy is very poorly, sweetheart. If the clever doctor at the hospital can help him, your dad might get better.'

Throwing Margaret a knowing look, Joy answered directly. 'I hear Mam crying all the time, and I see my dad growing weaker and weaker. They think, because I'm a child, I don't understand, but I do,' she insisted. Taking Margaret by the hand, she almost repeated the same words as her father had said, just hours before. 'I'm glad we've got you, Miss Margaret, you've made us all happy with your singing classes.'

Feeling yet another rush of tears, Margaret squeezed the child's hand. 'I think it should be me thanking you for your singing, sweetheart.'

They were interrupted by Arthur yelling across the lawn, 'Dinner's ready, we've got custard tarts!'

Sister Agnes had pulled out all the stops to please her young guests. Given the daily restrictions she faced – with rationing that was getting harder and harder with every passing week – she had managed somehow to make spam fritters, which she happened to know was the children's favourite. Light, crunchy batter wrapped around spam that had been flavoured with fresh herbs and pepper, served with mashed potatoes topped with a bit of Alf's tangy Lancashire cheese. Every single morsel disappeared off the children's plates, which they wiped clean with chunks of bread.

Arthur, who could never quite remember Sister Agnes's correct title, smiled his adorable gap-toothed smile at the doting nun. 'Thank you, Missus Agee, that were right tasty.'

Ever one to remember her manners and what her mother had taught her, Joy conscientiously asked, 'Thank you, can we wash up, miss?'

Arthur eyed the mountain of plates stacked on a trolley waiting to be taken into the kitchen. 'I don't want to wash up!' he burst out. 'We'd be in't kitchen all day with that lot.'

Agnes, who unapologetically adored cheeky Arthur, couldn't stop herself from bursting out laughing. 'You don't have to, lovie. Me and Sister Theresa have helpers who will see to the washing-up. But maybe you could give me a hand pushing the trolley?' she suggested.

Pleased as punch to be given a grown-up job, Arthur swaggered over to the loaded trolley – which he could barely budge.

'Give it a good shove,' Maisie laughingly called out, as she was finishing off her second helping of pudding.

Assisted by Agnes, Arthur managed to get the trolley rolling, passing smiling residents on the way, who fondly tousled his thick dark hair or patted him on the back.

'You're doing a grand job,' Agnes said.

Grinning, Arthur gazed up at the indulgent nun before cutely asking, 'When do we get our custards, miss?'

After pudding had been served, Maisie beckoned Joy to her side before the residents left the dining room. 'How do you feel about giving us a little sing-song?'

Joy turned to Margaret, who had overheard Maisie's request.

'I don't see why not,' she smiled.

Delighted, Maisie addressed the departing residents. 'Eh up, ladies, we've got entertainment in the sitting room, courtesy of Mary Vale's two little songbirds.'

When news spread through the Home that the Carter children were about to perform, as many of the staff as could be spared hurried into the sitting room to join in the fun. Sisters Theresa and Agnes abandoned the washing-up. Dora briefly left her helpers to it in the baby nursery, so she could nip down the hall to see what was going on, meeting Ada on the way. Giggling conspiratorially like naughty schoolgirls, the two women winked at each other.

'I did ask Matron if she could spare me,' Ada confessed.

'That was good of her,' Dora replied.

Ada grinned. 'Her only condition was that I return to the ward soon so that she gets a chance to hear the Carter children sing too.'

When Libby joined them, Dora chuckled. 'Looks like most of Mary Vale's staff are not quite where they should be.'

'I'll only stay for a few minutes,' Libby promised.

Outside, the garden was cold and frosty. But inside, all was warmth and good cheer, with a fire crackling in the hearth. Striking up the piano, Margaret accompanied Arthur's much-practised solos, 'Away In A Manger' and 'Silent Night', at the end of which the room resonated with the boy's high sweet notes. Margaret sensitively let the poignant moment linger before she played the opening chords of 'Oh Come, All Ye Faithful' followed by 'Hark! The Herald Angels Sing', which Joy and Arthur sang in perfect harmony.

After heartily applauding, the nursing staff hurried back to their posts, apart from Sisters Agnes and Theresa, who were having too much fun. After singing the popular Christmas song 'Walking In A Winter Wonderland', the thrilled audience demanded two encores. They could have sung 'White Christmas' all afternoon, if Joy and Arthur hadn't insisted on 'Rudolph The Red-Nosed Reindeer', which left the residents in jolly high spirits. As usual, the grateful residents (quite of their own accord) made a collection and presented it to the children at the end of their performance.

'Buy yourselves something nice,' Maisie said as she gave them both a big kiss on the cheek. 'You deserve it.'

Thrilled, the children gazed in delight at the coppers they'd been given.

'I'll buy our baby Susan a toy,' Joy happily promised.

After the entertainment had concluded, and the room was emptying out, Matron, who had replaced Ada, spotted Margaret looking quite worn out. Wasting no time, she briskly said, 'I insist you go upstairs and put your feet up, dear. You've never stopped all day, and you need to rest. I'll see that the children are looked after.'

Margaret, who really couldn't think of anything nicer, prevaricated. 'I'm fine,' she insisted.

Equally as insistent, Matron said firmly, 'Doctor's orders, off you go.'

After a welcome and very deep sleep, Margaret, somewhat bleary-eyed, went downstairs, where she could still hear merry singing. Curious, she hurried into the sitting room to find Sister Theresa sitting on the rug in front of the fire, with the Mary Vale cat purring on her lap and Arthur and Joy on either side of her, singing 'Jingle Bells'. The sight of them all, happy, relaxed and glowing in the warmth of the crackling fire, brought a smile to Margaret's face.

'What have you been up to?' she enquired. She tried her best to crouch down but found, because of her burgeoning tummy, she simply couldn't. 'Whoops,' she corrected herself, as she sat in a comfy chair instead.

Grabbing pieces of white card, Arthur explained. 'Sister Theresa's been helping us to make Christmas cards, look!'

Margaret stared at his scrawled crayon images of stars and Christmas trees, and then at Joy's more controlled, detailed seasonal images: Jesus in the manger, the Magi on their camels following a star, shepherds on a hillside watching their sheep.

'They're lovely,' she exclaimed.

'We're going to make a card for all of the ladies who live here,' Arthur excitedly told her.

'They're very kind to us,' Joy sweetly added.

'And they give us money whenever we sing,' naive Arthur said. 'We've made one for you too, Miss Margaret.'

Margaret threw him a teasing smile. 'Even though I don't give you money?'

'You do, miss. For our toffees and food and that. But anyway, that doesn't matter, miss, you give us the music instead.'

Touched by the thought that she supplied music in the children's lives, Margaret smiled to herself; it was something her parents had given her, and here she was in another part of the world, passing it on to other children.

Suddenly catching sight of the slanting sunlight fading in the garden, Margaret hurriedly checked her wristwatch. 'We'll have to leave soon,' she reminded her charges. 'I need to get you back home by bedtime.'

'Awww, miss, can we stay here tonight? It's lovely and warm,' Arthur begged.

Conscientious Joy frowned at her brother. 'Mother needs us at home,' she reminded him.

While the children packed up the cards and crayons that Sister Theresa had supplied, Margaret said to the young nun, 'Thank you for looking after them.'

Theresa's face lit up as she responded, 'Any time, Margaret. It's an absolute pleasure being with them,' she assured her. 'They taught me all their carols, even the ones I've never heard before. Really, I've had a wonderful afternoon.'

Gazing at Sister Theresa's innocent face glowing with happiness, Margaret thought, 'What a good woman she is – bless her.'

After the quick train ride into Grange, they were all freezing cold on the bus back to Allithwaite. By the time they had walked to the Carters' cottage, the children were chilled to the bone and tired.

When Mary opened the door to them, looking beyond weary, Margaret wished she had let the children stay overnight at Mary Vale, after all. Walking into the dank cottage, where the fire had gone out and Susan was miserably wailing, she saw all the joy of the day fade from Arthur and Joy's faces. Staring mutely at the empty bed their father had vacated, they turned to their mother for comfort.

Mary gave them both a brief hug before turning to Margaret. 'Thank you so much for looking after them,' she said.

'We had a very nice time,' Margaret reassured her kindly.

'We made Christmas cards, Mam,' Joy said.

Looking blank, Mary answered, 'That's nice, lovie.'

After stoking up the fire, Margaret urged the children to come and get warm. She watched Mary reach for a wailing Susan and hold the baby passively to her breast. Leaving the children by the fire, Margaret approached Mary, perched on the side of the bed.

'How was Sam when you left him?' she whispered.

'Better now that he's in there being properly looked after,' she answered, dropping her voice. 'The consultant fella didn't mince his words, though. He said he would do his best, but he warned me that if the disease has spread too far, my Sam might not make it till Christmas.'

24. Bed-Rest

Ordered to have total bed-rest, Beth had lain in her solitary room hearing the distant sweet sound of singing floating through the Home and reaching bed-bound patients like herself. Still a bit woozy from everything that had happened, when she heard sweet angelic voices Beth had thought that she was dreaming, but when she'd opened her eyes and could still hear them, she realized she wasn't dreaming at all. As the music continued in the background, Libby walked into her room.

'Who's been singing?' Beth asked.

'We've been enjoying a bit of unexpected entertainment in Mary Vale today. One of our residents is babysitting some children,' Libby explained. 'The kiddies are very popular with the residents, who always ask them to sing.' Approaching her pale-faced, weak patient, Libby asked, 'How are you feeling, dear?'

Beth's brow crinkled. 'Relieved to be here, and frightened about what might happen next,' she fearfully admitted.

Wanting to keep her patient as calm as possible, Libby said, 'Dr Reid will be here to examine you soon, Beth. Do you mind if I tidy you up a bit before he arrives?'

Scrambling to sit upright, Beth looked all set to hop out of bed.

'Stop,' Libby cried. 'You're confined to your bed until

the doctor says otherwise. I can wash and change you while you're lying there, you know.'

Soaping down Beth's thin pale body, Libby could see that the young woman must once have been lovely. Weight loss and abuse had taken its toll, but Beth's long legs, high breasts and slender shoulders hinted at the former attractive woman she must have been before Thorp destroyed her young life. After Libby had towel-dried her patient and freshened up her bedclothes, she brushed out Beth's long silver-blonde hair which, when not tangled, fell in soft silky waves around her shoulders. Though her face was still bruised, the witch hazel Libby had dabbed on to her cheekbone the night before had taken some of the lurid colour out of the bruise.

Used to seeing a haunted expression in Beth's arresting green eyes, Libby was relieved to see a spark of life there that she previously had never noticed. 'You're a very pretty woman,' she said warmly.

Beth looked positively surprised. 'I used to be,' she admitted, 'but I've not felt loved or beautiful in quite a long time.'

'Your circumstances have not been conducive to those kinds of emotions,' Libby answered realistically.

Beth gave a hard, mocking laugh. 'I was such a fool, Libby,' she groaned. 'Why did I ever think that marrying Thorp would be a good thing?'

'People do the maddest things when they're in love.'

'I just flew in the face of everybody's advice,' Beth confessed. 'Of course, I could see he was a hard, tough man, but that was a challenge. I thought I would influence him, change him for the better. The arrogance of youth,' she sighed. 'He lied about almost everything – his background, his family, his finances, his work – and I think he was a war dodger too. He said he had a bad leg, which was why he had never been called up. Believe me, there is physically absolutely nothing wrong with him at all, he's just a coward,' she ended hotly.

Libby rolled her eyes; of course the man was a war dodger. When most men were offering to fight for their country, unscrupulous Thorp, saving his own skin, would have been doing the exact opposite.

Purposefully turning to a brighter subject, Libby asked, 'Did you have boyfriends before you were married?'

'Plenty,' Beth smiled. 'Young lads from the Borrowdale valley; I'd grown up with most of them, gone to dances and kissed a few, before they were all called up when war broke out. Maybe it was the lack of local lads that attracted me to Ronnie. He was older than the boys I was used to, and he seemed like such a man of the world then, mature and sure of himself. I was flattered and infatuated by him, even though I was warned off him by my mother. When I look back, I can see clear as day that he was always after my money – well, my family's money – which, once we were married, he forced my poor father to hand over.'

'Why does that not surprise me?' Libby cynically wondered.

'What about you, Libby?' Beth giggled. 'Do you have a boyfriend?'

'ME?' she laughed. 'No!'

'Why not, you're a good-looking girl with a fine career.'

'It's the fine career bit that gets in the way of courting,' Libby explained. 'I love my work too much to want to swap it for a wedding ring and a family. It drives my mother to distraction; she'd love grandchildren and a devoted daughter close by.'

'It'll happen when Mr Right comes along,' Beth smiled.

'I hope that's not for a very long time,' Libby replied. 'I want to get Mary Vale's community nursing project well under way, and that means securing further funding in the New Year. I need to do some research, like investigate the county council to see if there's any possible funding there for Mary Vale – we can't always keep borrowing from the nuns in the convent.'

Looking surprised, Beth said, 'Did the convent pay for you to nurse me?'

'Yes, but don't tell them I told you,' Libby grinned.

'Well, I'm truly grateful,' Beth responded earnestly. 'I don't think I would have got through my pregnancy without your support and experience. If I had a pot of gold, I would certainly hand it over to the convent in deep gratitude for you.'

Touched by her kind words, Libby threw her patient a warm smile. 'You have been money well spent, dear,' she assured sweet Beth.

'I'm proud to be the patient who benefitted from Mary Vale's kindness. I hope the Home thinks it paid off,' Beth said nervously.

'I think they're glad that working in the community directed me to a patient in real need,' Libby answered diplomatically.

Beth vigorously nodded her head. 'God only knows what would have happened to me if you hadn't come knocking on my door, Libby.'

Their intimate discussion was brought to a halt when Jamie arrived.

Pleased to see Beth sitting up against her pillows, looking a thousand times better than when he had last seen her, Jamie smiled. 'How are we today, Mrs Thorp?'

Looking a little shy, Beth replied, 'I was just saying to Nurse Libby, I'm so grateful and relieved to be here, but frightened of what might happen next.'

'Hardly surprising, after your recent adventure,' Jamie responded. 'We were very worried about you, which is why we had to admit you as an emergency.'

'How is my baby?'

Now that Beth was safely under Mary Vale's roof, Jamie felt it was his duty to make the situation clearer to his delicate patient. 'I'm going to do some checks now, but I have to be honest, I have been concerned.'

Beth's hand flew to her mouth.

'Your baby's heart-beat was so weak when you were admitted, I thought we might have to perform an emergency Caesarean in order to save it.'

Alarmed, Beth cried, 'Why didn't you?'

'Because you were too weak, Mrs Thorp. You had lost blood – which is not what we want, in your anaemic condition – and according to Nurse Libby's notes,' he said as he glanced down at the medical chart hanging on the end of the metal hospital bed, 'you were running a temperature, and your blood pressure was high too. You were in no state to sustain surgery, so we did our best to stabilize you with round-the-clock monitoring and total bed-rest – which I hope is already making you feel stronger?'

'I certainly don't feel as weak and dizzy as I did,' Beth told him.

'With constant care, a good diet and total bed-rest, we should be able to build up your strength so that, with a bit of luck, we will be able to get you to full term.'

'That would be marvellous,' Beth exclaimed.

Taking out his stethoscope, Jamie said, 'Let's see how your baby is doing today.'

Using his own medical stethoscope instead of the Pinard model that Libby had previously used, Jamie listened attentively as he moved the instrument slowly and carefully over Beth's stomach. 'The heart-beat's a little better than it was,' he finally announced. 'Though I'd like it to be stronger,' he confessed.

'Surely, if I do everything you advise, my baby will grow stronger?'

'Your baby draws its strength from you, which is why you must rest, eat well and take great care of yourself. The same goes for your mental health; your baby will immediately pick up on any distress you might be experiencing. I appreciate that, in the past, it might have been difficult for you to maintain any equilibrium, but now that you're safely under Mary Vale's roof, you must concentrate on remaining as calm as possible, for your baby's sake.'

'Believe me, I feel calmer just for being here,' Beth fervently responded. But then, as fear got the better of her, she blurted out, 'Do you think my husband can force me to leave the Home?'

'He certainly wasn't happy yesterday when he heard that you had been admitted,' Jamie answered honestly.

'He was here!' Beth gasped.

'You were exhausted, which is why we moved you to a quiet private room,' Libby explained. 'You probably slept through most of what happened.' Not knowing just how much to say, she waited for Jamie to continue.

'Your husband wanted to discharge you,' he said.

Beth threw him a grim look. 'He would want me back, even if I was half dead.' Turning to Libby, she said with steely determination, 'I meant what I said, Libby, I would rather die than go back to living with Ronnie in Thorp Hall.'

Keen to avoid overexciting their patient, Libby spoke soothingly. 'I know, dear. I'm sure it won't come to that.'

Clearly not in the mood to be fobbed off, Beth insisted, 'What if he does come back again? My husband's not a man to be denied. How can I be sure that he won't drag me from out of this bed?'

'Right now, Mrs Thorp, it would be ethically irresponsible of us to discharge you in your weak condition. So far, we have managed to persuade your husband that a hospital environment is better for you.'

Awed by Jamie's calm professional summary of what had, in truth, been a charged and violent scene in the hallway, Libby marvelled at the doctor's ability to sidestep a question which he knew would trouble his patient.

'So, for the moment,' he concluded, with a cheerful smile, 'let's just concentrate on building up your strength, shall we?'

'I'll try my best, Doctor,' Beth promised.

'You have Nurse Libby here as your appointed nurse. I know she'll take the very best care of you.' Smiling as he left the room, Jamie said, 'I'll be popping by later to keep an eye on your progress.'

After he had left, Libby snugly tucked her patient up. 'Now, remember what the doctor said about eating well?'

Beth grimaced. 'I've not got much of an appetite,' she confessed.

'That's not the point, it's vital that you eat for two.'

Looking suitably chastised, Beth responded, 'I will eat more – even if it's liver, which I detest.' Clutching Libby's hand, she said with genuine desperation in her green eyes, 'I would do anything, absolutely anything, to keep my baby.'

Seeing her pain and the desperation in her patient's eyes, Libby squeezed her hand. 'We'll all do our best to take care of your baby, sweetheart.'

It might have taken Beth a lot longer to discover that one of the residents at Mary Vale had a direct connection with her husband, if she hadn't overheard Maisie and another resident, busy on cleaning duty, discussing the latest gossip in the ward corridor just outside her room.

'That brute of a man who came here, causing a commotion and disturbing the peace, is even more of a troublemaker than we thought,' Maisie announced as she slopped soapy water on to the floor, which she then vigorously mopped.

'Why, what's he done now?' her friend on the opposite side of the corridor enquired.

Obviously enjoying the bit of juicy gossip that she was about to impart, Maisie stopped mid-mopping to relish the moment. 'I've heard he's the one who's been threatening to evict those poor little kiddies that Margaret takes care of from their own home. The family's in a terrible state, with the father on his deathbed and the mother nursing a baby too.'

Flabbergasted, her friend gasped. 'He'd never go and do such a wicked thing!'

'You saw him with your own eyes yesterday, shouting and bawling, threatening nuns and anybody else who got in his way – I'd say the man's capable of anything. Look at the way he was with Glad. One look from him sent her into labour,' Maisie said dramatically. 'He's now't but a bully – going around threatening innocent women and children,' she added darkly. 'I'd say nothing's beyond a man like that.'

Continuing to chat, they carried on with their mopping, moving down the corridor and out of Beth's earshot as they did so. Desperate to get out of bed, to follow them and ask questions, Beth forced herself to lie still.

'They're talking about my husband. What on earth is he up to – evicting children from their homes?' she frantically asked herself.

By the time Libby arrived half an hour later to check up on her patient, Beth was in an agitated state.

Surprised that her patient's blood pressure was high again, Libby remarked, 'Your blood pressure has gone up since I left you, barely an hour ago – what's going on, lovie?'

Flushed and agitated, Beth came straight to the point. 'I heard some of the ladies discussing Ronnie in the corridor out there.' She nodded towards the door. 'They said he was going to evict a family, children that somebody here called Margaret looks after. Is it true?' she demanded.

Libby gave an inward groan; this was exactly the

emotional scenario that she and Dr Jamie were keen to avoid right now. Their priority was to keep their patient as calm and composed as possible, yet here was Beth demanding answers to questions that Libby knew would upset her.

Seeing her tense expression, Beth urged, 'Please, Libby, I will worry more if you don't tell me. I'd rather know the truth, particularly if it's from your own lips,' she said trustingly.

'I don't know much,' Libby prevaricated, 'but the family in question are tenants on one of the farms your husband manages.'

'And the children the ladies mentioned – the ones that the woman Margaret looks after?'

'Arthur and Joy Carter,' Libby told her. 'They were here today, you heard them singing earlier.'

'Those children!' Beth exclaimed in astonishment.

Libby nodded. 'They're in a choir that Margaret set up in the local school.'

Looking suddenly alert, Beth struggled to sit upright. 'Do you think I could meet this woman Margaret?'

Wary, Libby asked, 'Why?'

'Because I'd very much like to get to know the family my husband is planning to evict.'

25. A Fall-Back Plan

Before doing anything, Libby talked to Matron and Ada about Beth's request.

'She's asked to meet Margaret,' Libby explained. 'She's keen to get to know her, and the Carter family too.'

'She's got more than enough on her plate,' Ada protested. 'Does she really need to involve herself in more of her husband's dirty business.'

'I agree with you,' Libby responded. 'There's only so much anybody can take.'

'*But*,' Matron interjected, 'now that Beth is aware of the situation, she will worry anyway if we don't at least try to meet her halfway.'

Calling Matron by her first name – the one she used when they talked frankly, friend to friend – Ada said, 'You're so right, Ann, the worst thing we could do is leave her guessing.'

Coming in on the conversation, Libby added, 'Margaret Church is a highly responsible woman, I'd trust her to handle this tricky situation with discretion, especially if we brief her first.'

'I totally agree. Margaret is entirely responsible and mature enough to be sensible,' Matron concurred.

Later, when Libby encountered Margaret in the corridor outside the ante-natal ward, she seized the opportunity to pass on Beth's request.

Margaret responded in surprise. 'Goodness, if you think it's a good idea, but I really don't want to go stirring things up. From what I gather, the poor woman has been through enough as it is. Will hearing another horror story about her wretched husband help her peace of mind?'

'I totally agree with you, Beth's had a tough time.'

Having recently witnessed bombastic Thorp in the hallway, Margaret had no doubts about how extremely difficult that time would have been.

'She's highly emotional and very weak,' Libby continued, 'so tread carefully.'

Margaret raised an eyebrow. 'What if she starts asking a lot of awkward questions that might be difficult to answer?'

'Just do your best,' Libby urged, before ushering a cautious Margaret into Beth's private room.

After introducing the two women, who could not have looked more different – Margaret, in her thirties, dark-eyed, clever and dignified, and silver-haired, wide-eyed Beth, young and highly strung – Libby was keen to stay close to her patient and quietly busied herself about the room as they chatted.

'Thank you for agreeing to see me, Margaret,' Beth said politely. Then, showing unexpected composure, she asked a very direct question. 'I'm rather concerned about the Carter family, whom I gather my husband is planning to evict. Could you tell me more about their situation?'

Taking a deep breath, Margaret calmly related the events as objectively as she could. 'I gather Sam was a good, conscientious, hard worker who never took a day off until he unfortunately contracted TB and his health rapidly deteriorated.' Sticking only to the facts as they had been related to her, Margaret continued. 'Though advised to rest, Sam was so desperately in need of money to pay the rent and feed his family that he carried on, regardless of his illness, which did him no good at all.'

'Poor man, how awful for him,' Beth murmured.

Reaching the tricky bit of the narrative, where Thorp had systematically hounded the Carters, Margaret paused.

Seeing her hesitation, Beth said in a firm voice, 'Nothing you say about my husband will shock me, please continue.'

'When the Carters couldn't pay the rent, your husband constantly threatened them with eviction. He has given them no extra time to find the rent, or for Sam to get himself well enough to return to work.'

Remembering how she had suffered at the hands of her ruthless husband, Beth whispered, 'I feel so sorry for them all.'

'I only recently became acquainted with the family,' Margaret explained. 'Initially, it was through Arthur and Joy Carter, who sing in my choir, but then as I got to know Mary, the mother, I began to see quite how badly they are struggling, and I feel so sorry for them. I've visited them more often, with much-needed food and some warm clothing. Seeing them so destitute, and Sam so desperately poorly, I approached Dr Reid, who kindly agreed to visit Sam. To cut a long story short, Sam has now been admitted to Lancaster Infirmary, where he is being treated. But because of the severity of his advanced condition, it might be too late.'

'You mean he might die?' Beth gasped.

'Yes, there's a good chance that Sam might not recover.'

Having recounted the facts, Margaret fell silent.

'Thank you,' Beth said graciously. 'It's better to know the facts, rather than to imagine them. And,' she added, as she held Margaret's gaze, 'knowing my husband as well as I do, I expected nothing but bad news.'

'I only hope I haven't upset you?' Margaret nervously enquired.

Beth gave the weakest of smiles. 'Believe me, Margaret, I am well beyond being upset by anything Ronnie does,' she answered candidly. 'However, I would like to help the Carters, particularly the children, whom I heard singing recently. They sang so perfectly, I actually thought I was hearing angels in my sleep,' Beth confessed.

'They are truly amazing singers,' Margaret enthused. 'Though at times I wonder how they have the heart to sing, when their young lives are so relentlessly tough.'

After relating the Carters' grim story, Margaret visibly relaxed and the two women started to chat about their babies' due dates.

'Christmas time, if I can go that long,' Beth answered hesitantly.

'I'm the end of January,' Margaret said as she rolled a hand over her tummy.

'You're due after me, but I'm nowhere near as big as you,' Beth observed, with an edge to her voice.

Gazing across at the two pregnant women, Libby couldn't help but be struck by the sight of Margaret's full, round tummy – which was so heavy she was presently cradling it with both hands – while Beth's tummy looked so much smaller.

Hoping to avoid causing any concern to the anxious young woman in front of her, Margaret gave a reassuring smile. Telling a white lie, she replied, 'I think I've just piled on the weight – I was rather on the tubby side to start with.'

Seeing Beth looking suddenly tired, Libby approached the bed. 'I think it's time you had a nap now, dear,' she suggested.

Settling back down on her pillows, Beth said, 'Thanks for agreeing to see me, Margaret.'

'It's been a pleasure meeting you.'

Eager as a child to make a friend, Beth shyly asked, 'Please will you come back and talk to me some more? I get very lonely in here by myself all day.'

'Of course,' Margaret immediately agreed.

'And perhaps when Joy and Arthur are next in Mary Vale, I could meet them too?' Beth added. 'I'd certainly love to hear them sing again.'

'I think that can be arranged,' Margaret smiled.

After seeing Margaret out of the room, Libby drew her to one side in the corridor.

'I just wanted to thank you for keeping everything as low key as it can be in the circumstances, you got the tone just right,' she said.

'I certainly didn't want to upset the poor woman,' Margaret said with passion. 'What she must have gone through married to a monster like Thorp just doesn't bear thinking about.'

'How right you are,' Libby thought. Keeping further feelings to herself, she simply said, 'We're just so relieved that we managed to get her here.'

Looking worried, Margaret said, 'After hearing Thorp shouting and cursing in the hallway, I can't imagine that he's not going to come back for his wife. I have a strong suspicion that he is not the kind of man who ever gives up.'

'I know,' Libby responded grimly. 'Matron and Dr Reid have taken every precaution in the event that he does come back.'

'Let's hope it's enough to keep Thorp at bay,' Margaret said fervently.

'What do you think will happen to Mrs Carter and the children, now that Sam has been hospitalized?' thoughtful Libby enquired.

Margaret gave a heavy sigh. 'It's a conversation I need to have with Mary Carter, but talking about the future upsets her too much. The reality is, if Thorp carries out his threat and evicts the family before Christmas, where on earth will Mary and her children go?'

'It's a terrible thought,' Libby agreed. 'I don't understand the workings of Thorp's sadistic mind, he seems to delight in hurting others.'

'He's certainly had it in for the Carters.' Checking her little gold wristwatch, Margaret apologized. 'If you'll excuse me, I have a few jobs to finish off here before I get the train to Grange, I'm due at St Mark's this afternoon.'

When Ada discovered that Margaret was planning on going out for the afternoon, she stopped her patient in her tracks.

'I thought you were reducing your school hours, dear?'

'I have,' Margaret assured her. 'I only go into school once a week now, and that's to rehearse the choir.'

Keen to speak directly to Margaret while she was on

her own, Ada said, 'There's no doubt that you're pushing yourself. Have you thought about what might happen if you start to feel poorly, or just simply exhausted, around the time of your public carol services?'

Margaret gave a nervous little shrug.

'Expectant mothers tend to think that babies come on time, but they're sometimes early as well as late, especially if the mother pushes herself too hard. In my experience, nothing is predictable when it comes to childbirth,' Ada concluded.

Looking guilty, Margaret mumbled, 'I suppose I've just been hoping for the best.'

'Well, make sure you don't overdo it. You've not got long to go now, you know,' Ada said firmly.

On the train to Grange, Margaret carefully went over what Ada had quite rightly said. Her passion for the choir and her love of the children had driven all sense from her head. For all the reasons that Ada had stated she could quite easily take to her bed (just like Beth) and stay there until she gave birth, but then what would happen to all the arrangements she had made? Apart from disappointing the choir, who had worked so diligently and consistently, learning all the new pieces, with their complicated descants and harmonies, she would be letting the school and the community down too. She had already heard that plans were under way in Grange – the parish council were providing hot drinks in the town square during the carol service, and lighting little fires in braziers to keep the audience warm, and they had ordered the most magnificent Christmas tree to mark the occasion.

'I can't possibly disappoint all those good people,' Margaret fretted as she made her way down the little back streets to St Mark's School. 'Please God, I'll be able to enjoy the festivities, but Ada's right, maybe I need someone to help me with some of it, in case there's a day I don't feel up to a rehearsal. But who? It's a busy time of the year for everyone,' she berated herself. 'And it's not everybody's cup of tea, spending long hours with children in draughty halls and freezing town centres.' She had fitted perfectly into the role, but it wasn't to everybody's liking.

'Margaret Church,' she scolded. 'You cannot let these good people down – you need to sort something out right away, just in case.'

When the after-dinner play-time ended, Margaret gathered together her little group of sixteen children in the school hall where they regularly practised. As the eldest boy, Davie, rattled on about his dad and which pub they had graced with their company at the weekend, and how much money they had made, Margaret's eyes lit on Arthur and Joy looking distinctly down in the mouth. Normally, at the start of rehearsals, cheeky Arthur would be whizzing around the hall with his arms sticking out, pretending to be a Spitfire in pursuit of a Luftwaffe bomber, but today he just sat glumly on the floor beside his sister.

'What's the matter, sweetheart?' Margaret gently enquired. 'Aren't you feeling well?'

At which point, the little chap burst into tears.

Laying an arm across her brother's heaving shoulders, Joy explained, 'He misses our dad.'

Unable to physically hunker down beside the boy, Margaret leant forward to stroke his wiry dark hair. Murmuring sympathetically, she said, 'Of course you do.'

'That horrible shouty man's been banging on our door again,' Arthur added on a choked sob.

'He means the landlord,' Joy again explained. 'We heard him telling Mam he wants us out by Christmas.'

Margaret's heart sank. Her worst predictions were already becoming a reality.

'Where will we go, miss?' Joy asked as she too started to sob.

Seeing the other pupils getting restless, and afraid they might start to ask difficult questions, Margaret whispered to the two tremulous children, 'Would you like to sit the rehearsal out?'

'No, miss,' Joy insisted. 'Singing always cheers us both up.'

Margaret hoped that singing carols would help. Though Arthur lacked his usual breezy cheerfulness, and Joy stumbled a few times over her harmonies, they got through the rehearsal, after which Margaret slipped them a two-shilling piece.

'Buy something nice for tea on your way home, and make sure you buy something tasty for your mam too.'

Thrilled, the children hugged her. 'Thanks, miss,' they cried.

'Will you come and see our mam soon?' Joy asked, before she sped off after Arthur.

'Yes,' Margaret assured the anxious child. 'I'll come just as soon as I can.'

Watching the children walk away hand in hand, Margaret's thoughts flew to Thorp.

He simply delights in hurting people, she thought furiously. His wife, his tenants, innocent children, women, even baby Susan. What is wrong with the man, and where in God's name will it all stop?'

26. A Group Effort

The next day, though Mary Vale's doors were bolted, Thorp banged on them until Sister Agnes, afraid the thundering noise and continued shouting would upset the residents, reluctantly opened them. When Thorp came raging in, demanding to see his wife, Ada caught sight of him storming down the corridor, clearly intent on no good.

'Oh my God, Thorp's back!' she muttered to Libby, who had turned pale at the sight of the man she detested most in the world. 'Quickly, Libby,' Ada added under her breath, 'run and fetch Jamie.'

Libby did a startled double-take. 'Dr Reid?'

'We're urgently going to need him here to explain a few things,' Ada continued. 'Run down the back lane – tell him to come up quickly, with Catherine.'

Without a second's hesitation Libby went the opposite way down the corridor, avoiding Thorp, then out through the kitchen door, to speed down the farm track that led to Ada and Jamie's cottage.

'Ada's sent me to fetch you,' she gasped when Jamie opened the door. 'Ronnie Thorp's on the war path.'

Almost as if he had been expecting the news, Jamie moved calmly to collect his coat. 'Okay, I'll be right there,' he said as he attempted to pick up Catherine.

The little girl started to cry. 'Want to play with Teddy,' she protested as she wriggled in his arms.

Frantic Libby urged Jamie to be on his way. 'I'll take Catherine, please just go. We'll catch you up.'

'Thanks,' Jamie called over his shoulder as he ran out of the door, leaving Libby to collect Catherine's favourite toy.

'Let's take Teddy for a walk,' she said persuasively. 'We can see Snowball on our way, if we hurry.'

Hearing the name of her favourite pony, Catherine gurgled in delight. 'Gee-gee,' she said, and toddled out of the house as quickly as her strong little legs would allow.

Thinking he might need the prestige of his doctor's white coat, Jamie quickly grabbed it from his surgery. Then, breathless with running, he joined his wife in the corridor outside Beth's private room where Thorp was standing with a face like thunder.

Looking flushed but very determined, Ada politely addressed her husband. 'Doctor,' she said, with obvious relief. 'Mr Thorp here is keen to see his wife.'

'And this woman here is getting in my way,' Thorp growled.

Playing for time, Jamie checked his wristwatch. 'It's rather early for visiting,' he said blandly.

'I don't give two bloody figs about visiting time,' Thorp sneered. Glaring at Jamie, he added in a voice thick with fury, 'You're the interfering fella who came bothering me before, trespassing on my property and telling me what to do. Don't think you can start that baloney now.' Jabbing a stubby finger in the direction of Beth's door, he declared, 'I'm going in there to see my wife, whether you like it or not.'

As Thorp turned back to Jamie, Ada, terrified of how Beth might be reacting on hearing her husband's violent threats, slipped into the room to safeguard her patient.

'Mr Thorp, I'm sure you're aware that your wife has been admitted to Mary Vale for a number of very significant reasons.'

Waving his arms dismissively in the air, Thorp said, 'Aye, I've heard 'em all before. Starting with the snivelling midwife who put all sorts of soft fancy notions into my wife's head.'

'She was only doing her job, sir,' Jamie reminded him. 'Just like I am only doing mine now.' Looking at Beth's hospital notes, which he had brought along with him, Jamie repeated almost word for word what Matron had previously told Thorp. Running down the list of Beth's serious complaints, he then looked up from the notes and said, with great emphasis, 'We are treating your wife as best we can; she's been ordered to stay on bed-rest, which means under no circumstances can she leave, for fear of her haemorrhaging and losing the baby, who has a weak heart-beat and is underweight.'

Barging at the door, Thorp cried, 'I've had enough of this – to hell with the lot of you!'

When the door flew open, Thorp briefly stopped in his tracks. In the short time available to her, Ada had managed to lay Beth flat out on the bed, and pull the hospital bedding up to her chin. She had scraped the young woman's hair back from her pale face, revealing the shadow of a bruise Thorp had recently inflicted. The very sight of her raging husband had brought Beth out in a sheen of sweat, and her eyes were genuinely wild with fear.

Quickly recovering himself, Thorp strode to the bottom of the bed from where he growled at his trembling wife. 'So, you've finally got your own way, you snivelling sop of a woman, convinced this bunch of fools that you need special care and attention.' Seeing his wife weeping, Thorp scoffed, 'Go on, let's have the theatricals, they might wash with these fools, but they don't wash with me.'

Thoroughly outraged by the man's malevolent presence, Ada advanced on Thorp, her vivid-blue eyes flashing. Luckily, Jamie, who knew the extent of his wife's temper when faced with injustice, quickly stepped in.

'Mr Thorp,' he said, in a voice that was steely with determination. 'I'm afraid I have to ask you to leave.'

Beth's distress was growing, her tears now raining down her cheeks. 'Please,' she begged as she clutched Ada's arm, 'get him out of here.'

'Shhh, dear,' Ada soothed.

'Don't let him touch me!' Beth, now thoroughly distressed, was whimpering in her bed.

'Sir, you are doing more harm than good by staying here,' Jamie urged, worried for his patient's frail health.

'She's having you on,' Thorp roared. 'I've a good mind to drag her from that bed and show her who's the boss.'

Already pale, Beth went a ghostly white as Thorp threatened her with the thing she most feared.

'You cannot do that, Mr Thorp,' Jamie announced. 'I cannot let you remove my patient in this condition.' Then, appealing to any humanity that Thorp might possibly have, he whispered, 'If you carry out this threat, your wife and child will almost certainly die.'

Thorp lingered long enough to throw his wife a filthy

look. Then, barging into Jamie so hard he nearly knocked him over, he stormed out of the room, calling over his shoulder, 'Keep her – you're welcome.'

The second he had left the room, Ada ran to the door to slam it shut.

On the point of passing out, Beth cried, 'He'll come back for me, I know he'll come back.'

'No, he won't,' Jamie said through gritted teeth. 'If he ever tries to enter this building again, I'll call the police. The man's intent on evil,' he muttered under his breath. Turning to Ada, he whispered, 'Make absolutely sure he's gone, then lock and bolt the door. Tell Sister Agnes, and everyone else, that under no circumstances – I repeat, *no circumstances* – must the door be opened to Thorp again.'

Leaving her husband attending to the patient, Ada slipped out of the room and made her way along the corridor. Keeping her distance, she silently followed Thorp. He finally left the building, thunderously slamming the door closed behind him. After dashing forward to lock and bolt it, Ada slithered to the ground trembling, which was where Libby and Catherine found her a few minutes later.

'Mama!' Catherine cried in delight, as if finding her mother crouched on the ground was an everyday occurrence.

'Hello, sweetheart,' Ada said feebly as she struggled to her feet and cuddled her daughter. Realizing she was shaking with nerves, she turned to Libby. 'Thank God in heaven – he's gone.'

Libby gave a grim nod. 'We saw him leave. I must admit, we hid,' she confessed. 'When I saw him storming out with a face like thunder, I grabbed Catherine and we hid behind the kitchen wall.'

Ada gave a weak smile. 'Wise move – the mood he was in, he would have picked a fight with the Devil himself.'

Looking tense, Libby asked, 'Is Beth all right?'

Ada shook her head. 'She all but fainted in fear when Thorp burst in on her.' Shuddering as she recalled the words and insults Thorp had thrown at his wife, she added, 'I have never witnessed such a scene of complete abuse in all my working life. The man is simply a monster.'

'What's a monster, mama?' Catherine innocently enquired.

'Not a very nice person, sweetheart,' Ada answered as she kissed her pretty daughter on both of her rosy cheeks. Turning to Libby, she said, 'You get back to Beth, Jamie's with her now, I'll take care of Catherine.'

Looking relieved, Libby set off down the corridor.

'Thanks for acting so promptly,' Ada called after her.

Creeping into Beth's room, Libby felt tears sting the back of her eyes.

Sweet Jesus, she thought. How much more can this wretched woman take? Hurrying to Beth's side, she took hold of her limp hand and, without even realizing what she was doing, she quite instinctively felt her pulse.

'It's rapid again,' Jamie said grimly. 'And her blood pressure, usually so low, was sky high after the stress of Thorp's arrival. And no wonder,' he added, with huge compassion. 'I think she genuinely fears for her life when he starts on at her.'

Gazing at Beth, now dozing fretfully, Libby answered softly, 'She looks completely worn out.'

'God in heaven!' Jamie finally gave vent to his anger.

'What beast of a man would do this to a poor helpless woman who is, after all, carrying his child?'

Libby gave a deep, heartfelt sigh. 'My exact feelings since I first laid eyes on Thorp. *But*,' she added in defiant pleasure, 'Beth's still here, you beat Thorp down, quite an achievement, Dr Jamie. I saw him leave just now, and he was livid,' she said, with undisguised glee.

'I've just told Ada to alert the staff – Thorp's never to be allowed entry again. I won't allow him back in, even if I have to fight him off with my bare hands. I will not allow him to treat Beth – or anybody else, for that matter – the way he did just now.'

Turning to her beloved patient, Libby murmured, 'Is she going to be all right?'

Looking miserable, Jamie responded, 'All the good work we've done here – bed-rest, constant care, coaxing her appetite – could be for nothing if that man has sent her back to square one.'

Choking back her sadness, Libby said, 'And the baby?'

Jamie answered with professional frankness. 'If she doesn't rally from Thorp's onslaught, the baby's chances are minimal.'

The following day was Libby's day off. But before she even visited Snowball, whom she planned to ride that day, she hurried to see Beth. Gently opening the door, dressed in her riding slacks and woolly jumper, she stepped inside the quiet room and crept up to her patient.

Hearing Libby's approach, Beth's eyes flew open. 'Hah!' she gasped. 'Has he come back?'

'No, no,' Libby answered gently. 'Dr Reid won't be

allowing your husband back in a hurry,' she assured her edgy patient. Perching on the side of the bed, she whispered, 'How are you feeling today, sweetheart?'

'Happy to see you,' Beth answered, with the sweet honesty of a child. Noticing that Libby wasn't wearing her nurse's uniform, she added, 'Why are you dressed like that?'

'It's my day off, and I'm going riding,' Libby announced, with a bright smile.

'Enjoy yourself,' Beth said warmly. 'I used to love riding; I had a sweet fell pony that my father gave me. I rode him the length of the Borrowdale valley.'

The yearning in her voice made Libby's heart ache. 'You'll ride again, Beth, for sure,' she said heartily. 'Rest now, and get your strength back,' she urged as she rose to go. 'Ada's on duty, so you'll be well taken care of.' Wagging a finger, she teased, 'I shall check with her that you've eaten your dinner.'

'Bye, Libby,' Beth smiled. 'Enjoy your day off.'

27. Libby's Day Off

As soon as she had said goodbye to Beth, Libby gathered up her warm coat and riding boots, and hurried to the kitchen to collect the picnic that Sister Agnes had kindly prepared for her.

'There's a letter arrived for you,' the cheery nun said as she handed over both the picnic parcel and the letter.

'Thank you, Sister,' Libby gratefully replied as she stuffed the letter into her coat pocket. 'I recognize the writing, it's from my mother.'

'Aren't you going to read it?' Agnes asked.

'I will later,' Libby told her. 'I just want to get going, I've already wasted half the morning as it is.'

Following her to the back door, Agnes mused, 'Your mother must miss you.'

'She does,' Libby agreed. 'It's worse for her with us all gone from home now.'

The nun gave a sympathetic cluck of her tongue. 'What with you working here, and your brothers away fighting for their country, your mother must be a very proud woman.'

Libby's big violet-blue eyes were full of concern. 'She is proud, but she's lonely too, and worried sick about my brothers most of the time.'

'I'll say some prayers for her,' Agnes promised.

'Please do,' Libby begged. 'And thanks again for the

picnic,' she said hurriedly as she ran down the back lane to the farm.

Watching her tear down the track, with her long golden-red hair flying in the cold December wind, Sister Agnes smiled fondly. 'God love the girl,' she said. 'She certainly deserves a day off.'

Snowball welcomed his mistress with a rapturous neigh. Having fed and groomed her earlier that morning, Libby quickly tacked her pony up.

'It's a beautiful day,' she chatted as she tightened Snowball's girths, and got a nudge in the stomach from her protesting pony. 'Bright and crisp and clear, perfect for a ride out.'

Mounting, she gathered up the reins, and set off out of the farmyard with an excited smile on her face. Hearing the sound of Snowball's clip-clopping hooves, Alf came hurrying out of the cowshed.

'Aye-aye,' he grinned. 'Off out, are we?'

Libby nodded. 'I thought I'd skirt around the woods, then take the coast path along the edge of the marsh. I fancy a long ride by the sea,' she told him.

'Sister Agnes has asked for some mackerel,' Alf grinned. 'I might do a bit of fishing down there myself, though it's a proper cold day. I hope you're well wrapped up?' he enquired. 'There's no hiding from the chill wind out on yonder marsh.'

'Hopefully it will blow the cobwebs away,' Libby laughed. 'I feel like I've been cooped up for too long.'

As Libby clicked Snowball on, Alf called a warning

after her. 'Don't forget how short these winter days are. You don't want to get lost in the dark.'

Waving her thanks, Libby trotted off down the farm track. After a long gallop over open fields, she slowed her pony so they could take in the tranquillity of the peaceful day. As Alf had predicted, it was chillingly cold.

Cold enough to snow, Libby thought.

Once they were close to the woods, dense with enormous ancient beeches and oak trees, the air felt milder. Finding a sheltered spot close to a bubbling beck, Libby led Snowball to a shallow part of the stream where he could drink his fill of sweet, cold water while Libby relished the delicious taste of Sister Agnes's tangy, sharp Lancashire cheese and home-made piccalilli sandwiches. After giving Snowball the apple that Sister Agnes had packed, Libby poured hot tea from the Thermos she had brought along with her. Then, settling down with her back against a stout tree, she read her mother's letter.

My dear Libby,

Just to let you know our Tom had a nice leave at home recently, but it was terrible having to say goodbye to him. Three days just flew by, not that I'm complaining, three days is better than none at all, but it was so hard to see the lad go, especially looking so thin and tired as he does. He's returning to his Army base, with no clear idea of where he'll go next. Have you been following the news, lovie? Your dad and I have been hearing on the wireless of the Germans' attack on the Allied forces in a massive forest somewhere in Belgium.

Feeling guilty that she hadn't even had a moment recently to sit and listen to the wireless in order to catch up with war news, Libby eagerly read on.

They're calling it the Battle of the Bulge. Your dad explained it's got that name because of the Germans trying to push through and break the enemy line, which after all this time of the Allies gaining ground in that area would be a terrible loss. It must be so demoralizing for our lads, losing territory they fought so hard to gain. Thank God bad weather is hampering the Germans, long may it stay that way, I say.

On the brighter side, our Tom was telling us some good war news. Evacuees are being allowed to return home to areas that are unaffected by the V-rocket attacks. Imagine that! How many happy children must be going home at last? I can't wait for my precious boys to come safely home. The fact that they've survived so far is a blessing, but every day the war continues is another day of fear. With the Germans suffering so many recent defeats, the shoe is definitely on the other foot, we've really got Gerry on the run. The end must surely be in sight but, in truth, nobody dares to get their hopes up.

We've not heard much from you lately, Libby. I suppose you must be rushed off your feet. Try and spare a minute to write home. We miss you so much.

Your ever devoted,
Mum and Dad

After folding up the letter and returning it to her pocket, Libby sighed. She really should have spent some of her day off writing back to her mother, instead of galloping around the countryside thinking only of her own pleasure.

Remounting Snowball, she trotted off in thoughtful mood. Having lived so long with war, she let her mind wander to the possibility of conflict ending. What would it be like to finally live in peace? The thought made her flesh tingle, but what was the reality? There wouldn't suddenly be a miraculous amount of food available; she had read that rationing would go on for years, until the country got back on its feet. Here in the Lake District, far away from most of the bombing (though the Barrow-in-Furness shipyards were constantly targeted by the Luftwaffe), most towns had remained intact, but what of cities like Manchester, Liverpool, Coventry? Reduced to smouldering ruins over years of heavy bombing. Cities would have to grow again, be rebuilt, to provide homes for the heroic men who had fought for the nation's freedom. And what about those who had lost their lives in the cause, leaving behind widows and children whom the state had a duty to care for? Libby shook her head at the immensity of what lay ahead.

'Just pray the war ends soon, and worry about the rest later,' she told herself as she moved Snowball into a steady canter.

By the time she reached the coastal track, the sun was starting its slow descent over the Irish Sea. Knowing she had a few hours of daylight left, Libby wasn't unduly worried; she could enjoy the ride over soft sandy ground, while admiring the marsh where the tide was slowly going out, leaving sand dunes and rock pools in its wake. As little rivulets trickled away from gullies and inlets, Snowball was tugging at tough grasses growing by the side of the track and Libby watched sea-birds squabbling with each other over morsels left in the tidal rock pools. Squawking and screeching in the shallows, long-legged redshanks, oystercatchers and piping curlews dibbled eagerly with their long beaks for worms and molluscs washed in by the tide. Even though the wind was freezing her face, Libby stopped briefly to admire the blazing sun's scarlet and orange rays reflected in the rippling waves. Warming her hands under Snowball's thick silver mane, she shivered. Feeling the cold too, Snowball stamped his hooves impatiently.

'Righty-ho,' she agreed as she gathered up the reins. 'Time to head for home.'

Needing no urging, Snowball tossed his pretty little head, then trotted briskly up the path hedged by bushes and shrubs, with occasional breaks where tidal streams leading to boathouses and abandoned sheds sliced into the land. In places where inlets cut deep, the coastal path turned and twisted through narrow lanes and alleyways that were off the beaten track. It was in one such place that, dipping her head to avoid overhanging branches, Libby spotted what she thought in the fading light was an abandoned car. Thinking little of it, she would have moved on, but a light flashing on in a cobbled yard, followed by the sound of a car door opening, caused her to pause and note that the car was, in fact, not abandoned but actually quite smart-looking. Leaving at speed, it pulled out on to the footpath, right in front of her. Screeching sharply, the driver slammed on his brakes before blazing away down the track.

But in the brief moment before he screeched away, Libby saw who the driver was. 'Thorp!' she gasped.

By now thoroughly spooked by the sudden noise and flashing car lights, Snowball reared, and Libby held tightly on to his reins, struggling to keep him under control.

'Whoa there,' she soothed, 'Whoa there, now.'

Once Snowball was calm, Libby, curious as to what Thorp might have been up to in such a lonely isolated area, turned into the yard and swept her keen blue eyes over the cobbled entry leading up to an apparently run-down warehouse. With twilight descending, Libby knew she should be on her way, but realizing that the building before her was in some way connected to Thorp was an irresistible draw. Determined to investigate further, she led Snowball back on to the coast path to tether him up beside a patch of grass that he could nibble.

'Be a good boy,' she told him. 'I'll just have a quick snoop around. Back in a jiffy.'

Clearly annoyed that he wasn't, in fact, returning to a warm stable and a fresh net of hay, Snowball protested with an indignant neigh. Whispering over her shoulder as she went, Libby said, 'I won't be long – promise.'

Not surprisingly, the warehouse door was locked, and Libby's efforts to peep through the ground-floor windows were marred by blackout blinds. With her curiosity thoroughly aroused, Libby made her way along the side of the building, only to find there were no windows at all. Round the back there were several more blacked-out windows and a back door, which was also locked. Frustrated, but aware of the growing dark, Libby turned to leave, noticing as she did so that one of the windows had been smashed. On closer inspection, she saw that the hole in the window was large enough for her to poke her hand through and lift the latch. With her heart now beating wildly, Libby eased open the window as wide as it would go, then climbed carefully on to the sill from where she lowered her body down. Stretching out with her feet, Libby wriggled around as she tried to feel the ground; too late, she realized there was no immediate solid ground to land on. But by that time she had released her grip and consequently fallen a good five feet into a gloomy semi-basement. Groping around on her hands and knees, Libby cracked her head against a couple of low shelves, until she finally reached a wall where she pulled herself into an upright position. Feeling her way along the wall, she came across more shelves, loaded with boxes and cases, all smelling heavily of alcohol. Frightened by the cloying darkness, Libby gasped in relief when she felt a light switch on the wall. But just as she was about to throw it, she heard the sound of a car pulling up at the front of the building.

'NO!' she muttered.

Frantically groping in the dark, she had no idea where she could hide; she was also terrified that, if Thorp entered the room, he would notice the open window she'd climbed through. Falling to her knees, she crawled under a low shelf where she lay with her face pressed against the floor. When the door flew open and a shaft of light illuminated the semi-basement space, Libby saw with relief that Thorp didn't seem to have noticed the window.

Worried her legs might be visible, Libby wriggled further underneath the shelf and held her breath while she curled herself up as small as the restricted space would allow.

'It's all in here, as much as you want,' Thorp's loud swaggering voice boomed out.

'How many cases?' a deep growly voice responded.

'Like I said, as much as you want,' Thorp answered gruffly.

'And fags?'

Thorp gave a deep satisfied laugh. 'As many as you can handle.'

'What about the delivery?'

Thorp's reply was brusque and to the point. 'I arrange that. Once you've paid up front – in notes – I ship the goods out across the bay overnight.'

Libby smothered a cry of surprise. 'Oh my God! Thorp's running a black-market business, right under our very noses.' Hardly daring to breathe, Libby listened intently from her cramped hiding place.

Suddenly suspicious, the man said, 'If it don't arrive, you might find a knife in your back.'

Turning nasty, Thorp snarled, 'And you might find a gun at your head, if you should so much as breathe a word about this place.'

'I think we understand one another,' the man said coldly. 'When will I know you've made the drop?'

'When I tell you,' Thorp answered curtly. 'I'll leave a message at your office. Now, if we're done,' he said as he switched off the light, 'let's lock up and get out of here.'

When the door closed behind the men, Libby was once more cast into near total darkness. It was only after she heard the front door slam shut that she even dared wriggle out from her hiding place. Now completely desperate to get away, Libby scrambled back to the window – which, to her horror, she realized she couldn't reach. No matter how many times she tried jumping up to grasp the sill, she couldn't catch hold of it.

Slumping breathless on the ground, Libby cursed her own stupidity. 'What in God's name was I thinking of?' she raged at herself. 'I could be stuck here all night, possibly longer, if I can't find a way out of here.'

Remembering the boxes she had tripped over, Libby groped yet again in the murky darkness until she located them. Heaving and tugging, she lugged several of them to the window and stacked them one on top of the other. If she stood on her tiptoes, she could reach the sill, and just about peep over, but she could find nothing to grip in order to lever herself up. After trying at least half a dozen times, Libby fell back to the floor, utterly exhausted. Lying there on the verge of tears, she heard the distant sound of Snowball neighing.

'Poor lamb,' she fretted. 'Snowball's stuck, just like me.'

Now thoroughly wretched and worried sick about her pony, who would be so cold and hungry, Libby began to cry. With her head in her hands, she didn't at first see a flash of light, but she did hear a hoarse voice. Thinking Thorp was back, Libby gasped in fear and crouched low.

'Are you there, lass?' she heard somebody call.

'That's not Thorp,' she exclaimed as she jumped on to the piled-up boxes.

'Libby, are you there?'

The familiar sound of Alf's deep warm voice sent a

shot of pure adrenalin through Libby, who cried out, 'Alf! I'm over here.'

Shining a torch, Alf located Libby's head peeping out of the basement window. Flabbergasted, he cried, 'What the 'ell are you up to?'

'It's a long story, Alf,' she whispered. 'Please,' she begged. 'Just get me out of here.'

'Here, take this,' Alf said as he thrust the torch into her hands. 'Shine it down on to me, then I can see where I'm going.'

Doing as he instructed, she directed Alf to the window. 'I'm stuck,' she confessed. 'You'll have to drag me out,' she told him. 'Can you mange that?'

Alf's response in the semi-darkness was resoundingly indignant. 'I've lifted hay bales heavier than you,' he declared. 'Give us your hands.'

Still holding tightly on to the torch, Libby stretched as far as she could, extending her hands.

Alf gripped them fast. 'Ready?'

'Yes,' she cried.

'One, two, three . . . pull!'

Astonished at how strong Alf actually was, Libby felt her body rise, and as soon as she was high enough up, she grasped the widow casement. Then after briefly balancing her weight against it, she jumped to the ground and flung her arms around the old man who – clearly relieved that she was safe and sound – briefly clutched her close to his chest.

'Oh, Alf,' she sobbed. 'I'm sooooo glad to see you.'

Riding home on Snowball, with Alf leading the pony

along the now pitch-dark track, his fishing rod over his back, Libby listened as the farmer related how he'd happened across the warehouse.

'I'd done a bit of fishing, as I mentioned I might. But when it grew too cold to stay out any longer, I set off for home. I couldn't believe my eyes when I stumbled across Snowball tethered by the track.'

'Poor lad,' Libby said as she leant forward to bury her face in her pony's thick warm mane. 'I'm so glad I left him on the track; if I'd taken him into the warehouse grounds, you would have missed him altogether.'

'I can tell you, he weren't happy, stamping his feet and snorting, he was. Knowing how attached you are to Snowball, I was sure you wouldn't be far away, so I took out mi torch and came looking for you.'

'Thank God you did, Alf,' she said, with heartfelt gratitude.

Back at the farm, after she had groomed, fed and watered Snowball and left him warm and cosy in his stable, Libby rushed over to Alf's cottage to find he'd already brewed a pot of tea and stoked up the fire.

'Get theeself warm, lass, and then there'll be time to explain yourself,' he urged as he poured scalding-hot tea into pint pot mugs and added milk.

Cradling the hot mug in her freezing-cold hands, Libby proceeded to explain why she had sneaked into the warehouse. 'I know it was stupid and dangerous, going into that empty place in the dark, but you see, I saw Thorp down there and it sparked my curiosity.'

'That's as maybe,' Alf scolded. 'You could've waited for

somebody to accompany you, instead of being so damn foolhardy, you were asking for trouble.'

Trying to justify herself, Libby added, 'I thought I'd be okay.'

Alf shook his head in despair. 'Bloody headstrong, if you ask me.'

'I'd just seen Thorp drive away,' Libby cried. 'I simply had to find out what was going on. When Thorp came back with another man, I was terrified. Can you imagine what he would have done if he'd found me sneaking around in there?'

Rolling his eyes, Alf grunted, 'I'd rather not, to be honest.'

Now thoroughly excited, Libby pushed on. 'But Alf, the place is stuffed with black-market goods. Thorp was arranging a deal right under my eyes – I heard every word.'

'You heard him?'

'Every word,' she assured him. 'And I saw his stash too – cases and cases stacked up in that basement.'

'But it were nearly pitch dark,' Alf recalled.

'When Thorp came back with a customer, he switched on the light so the man he was with could make his order.'

'Where were you when all this ordering was going on?'

'I was on the floor, squashed under a shelf, I could barely breathe,' she told him. 'But I could see floor-to-ceiling shelves full of boxes and crates.'

Sitting back in his old wooden chair, Alf lit up his pipe and puffed thoughtfully on it for several minutes. 'I heard folk say Thorp was up to no good,' he ruminated. 'Did you pick up on anything else, lass?'

Libby nodded eagerly. 'He ships the stuff out himself, overnight, to the other side of the bay.'

'The bugger's got it all figured out,' Alf reflected. 'If you hadn't stumbled across his hidey hole, nobody would be any the wiser.'

Impatient and restless, Libby asked, 'So, what do we do now?'

Laying his pipe aside, Alf stood up. 'We notify the police, of course. Come on,' he said as he grabbed his old jacket and headed for the door.

'Where are we going?'

'To ask Matron if we can use her phone.'

28. Sisters of Charity

While Libby was uncovering Thorp's black-market stash, Margaret, with Ada's warning words ringing round her head, was in the process of finding somebody who could help her with St Mark's choir through the Christmas festivities. Aware that Sister Theresa usually did a morning shift in the kitchen, after which the young nun helped out on the wards before returning to the convent for evensong, Margaret lingered just after dinner-time. Spotting Theresa heading down the corridor that connected the hospital wing to the main house, Margaret hurried (as much as her baby bump would allow) after her.

'I'm so sorry to trouble you, Sister,' she said, rather breathlessly, 'but I wondered if I might have a word with you?'

Smiling sweetly, Theresa replied, 'Of course.'

'I have an enormous favour to beg of you,' Margaret started. 'You see, I may well need help with my little choir.'

Looking surprised, the nun said, 'Oh, I do hope everything is all right?'

'The choir is fine,' Margaret quickly assured her. 'I'm just finding it a little tiring, and would love a bit of help.' She outlined what Ada had spoken to her about a few days earlier. 'To be blunt, Sister, I think it would be wise to have someone helping me with this, just in case I ever have to miss a rehearsal if I'm not feeling up to it.'

Theresa gave an understanding nod. 'Sister Ada is quite right, you are well advanced in your pregnancy,' she observed.

'I'm actually really grateful to Ada for her advice. If the truth be known, I am beginning to feel a little tired these days,' Margaret confessed.

'I'm not at all surprised, you've certainly been pushing yourself.' Sister Theresa smiled kindly. 'It would be such a pity if this lovely project made you unwell. I quite see your point, dear – they are really an adorable group of children, and talented too.'

Seeing the nun's caring expression, Margaret came straight to the point. 'Forgive me for asking, but I wondered if *you* would consider helping me, Sister?' Having managed to actually articulate her request, an embarrassed Margaret stumbled on. 'You're so good with children, you would be perfect – that's if you could possibly spare the time, of course.'

Willing Theresa didn't hesitate. 'I'd be delighted,' she responded. 'I had such a sweet time with Arthur and Joy the other day; they taught me all their carols and made me sing in harmony with them. I loved it.'

'Actually,' Margaret quickly added, 'we're having an after-school practice later, it would be a perfect opportunity for you to get to know the choir. Would you care to come along, if you can be spared?'

'I should have finished my ward duties by then, but I will have to get permission from Reverend Mother to leave the convent,' Theresa pointed out. 'I'll check and get back to you right away,' she promised.

Shortly after, while Margaret was having a rest and

reading the paper in the sitting room, Theresa appeared with a bright smile on her face.

'Reverend Mother has granted me permission to attend your choir practice,' she announced. 'Just so long as I'm back in time for evening prayers.'

'That's marvellous,' Margaret declared, then quickly added, 'I should have mentioned before that I'm bringing the Carter children back to Mary Vale after the rehearsal. Mary is visiting her husband in Lancaster Infirmary, and children are not allowed on the ward. She might not get back till late, so I've arranged with Matron for Arthur and Joy to stay overnight at Mary Vale. They're very excited.' Margaret smiled. 'I just hope I can get them to bed early, and they don't disturb the residents.'

Theresa threw her a knowing look. 'Try telling that to cheeky Arthur Carter,' she chuckled.

When the two women arrived at St Mark's, they found the pupils in a high state of festive excitement. Throughout the day they had been busy making paper chains which were now hanging up in all the classrooms, and in the corridor too. The windows had been painted with white blobs, so it looked like it was snowing outside, and there was talk of Father Christmas visiting the school soon.

'He's got toys in his sack, and his pockets are full of toffees,' Arthur announced.

Smiling in delight at the charming little boy, Sister Theresa fondly stroked his wiry dark hair. 'I'm sure he'll have something very special for you, dear.'

Surprised that the Mary Vale nun was in his school, Arthur asked in his usual forthright manner, 'What're you doing here in my school? You live with Jesus, miss,' he reminded her.

'I've come to help Miss Margaret with the choir,' Theresa explained.

'Will you sing with us, miss?' Joy asked.

'I'm nothing like as talented as you two songbirds,' Theresa praised the glowing children. 'But I'll certainly join in the parts that we all sing together.'

'What's your favourite carol, miss?' Joy enquired.

'"Away In A Manger",' Theresa answered. 'It always reminds me of the babies sleeping peacefully in their little cribs in Mary Vale's nursery.'

In the hall, also strung with coloured paper decorations adorned with bits of silver tinsel, Margaret took the children through the carol service, concentrating mostly on Arthur and Joy, who had the most complicated musical pieces to sing. Suddenly, and rather alarmingly, as she was playing the piano Margaret felt a sharp twinge in her side. Readjusting her position on the piano stool, she soldiered on. But the twinge didn't go away – in fact, it felt even more uncomfortable.

Turning to Theresa, who was standing by the side of the piano, Margaret whispered, 'I don't feel too good.'

'That's all right,' the nun calmly responded. 'I'll take over until you feel better.'

Excusing herself, Margaret left the hall and slowly paced up and down the corridor until the pain eased and she could breathe more easily. You really have been pushing your luck, she thought. Cradling her enormous tummy, Margaret made a promise to her unborn child. 'I'm sorry, sweetheart, I'll take more care from now on.'

When she returned to the hall, Margaret was flabber-gasted to find the choir, led by Sister Theresa, doing the 'Hokey Cokey'!

Seeing her astonished face, Theresa quickly explained. 'I'm so sorry – we just thought we'd take a break.'

'Please don't stop – festive fun is in the air,' Margaret laughed. Sitting down, she watched the young nun con-tinue the dancing and the singing with such contagious joy.

Picking up on her vibrant mood, the children roared out the last line of the song, bending their knees and stretching their arms with happy abandon, before they regrouped around the piano to finish their rehearsal, con-cluding with a thunderous rendition of 'Rudolph The Red-Nosed Reindeer'.

When the session ended, the choir disbanded, leaving only Arthur and Joy in the hall, along with Margaret and Sister Theresa.

'Mam said we're coming home with you, miss,' serious-faced Joy said.

'You certainly are, dear.' Margaret smiled as she but-toned up the second-hand overcoat she had recently bought for Arthur at yet another local jumble sale.

'Are you warm enough?' Theresa asked Joy. 'It's a cold night.'

'I'm all right, thank you, miss,' the girl replied. 'Marga-ret gave me some mittens and a scarf that one of the Mary Vale residents had knitted for me, they're very cosy.'

'Are you looking forward to spending the night at Mary Vale?' Sister Theresa enquired as they all headed off to the railway station.

Solemn, earnest Joy answered with the shyest of smiles. 'Yes, miss. It's the nicest place in the world.'

When they got back to the Home, Sister Agnes had kept back tea for them all, which she served in front of the Aga in the cosy kitchen. In her element, she clucked over the children like a doting mother hen.

'Come along now, dears,' she said as she settled them at the table. 'You must be starving.'

Arthur gazed in awe at the little cheese pasties and coconut cakes that the nun had provided for their tea. 'Is this *all* for us, Sister Agnes?'

The happy nun nodded. 'For you, and Margaret, and your sister too.'

'What about Sister Trees?' Arthur asked, as he turned to the nun he had spent the afternoon with.

'I have to go back to my sisters in the convent,' she explained.

'Will they have kept a nice big tea waiting for you?'

'I'm sure they will,' Theresa replied. 'But I won't eat it straight away.'

'Why not, aren't you hungry?'

'I am,' she assured him. 'But first I have to say prayers in the chapel.'

Arthur glanced at the dark sky, visible through the kitchen window. 'Will you say goodnight to Jesus?'

'I certainly will,' Theresa smiled. 'And I'll say lots of prayers for you and your sister too.'

'Please will you pray for our dad?' Joy whispered. 'Please will you ask God not to take him to Heaven?'

Batting back the tears that rushed to her eyes, Theresa

nodded. 'Of course, darling, I'll make that my biggest and best prayer of the evening.'

After the children had eaten their fill of Sister Agnes's delicious supper, she suggested they had a hot bath.

'And then you can put on the nice clean nightclothes I've got for you.'

While the nun was busily running a bath for the children, who loved the luxury of hot water and soap bubbles, Margaret slipped on to the ward to pay a visit to Beth.

'Hello,' Margaret said quietly as she approached the bed, finding Beth wide awake. 'Sorry it's late, but I've been at St Mark's most of the afternoon.'

'It's nice of you to spare the time to come and see me,' Beth shyly responded.

'How are you feeling?' Margaret asked.

'No improvement, unfortunately,' Beth replied. 'My husband came back. He was so rude to the Mary Vale staff, especially Dr Reid, and then he turned on me.'

Appalled that Thorp could still intimidate his wife, even when she was in a hospital bed, Margaret commiserated. 'I'm so sorry, Beth, you deserve better than that.'

'He really set me back,' the young woman admitted, with tears in her eyes. 'I lie here in this room, forbidden to even get out of bed, because walking around might harm my baby, and still my husband bullies and threatens me.'

Determined to rally Beth's fading spirits, Margaret urged, 'The best thing, dear, is that you're here in the Home, you and your baby are protected and monitored, there's no safer place for you right now than Mary Vale.'

Forcing a weak smile, Beth agreed with her visitor. 'How right you are, and how lucky I am to be here, surrounded by kind people who genuinely care for us all.'

'Now, if you're not too tired, I have a little surprise for you,' Margaret continued. Beth's face registered curiosity. 'Oh, what's that?' she asked.

'You mentioned that when the Carter children were next here, you would like to meet them.'

'I certainly would.'

'Well, they're downstairs with Sister Agnes at the moment, having a bath before bed,' Margaret smiled. 'I can bring them up to say goodnight, if you're not too tired.'

'I'd love that,' Beth replied.

Ten minutes later, washed and scrubbed within an inch of their lives by Sister Agnes, Arthur and Joy stood before Beth's bed.

Beth smiled at Arthur's dark wiry hair, which had been brushed and was standing on end. 'You look very clean.'

Arthur grinned his gap-toothed smile. 'Sister Agnes loves scrubbing us.'

Agnes looked self-conscious. 'They come up so bonny after a good wash.'

Leading the conversation on, Margaret added, 'This lady, Beth, lives quite near to Allithwaite Farm.'

Joy gave a proud smile. 'Our dad is head shepherd there,' she said, before her smile faded and she added, 'that's when he's not in hospital.'

Keen to get in on the conversation, Arthur blurted out, 'We live in a cottage that's owned by a shouty man who doesn't like us.'

Listening intently, Beth gave a sympathetic nod. 'Some people are not very kind.'

'He shouts at mi mam a lot, now that mi dad's not there to stop him,' Joy elaborated.

'I hate him,' Arthur growled. 'When I get stronger, I'm going to thump him,' he vowed.

Covering her mouth with her hand to hide her smile, Agnes murmured, 'Now then, son, that's not a very kind thing to say, is it?'

'I don't care, Sister,' Arthur declared.

Treading carefully, Beth enquired, 'Do you know why the nasty man shouts so much at your mother?'

'Because we've no money,' Arthur said, without a hint of shame.

'And we can't pay the rent,' Joy said bluntly.

'That's a pity,' Beth sympathized. 'Perhaps I can give your mother some money to pay the rent, and then the nasty man will go away and leave her in peace.'

As if all his problems had miraculously been solved, Arthur beamed his thanks. 'Can you give Mam the rent money soon, miss? Mi mam says if we carry on the way we are, we'll be on the streets by Christmas.'

Shocked by her brother's forthright manner, Joy hissed, 'Shhh! You're showing us up.'

Wide-eyed with indignation, Arthur protested, 'Well, it's true! I've heard Mam say as much to Miss Margaret, plenty of times,' he declared.

Quickly stepping forward, Margaret said, 'I don't think you need trouble yourself with any more thoughts of that nature, Arthur.' Worried what the child might say next, she suggested they should leave in order for Beth to get some sleep.

Thoughtful Joy said, 'Shall we sing to you before we go, miss?'

'That would be lovely,' Beth replied.

After a sweet chorus of 'Greensleeves', the two children were ushered away by Sister Agnes, leaving Margaret alone with Beth.

'I will pay their rent,' Beth immediately said, the moment they had left the room. 'I have money in my purse; you can take it now for Mrs Carter to give to my wretched heartless husband. Here, take it,' she insisted, as she pulled her purse out of the bedside locker and pulled out a handful of notes. 'This wicked cruelty must stop.'

Agitated, Margaret asked, 'What if he finds out where it's come from?'

Beth gave a bitter knowing laugh. 'Believe me, Margaret,' she said, 'Ronnie's only interest is money and what it can buy – he doesn't give a damn about where it might have come from.'

29. The Marsh

After notifying the local Grange police of their discovery, Libby and Alf were asked to show them Thorp's warehouse on a freezing-cold December afternoon. On their way there, accompanied by two policemen, Libby mentioned something that had been troubling her.

'Thorp's nothing but a bully, he'll try and dodge the law,' she said knowingly. 'How can you be sure you'll get him?'

Trudging through the pouring rain that was fast turning to sleet, the senior officer confidently answered her question. 'There's bound to be documentation we can trace, either in his home or in the warehouse. Anyway, we have your sworn evidence, miss – we've recorded what you saw and heard on the night you broke into the warehouse – be assured, that will go a long way in a court room.'

Making their way around the edges of the marsh, Alf had his head down to protect against the strength of the bitter wind that blew straight off the Irish Sea. Raising his voice, he asked the question that had been on his mind for some time.

'Everybody knew Thorp were up to summat. You can't go around in an expensive new car without getting noticed round here, where folks are just about scraping a living. If we local folk had our suspicions, you bobbies must have had 'em too!' he exclaimed.

'You're right there, Mr Arkwright,' the senior officer responded. 'We've certainly had our suspicions concerning Ronnie Thorp, never a popular man at the best of times.'

'That's putting it mildly,' Libby scoffed. 'I've yet to hear a good word said about him.'

'Our problem's been finding something concrete to pin on him. Idle talk is not going to put a man behind bars,' the senior officer said wisely.

Chipping in, the younger policeman added, 'To be fair, we have been keeping an eye on the local black-market situation. There's evidence that a lot of stuff is being shifted in this area, but we've had no luck in tracing the ringleader until you showed up, miss.'

'Aye, we can't arrest a suspect based on rumour alone. Your information is vital, miss,' the older man added.

'I don't think you'll have a problem arresting Thorp once you've seen the stash of goods he's got squirrelled away in his warehouse,' Libby informed him.

'You say it's right here on the marsh,' the officer said as he glanced around the wind-swept terrain. 'After a couple of recent tip-offs, we did check out the area. Fishing shacks, jetties, boatsheds, we never found anything of any significance.'

'To be honest, I wouldn't have stumbled across the warehouse myself,' Libby admitted. 'It's set well back from the coast path, hedged in with trees and bushes. I would have ridden right past it, if Thorp hadn't almost run me over when he roared away in his car. If I hadn't recognized him, I really don't think I would have given the warehouse a second glance. It was seeing *him* at the wheel that caught my attention.'

'Why is that, miss? Have you had personal experience of Ronnie Thorp?' the younger man enquired.

'Yes, I'm his wife's midwife, I've visited his home several times. He's a very cruel and dangerous man,' she added bluntly. 'I wouldn't trust him as far as I could throw him.'

When they reached the warehouse, the sleet had turned to snow, and the ground underfoot was slushy.

Hesitating, Alf said, 'So, what do we do now, officer?'

'We try and gain entry the polite way, by knocking on the door – if that fails then we'll just break into the building.'

When nobody answered to his knock, the officer turned to Libby. 'Did you say there's a back door?'

Libby nodded. 'And a broken window that I left ajar.'

'Let's not tamper with the front door,' the senior man said to his colleague. 'Thorp might pop by. If he sees that the front door's been damaged, it will immediately arouse his suspicions.'

After they had located the door at the back of the building, the junior policeman put his shoulder to it; after three hefty shoves, the lock gave way. When the door swung open Libby quickly located the light switch, and the room was suddenly illuminated by a dangling bare bulb. Letting out a long whistle, the senior officer's eyes raked the line of shelves containing cases of sprits – whisky, brandy, gin, vodka, martini, sherry, wines, even champagne. There were hundreds of boxes of cigarettes, chocolates, nylons, lingerie, make-up and luxury foodstuffs – jam, marmalade, tins of fruit, beef, salmon, caviar and packets of biscuits.

Waving his hands in the direction of the loaded crates,

the junior policeman exclaimed, 'My word! What a hoard! Thorp must have been trading for a very long time to have stored this lot away.'

Galvanized, his senior colleague said decisively, 'Let's try Thorp's home – with this lot as evidence, we could nail him on the spot.'

Determined to be in on Thorp's arrest, Libby begged the senior officer to allow her and Alf to accompany them to Thorp Hall.

'You're taking this very personally, miss,' the senior officer grinned.

'I know,' Libby agreed. 'I just want to see what happens with my own eyes, it would give me the greatest satisfaction.'

Staring into her delicate heart-shaped face dominated by big violet-blue eyes, the younger officer was taken by her passionate determination. 'The fella's clearly got on the wrong side of you, miss,' he mused.

'As I said, he's a cruel man – I'd very much like to see him brought to justice, plus it would give me great pleasure to be able to tell his wife that he won't be troubling her for a long time.'

Though the police granted her request to accompany them in their official car to Thorp Hall, they were adamant that Alf and Libby should stay well out of the way when they actually made their arrest. 'You cannot get involved, young lady,' the senior officer said firmly.

'I understand that,' Libby immediately agreed.

'Whatever happens, stay out of the way and – I repeat – *don't* get involved.'

'Right,' she nodded back.

As the burly policemen approached the hall, Libby and Alf ducked into a garden shed, almost opposite the front door, where they crouched low before cautiously peeping out.

'Hell fire, lass,' Alf muttered. 'I don't know how you've got away with this.'

'Charm and persuasion,' Libby smiled. 'And a determination to see Thorp's face when he's taken away in a police car,' she added, with undisguised glee.

'Shhh!' Alf hissed as the front door swung open.

Seeing the granite-faced housekeeper barring the police's entry, Libby muttered, 'Oh-oh, Mrs Grimsdale.'

Though they couldn't hear every word that was exchanged, they could certainly see the action. Clearly furious, the housekeeper waved her arms about in protest, but to no effect. Having listened long enough, the young officer politely moved the protesting woman to one side then stepped inside the hall, followed by his colleague. Red-faced and shouting at the top of her voice, Mrs Grimsdale followed the policemen, slamming the door shut as she went.

With the snow falling down in a thick blanket, Libby huddled close to Alf. 'Let's hope Thorp's at home,' she whispered.

'Looks like it, his car's over yonder,' Alf pointed out.

After a tense pause, Libby said, 'If he is at home, I can't see Thorp going peacefully, can you?'

Alf couldn't help but grin. 'That's definitely not his style.'

They both stopped short when the front door was suddenly thrown open with considerable violence.

'Stop, Thorp,' the senior officer's voice rang out. 'Stop, you're being a bloody fool!'

To Libby and Alf's horror, they saw Thorp bolting from the house while a hysterical Mrs Grimsdale threw herself on the policemen, landing punches and screaming at them.

Watching the struggle on the doorstep, Libby gasped. 'He's going to get away!' Leaping to her feet, she barged out of the shed, right into Thorp's path. 'NO!' she cried. 'NO!' Without a moment's hesitation, she ran forward, intent on tackling Thorp single-handed.

'Get out of my way, you stupid interfering little bitch!' he roared as he wrestled her to the ground, only to find himself confronted by stocky Alf.

The farmer threw a heavy blow that connected with Thorp's jaw.

'You old bastard!' Thorp bellowed, and moved forward to thump Alf in the face. He found that his legs were held tight in Libby's strong grip. 'Bitch!' he hollered as he frantically tried to kick her off.

Slipping and sliding in the slushy snow, Thorp continued throwing punches at Alf until Libby bit into his leg.

'ARGHHH!' he hollered, by which time the two policemen were upon him.

Tackling him to the ground, the younger officer quickly secured handcuffs to the struggling Thorp's wrists, then breathlessly issued a warning. 'You do not have to say anything, but anything you do say will be taken down and may be given in evidence.'

After relieving Thorp of the contents of his pockets, the officers thrust him, swearing and cursing, into the police car. The senior officer turned to address Mrs Grimsdale, who was screaming blue murder on the front doorstep.

'I shall report you to your senior officer,' she threatened.

'I *am* the senior officer,' he calmly addressed the hysterical woman. 'I suggest, madam, that you keep what you have to say to yourself until you are called to give evidence in a court of law.'

Incandescent with rage, Mrs Grimsdale turned her vitriolic wrath on Libby, who was busy helping Alf to his feet.

'YOU!' she ranted. 'You've been nothing but trouble since you arrived in this house.'

Dusting snow off his overcoat, Alf shook his head. 'Ignore her,' he warned Libby. 'She's a bitter old woman who's finally got her comeuppance.' Suddenly noticing that the junior officer was holding a set of car keys in his hand, cunning Alf remarked, 'Are those Thorp's keys to that smart new Daimler?'

'That's right, we've just emptied his pockets.'

With a glint in his eye, Alf said, 'You won't be needing them right away, I'm thinking?'

The officer grinned. 'Depends what you have in mind?'

'I thought I might give the young lady a lift home,' Alf winked. 'Don't fancy walking home in a snowstorm,' he added. 'And I've got gloves on,' he said as he raised his leather-clad hands in the air. 'So no fear of fingerprints, if I was to take Thorp's posh car out for a spin.'

'Go on, then,' the indulgent officer said as he handed over the keys. 'We'll collect it just as soon as we've booked Thorp in at the station.'

*

It was dark by the time they drove home through the falling snow in the big black Daimler, with its comfortable deep leather seats and shiny chromework.

At the wheel Alf chuckled, despite his bleeding nose and bruised cheek. 'You know the old saying, there's a silver lining to every cloud?'

'And what might this one be, Alf?'

With a crooked grin on his lips, Alf replied, 'I've always had a fancy to drive one of these smart buggers!'

As soon as they reached Mary Vale, Libby went in search of Matron while Alf drove the Daimler down to Ada's cottage to pick up Jamie. Libby thought he might be needed when they told Beth of the day's events. Sitting in Matron's office, with tangled hair and still filthy dirty from her fight in the snow, Libby related the tale of Thorp's arrest.

Matron looked visibly relieved. 'Thank God,' she murmured as she sank into the chair behind her desk. 'Thank God,' she repeated as she made the sign of the Cross, her hands moving reverently over her breast.

'I hope you don't mind, Matron, but I took the liberty of asking Alf to fetch Dr Jamie. If you decide to inform Beth, I think he might be needed,' she added cautiously.

'Quite right, dear, good thinking,' Matron quickly agreed. 'Beth must be notified immediately.'

Arriving within minutes, a breathless Jamie joined them. 'Alf's just told me the news,' he said. Turning to the dishevelled young nurse, he smiled. 'You are a very brave woman, Libby. You showed great courage and determination today.'

With tears in her big blue eyes, Libby staunchly answered,

'I couldn't have done it without Alf. He can still pack a mighty punch. And the police officers were marvellous,' she enthused. 'It turned out to be a very satisfactory day,' she added, with obvious pleasure.

Rising, Matron solemnly opened her office door. 'I think the sooner Beth hears your news, Libby, the happier we will all be.'

Beth was dozing when they walked into her room. Gazing down at the slip of a girl, with her long silver-blonde hair spread across her pillow and her arms flung out like a child, Libby's heart ached. All she had ever wanted to do was to protect this lovely person from harm, and now she hoped she had achieved her greatest wish.

Hearing them entering the room, Beth drowsily opened her eyes, instinctively alert for danger. 'Is he back?' She asked the habitual question that was always on her lips when she was taken unawares.

'No, dear,' Libby responded as she helped her patient sit upright.

Taking command of the situation, Matron said, 'Beth, dear, Libby has quite a lot to tell you.'

Nearly an hour later, Libby concluded her long, rambling tale, from the moment she had first spotted Thorp's warehouse while riding out on the marsh on Snowdrop, to getting locked in the basement, to the police's arrest of Beth's husband that afternoon. Not even attempting to hide her delight at the outcome of events, Libby concluded by saying, 'Your husband is probably at this very moment behind bars in Grange's police station.'

Silence fell.

With all eyes on her, Beth gazed in disbelief from Jamie to Matron, then back to Libby. 'He's been arrested?' she gasped.

Libby nodded. 'I saw it happen with my own eyes.' She couldn't help but smile. 'He didn't like it one bit,' she couldn't resist adding.

Beth's smile broadened to a grin. 'I bet he went berserk.'

'Something like that,' Libby grinned back.

Leaning forward, Beth gripped her midwife's hands in delight. 'And Mrs Grimsdale?'

'She screamed like a banshee but the police quickly put her in her place,' Libby replied.

Now hugging her knees, Beth drank in the sheer joy of the moment. 'I'm safe at last. Ronnie can't come and take me away from here any more,' she murmured in disbelief.

'That's right, Beth,' Jamie reassured her. 'Black marketeers are not looked upon kindly, so your husband won't be bothering you – or anybody else, for that matter – for quite some time.'

As one thought quickly followed another, Beth asked, 'Will I have control of his estate?'

'I would hope so – you are his wife, after all.'

'And it was my family money that paid for Thorp Hall – so it's mine by rights,' Beth declared.

Seeing her patient getting flushed and agitated, Matron quickly soothed. 'I'm sure all these questions will be answered in the fullness of time, dear.' She glanced across at Jamie, adding, 'It's been quite an eventful day, let's just take one step at a time, shall we?'

Libby urged her patient to lie back. 'With Matron's permission, I'll make us a nice cup of tea before I take myself off,' she said. 'I could certainly do with one.' She smiled as she left the room.

'Dr Jamie,' Matron enquired, 'shall we examine Beth before we leave her to enjoy her cup of tea?'

'Certainly,' he answered.

After Matron had taken Beth's blood pressure, temperature and pulse, Jamie gently examined her pelvic area, moving his hands around her abdomen. 'Are you still having some spotting?'

'I thought it had stopped,' Beth wriggled in discomfort. 'But it does feel uncomfortably damp down there right now, so I hope I'm not bleeding again –'

She was interrupted by Libby walking in bearing a tea tray. 'Here we are,' she cheerfully announced as she laid the tray on the bedside table.

Looking up, Jamie said grimly, 'We won't be needing that right now, Libby. Beth's waters have just broken.'

30. God Rest Ye Merry Gentlemen

There was a great deal of discussion the following morning on the well-being of Mary Vale's newest arrival, who had been in labour all night.

'Sounds like the poor kid's had a lot to contend with,' Maisie sympathized as she helped herself to several slices of bread.

Gladys, who had recently given birth to a strapping baby boy with a voice almost as loud as her own, immediately moved on to her favourite subject, which was all men being bastards. 'Men!' she scoffed. 'Give 'em an inch and they'll take a yard.'

'Well, I hope the lass will be all right,' a less aggressive resident added to the conversation. 'They say she's nothing but a slip of a thing.'

Gladys's booming laughter sounded out. 'Eh, not like me,' she declared as she smeared her allotted quota of butter on to her pile of toast. 'I could have eaten a horse all the time I was pregnant.'

Maisie chuckled as she nodded towards Gladys's heaped plate. 'Looks like you still could, Gladys, love,' she teased.

Good-natured Gladys responded with a cheeky grin. 'Shurrup!' she scoffed. 'I need to build up mi strength.'

'I bet you're glad it's over?' the quieter woman nervously enquired. 'I must say,' she murmured as she gazed at her huge tummy, 'I'm dreading it.'

'There's no point in saying it dun't hurt,' Gladys answered cheerfully. 'It hurts like buggery, but by the time you're in that delivery room, with your legs up in the air, all you can think of is – get this baby out of me!'

'You had Sister Ada all the way through the delivery, didn't you?' Maisie asked.

'Aye, she were belting,' Glad announced. 'Calm, strong, cheerful, she knew what she were doing.'

'I hope I get her when my time comes,' Maisie sighed. 'Though, to be honest, they're a great set of midwives here at Mary Vale; even that new young Nurse Libby comes across as very caring and experienced.'

After draining her teacup, Gladys filled it up with fresh tea from the pot that always stood in the middle of the table. 'I'm off to see Father Ben this afternoon,' she told her chums. 'He's found a couple from Wigan who are keen on adopting my little lad.'

A silence fell as residents in the room, some of whom would soon be making the same grave decision as Gladys, grew thoughtful.

'I've heard the priest is good at his job, very conscientious,' Maisie said. 'He was kindness itself when I went to see him.'

Gladys lit up a cigarette thoughtfully. 'I trust him to find good parents for my boy, he takes his time and "matches people up", those were the words he used,' she explained. 'As long as he gives my son the opportunity to have a better life than if he'd stayed with me, dirt poor in Huddersfield, I'll be grateful to Father Ben for ever.'

'How much time have you got left with your baby?' the quiet woman asked.

'I'll be going back home after Christmas,' Gladys told her, with a grimace. 'Just a bit longer with the little lad, that's something.'

Seeing the glint of a tear in her friend's eye, Maisie quickly changed the subject. 'Only a few days to go till Christmas, eh? Anybody up for going to listen to Margaret's little choir in Grange tonight?'

'I thought about it,' the quiet woman responded. 'But I don't fancy the train journey to Grange at this time of the year, in the dark and freezing cold.'

Gladys gave a dismissive wave of her hand. 'Come on now, ladies, them little kiddies deserve an appreciative audience. We should make an effort for them, and for Margaret too. No doubt she'll be there, big as she is, with her baby due any time soon.'

'I shouldn't think wild horses would keep Margaret away from tonight's carol service,' Maisie declared.

Later that afternoon, before she left to meet up with the choir, Margaret waylaid Libby in the corridor.

'How's Beth getting on?' she asked.

Libby pulled down the corners of her mouth. 'Contractions coming and going, but not much significant progress so far.'

'Poor girl, I hope it won't be too hard for her. She's weak enough to start with, and she's already been labouring a long time,' Margaret commiserated.

Libby dropped her voice to a whisper. 'I do have some good news,' she grinned. 'Thorp was arrested yesterday.'

'Really?' Margaret gasped.

Libby nodded. 'Beth's waters broke just after she was

told, must have been the shock.' Smiling proudly, Libby continued, 'It was me and Alf who alerted the police. Oh, Margaret,' she cried. 'It was such a sight to behold – Thorp being carted off, handcuffed in a police car, I could have danced for joy!' she gloated. Checking her fob watch, she looked up and said apologetically, 'I must get back to Beth – who, by the way, is determined to make amends to Mary and her family.'

'She said as much to me,' Margaret responded. 'She even gave me money from her own purse to pay the Carters' rent.'

Libby grinned. 'Mary won't have to worry about that, now that Thorp's behind bars.'

'I know it's wicked to gloat,' Margaret confessed, 'but it really is the best possible outcome. So many people will be better off without his malevolent presence.'

'By the way,' Libby warned, 'don't mention a word of this to anybody – especially Mary. Beth will have to get her strength back before she starts sorting things out, but I bet the Carters will be at the top of her list of priorities.'

After Libby had hurried away, Margaret gazed out at the winter lawn, spiky with frozen grass. An incredulous smile spread across her face. Could it really be true that Beth would make amends to the Carter family? Repair the damage her cruel husband had relentlessly doled out? Thinking of the Carters' cottage the last time she had seen it, made Margaret shudder. The walls were running with damp; no matter how high Mary stoked the fire, the heat didn't even reach halfway across the room. To keep warm Mary slept with the children and baby Susan in the bed that Sam had vacated. Knowing how much colder it would get as winter progressed, Margaret prayed that Beth would soon have the strength to release the Carters from their misery and offer them decent accommodation at a price they could afford.

'At least they're not hungry any more,' Margaret comforted herself.

With dear Sister Agnes's help, there was some food on the Carters' table every day: pasties, spam fritters, bread, a tin of beans, a rice pudding, all eked out from Mary Vale's kitchen by Agnes. She didn't let a day go by without putting something aside for her beloved kiddies. The residents, of their own accord, had got into the habit of sacrificing something from their own plates – a sausage or a slice of pie, a baked potato or a scone. These precious morsels were all carefully stored away by Sister Agnes, who regularly cycled over to Allithwaite with all of Mary Vale's donations.

Seeing the buxom nun wobbling around on the icy roads, big-hearted Alf had offered to do the delivery himself. 'I can ride over there in the horse cart and drop yon stuff off,' he'd volunteered. 'Save you the trouble of cycling in all this cold weather.'

'I try and make the effort,' Agnes had explained, 'as it gives me the chance to help Mrs Carter with baby Susan. The poor woman is at her wits' end, what with the state of that hovel they live in, and her husband on death's doorstep. She needs all the help she can get.'

With a biting wind blowing off the marsh, Margaret and Sister Theresa (wrapped up warm for a long night outdoors) met up with the choir in St Mark's church hall. Wildly overexcited, the children were running around chasing each other, with Arthur in the middle of all the action, as usual pretending to be a Spitfire shooting down Luftwaffe planes.

Clapping her hands, Margaret called them all to attention. 'Come along now,' she called. 'We don't want you hoarse from shouting – please calm down and line up in twos by the door.'

As Arthur grabbed his sister's hand and joined the queue, he turned to Margaret. 'Are we taking your piano, miss?' he asked sweetly.

Smiling, Margaret shook her head. 'No, dear, the mayor of Grange is supplying me with a far smarter piano, so we can leave our school piano right here in the hall.'

'Will you play it outside, miss, under the tree in the marketplace?' he asked.

'I certainly will, Arthur.'

'Will you get cold, miss, sitting there all night?'

Thinking the irrepressible little boy would never stop asking questions, Margaret moved to the front, ready to lead the line of chattering children, while Sister Theresa brought up the rear.

When they reached the marketplace, the choir and their minders all gasped in delighted unison.

'Wowee, miss,' Davie declared. 'I never imagined ow't as good as this.'

The scene before them was a fairyland of coloured lights and brightly coloured decorations looped around the lamp posts and trees that enclosed the square. The tall Christmas tree, with a bright glowing star atop, was decorated with twinkling tinsel and paper chains. A circle of braziers containing coal and logs marked out and warmed the circled area where the children were to perform. And as Margaret had promised, a fine piano had been wheeled out for her to play. A good crowd had gathered for the event; true to her word, Gladys was there with as many residents as she could drag out of the Home on such a frosty night. Families and relatives were given seats near to the front, so they could get a good view, while teachers and staff from St Mark's stood among a great many townspeople who had turned out for the festive event.

After Margaret had taken her seat, and Sister Theresa had arranged the choir close to the piano, Grange's mayor, a stout man with a twirly grey moustache, stepped up on to a small platform from where he addressed the large and increasingly jolly crowd.

'I'd like to thank you all for coming out on such a chilly night,' he started. 'We've not had many opportunities in the last years to get together and celebrate, but this year, thanks to St Mark's School . . .' a smattering of applause followed, 'we can look forward to a treat from this little choir who've been working hard to entertain us. Let's hear it for them, folks.' After another enthusiastic round of applause, the mayor continued. 'There'll be a short interval halfway through the service, so that you can all get warm, and the choir can have a bite to eat, then we'll continue. All I can say for now is – take it away, St Mark's!'

At which point, Margaret struck up 'We Wish You A Merry Christmas' and the choir ripped into the first song, with great verve and energy. As they went into the second verse, Sister Theresa (unusually forthright) urged the audience to join in, which they did with enormous enthusiasm – especially the children at the front, who roared out the chorus. The second carol, one of Arthur's solo pieces, followed. As soft snow slowly started to fall, Theresa led Arthur forward, positioning him in front of the towering tree, glowing with lights, where the little boy (with no song sheet) sang 'Away In A Manger' to Margaret's gentle accompaniment. Total hush descended as Arthur's innocent voice soared high into the dark sky, where his piercing high notes resounded in the crisp, cold night air. When the music stopped and the carol faded like a dream, the silence that followed lingered for so long that Arthur worried something had gone badly wrong.

'Did they like my singing, miss?' he whispered loudly to Sister Theresa.

Stooping to give him a big hug, the nun was quick to reassure Arthur, tears in her eyes. 'They LOVED it, darling!'

Clapping and cheering immediately broke out.

'Marvellous!'

'Well done, lad.'

'Give us another!'

Enjoying the jolly mood, Margaret went straight into the opening bars of 'Oh, Little Town Of Bethlehem', which the choir sang beautifully, followed by Joy's melodic 'In Dulce Jubilo'. When it was time to stop for a break, Margaret gratefully stood up and stretched her aching back.

'Are you all right?' Sister Theresa anxiously asked when she saw Margaret grimace.

'I think so, the piano stool is very high, and I could

barely get my tummy close to the keyboard. I'll be fine once I've had a little walk about.'

While Margaret stretched her legs, Theresa kept her eye on the excited children who were eagerly accepting mugs of hot Bovril and bags of scalding-hot chips.

As the second part of the service got under way, there couldn't have been more delight when snow suddenly started to drift down from the winter sky in gentle swirls around the choir's upturned faces, completing the sense of Christmas magic. 'Silent Night', sung by Joy and Arthur, brought a tear to everybody's eye, swiftly followed by Davie's thundering rendition of 'Jingle Bells', which had all the kiddies in the audience on their feet dancing and clapping. Regrouping the overexcited choir, Sister Theresa hushed them with a few gentle words for the final carols, 'Oh Come, All Ye Faithful' and the tumultuous 'Hark! The Herald Angels Sing', both sung with such fervour and passion by the entire crowd that the rooftops of Grange rang and echoed with festive joy.

Wrapping up with 'God Save The King', Margaret sighed with relief. Thank God it went so well, she thought, as the pain in her back noticeably increased. Standing up, she supported herself against the piano while listening to the mayor's closing speech.

'I think we can safely say that this has been one of the finest performances Grange has heard in years. St Mark's choir is positively outstanding, and I think we have Mrs Margaret Church to thank for that.'

Taken aback that her name had even been mentioned, Margaret was glad to be largely hidden by the piano she was standing behind.

'The dedication and talent that we have witnessed takes some beating.' Beaming at the choir, who were lapping up his praise, the mayor continued. 'Some of these kiddies are genuinely gifted.'

'Aye, aye, you're right there, Mr Mayor,' an eager woman in the crowd called out.

'They could go far,' he added, with a flourish of his beefy hands.

After the mayor's speech concluded, little brown paper bags of boiled sweets were given to the choir who, now tired out, were taken home by their parents. While the crowd slowly dispersed, the mayor approached Margaret as she was buttoning up Arthur's warm woollen overcoat.

'I meant what I said just now, Mrs Church.'

Margaret didn't correct his misuse of her title – in fact, in the circumstances, she was grateful he had used it.

'There are sponsorships and awards for little lads like this one,' he said as he ruffled Arthur's hair, now speckled with falling snow. 'And the big lad too, he's got a grand voice – as has the young lass with the long plaits who sang all them beautiful harmonies.'

Margaret smiled proudly. 'You're quite right, your worship, we have a number of very gifted children in our choir.'

'I shall follow this through,' the mayor promised. 'We can't let local talent go to waste, it's something we must nurture.' Seeing that Margaret was visibly drooping, he quickly added, 'Would you like a lift, Mrs Church, I have a car at my disposal.'

Utterly exhausted, Margaret longed to accept but shook

her head. 'That's very kind of you, sir, but Sister Theresa and I have promised to get Arthur and Joy home to their mother in Allithwaite. She's presently very poorly.'

'It's a pity she couldn't attend the concert,' the mayor commiserated. 'Any mother would have been proud of tonight's performance.'

'Yes, it's a great shame that Mrs Carter had to miss her children's concert,' Margaret agreed.

'Anyway, let's drop the kiddies off, then I'll drive you and your companion home. Come along, let's not waste time standing here in the freezing cold, you look quite worn out.'

Loving the ride home in a posh car, the children raced indoors when the mayor drew up beside their front door.

Seeing Margaret looking distinctly unsteady, the big-hearted mayor said, 'Take your time, I'll wait here until you're done.'

Supported by Sister Theresa's guiding hand as she stepped out of the car, Margaret said gratefully, 'We shouldn't be long.'

When they got indoors, the sight awaiting them took away all thoughts of returning quickly to Mary Vale. Sister Agnes was pacing the room, holding baby Susan in her arms, with an agonized expression on her face.

'I got here about an hour ago with some food,' she whispered. 'I found them both on the bed, Mary coughing and coughing, the baby stone cold. Dear Jesus, help this wretched family,' she prayed.

Hurrying to their mother's side, Arthur and Joy took

hold of her hands which they stroked and kissed. 'Mam, Mam,' they urged. 'Mam . . . ?'

Joining them, Sister Theresa felt Mary's sweaty brow and then her pulse. 'Mummy's a bit poorly,' she said. 'I'll take care of her while you get something to eat. Look,' she said, pointing to the food that Agnes had laid out on the table. 'A nice supper before bedtime.'

While the children tucked into some pasties and baked beans, Margaret heaped up the fire.

'I got the shock of my life when I first saw the baby lying on the bed beside Mary,' Sister Agnes whispered. 'Honest to God, I thought she was dead.' Rocking the baby gently while rubbing her pale skin, Agnes added, 'She's warming up a bit now.'

Whispering too, Margaret confided, 'I knew Mary was poorly, which is why I volunteered to bring the children home, but I had no idea that she was quite so sick.'

Agnes, who had been the most regular visitor in the last few days, explained, 'She was complaining of feeling feverish, but then she got a bad cough – and no wonder, when you look around the place. Cold earth floors and running with damp. The fever must have got the better of her, and she took to her bed, maybe passed out. Thank heavens I got here when I did.'

'Thank God,' Margaret fervently agreed.

Joining the women by the fire, Sister Theresa had a worried crease on her white brow. 'What are we going to do? This family needs caring for, we can't leave them, not like this.'

Regardless of her own discomfort, Margaret instantly said, 'I'll stay with them.'

'You certainly will not!' Theresa said, with more force in her voice than Margaret had ever heard before. 'You're going back to Mary Vale – I'll stay.'

'Can't we all go back?' Margaret implored.

'I've just got Mary off to sleep, she's too weak and exhausted to move, and anyway we can't just turn up at the Home with an entire family,' Sister Theresa realistically pointed out. 'There might not be room for them all.'

Looking mutinous, Sister Agnes said, 'I don't care what you say, Theresa, I'm taking Susan back to Mary Vale. There's only one safe place for her right now, and that's Nurse Dora's baby nursery.' Turning to Mary, now tucked up fast asleep under a pile of blankets, Agnes added, 'Mary's in no state to feed a baby.'

So, it was quickly decided that Margaret, Agnes and Susan would return to Mary Vale, leaving the children and Mary in Theresa's expert care.

'I'll make a bed up for the children by the fire, and sit with Mary,' Theresa told her friends before they left. 'I'll need to monitor her temperature and breathing throughout the night.'

'We'll be back first thing,' Margaret assured the valiant little nun.

'Ask Reverend Mother as soon as you can about housing the family in the convent,' Theresa urged. 'Stress how disgraceful this cottage is – tell her that the Carters cannot spend another day here.' Seeing Margaret's drained and weary face, she added earnestly as she turned to Sister Agnes, 'Look after this lady, she's done far too much tonight.'

Sister Agnes quickly agreed with her colleague. 'Don't you worry, Theresa, I'll make sure she goes to bed as soon as we get back to the Home.'

Cradling Susan, wrapped in a big woolly shawl, Agnes, with Margaret leaning heavily against her, walked through the drifting snow to the mayor's waiting car.

Once back at Mary Vale, Agnes left Margaret to thank the mayor for his kindness while she dashed off to the baby nursery, still clutching Susan, who was making little mewling sounds of hunger.

'Take care of this little mite,' she begged Dora. 'She needs feeding and cleaning right away.'

'I'll see to her, don't you worry, Sister,' Dora assured the flustered nun, receiving the baby into her own arms with professional calm.

Having safely delivered Susan to the baby nursery, Sister Agnes went straight back to Margaret, who was hanging up her coat in the hallway. In her firmest yet kindest voice, she said, 'Come along now, Margaret, let's get you into bed, dear.'

Not for a moment did Margaret argue; tired beyond words, all she wanted was to lie down on her bed and get warm under her cosy eiderdown. Nevertheless, now that she was safely home, Margaret was determined to catch up on Beth's progress.

'Will you try and find out how Beth is progressing, Sister?'

Worried that Margaret might take it into her head to go on to the ward and find out for herself, Agnes quickly assured her, 'Of course, dear. You get yourself into bed.

I'll pop by later with an update on Beth, and a nice cup of tea too.'

Back in the quiet nursery, Dora was skilfully bathing and changing Susan, who had been very uncomfortable in a damp and dirty nappy.

'Poor little soul,' she cooed as she deftly inserted safety pins into Susan's fresh terry-towelling nappy, then slipped a clean cotton nightie over her head. 'Now let's see about getting some food inside you.'

By the time Sister Agnes reappeared, Dora was successfully feeding the hungry baby.

'There, there, clever girl,' she coaxed, as Susan settled down and sucked with vigour from the bottle Dora was holding. 'She's doing well,' she assured Agnes. 'Took to it like a duck to water.'

Smiling with relief, Agnes let out a long sigh. 'What a night we've had with the Carters. Theresa's still there with them, keeping an eye on them all, but I couldn't leave Susan there with the mother barely conscious. Promise you'll call me if Susan starts to fret,' Agnes fussed. 'I couldn't bear for the poor little mite to suffer any more than she already has.'

Dora threw the nun a reassuring smile. 'She'll settle after this, and I'll keep an eye on her, I promise.'

Before she turned to go, Sister Agnes dropped her voice. 'By the way, how's Mrs Thorp progressing?'

Dora shook her head. 'Still in labour, really slow progress.'

Agnes gasped in dismay. 'Poor woman, she must be quite worn out by now.'

'If you ask me, she can't go on the way she is for much longer,' Dora whispered. 'I wouldn't be surprised if they called in a surgeon to deliver the baby.'

Agnes crossed herself. 'A Caesarean – God bless the poor child,' she murmured fervently.

After quickly making tea for Margaret, and for herself too, Agnes made her way up the stairs to Margaret's room, where she found her washed and in her nightgown.

Sitting on the edge of her bed, Margaret gratefully sipped her hot tea, eager for an update on Beth. After the nun repeated what Dora had told her, Margaret said sadly, 'Heavens, poor Beth must be exhausted.'

Hoping to soothe Margaret, Agnes added, 'Let's pray it will soon be over with, and that her baby is born strong and healthy.'

'Amen to that,' Margaret added, with a heartfelt sigh.

Before she finally settled down, Margaret remembered that Sister Theresa had asked her to speak urgently to Reverend Mother about the Carters.

Determined to get overanxious Margaret into a peaceful frame of mind, Agnes said, 'Get some rest, lovie, we can discuss all of this first thing in the morning.' Stooping to kiss Margaret on the top of her head, she added, 'God bless you for all you've done for the Carter family.'

Overcome with weariness, Margaret finally snuggled down. 'Oh, Sister Agnes,' she exclaimed, 'I only wish I could have done a great deal more.'

31. Shelter From the Storm

When Libby saw Sister Agnes first thing the next morning, she was shocked to see her looking so exhausted.

'Are you all right, Sister?' she gently asked.

Wiping a hand across her furrowed brow, Agnes murmured, 'I hardly slept a wink all night. The Carters' situation has gone from bad to worse.'

'I know, I heard about it from Dora,' Libby commiserated.

Agnes shook her head in despair. 'It was awful,' she admitted. 'I'm worried to death. If things continue as they are, I fear one of the Carters won't see Christmas. At least baby Susan's here in Dora's tender care.'

'Well, that's got to be a comfort,' Libby responded.

'But Mary and the children, what's going to happen to them?' Agnes continued to fret. 'That house is uninhabitable, not fit for pigs. Sister Theresa thinks we should try and bring them to Mary Vale.'

Libby looked genuinely surprised. 'Bring them here – is there anywhere suitable for them?'

'I'm on my way to ask Reverend Mother that very question. I'm trying to get there before Margaret does. I've insisted that she stays in bed. The poor woman's worn herself ragged recently.'

Libby nodded in agreement with the nun. 'She's been doing far too much.' Seeing Agnes looking distracted, she hastily added, 'Sorry, Sister, I shouldn't be holding you up like this.'

'You're not holding me up, dear. To tell the truth, I'm trying to work out exactly what I'm going to say to Reverend Mother.' Shuffling uneasily, Agnes said, 'I'd hate her to think I was talking out of turn.'

'Nobody would think that of you, Sister,' Libby assured the edgy nun. 'There's nothing but goodwill in your request to house the Carters, it would be an act of great charity.' Seeing the nun still looking tense, Libby quite spontaneously said, 'Why don't I approach Reverend Mother instead of you?'

Agnes looked flabbergasted at the idea.

'I'm not part of your order, I'm a Mary Vale midwife,' Libby said, 'and I'm quite sure I can put forward a good argument for taking in the poor Carter family.'

Agnes dithered uncertainly. 'I suppose you have a point . . . that's if you don't mind?'

'I *really* don't mind.'

Having made her mind up to hand over the baton of responsibility to Libby, Agnes gave a big smile. 'I'd be grateful, dear – but please can you go to Reverend Mother right away, while I keep Margaret at bay.'

Briefly leaving her patient Beth with Dr Reid, Libby headed purposefully towards the convent that was connected to Mary Vale by an oak-panelled corridor with a large, silver and blue statue of Our Lady, Star of the Sea at its entrance. Sitting thoughtfully outside Reverend Mother's study, Libby wondered which way the discussion might go. If the Mother Superior refused, the Carters would probably end up in an institution. Though Beth seemed to have the best intentions, and wanted to make amends to the Carter family, she was presently in labour and in no position to set the world to rights. Nothing could be done to help the Carters until Beth had given birth and regained her strength. Deep in thought, Libby was startled when Reverend Mother opened the door to her.

After politely introducing herself, Libby passionately related the Carters' dire circumstances. Then, taking a deep breath, she came straight to the point.

'I'm here to implore you to help the Carter family – *all* of them,' she added pointedly. 'If they remain any longer in their wretched cottage, their situation will go from bad to worse. Already we have Susan in Mary Vale's baby nursery, while Sister Theresa was obliged to stay overnight at the Carters in order to nurse Mrs Carter and her children.'

'I know, Sister Agnes informed me of the events last night, before we said our evening office.' Looking deeply troubled, Reverend Mother continued, 'It truly is an awful situation, but as to the convent housing an entire family . . .'

Libby responded with genuine urgency. 'Reverend Mother, I truly believe it would only be a short-term arrangement.'

'How can you be so sure?'

When Libby's eyes locked with Reverend Mother's piercing gaze, she could do nothing but speak the truth as she understood it. 'I believe that the Carters' domestic arrangements will change for the better, early in the New Year.'

Reverend Mother cocked a quizzical eyebrow.

'One of Mary Vale's present residents is due to take over the running of her convicted husband's estate. At the moment, she's not strong enough to do so, but she has expressed a great desire to ease the Carters' burden by rehousing them at a rent they can manage, just as soon as she is able.'

Sitting back in her chair, Reverend Mother responded. '*If* the arrangement is as short-term as you suggest then we could let the family have our two available guest rooms in the convent, though they would have to respect our times of silent prayer and adoration.'

Just thinking of Arthur tearing around the convent, pretending to be a Spitfire bombing every Luftwaffe plane in sight, made Libby's heart sink into her boots. But she pushed the thought to one side. 'I can assure you I will do everything in my power to make them respect your convent rules.'

'In that case, I suggest you waste no further time – get over to the Carters' home as quickly as possible, and bring them back here before they all die of pneumonia.'

After gratefully thanking Reverend Mother, Libby made a beeline for Mary Vale's kitchen, light-hearted with relief. Breathless from running, she burst into the room.

'She agreed!' she announced.

Throwing her hands up in the air, Sister Agnes cried, 'Thank all the angels in heaven.'

'The Carters can use the convent's guest rooms for a short period, as long as they all behave themselves.' With her thoughts racing, Libby muttered, 'Now, I must find Matron and ask her if she'll allow me to ride over to Allithwaite.'

'But you're on duty, child,' Agnes reminded her.

Thinking fast, Libby responded, 'Perhaps Ada could cover for me, I shouldn't be that long.'

'Hold on a minute,' Sister Agnes protested. 'How on earth are you going to get Sister Theresa and all the Carters back here?'

'In Alf's cart – if he can transport Sister Theresa, Mary and Joy, little Arthur can ride with me on Snowball,' Libby confidently announced.

At which point, Margaret walked into the kitchen, pale-faced. Feeling the tension in the air, she turned from Agnes to Libby and back again. 'What's going on?' she demanded.

Sister Agnes quickly explained the situation.

'With Matron's permission, I'll ride over to Allithwaite right away to fetch the Carters here,' Libby added.

Margaret's response was immediate and characteristically selfless. 'I'll come with you.'

Libby's retort was firm and professional. 'No, Margaret. No more gallivanting around the countryside for you. You're staying right here.'

'B-b-but . . .' Margaret blustered.

Looking harassed, Libby urged, 'Listen, Margaret, even if you were fit enough, there's just not enough room for another person. Now, if you'll excuse me, I've got to find Alf and ask him to help me with transporting the Carters – and then I've got to see Matron.'

Finally agreeing with Libby's reasoning, Margaret didn't waste time by arguing further. 'All right,' she agreed. 'Can we do anything to help now?'

'Could you please fetch some blankets from the bed

store. And, Sister,' Libby added as she turned to Agnes, 'can you fill some flasks with hot tea?'

Picking up on the urgency of getting the Carters to a safe warm place, Matron suggested that Ada, presently at home looking after Catherine, should bring Catherine to the kitchen to help Sister Agnes make mince pies, thus freeing her mother to replace Libby.

'We can cover this,' Matron assured Libby, who was clearly desperate to be on her way. 'And don't worry, Libby, we'll keep a careful eye on Beth in your absence.'

Ten minutes later, kitted out in warm clothes and wearing leather gloves, Libby was in the stable saddling up Snowball. On such a bright, cold and frosty morning the little pony was ready for a gallop.

'Behave yourself,' she whispered fondly in his ear, before turning her attention to tightening his girths, a procedure which always ended with her getting a disapproving nudge in the tummy. 'We've got seriously important work to do today.'

When she made her way out of the stables, she found Alf already up on the seat of his cart, with Captain's reins held loosely in his gnarled old hands.

'Thanks for doing this, Alf,' Libby said as she threw him a grateful smile.

'Not a problem, lass.'

Margaret had walked the short distance down the back lane to the farm. She now placed the blankets and Thermos flasks in the cart. 'That should be enough to keep them warm on the journey back here,' she said anxiously.

As Alf and Captain set off up the lane, Libby reined Snowball in so she could speak quietly to Margaret. 'Promise me you'll go straight back to the Home.'

Margaret nodded her head. 'Have no fear, Libby, after yesterday I know I've got to take it easy,' she assured the worried nurse. 'Believe me, my thoughts will be with you all day. God be with you.'

Riding quickly through the frosty countryside, hot as she was with the exertion of cantering along the bridle paths behind Alf in his cart, Libby noticed how the temperature was dropping and heavy snow clouds were gathering over the higher fells. Frosted fields and hedges laced with icicles sparkled in the slanting rays of the low-lying midwinter sun. Snowball's breath came in great icy puffs and his feet clip-clopped sharply over the hard, snow-packed ground.

Alf called over his shoulder to Libby. 'It's turning right proper cold, lass. We should try our best to get the Carters back to Mary Vale before dark descends.'

'You're right, Alf – the sooner we're back at Mary Vale the better,' she agreed.

Though their plan was to get under way on the return journey as soon as possible, fate conspired against them. When they arrived at the cottage, snow was falling fast and the drifts from the night before were stacked high against the wall, which resulted in the temperature inside being almost as cold as outside. The children were blue with cold and tearful by the time Libby walked in, leaving Alf tethering the horses under an old oak tree to provide them with some shelter.

Sister Theresa looked fraught, with dark circles under

her eyes, and greeted Libby with bad news. 'I'd be grateful if you could examine Mary. Her fever is high, and I'm concerned that Joy might be picking up the same chest infection. I'll stoke up the fire while you attend to them.'

Libby, clutching her nurse's bag, nodded quickly. 'Sister Agnes has sent some pea soup. Please warm it up for the children, then we should leave as soon as possible,' she urged.

Rubbing his tired eyes, weary little Arthur asked, 'Where are we going, miss?'

'To Mary Vale,' Libby announced, with a bright smile.

'Good,' he smiled back in relief. 'It's nice and warm there - and there's always summat to eat.'

Seeing Joy looking pale and weak, Libby gave her a hug.

'My throat hurts, miss,' the girl said huskily.

'Don't worry, lovie, we've got some good cough medicine at Mary Vale, you'll feel better soon,' she promised.

From the bed Mary feebly croaked, 'How's our Susan?'

'Absolutely thriving,' Libby assured her. 'I'm told she took to the bottle and has been feeding regularly ever since her arrival at the Home.'

'That's good,' Mary smiled feebly. 'My milk's so weak, there's no nourishment in it these days.'

Seeing Alf standing by the door, Theresa urged him to take a seat and accept a cup of tea.

'Aye, lass, I'd be grateful. But,' he rolled his eyes towards the snow falling outside, 'we must be making tracks soon.'

By the time Mary and the children were fed and dressed and had visited the outside privy, it was well on into the afternoon. After loading Mary and Joy in the cart, Libby tucked them up under the warm blankets they had been keeping warm by the Carters' fire. Alf improvised a make-shift tarpaulin roof that provided his passengers with some protection from the swirling snow.

'You'll be travelling beside me, on the passenger seat,' he told Sister Theresa, who had borrowed Mary's old shawl and coat to keep her warm.

'If you get cold, there's some tea in a Thermos,' Libby told the nun before turning to Arthur, muffled up in an overcoat with a thick scarf tied across his chest. 'Put on your woolly hood and mittens,' she told him briskly. 'You'll be riding with me, son.'

'On the hoss!' Arthur gleefully exclaimed. Peering at Snowball, who was irritably stamping his shod feet on the icy ground, Arthur was suddenly wary. 'Is there really room up there for me?'

'Plenty of room,' Libby replied. 'You can sit in front of me, and I'll keep you snug and warm.'

Popping Arthur on to the saddle, Libby swung up after him and then, gathering in the reins, swiftly trotted after Alf who was already on the move. Guiding Snowball around the side of the cart, she came up along-side Alf.

The farmer was looking distinctly grim. 'I wish I could get old Captain to put a spurt on,' he mumbled. 'Just look at that sky up ahead.' He nodded in the direction they were heading. 'That's a damn blizzard over yonder, and we're riding straight into it.'

Libby's heart sank. Transporting vulnerable passengers in the cold was hard enough, but making a hazardous journey in a snowy blizzard was downright terrifying.

'Would it be safer to go back and avoid the blizzard altogether?' she asked.

Alf vehemently shook his head. 'Nay, lass, that would be the worst thing we could do, the Carters' cottage could be locked in deep snowdrifts for days, the best thing we can do is keep on moving – as quickly as we can,' he urged. 'Keep Snowball up ahead of us, Captain might quicken his speed if he tries to keep up with him.'

With the lively little pony leading the way, Captain did indeed increase his speed. They made good progress, until the blizzard hit and the snowstorm that engulfed them turned the entire world white and bewildering.

'Don't stop, keep moving, I don't want the cartwheels to get rutted in the drifts,' Alf yelled over the wind that was ripping at the tarpaulin sheltering Mary and Joy, huddled together in the back of the cart.

With the biting wind in her face, Libby was concerned about Arthur, who was in the teeth of the gale. 'Sweetheart,' she instructed, 'pull your hood down as far as you can over your face, and duck your head down to avoid this nasty cold wind.'

'Right, miss,' he said obediently.

Plodding on along the path that was banked up with deep snowdrifts, Libby seriously wondered if they had made the right decision. 'Trust in God, and keep moving,' she said through gritted teeth.

As the wind howled around them, showering swirls of snow in their faces, the ground underfoot became treacherously slippy. Feeling Snowball starting to skid and slide, Libby reassuringly patted his warm neck. 'Good lad,' she said, 'Steady, boy.' When she heard an echo of her own voice, she glanced down to find little Arthur valiantly repeating her words.

'Good lad,' he squeaked as he leant forward to pat the pony's neck. 'Steady, boy.'

Somehow, Arthur's cheerful confidence in her and her pony revived Libby's flagging spirits. If a six-year-old could believe in a miracle at a time like this then so could she. Clicking softly, she guided Snowball around the drifts, constantly reassuring him. Glancing quickly over her shoulder, she caught sight of Alf, perched on his cart and covered in snow, while poor Captain, too old to be on such a journey, plodded steadfastly forward. Libby's heart filled up with love at the sight of them both; how lucky she was to have Alf's friendship. Not only had he helped her uncover Thorp's black-market ring, but now here he was, risking his life to save a family in need.

Doubling back, she rode alongside Sister Theresa. 'Have you checked Mary and Joy?'

Theresa nodded. 'The tarpaulin's keeping some of the snow off them, let's hope it doesn't get torn away by this wretched wind.'

Libby moved back up to the front of the procession. Now unable to see anything but the swirling and blinding snow, she and Snowball doggedly followed the path, which grew narrower as snowdrifts settled – and darker too as the midwinter light faded. Squinting and disorientated, Libby tried to make out familiar landmarks. But seeing none, she panicked that she might have taken the wrong turn and was leading the little party into unfamiliar territory.

Firmly taking herself in hand, she muttered out loud,

'You've been along this way dozens of times, you know it, just stay focused and follow the path.'

With the wind tearing at her long hair and biting at her cheekbones, Libby wasn't immediately aware of Arthur singing; hearing him now in a vast, silent snow-blasted world verged almost on the miraculous. Blinking against the snow that was stinging her eyes, Libby gazed down in awe at the little boy, with his woolly hood pulled down over the upper part of his face, leaving only his mouth exposed.

'*Alas, my love, you do me wrong to cast me off discourteously* . . .'

His innocent voice, sweet and high, soared out from his small body like a prayer. The beautiful romantic words, combined with his breathtaking high notes, rolled into the snowy air where they seemed to hang, briefly suspended, before being tossed away on the wind.

Giving him a quick squeeze with her free hand, Libby whispered in his ear, 'Thank you for the singing, Arthur, it's making me feel very happy.'

'Shall I sing some more, miss?'

'I'd love it, if you want to,' she responded.

'I feel better when I sing, especially when I'm cold.'

And so, singing together, they continued through the storm until they saw, very faintly up ahead, tiny specks of golden light.

Thinking she might now be snow-blind and hallucinating, Libby said, 'Arthur, can you make anything out up ahead of us?'

'Yes, miss, some lights.'

'Thank God,' Libby virtually sobbed.

Sensing they were close to home, Snowball tossed his pretty head and increased his speed.

'Yeah, faster, faster!' Arthur cried out in delight as he bounced up and down in the saddle.

'Whoa, boy,' Libby cautioned. 'We don't want you slipping and breaking a leg.' Turning round, she called out to Sister Theresa and Alf, 'We're nearly there!'

'Mary Vale!' Arthur cried out excitedly.

Smiling, the young nun whispered, 'Thank God, we're home.'

Drifts were piled high in Mary Vale's drive, but somebody had been out and shovelled a path through the snow. Was it Sister Agnes? Out with a posse of pregnant women, all issued with shovels and instructions to keep the drive clear? Libby smiled to herself. I wouldn't put it past her, she thought fondly.

Before Libby had even dismounted from Snowball, Mary Vale's front door was thrown open and out rushed Sister Agnes and Ada, followed by little Catherine.

'You made it!' Ada exclaimed in delight.

'We've been worried sick,' Sister Agnes said as she scooped Arthur into her arms and hugged his snowy body close.

'Poor cold horsie,' Catherine cried as she stroked Snowball's sodden neck.

'Let's get you all inside,' Agnes urged.

Between them Libby and Sister Theresa helped Mary out of the cart, then led her indoors while Alf lifted Joy in his arms. Once inside the Home, the travellers blinked in wonder at the Christmas tree that had gone up in their absence, feeling dazed and still slightly snow-blind. Glittering with silver threads of tinsel and bright with softly glowing, jewel-coloured lights, it seemed to the weary travellers an apparition of perfect beauty.

Still in Alf's steady arms, weak little Joy gasped, 'Is it real or am I dreaming?'

'It's real all right, lovie,' Alf told her. 'A nice surprise for Christmas.'

Thawing out, and wildly excited now that he was safely indoors, Arthur (trailed by an overexcited Catherine) skipped around the base of the tree, quite spontaneously breaking into song.

'*Oh, Christmas tree, oh, Christmas tree, how lovely are your branches . . .*'

Urging them to remove their dripping outer clothing, Agnes gathered them all into the sitting room, where a fire blazed in the hearth.

'Oh, this is wonderful,' Libby sighed as she rubbed her freezing hands in the welcome heat. 'Alf,' she called to the farmer. 'Come and get warm.'

Alf was heading towards the door. 'Nay, lass, I've got to get the horses back.'

'Wait, I'll come with you.'

Hurrying after Alf, Libby spotted Ada on her way out. 'Ada,' she cried as she ran up to her. 'How's Beth?'

Ada's beautiful smile immediately put Libby's mind at rest. 'She finally gave birth to a gorgeous baby girl this morning, just after you left.'

'Oh, how wonderful!' Libby cried. 'How is she?'

'Weak – the labour was long, because the baby got stuck due to the placenta being low. When there was a fear of the placenta breaking up, there was no choice but to operate. In the end Jamie called in the surgeon from the local cottage hospital, who did a fine job. Thank God, mother and baby are well, though it was touch and go at one stage.'

'How is the little girl coping?' Libby nervously asked.

'She's presently with Dora in the baby nursery. Beth's in no state to feed her. The little girl's doing well, considering everything she has been through – though, as you can imagine, she's very much on the small side.'

'I'm longing to see them both,' Libby said excitedly. 'But first, I must help Alf stable the horses.'

'Don't tell Catherine that,' Ada grinned. 'She'll be after you like a shot, if she knows you're going to the farm.'

After grooming her pony and covering him with a snug blanket, Libby made both Snowball and Captain a warm bran mash, which they ate with relish before turning their attention to their full hay nets.

'They've both been wonderful today,' she said to Alf. 'We'd never have made it without the horses.'

Alf, who was fastidiously drying Captain off with hand-fuls of straw, nodded. 'Good beasts,' he murmured.

Seeing his weary wind-blasted face and tired old eyes, Libby said, 'Please, Alf, promise me you'll go home just as soon as you've locked up the stable for the night?'

'Don't you worry, lass, I'll be on my way soon,' he assured her.

'And thank you again for being such a wonderful friend,' she said, with tears in her eyes.

Embarrassed, but clearly touched by her words, he muttered, 'Get away with you, lass.'

Then, before she could stop herself, Libby kissed him on the cheek. 'You're a hero!' she declared.

Back in the sitting room, Sister Agnes was pouring tea and handing around hot buttered toast.

Seeing her colleague working so hard, Sister Theresa automatically sprang to her feet to assist her. 'Here, let me help.'

'You'll do no such thing,' Agnes scolded. 'Stay right where you are and get warm, dear.'

Though weak and utterly exhausted, Mary was anxious to see Susan.

'I'll take you to the baby nursery,' Matron volunteered. 'Though I would advise that you peep at your baby through the window, we're anxious that you don't pass any infection on to her.'

Mary immediately nodded in agreement with Matron. 'It will put my mind at rest if I can just see Susan.'

Leaving her children in Sister Agnes's devoted care, Mary followed Matron to the baby nursery while Sister Theresa made her way to the convent in order to report back to Reverend Mother.

'Put two hot-water bottles in the guest-room beds,' Agnes instructed the young nun before she departed. 'I'm going to give the kiddies a bath before I put them to bed. I'm hoping the hot steam might ease Joy's wheezy chest,' she added fretfully.

Hurrying back to the convent, crossing herself as she passed the silver and blue statue of Our Lady, Star of the Sea, Theresa thought back over the last twenty-four hours.

It had been nothing short of a miracle that they had got safely back to Mary Vale all in one piece. Sighing, she thanked God for his many blessings – Mary could now be properly nursed, baby Susan would soon be flourishing under Dora's doting attention, and Sister Agnes could shower Joy and Arthur with love, cuddles and as many treats as she could dream up, given rationing shortages.

Slipping into the incense-perfumed darkness of the silent chapel, glowing with rows of candles flickering on the high altar, Theresa fell to her knees and with her head buried in her hands she thanked God for a peaceful end to a terrifying, turbulent day.

Mary Vale had, yet again, provided sanctuary for travellers in the storm.

32. Sleep in Heavenly Peace

Though she had been cautioned about not exerting herself, Margaret decided that going over to the convent to see Mary and the children could not possibly do her any harm. Having asked Sister Agnes for directions to the convent's guest rooms, Margaret self-consciously crept through the empty, silent winding corridors until she heard the unmistakeable sound of Arthur giggling. Following the noise, she came to a door and gently tapped on it.

Throwing it open, Arthur, clearly back to his old confident self, beamed. 'Hello, Miss Margaret, come in!'

Margaret was thrilled to find sweet Sister Theresa with the Carters, who all looked radically better and brighter than when she had last laid eyes on them.

'Margaret,' Mary smiled, 'how lovely to see you.'

'What a relief it is to see you all again,' Margaret cried as she gripped Mary's hand. 'How are you feeling, dear?'

'So much better, thanks to all the care and attention I'm getting here – being warm and well fed helps too,' Mary said gratefully, before adding, 'I know we put your friends to so much trouble yesterday, but really I don't think we would have survived another week in that hovel of a cottage.'

'Let's not worry about that now,' Sister Theresa urged as she spooned cough medicine into Mary's mouth. 'You're here, safe and sound at Mary Vale, for the time being.'

'As soon as I'm on my feet, I must see my husband,' Mary fretted. 'He doesn't even know we've left the cottage.'

Concerned that Mary was already thinking of going on a hospital visit, which she certainly wasn't fit enough to do, Margaret quickly made a suggestion. 'I'm sure we can phone the ward and ask to speak to Sam, or at least leave a message for him. You are in no state to go outdoors at the moment, Mary.' Turning to Joy, who was lying on her little narrow single bed, Margaret gently asked, 'How are you, darling?'

'I feel better now that Sister Theresa is looking after us, Miss Margaret,' the girl replied. 'She's got some good cough medicine that tastes of oranges.'

'You'll all be on your feet soon,' Margaret said, with a bright smile. 'We're hoping you'll come to the Home's Christmas dinner tomorrow; the residents are longing to see you children again, and longing to hear you sing again too.'

'Can I come back with you now, miss?' exuberant Arthur asked. 'We could build a giant snowman.'

Margaret looked down at her tummy, bigger than ever, and burst out laughing. 'Arthur, I'll happily watch you build a snowman, but I honestly don't think I can even bend down these days.'

'When's your baby coming, miss?' he asked.

Margaret smiled. 'Not too long now,' she told the charming little boy.

Leaving Mary and her daughter to rest in their room, Sister Theresa walked back through the convent with Margaret, who held Arthur firmly by the hand. Stopping by the statue of Our Lady, both women genuflected but not before Arthur, keen to run across the entry hallway, tried to release his hand from Margaret's.

'No, dear,' she firmly told him. 'This is a quiet, peaceful place that we must respect. You can play outside, if you like, or we can sit by the sitting-room fire and do a jigsaw.'

'I want to build a snowman,' Arthur announced.

'I thought you might say that,' Margaret chuckled. Turning to Sister Theresa, she added, 'You seem to have bounced back after yesterday's terrifying journey.'

The young nun grinned. 'I have to admit, I was scared stiff. The snow swallowed up all the familiar landmarks and there was one point, as the light was fading, when I thought we would be going around in circles all night long. If I hadn't been sat next to Alf, who was completely unflappable, I would have been in tears. I've never known a storm like it.'

'I won't ever forget hearing that you'd turned up at the front door, covered in snow – I don't think I've ever been so relieved in my life,' Margaret recalled.

'It was so wonderful to walk into the heat, and to thaw out. And the sight of that splendid Christmas tree – it was such a wonderful surprise.'

'We'd planned to get the Carter children to help us decorate it but, as it happened, things turned out otherwise,' Margaret smiled. 'Nevertheless, it was a joy to see their faces when they walked in and saw it all set up for Christmas.'

Once back in the Home, Sister Theresa hurried into the kitchen where, with all the Christmas dinner preparations under way, she was urgently needed. Meanwhile, Margaret slipped on her warmest coat and stoutest boots so she could supervise Arthur building his snowman, all the while singing 'Frosty The Snowman'.

Eventually, when his hands were numb with cold and he needed a carrot for the snowman's nose, Arthur agreed to go indoors on condition that his snowman didn't go for a walk in his absence. Charmed by the little boy's vivid imagination, Margaret assured him that 'Frosty' would definitely be there for him to play with later in the day. 'It's too cold for him to go anywhere today.'

Smelling the rich spicy aroma drifting from the kitchen, Arthur bade a hasty goodbye to Margaret, who seized the moment to visit Beth on the post-natal ward.

After checking with Libby that it was a convenient moment to visit her patient, Margaret asked, 'Is she all right?'

'She's very weak, and in pain too from her op, but I'm sure she would love to see you, Margaret. But please try not to overtax her.'

Creeping into the room, Margaret gazed at Beth, whose eyes were closed. But the minute she heard footsteps, her eyes flew open and a smile lit up her pretty, pale face.

'I'm so pleased to see you,' she said.

'I've been wondering how you are, dear.'

'Exhausted, if I'm honest,' Beth confessed. 'And in pain from the Caesarean – it's difficult to get about, and the stitches hurt.'

'But how wonderful that your baby is born,' Margaret exclaimed.

Proud love suffused Beth's face. 'My little girl, Holly,'

she declared. 'She's so lovely but very small. They're keeping her in an incubator for the time being and bottle-feeding her. I can't sit long without being in pain, so bottle-feeding suits me, and I'm told it suits Holly. Nurse Dora's in charge of her, and she pops in regularly to report on Holly's progress. When I'm strong enough, they'll take me in a wheelchair to see her.'

'Be assured,' Margaret said, 'there is no better person than Dora to look after your baby.'

'She told me that the Carters' baby is in the nursery too,' Beth continued. 'Thank God Libby got them out of that terrible cottage.'

'She was so brave, riding all the way over to Allithwaite and back in that awful snowstorm,' Margaret said.

'Libby's a very special woman, I've never known anybody quite like her,' Beth said, with a lump in her throat. 'She certainly saved my life, and my baby's too. She's a wonderful midwife, even though she wasn't with me when I finally did give birth, which is what I had always hoped for, but it wasn't meant to be.' Leaning closer, Beth confided in Margaret. 'Dr Reid looked after me when my waters broke; the shock of hearing that Ronnie had been arrested set me off.' Beth gave a heavy sigh. 'Don't get me wrong, I knew my husband was a bad 'un, but it never crossed my mind that he was actually trading black-market goods. No wonder he was hardly ever at home,' she exclaimed. 'And no wonder he appointed Mrs Grimsdale to guard me – if he couldn't be there, somebody else had to control me,' she said bitterly. 'Can you believe, all the time we were married Ronnie was storing illegal goods in a warehouse in Kents Bank? Libby told me she had actually seen it,' she exclaimed. 'Stuffed full of contraband – which, apparently, he shipped across the bay under cover of darkness.'

Margaret, who could well believe anything bad about Ronnie Thorp, gave a little shrug before she said, with undisguised pleasure, 'Well, at least you're free of him, Beth.'

With not a hint of sadness at her husband's conviction, Beth spoke frankly about her feelings. 'I can't believe my luck!' she confessed. 'The thing I've most wanted, most prayed for – that Ronnie would disappear out of my life and, to be truthful, I really didn't care how – has come to pass. It might sound like a heartless thing to say, but he killed the love in me long ago. He's a cruel, ruthless, unscrupulous man, and now he'll go to prison for a very long time,' she said, with some satisfaction.

'I've not heard much officially about his arrest, but news of a local scandal like this one spreads like wildfire,' Margaret remarked. 'Sister Agnes tells me that her sister, who lives in town, says everybody's talking about it in Grange.'

'Hardly surprising. Ronnie was never a popular man – he was always too busy trying to prove he was better than others – but now he's been proved to be a complete scoundrel.' With a determined gleam in her green eyes, Beth continued. 'Once I'm back on my feet, I'm going to take over the running of the estate that Ronnie bought with my family's money – by rights it's mine, it belongs to me. I'll make it my business to put a lot of things right, Margaret. The Carters will be rehoused in a decent place for a reasonable rent, and I'm going to make sure that Sam Carter is properly taken care of. Wait and see,' she predicted. 'Things will change on the Thorp Estate. I don't want my daughter growing up in a valley where she has to pay every day for the sins of her father. It'll take time and a lot of healing, but the Thorps of Allithwaite will have a good name under my rule. That's the promise I made to myself, the minute I first held my baby daughter in my arms.'

Thrilled that all these changes might be imminent, Margaret was nevertheless concerned that she had allowed Beth to overexert herself. 'I should be going now,' she said as she rose to go. 'You need to get some rest so that you can carry out all these wonderful plans of yours.'

Gazing at Margaret's enormous tummy, Beth smiled. 'You'll be a mother soon too. It's the most powerful feeling, holding a new life in your hands, all you want to do is protect and love your baby for ever.' Beth's smile faded as she realized what she had said. 'I'm sorry, Margaret, I don't know what your plans are for your baby, forgive me if my words were out of order.'

Margaret gave a heavy sigh. Stroking her tummy, she said, 'I'm having my baby adopted, Beth.'

'Oh, I'm sorry . . .'

Weary of forever hiding her emotions, Margaret suddenly burst into tears. 'I would love to keep my baby,' she sobbed. 'I've gone back and forth in my mind, trying to think how I could manage it. I haven't got either a home or a job, and I've little money. I don't know where I'll live, or what I'll live on; what kind of existence is that for a new-born baby?' she asked, with tears streaming down her face. 'Not to mention the stigma of being born out of matrimony – a bastard.'

'What about the father, can he help you?' Beth cautiously asked.

'He's married with a family. He never deceived me; I knew full well about his situation when I fell in love with him. He doesn't even know that I'm pregnant with his baby.' Dabbing her red eyes, Margaret stifled her sobs. 'I've made my mind up to do what's best for the baby – he or she never asked to be born.'

Repeating herself, Beth murmured, 'I'm so very sorry, Margaret.'

'Me too, Beth, me too.'

In the Home's hallway, dominated by the splendid, sparkling Christmas tree, all was excitement and joy. The thoughtful residents had secretly left little presents at the base of the tree for all of the Carter family.

'Look, Miss Margaret,' Arthur cried when she reappeared after her visit to Beth. 'There are gifts for me and Joy, and some for Mam too. Ooh, I am excited,' he cried as he flung his arms around Margaret and kissed her hard on the check. 'I love Mary Vale,' he said. 'I wish I could stay here forever.'

Margaret clung to the little boy. 'I love Mary Vale too,' she gulped as she struggled to hide her clamouring emotions.

God, how I love this place, she thought to herself. The friends she had made, the women she had met: Gladys, Maisie, Mary, Beth, Sisters Theresa and Agnes, Libby,

Dora, Matron, Ada. Even if she left tomorrow, she would carry these women in her heart. Brave, strong, outspoken, big-hearted – and, above all, compassionate and non-judgemental. But best of all she loved Mary Vale, because here in this place her baby was safe inside her; while she was in the Home the baby she loved was, just for now, completely hers.

33. We Wish You a Merry Christmas

Christmas morning dawned, with yet another flurry of snow transforming the already wintry garden into a wonderland of deep drifts and trees glittering with icicles.

Straight after breakfast, everybody – including Mary, Joy and Arthur – gathered around the Christmas tree where presents were distributed. Though money was short, and basic commodities were hard to come by, the residents had ingeniously created surprise presents for one another, and for the children too. Joy was given several little peg dolls with knitted hair and painted peg legs; Arthur had a little home-made wooden train attached to a length of string; and Mary loved the red scarf and matching gloves Sister Agnes had knitted for her. Sister Theresa's gift of wild-bird colouring books delighted the children, and Margaret's Beatrix Potter picture books were received with gasps of surprise and pleasure. As well as the gifts, there were stockings (hung on the fireplace in the sitting room), filled with nuts and an apple in the toe, a small bar of chocolate, a few boiled sweets and, peeping out of the top, a knitted giraffe for Arthur and a knitted fairy waving a wand for Joy. Amid much laughter and cries of excitement, presents were opened and smiles of gratitude were lovingly exchanged.

Desperate to run out into the garden and build an igloo, Arthur, knowing his sister wasn't yet well enough to play outdoors, begged the residents to join him. Laughing and giggling, several of them willingly donned warm coats and boots and hurried after the little boy. Well wrapped up in his warm tweedy overcoat, he organized them to dig tunnels in the show drifts with shovels they found in the garden shed. Though Sister Theresa was needed in the kitchen, she made an excuse to briefly join in the dig, taking mugs of hot Bovril into the garden and borrowing a shovel to join in the digging.

'Can I sleep out here tonight, Sister Trees?' Arthur asked in all innocence.

'Darling,' she cried, 'you'll freeze.'

Pointing at the snowman he had previously built with Margaret, Arthur protested, 'But my snowman sleeps out here.'

'He's made of snow, you're made of skin!' Theresa laughed as she hugged the little boy. 'Anyway, we would miss you if you stayed out here.'

Leaving Arthur playing snowballs with some jolly residents, Theresa hurried back indoors. When she arrived in the kitchen, she was delighted to find that Ada and Catherine were there too.

'Jamie's coming later,' Ada explained. 'I thought you and Sister Agnes might need a hand, plus Catherine here is desperate to give you your home-made Christmas presents.'

Presenting a gingerbread donkey to Sister Theresa and a gingerbread duck to Sister Agnes, the little girl told them proudly, 'Daddy's got a pig.'

'I've never had a gingerbread donkey,' Theresa admitted as she smiled at the donkey's wonky legs and broken ears. 'Thank you, Catherine, it's perfect.'

On hearing that Arthur was playing in the garden, Catherine, who hero-worshipped the little boy, was keen to join in the fun. 'Come,' she said to the two nuns who were basting pheasants. 'Come and play,' she implored.

'We can't, my sweetie,' Agnes, flushed from the heat of the oven, replied. 'We have to cook your dinner.' But seeing the child's deflated expression, Agnes relented. 'All right then, just for five minutes.'

With her dark-blue eyes sparkling with amusement, Ada urged the nun to go and enjoy herself. 'I'll take over here,' she promised.

While Sister Theresa mixed chopped wild herbs with onions, breadcrumbs and dripping fat to make a tasty stuffing, Ada put the Christmas puddings on a low light to simmer.

'They look nice and dark and shiny,' she commented.

'To be honest, it's just a big dash of gravy browning that gives the puddings a nice dark colour,' Theresa admitted. 'There's not much fruit in any of them, they're mostly breadcrumbs mixed with spice and as many currants and raisins as we could scrounge.'

Ada gave an appreciative sniff. 'They smell lovely anyway.'

'They'll be fine served up with white sauce and a splash of brandy that Sister Agnes squirrels away in her pantry,' Theresa grinned.

When the kitchen door swung open and Margaret walked in, the two women smiled a warm welcome.

'Merry Christmas, Margaret,' Ada cried. 'How are we feeling this morning?'

'Fine,' Margaret beamed. 'I just wondered if you might need help in here?'

Ada shook her head. 'You can sit at the kitchen table and watch us, but you're not doing anything.'

'I'm a very good peeler,' Margaret hinted.

Plonking a basin of carrots and sprouts on the table, Theresa said, 'As long as you don't get up from that chair, I'd be grateful if you could peel that lot.'

As the women worked in easy companionship alongside each other, Libby dashed in to make Beth's breakfast.

'Heavens!' Theresa exclaimed. 'Half of Mary Vale will be in here soon.'

'Happy Christmas, all!' Libby called cheerily. 'Will I get in your way if I make Beth a hot drink and some toast? She's just woken up from a good sleep and announced that she's starving, which is wonderful news, as normally you can't get a thing down her throat.'

Margaret eagerly asked, 'How is Beth?'

Libby did a little twirl of happiness in the middle of the kitchen. 'A changed woman,' she announced. 'It's like a miracle. She's eating, smiling, sleeping and talking about the future. And best of all, she's fallen completely and hopelessly in love with Holly, who is really the sweetest, dearest baby imaginable. Dora's done a great job with bottle-feeding her, she's put on a bit of weight already, and Beth's getting plenty of rest while Holly's being looked after in the baby nursery.'

'I'm so pleased,' Sister Theresa said. 'If anybody deserves happiness, it's Beth Thorp.'

'Has she said much about her husband?' Ada asked.

'Not much,' Libby answered. 'And when she does, it's always with a huge sense of relief that he's safely behind bars.'

Thinking how much she adored her husband, and how intolerable life would be without Jamie at her side, Ada sighed. 'How awful to have absolutely no affection for the man you married.'

'I think any affection she might have had was beaten out of her long ago,' Libby answered knowingly.

Sister Theresa paused in her work. 'I do worry what will happen when Thorp is released from prison,' she said anxiously.

'That won't be for years,' Margaret responded. 'Black-market dealing is seriously frowned on, and quite right too. Making a profit from selling illegal goods, while the rest of society is living on the breadline, is downright despicable behaviour.'

'I quite agree,' Libby responded robustly as she put a pot of tea and a plate of toast on a tray. 'Now, if you'll excuse me, I'd better get back to my patient.'

Having finished her task, Margaret asked, 'May I come and see Beth?'

'Of course,' the young nurse replied.

Though still thin and pale, there were nevertheless notice-able changes in Beth's looks. Her long silver-blonde hair, recently washed and brushed, swung in curling waves around her slender shoulders. Her lovely green eyes shone with a new light, and when she talked about her baby a tender smile played constantly on her lips.

'Oh, Margaret,' she sighed, 'I'm so lucky – I just can't

believe it. Being a mother is such a wonderful experience.' Seeing a shadow of sadness flash across Margaret's face, Beth reached across to take her hand. 'Margaret, I've been thinking,' she started hesitantly. 'I'll soon be looking for somebody I trust to look after Thorp Hall. I certainly don't want Mrs Grimsdale living there one minute longer than she has to,' she grimaced. 'I plan to improve it, do it up, and make it into a lovely home. Presently it's dark and dreary, but it could be beautiful. It has a wonderful garden with a grand view of the fells –' Cutting herself short, she came to the point. 'Anyway, would you ever consider living there and helping me?'

Utterly speechless, Margaret could only gape at Beth.

'I intend to go back and forth between the Hall and my parents' farm to start with,' Beth elaborated. 'I want Holly to grow up, like I did, with an appreciation of family and farming. In effect, we would be sharing Thorp Hall – really, it's big enough to house three families, so we wouldn't get in each other's way.'

Margaret held up a hand to stop Beth mid-flow. 'Beth, this is an amazing offer, but why on earth are you suggesting this to me?'

Looking self-conscious, Beth said, 'I'm offering you a home. So you can keep your baby,' she added, with genuine affection. 'Having just become a mother, having given birth to Holly, I know the joy of motherhood, and I want you to know it too . . . if that's what you want, of course.' She paused before she added, 'I felt I really had to say something, I hope I haven't caused any offence.'

Totally overwhelmed by Beth's immense generosity, Margaret started to cry. 'I don't know what to say.'

'Don't say anything,' Beth begged. 'Just think about it for now. Please, will you do that?'

Margaret nodded. 'Yes, I'll definitely do that, Beth. And thank you from the bottom of my heart for your offer, it's given me hope for the first time in a long while.'

34. Unto Us a Child is Born

After having built as many igloos as they could endure in the freezing cold, children and residents alike hurried indoors to get warm by the sitting-room fire and to help with the Christmas dinner preparations. Margaret took charge of both Arthur and Catherine, leaving Ada free to help in the kitchen. Libby, on duty with Matron and Dora, was surprised when Jamie walked on to the ward.

'I thought you were off duty today, Doctor,' Libby said when he walked into Beth's room.

Turning to Beth, now sitting up on her bed, Jamie thought, My God, she's unrecognizable from the woman I visited at Thorp Hall. Smiling, he said, 'I am off duty, but I wanted to see how my patient is feeling this morning?'

Beth virtually glowed. 'Libby's taking me in a wheel-chair to the baby nursery, to see Holly before dinner. I just can't wait to hold her.'

Libby quickly added, 'I thought it might be wiser for Beth to have Christmas dinner in her room, rather than the dining room, which might be a bit loud and crowded today.'

Jamie nodded. 'Let's not go overdoing things just because it's Christmas,' he warned. 'We don't want to put too much strain on those stitches – which, if you don't mind, I'd quite like to take a look at, Beth.'

'Of course, Doctor,' Beth agreed.

After Jamie had examined Beth's tummy, assuring her that the stitches were healing nicely, he went on his way to find his wife and daughter, leaving Libby gently settling Beth into a wheelchair.

'Off we go,' she said as she pushed the wheelchair down the long winding corridor to the post-natal ward where tiny Holly was lying, sleeping peacefully in an incubator.

In a rapture of joy, Beth gazed at her sweetly sleeping daughter. 'She's so perfect,' she sighed. 'Smaller than the other babies, but perfect, just look at her tiny hands and little pink fingernails.'

'She is a gorgeous baby,' Libby fondly agreed.

'To think I might have lost her,' Beth murmured. 'If it hadn't been for your intervention, she might have died, Libby.'

'We were lucky, dear, everything worked out for the best in the end. Blow a kiss to your little girl, and I'll get you back into bed.'

'One more minute,' Beth begged as she turned her gaze back to Holly. 'Merry Christmas, my darling,' she whispered. 'The first of many more to come, please God.'

As many residents and staff as possible gathered for Christmas dinner, leaving only a few in the post- and ante-natal wards, Beth included. With her patient safely tucked up in bed, Libby hurried to join in the fun and games in the dining room, where home-made paper chains had been strung criss-cross from the ceiling and little candles flickered on the windowsills, shedding a gentle light in contrast to the stark white of the constantly falling snow outside. Sitting down between Alf and Margaret, Libby smiled at the happy faces all around: the Carters across the table opposite her, Ada and her family, Dora and her shy husband, Matron, Father Ben, Gladys, Maisie and the other residents, all wearing home-made paper hats and pulling home-made Christmas crackers.

After Father Ben had said grace, Sisters Agnes and Theresa swooped in, bearing platters of roast potatoes, game pie (bulked out with rabbit and pigeon), boiled ham (courtesy of a neighbouring pig-farmer friend of Alf's), festive stuffing, sprouts, leeks, carrots and jugs of rich brown gravy. In between the chatter and laughter Libby's thoughts drifted to home, Newby Bridge. She knew her parents would be sharing Christmas dinner – in their case, a hand-reared goose – with relatives, but neither of their sons would be there, and nor was Libby. Maybe next year, she thought guiltily. This year was her first Mary Vale Christmas, and she was happy and privileged to spend it with the women she loved and had cared for in recent months, even if she missed her family. Knowing she was deeply missed at home, and to make up for her absence, Libby would make sure to plan a visit just as soon as she could.

Seeing Margaret at her side, wriggling rather uncomfortably, Libby whispered, 'Everything all right, dear?'

Looking a little flushed, Margaret replied, 'Yes, I just feel very full.' She rolled a hand over her very large tummy. 'The food is delicious but it's too filling for me.'

Catching sight of Margaret's unfinished meal, ever-hungry Gladys cried, 'Waste not, want not, pass it down here, lovie.'

After Margaret had shared her meal with Gladys and others, Libby suggested that she go for a lie-down.

'I'll wait until the meal's over, then I'll go,' Margaret replied.

When the dinner plates had been cleared away by grateful residents, the Christmas puddings were carried in by a smiling Jamie who placed them before Matron. Pouring Sister Agnes's precious brandy over the steaming puddings, much to Catherine's delight, Jamie set light to them, and as they briefly blazed all sang.

> *Now bring us some figgy pudding*
> *Now bring us some figgy pudding*
> *Now bring us some figgy pudding*
> *And bring it out here!*
>
> *Good tidings we bring*
> *To you and your kin,*
> *We wish you a Merry Christmas*
> *And a Happy New Year.*

Raising their glasses of home-made root beer, and dandelion and burdock – another of Alf's contributions – the diners cried, 'Here's to the cooks!'

Blushing and overwhelmed, Sister Theresa fled into the kitchen, but Sister Agnes took a bow before she served the fragrant pudding with white sauce. Joy and Arthur Carter, who had never seen so much food in their lives, simply couldn't believe their eyes when they saw the blazing puddings.

'Mam, why has Dr Jamie set our dinner on fire?' indignant Arthur cried.

'He's just warming it up, lovie,' Mary explained.

'Are you enjoying your meal, Mrs Carter?' Matron, just across the table from her, enquired.

'I certainly am,' Mary assured her. 'It's a feast fit for a queen. We've not eaten so well in years,' she finished gratefully.

'Have you had much communication with your husband recently?' thoughtful Matron asked.

'Hardly any,' Mary told her. 'I've tried phoning his ward, just to tell him of our whereabouts – he doesn't even know that we've moved into Mary Vale. When I phone, he's either asleep or not strong enough to speak. We did manage to post him a Christmas card, though.'

'He's in safe hands,' Matron comforted her. 'I know Dr Reid has a high regard for the consultant taking care of your husband.'

'I appreciate that, Matron. The question is, how long can they keep him on that ward? And where will he go when he's discharged?'

Joy interrupted them, turning Mary's attention to other things. The solemn-faced girl, with her long hair neatly plaited, said, 'We're going to see our Susan in the baby nursery, now that we're not coughing so much.'

'How lovely,' Matron exclaimed. 'I saw her only this morning, she's thriving.'

'She is that,' beamed nearby Dora. 'A little sweetheart you've got there, Mrs Carter.'

'I've missed her so much,' Mary confessed.

'Well, as soon as you've got your strength back, your baby will be joining you,' Matron assured the anxious mother.

Overhearing the conversation, Libby and Margaret exchanged a knowing look.

'Mary still hasn't a clue about Beth's plans for her family,' Libby whispered.

'I know,' Margaret agreed. 'I'm just wondering when she's going to tell them, I really hope it's sooner rather than later. You heard what Mary just said; she's worried about what happens next to them all.'

'I don't believe it will be long – Beth's getting stronger by the day,' Libby assured her.

Lowering her voice, Margaret added, 'Beth's come up with an interesting plan for me too.'

Wide-eyed, Libby gazed at her. 'What do you mean?'

'She asked if I'd like to take over Mrs Grimsdale's job.'

Libby burst into peals of laughter. 'You mean, live in Thorp Hall and ban anybody from entering?' she joked.

'I hope not,' Margaret smiled. 'Beth's idea is that we both live there together. She said the place is big enough to house three families.'

'Oh, believe me, it's enormous,' Libby assured her.

'Beth's planning to go between Thorp Hall and her parents' home in the Borrowdale valley; she wants somebody permanently in the Hall, to keep an eye on the place.'

'It would do Beth the world of good if she could spend time with her family in Borrowdale. She missed them terribly, especially when she was pregnant, but Thorp restricted their visits.' Looking thoughtful, Libby asked, 'Are you seriously considering Beth's offer? It's a bit of a dreary place, dark and gloomy – like a prison, to be honest.'

'Beth's got plans to transform it into a proper home,' Margaret explained.

'It would improve with a lick of a paint,' Libby replied.

'It's certainly never been a home, not with Thorp and his housekeeper guarding it like a lion's den. But,' she added, 'it has lovely gardens and great views of the fells. It's a very generous offer.'

'It's a wonderful offer,' Margaret exclaimed. 'If I had a home, I could seriously think about keeping my baby – which, in truth, is all I've ever wanted. It could be a dream come true for me.'

'Dear, sweet Beth,' Libby murmured. 'She really is on a mission to do good. Talking of which,' she said as she rose from the table, 'I'd better get back to her and to the other patients on the wards.'

'You work so hard on our behalf,' Margaret smiled gratefully.

Wagging a finger in the air, Libby said with a teasing smile, 'Don't forget to go for a lie-down, lady.'

Margaret's lie-down never happened. As soon as dinner was cleared away, the residents moved into the cosy sitting room where a fire crackled in the hearth, and Gladys declared it was time for a sing-song. 'Come on, kiddies, gather round the piano.'

Realizing that this was certainly not the time to go and have a rest, Margaret perched awkwardly on the edge of the piano stool to play the opening chords for 'Silent Night'. After all the favourite carols had been sung, the residents begged for the more popular festive numbers – 'White Christmas', 'Rudolph The Red-Nosed Reindeer' and 'Jingle Bells' – which sent Catherine skipping around the room, hand in hand with giggling Arthur.

Suddenly feeling utterly weary, Margaret rose to stretch

her aching back. At which point, a stabbing pain shot down her back and then gripped her abdomen as tight as a vice.

'HAHHH!' she gasped.

Hearing her cry, and seeing the startled expression on her face, Gladys gave her a knowing look. 'Sit yourself down on the sofa, lovie.'

Still gripping her back, Margaret demurred. 'I'll just pop up to my room,' she murmured, just as Sister Theresa entered the room.

'Maybe you should take a look at Margaret,' Gladys urged. 'She's having a funny turn.'

Gently steering Margaret out of the room and away from the residents, Theresa suggested they go on to the ward, where Matron or Libby could examine her. Relieved that she didn't have to walk up two flights of stairs, Margaret immediately agreed. Feeling strange and oddly heavy, Margaret was grateful for Sister Theresa's firm hand on her elbow.

When she guided Margaret on to the ante-natal ward, the first person Theresa saw was Libby.

'Hello,' the nurse said, somewhat surprised.

Sister Theresa threw Libby a knowing look. 'You may need to examine Margaret,' she said quietly.

By the time Libby had settled her patient into a freshly made-up bed, Margaret had regular pains in the base of her back. With sweat breaking out on her brow, Margaret told Libby she had pains in her tummy too.

After a brief examination, Libby said, cool as a cucumber, 'The baby's head is well down, and you have a bloody mucus discharge. I think you're having contractions. Now, let's get those clothes off and put you in a nice fresh nightdress.'

Panicking, Margaret cried, 'But it shouldn't be now – I'm not due till January.'

Libby gave her a steady look. 'I think we can safely say, Margaret, that you are going into labour, dear.'

'B . . . b . . . but, it's too early,' Margaret said tremulously.

'You're nearly in your ninth month, Margaret,' Libby soothed. 'You should be okay.'

Still fearful, Margaret asked, 'Will my baby really be all right?'

Assuring the anxious mother, Libby answered calmly. 'We'll take the best of care of you and your baby. And really,' she gently smiled, 'there's nothing we can possibly do now to stop this little one coming out.'

After the effort of getting changed, Margaret had little time to ask further questions. Lying back down on her bed, she felt deep pain in her pelvic region.

'OUCH!' she cried.

'Your contractions are getting stronger,' Libby explained. 'You're in the early stages, but be prepared for them to speed up.'

Margaret gave an obedient nod. 'Is it really happening?' she asked incredulously.

Libby smiled. 'I'd say yes, it is.'

Thinking she needed to notify Matron of Margaret's condition, Libby briefly left the room only to return within minutes, accompanied by Matron whose very presence exuded a calm sense of authority.

'Libby tells me your labour has started.'

Margaret gave a bleak smile. 'I wasn't expecting it quite so soon,' she said ruefully.

'Babies have a habit of coming when they want to. Don't worry, we'll take care of you,' Matron confidently responded. 'Now let's have a little look at you, shall we?'

After she had examined Margaret, Matron explained. 'Your cervix has to be well dilated before baby can pass through. If you can manage it, don't waste your strength thrashing and protesting in between contractions. It'll wear you out, and you need to keep your energy for the next stage, when your baby is on the way out.'

Feeling a mixture of nervous excitement and fear, Margaret said, 'I'll try my best.'

'You won't be short of company,' Matron told Margaret. 'I'm on duty, and so is Libby, and even Ada and Dora are here in the building, so you're not without midwives.'

Beginning to feel a lot calmer, Margaret responded, 'The best midwives I could ever hope for.'

When Matron and Libby left to check up on their other patients, Margaret suddenly felt she could somehow sense Peter's presence; was she imagining his closeness, or had their souls reached out to each other as their child was about to enter the world? She hoped with all her heart that her lover was well and happy; oddly, she felt no anger or bitterness. Now it was her, alone with her baby, and her only thought was to deliver it safely, and to love it and care for it for as long as she could. A tight spasm across her tummy took Margaret's breath away; feeling the muscular contraction ripple down from the top of her uterus to the bottom, Margaret took deep steady breaths until the sensation had passed.

As the wintry afternoon sunlight faded from the garden Margaret's contractions increased, but all the time she was monitored and reassured by Matron or Libby. Even Ada called in to see Margaret before she and Jamie took Catherine (utterly exhausted after her thrilling day) home to bed. Darkness descended and a deep silence filled Mary Vale, shrouded in thick snow, standing as it had done for centuries on a high rocky promontory overlooking the Irish Sea where innumerable wintry bright stars were reflected in its rippling waters. All the frantic activity, preparation, laughter, chatter, singing and banter faded away like a dream; the only thing that was real was Margaret's labour. Clutching Libby's hand, she flopped back, exhausted, after riding out one contraction after another.

'You're doing so well,' Libby frequently told her. 'You're nearly there, you'll soon be pushing your baby into the world.'

When the time eventually came to push, after a long night of labouring, Margaret wondered if she would have enough strength left in her for this huge final burst of energy. But under Libby's steady, expert guidance she safely and comparatively easily delivered her baby into the world, just as the sun rose over the eastern fells.

'A little girl!' Libby exclaimed. 'A perfectly beautiful little girl,' she added as she laid the tiny swaddled body in Margaret's arms.

Staring into her daughter's milky-blue eyes and kissing her pearly-pink teeny fingernails, love flooded through Margaret like a river through a desert. Stroking her daughter's wispy hair, she gazed adoringly at the baby's sweet cupid-bow rosy lips and tiny nose.

'Oh, my sweetest darling,' she whispered. With tears rolling down her cheeks, Margaret turned to Libby. 'I never thought I would feel like this,' she confessed.

Moved beyond words by the bonding she had just witnessed between mother and daughter, Libby also had tears in her eyes. 'How do you feel, dear?' she gently asked.

'In love, besotted, amazed, grateful, and *so happy*,' Margaret marvelled, as she held her daughter close to her breast and kissed the top of her small head. 'Libby,' she said, with a determined glint in her eye, 'I'm so grateful to Beth for giving me a chance to keep my baby – now I've got her, I know for sure that I am *never, ever* going to let her go.'

On Boxing Day afternoon, after Margaret had successfully breast-fed her daughter for the second time, Libby wheeled Beth with Holly in her arms on to the post-natal ward.

'You have a visitor,' she announced.

Both women smiled rapturously at each other, each holding their baby.

'How are you?' Beth smiled.

'Never happier, never more grateful,' Margaret told her. Moving the shawl that obscured her daughter's little face, she said with a proud smile, 'Meet Ivy, my baby daughter.'

Looking from one new-born to the other, Beth tenderly said their names.

'Holly and Ivy, Mary Vale's beautiful Christmas babies.'

35. Happy Valley

In the early spring of 1945 when the snow had finally melted, flooding the becks, rivers and streams, Margaret pushed her second-hand Silver Cross pram up the sweeping drive that led to Thorp Hall, thoroughly transformed by builders and decorators. The dreary corridors and gloomy rooms, now painted in pale pastel colours, were warm and welcoming, colourful heavy drapes graced the elegant windows, and pretty furniture added a soft feminine touch. Though the weather was still wintry cold, there was a promise of spring in the air. Primroses and snowdrops poked through the dark damp earth, bright yellow catkins turned golden in the rays of the slanting sun, and birdsong rang out from every treetop. Thinking of the thrills to come, of exploring the world afresh with her daughter, Margaret's heart fluttered with pure joy. Soon there would be ducklings and chicks, scampering lambs in the meadows, trees decked with fragrant blossom, and then hot summer days, sunshine, warm rock pools, sandcastles and picnics on the beach.

'We're going to have such fun together, sweetheart,' she told Ivy as she bent down to kiss her little daughter for the tenth time that morning.

Not only was there new hope in Margaret's life but there was a sense of hope in the air for the entire nation. People were actually starting to talk about the real possibility of peace. In January, Soviet troops had captured Warsaw and liberated Auschwitz, where atrocities beyond all human comprehension had been revealed. Only recently, Dresden had been totally destroyed by a firestorm after Allied bombing raids. Thinking sadly of all the thousands of innocent men, women and children who had died in the Dresden raid, Margaret prayed for all the victims of war. When it was over, how many millions of lives would have been claimed? How many families utterly destroyed, how many widows left to weep and children left to grow up without the loving guidance of a father? Even now, British Commonwealth troops and their allies were continuing to fight a bitter war against the Japanese in Asia, fighting a brutal enemy in malaria-ridden jungles during drenching monsoon rains, and on remote islands in searing tropical heat. But, Margaret prayed, with peace talks between Stalin, Roosevelt and Churchill taking place, surely the end was in sight.

Approaching the Hall, now her home, Margaret thanked God for Beth Thorp's incredible generosity. True to her word, once she had rallied and regained her strength, Beth had set about making amends for the sins of her convicted husband. When Margaret's time at Mary Vale came to an end, she and Beth agreed that Margaret would move into Thorp Hall right away. Wild with excitement, Margaret was slightly nervous too about being on her own after so long a time at Mary Vale, which had become her beloved second home. She would never forget the day she had left, with Ivy cradled in her arms. Behind her on the doorstep stood her dear friends, waving and smiling, wishing her well: Ada, Dr Reid, Dora, Matron, Libby, darling Sisters Agnes and Theresa, even Father Ben (who had withdrawn Ivy's adoption papers once Margaret announced her change of plans). Before her stood Alf in his cart that was tethered to aging Captain, waiting to transport Margaret and baby Ivy to a new home, a new life and a new future.

When Alf pulled up outside the Hall, only to find the builders already under way with restoration work, he voiced some concern. 'Lass, are you sure you're doing the right thing, moving in with men working in the house, making a racket and covering the place in muck and brick dust?'

'Really, it's fine, Alf. The drawing room at the back of the house is untouched, I can camp out there until my own rooms are ready. It's light and airy, with a big fireplace. When the fire's lit, it keeps the room warm, and there are French doors that open out on to the garden. And best of all, for the time being at least, it's free.' Cradling her baby in her arms, Margaret grinned at the old man. 'Really, what more could I want?'

'Well, if you put it that way, I can quite see your point,' Alf smilingly agreed.

Once Beth had been discharged, and Holly was strong enough to be bottle-fed by her mother, Beth had taken her new baby home to Borrowdale where her grandparents doted on her from dawn till dusk. Though Beth was away for almost two months, Margaret had never felt lonely, not with so many wonderful things happening in her life. Early in the New Year, the Carters – including Sam (still weak and poorly but at least now able to sit up in bed and take an interest in life, and recently discharged from Lancaster Infirmary) – moved into a nearby fine grey-brick and slate three-bedroom farmhouse on the Thorp Estate, with an indoor toilet and a bathroom. It had taken weeks for Arthur to get over the novelty of using a toilet with a flush, and washing his hands in warm water. Though temporarily living rent free, Mary had vowed that she would pay Beth some rent for their wonderful new home just as soon as she could, insisting that they couldn't always be living on Beth's amazing generosity and goodwill. Living so close to each other, and knowing that Mary had Sam to look after, Margaret offered to keep an eye on Susan from time to time; she was as happy looking after two babies as one. As the weeks passed, the two women, now firm friends, established baby-sitting swaps that suited them both very well and conveniently freed up time for Mary to spend looking after her still-ailing husband.

Because of the two households' convenient proximity, Arthur and Joy were constantly running up the hill to the Hall to visit Margaret, often bringing with them thoughtful little gifts: a bunch of scented wild violets, or a clump of the first fragile snowdrops. They always came with some news too, usually blurted out by Arthur.

'I've been to the lav four times today!' he announced triumphantly.

Modest, blushing Joy hissed him a warning. 'Shhh! It's rude to talk like that.'

Completely ignoring his sister, Arthur explained. 'It's so much better than our old outside privy where I was always frightened of dropping down the big dark hole into the earth. We're posh now,' he informed Margaret, with a little swagger.

Another nugget of information imparted by Arthur was that one of St Mark's teachers was leaving.

'She's being posted overseas with her husband,' Joy explained.

When Margaret heard this piece of information, her ears pricked up. Would she ever be considered for a full-time post? she wondered. And anyway, who would look after Ivy? The headmistress and staff liked her well enough, but she still remained an unmarried mother – which carried a big social stigma. Dismissing the subject, Margaret was surprised when she received a letter from Mrs Temple, the headmistress, inviting her to pop into the school at her earliest possible convenience.

Leaving Ivy with Mary and Susan, Margaret, now the proud owner of a rather fine bicycle that she had discovered in the Thorp garage, cycled into town on a cold but bright day. Feeling the wind sweeping her long dark hair loose around her face, Margaret felt fitter and happier than she had done in years. How she loved this part of England where the sea met the land, and there was beauty on every side: the rolling fertile farmland, the sweeping marsh loud with the wailing calls of sea-birds, and the vast golden bay that enclosed the entire peninsula.

'I never want to leave,' she said out loud as she cycled full pelt down the hill into the town of Grange.

Once settled with a cup of tea in the headmistress's office, Margaret, quite expecting Mrs Temple to ask her to restart the music lessons she had so recently abandoned, was staggered when the headmistress offered her a full-time teaching post instead.

379

With trembling hands, Margaret laid down her cup and saucer. 'Excuse me, Headmistress, I have to point out that by appointing me to the post you could, in fact, be creating a problem for yourself – and the school too.' Looking her straight in the eye, she made it perfectly clear what she meant. 'You know I am an unmarried mother.'

Mrs Temple gave a brisk, businesslike nod. 'Of course, Margaret, I'm well aware of your situation. But really, how is it any different to when you were recently teaching here?'

'I was previously teaching here on a voluntary basis,' Margaret reminded Mrs Temple.

'And during that time, we said your "husband",' the headmistress smiled politely, 'was fighting for his country. How has that changed, dear?'

When Margaret thought about it, nothing had changed. But she had another question.

'What happens when peace comes, which might be soon. How do I explain my husband not returning home?'

'He could continue fighting in the Far East, as many men are. Why don't we reassess the situation when peace is actually declared?' Mrs Temple, clearly impatient with all the 'ifs and buts', came quickly to the point. 'Margaret, you are an excellent teacher, your musical skills have lifted the school's reputation across the entire county of Westmorland, the staff like you, the children love you, and I would consider it an honour to have you as a member of my staff. There, the offer's on the table, think about it, but be aware the post starts after the Easter holidays.'

Suddenly on her feet, Margaret heard herself saying, 'Just as long as I can make arrangements for my baby, the answer is definitely YES!'

Looking thrilled (and a little surprised), the headmistress beamed. 'What a relief. I was worried sick you might turn it down because of your marital status,' she confessed.

Suddenly carefree, Margaret shrugged. 'As you say, let's worry about that later,' she smiled. 'Right now, my priority is sorting out childcare for Ivy right away.'

'We will help in any way we can,' the headmistress assured Margaret, before adding, 'of course, we'll have to get references from your previous school.'

'Certainly, but please could I beg you to ask St Chad's School to keep my whereabouts private? It's important that I have no links with that school – for deeply personal reasons, I have no wish to re-establish contact.'

The headmistress gave a diplomatic nod. 'I'll make sure that's taken care of,' she said. 'By the way, good news from the town's mayor, he's kept his word about exploring funding for Arthur. There are musical scholarships available in Lancaster and Penrith, which he's sure Arthur could apply for. Could you let Mrs Carter know the mayor's news, then perhaps we can make arrangements for Arthur to be auditioned for a scholarship in the near future?'

'Wouldn't that be wonderful!' Margaret exclaimed as she stood to leave. 'Angelic Arthur a chorister,' she laughed.

'Not so angelic,' Mrs Temple recalled. 'But highly gifted, something that would have gone unnoticed but for you coming here, Margaret dear.'

Straight after her interview, Margaret cycled to Mary's house to pick up her baby. Finding both girls peacefully sleeping in their prams, Margaret gratefully accepted a cup of tea from Mary. Sitting at the kitchen table in her friend's spotlessly clean kitchen, she eagerly announced her news.

'I've been offered the teaching job at St Marks' school,' she told Mary who was busy pouring tea for them both.

'That's marvellous,' Mary exclaimed.

After taking a sip of hot tea, Margaret cautiously added, 'I will need to arrange childcare . . . and I was wondering if you might be available to mind Ivy full-time? I honestly can't think of anybody better – she already knows you and loves being with your Susan.'

Smiling, Mary nodded her head. 'I'd love to, Margaret,' she warmly responded. 'I'm quite sure we can come to a suitable arrangement.'

'Oh, what a relief,' Margaret smiled back. 'I'd pay you the going rate, of course.'

'The money will certainly come in handy,' Mary said gratefully.

Touching on a rather delicate subject, Margaret asked, 'Will you be able to manage two babies, with Sam to take care of?'

'I've been taking care of my Sam almost since Susan was born,' Mary answered realistically. 'I think I can manage. You never know,' she grinned. 'Two babies might work better – at least they can entertain each other.'

After her meeting with Mary, an excited Margaret took Ivy home to Thorp Hall. Leaving the big pram in the hallway, she scooped her gurgling baby into her arms and entered the drawing room, where she smiled in delight at the sight that awaited her. Before a crackling log fire sat Libby, bouncing Holly on her knee, and chatting to her was Beth, who had recently returned from her family in the Borrowdale valley.

'Margaret!' Libby cried as she hurried over to greet her. 'And darling Ivy, how are you, sweetie?' she said as she kissed the top of the baby's head. 'Beth's just been telling me about her time on the family farm.'

'I loved every minute with my family,' Beth declared. 'But it's nice to be back here with Margaret and Mary. To be honest, I was glad to be in the middle of nowhere during Ronnie's trial. We followed the court case, of course,' she added. 'I almost felt sorry for Ronnie when he was sentenced to so many years behind bars.'

Laying Holly on a blanket in front of the fire, Libby said matter-of-factly, 'Sorry to say this, Beth, but he deserved it.' Patting Beth gently on the arm, she continued brightly. 'You're doing a great job here, just as you promised, restoring local trust in a very short space of time.'

'I was determined to make changes,' Beth declared. 'With Margaret and Mary's help, things have happened quicker than I ever expected.'

When Ivy was settled on the blanket beside Holly, the women watched in delight as the two little girls kicked their legs and gurgled at each other.

'Who would have thought that life could ever be so good?' Margaret marvelled, bubbling over with excitement. 'I've been offered a teaching job at St Mark's – which I've just accepted.' After she related the events of her exciting day, her friends congratulated a glowing Margaret who confessed, 'I have to keep pinching myself to make sure I'm not dreaming – I never imagined I could ever be so happy, so fulfilled.'

Gazing at her friends, Beth gave a secret little smile. 'I think life might get even better for Sam and Mary,' she quietly announced.

'Have you managed to get a district nurse to visit Sam?' Libby eagerly asked.

'Better than that,' Beth smiled. 'I've secured him a place in one of the big sanatoriums in Grange.'

Libby and Margaret gazed incredulously at Beth.

'You've what?' Libby cried.

'Realistically, he wasn't showing enough signs of improvement once he was back home with the family,' Beth pointed out. 'He needs specialist care if he's to stand any chance of surviving, so I booked him into Sunningdale Sanatorium,' she said, with real satisfaction.

'I can hardly believe it,' Margaret gasped in delight. 'What a relief it will be for Mary, knowing that her husband will be nursed properly, and taken good care of.'

'It will be easy for the family to visit too — not miles away, like Lancaster,' Beth continued happily. 'It's perfectly placed on the front, with sea-facing balconies where patients' beds can be wheeled out and they can breathe in all that good fresh sea air.'

Nibbling her lower lip, Libby blurted out what was troubling her. 'Beth, dear, I know you are on a mission to right the world, but have you considered how much money you're spending in making all these vast, sweeping changes?'

Beth threw her best friend a loving smile. 'I spent hours and hours at home with Dad going through the Thorp finances — remember, most of it is our own family money. There's no getting away from the fact that Ronnie spent a great deal of it – the wretched Daimler car for a start – but Dad's guiding me and advising me on what I can afford to do and what I can't afford. I completely trust him when it comes to making major decisions,' she concluded.

'Well, if you say so, dear, then I believe you,' Libby said as she crossed the room to hug Beth. 'You are a saint,' she announced, with tears in her eyes. 'A true saint.'

A few days later, pushing their babies in their prams, the two new mothers strolled the short distance to Mary's house. Libby, who took every opportunity to visit her favourite babies, Holly and Ivy, whenever she had any free time, was walking happily in between them.

When they got there, Beth asked if she might speak to Sam. Leaving the babies outside with Libby, the two women approached Sam, who was still thin and pale but presently sitting upright on a neatly made-up single bed in the sitting room of his new home.

'How are you, Sam?' Beth immediately asked.

'All the better for being here, missus,' Sam said, with a grateful smile. 'This house is like a palace, compared to our old cottage.' Smiling at Margaret, who was standing beside Beth, Sam added, 'It's lovely to see you, Miss Margaret.'

Margaret, who knew Sam far better than Beth, sat down on a bedside chair and said, 'Mrs Thorp has come up with a wonderful plan for you, Sam.'

Sitting down on the other side of the bed, Beth added, 'I wondered if you would like to spend some time in one of the big sanatoriums in Grange, one of the new ones overlooking Morecambe Bay?'

Utterly speechless, Sam looked across to his wife,

standing at the end of the bed. 'Mary,' he spluttered. 'What's going on?'

Equally as bewildered, Mary answered, 'I've no idea, Sam.'

'Let me explain . . .' Beth started. 'I know how badly my husband treated you. It can't have helped your condition; in fact, I know that it worsened it, for which I'm truly sorry.'

Sam held up a protesting hand. 'Mrs Thorp, it was no fault of yours.'

'Well, in a way it was, Sam. I was married to Ronnie, and now I want to make amends, to give you back something my husband so cruelly took away from you.'

Half an hour later, with tears coursing down his pale face, Sam accepted Beth's very generous gift. 'I can never thank you enough,' he sobbed.

Beth smiled brightly. 'Yes, you can,' she announced. 'You can get better – that would be the best gift you could ever give me.'

Once outside on the garden path, Mary threw herself into Beth's arms. Repeating her husband's own words, she just cried over and over again. 'Thank you, thank you, thank you. You're too good to us!'

Luckily, the children returning home from school broke the highly emotional mood.

'MAM!' Arthur bellowed in his rich, strong young voice. 'We heard in assembly we've got a new teacher . . .' Pausing, with an impish grin on his cheeky face, he cried, 'You'll never guess who she is!'

Exchanging a conspiratorial look, Mary and Margaret waited for the children to pass on the latest school news.

Joining the group, Joy said in a quieter voice than her

noisy brother, but with a radiant smile on her plain honest face, 'It's Miss Margaret!'

Grinning, Margaret exclaimed, 'I'm so sorry I couldn't tell you sooner.' She apologized to the giggling children. 'I had to wait until my references had been approved, and I also had to talk to your mother about an important business arrangement.'

The children looked expectantly at their mother, who explained, 'Margaret has asked me to look after Ivy while she's teaching at St Mark's.'

Ever the pragmatist, Arthur said, 'Who'll look after our Susan while you're looking after Miss Margaret's Ivy?'

Mary laughed. 'I'll look after *both* babies; they're already on the way to becoming the best of friends – they'll keep each other company.'

'More wonderful news,' Libby laughed. 'This place is turning out to be a real happy valley,' she joked.

Margaret gave a radiant smile. 'I'm more than happy for Ivy and Susan to grow up together – and Holly too, I hope. They're going to be the best of friends, I'm sure.' Turning to Joy and Arthur, hugging them both tightly, Margaret added, 'We're going to have such fun – we're going to make St Mark's school choir the best in the whole of Westmorland.'

Leaving Beth and Libby to walk around the estate, with Holly still sleeping in her pram, Margaret went to sit on her favourite bench with Ivy. Perched on high ground in a part of the garden that sloped steeply up to the ever-rising fells where dull-brown faded bracken was sending forth fresh green vernal shoots, Margaret sighed deeply. Gazing yet again in wonder at her daughter, at her dark eyelashes fanning her small heart-shaped face, at the way her brown hair (the exact same colour as Peter's) curled around her ears, at her tiny hands and sweet cupid-bow lips, Margaret marvelled. Was a baby ever more perfect than this child whom she had thought she would be forced to give away?

Life had been more than good to Margaret; she had a family, a future, true loyal friends, and a home in the Lake District. Margaret knew that this beautiful part of the country, though now weary and devastated by six years of war, would with God's help and local folks' hard work rise again, phoenix-like.

England would prosper, rebuild and overcome.

Life would go on, and peace would return.

Acknowledgements

With many grateful thanks to Dr Aditi Vedi, Consultant Paediatric Oncologist at Addenbrookes Hospital, Cambridge, and to Dr Clive and Patsy Glazebrook. I'll be forever grateful to you all for the time you spent addressing the many medical issues in *Christmas with the Wartime Midwives*. I'd like to thank Selwyn Image (Cambridge) for the cups of tea and glasses of wine that always accompanied my visits to pick his brains on anything to do with the Second World War: from rationing to the North Atlantic Blockade, Bomber Command and the D-Day landings. A big thank you to Shan Morley Jones, my copy-editor, and to my fantastic, supportive editorial team at Penguin Random House – Rebecca Hilsdon and Clare Bowron. Finally, with a full heart I want to thank all the millions of conscripted women who fought for their country during the Second World War, and all wars in fact. The women I write about are a ceaseless inspiration to me. God bless them all, living and dead.